Jozadak

Louise Furley

Jozadak

ISBN- 978-1-7369376-0-0 (Paperback)
ISBN- 978-1-7363452-9-0 (eBook)

Cover design by Pixel Mischief Design

The characters and events portrayed in this book are fictitious. Any similarity to real persons, living or dead, is coincidental and not intended by the author.

ALSO BY LOUISE FURLEY

A Mafia Romance series

Distilled Duplicity
His Winnings
Adara
Jozadak

Satan's Brood series

Devil's Prince
Devil's Seed

Dutch Military Special Forces series

Jungle Treasure
Jancarlo

Stand alone titles

Jezábel and the Assassin

Solitar

Halo Valley

Isle of Orainn

Louise Furley

JOZADAK

Chapter One

"So, what did you find out? Was the information from the stoolie accurate?"

The luxuriant, burgundy leather chair was large scale, but Jozadak Kane's broad shoulders easily filled the rounded upper wings. With an ankle over a knee, brawny forearms settled along the cushioned chair arms, he appeared relaxed lounged against the rich buttery leather.

But it was a deceptive contrast to the restrained dynamism in his blue eyes.

Watching Scottie's brown gaze skitter down to stare at the smoky grey carpet, Joze held a glass of scotch with his thumb and two fingers draped over the end of the arm of the chair.

He lightly twirled the liquid, took a sip, but didn't take his eyes off the scrawny runt standing in front of him shaking in his chukka boots.

Joze stayed silent, no one else in the room spoke.

Five of his closest friends, the top members of his team, his captains, sat clustered around him in leather-tufted chairs waiting unperturbed.

It took several awkward moments before Scottie got the balls to raise his head and answer Joze.

At only 27, Joze Kane was the head of Chianina, a notorious criminal organization, handed down to Joze from his father, Mathius Kane, AKA Boa. As in the constrictor.

Scottie wasn't the only man to fear father and son. The name Chianina alone, a type of bull, emphasized the strength, the danger, and the ruthless power of the family.

"Uh, yeah Boss," Scottie managed to croak out. His blond hair stood in unruly spikes on the top of his head.

When Scottie wasn't more forthcoming, Joze's dark brows drew down over brilliant but emotionless ultramarine eyes encircled by long lashes.

Scottie quivered at the vivid deadened orbs directed at him.

When angry, Joze's pupils enlarged, completely taking over the piercing blue irises. Such an eerie transformation startled most people into a fearsome double-take when Joze directed his enigmatic gaze at them.

What made him appear even freakier was the white-blond hair. With his voltaic eyes morphing into black discs they were a discordant clash with his hair.

He kept the darker sides trimmed extremely short; the top was longer thick waves. The rest of the hair on his body, his brows, scruff, the hair on his chest were contrasting dark brown. Well aware people call him a vampire behind his back, he doesn't give a *shyt*.

"Fucking speak up, Scottie." The implied threat was crystal. Joze's Welsh accent thickened when disturbed, the sometimes unintelligible words coming across even more fierce and threatening than his glacial voice.

His family was from an island off Wales. During the mining strikes in the 1420's, the Russians helped feed the starving families. Some stayed and mated with the Welsh islanders creating their own bastardized Welsh dialect, a mix of Welsh and Russian and Island.

Muttering, "Uh," legs unsteady in brown cords, clutching his hat with a death grip, Scottie cleared his throat. "Yeah, Drake told me there's been recon on some of your businesses to find out where you hang out. He says there's an undercover cop supposed to spy on you, see if he can get some shit, to uh, hang you."

Waiting for more, Joze stared silently at the terrified man.

Scottie gulped hard, trying to maintain eye contact with one of the scariest men he's ever known.

The black leather trench coat Joze normally wore that went to his ankles, with the freaky eyes and the white-blond hair made Scottie think of zombies or vampires or something alien. Whatever, they were all deadly.

Joze sipped his scotch, barely stifling his annoyance at the *frota pidyn*, stupid dick, standing there quaking, about to piss his pants. Joze slid a side-glance to his 2nd in command, Lincoln Lintz.

Both men loomed over 6'5". As big and muscled as Joze, Linc left his tawny curly hair a little long, almost to his collar, but he kept his scruff close trimmed. He used his Harvard earned law degree in the business, otherwise, it wasn't obvious in his laid-back countenance or patient drawl. Handsome with a strong square chin, a corner of Linc's mouth twitched.

Joze's attention flicked back to Scottie. If the creep hadn't known a snitch in the Chie Texas Police Department, he would have dumped the *cwd capatr*, scrotum scratching, scaredy-cat long ago.

"Well?" Joze sighed irritably. "Did Drake say who the cop is? He give a name?"

Scottie shook his head, swiped at beads of sweat on his forehead with the backs of his skinny, hairless hands. "No. That's all he knows." His nervous eyes bounced from his frightening boss to around the luxurious office.

The purely masculine room was a blend of contemporary and classic, with gold trimmed, Santos mahogany paneled walls and dark cherry bookcases.

Smoky grey carpeting partially covered a white and gold veined marble floor. The fireplace anchoring one end of the office was made with the same marble.

Dark aqua curtains pulled back to let the sunlight in from the floor to ceiling windows that stretched in front of the mahogany and gold gilded desk.

Joze's preternatural orbs seemed to slice right through Scottie's small brain seeking more information. Seeing less than zero activity

3

there, Joze tossed back the rest of his drink. "All right. Get back with Drake, tell him to spread the word that I hang at the Seraphim Saloon in Dustin."

Ignoring his team's raised brows, sighing while frowning, he jerked his jaw, indicating for Scottie to leave.

Scottie's tiny brown eyes flashed around the room, the other men stared blankly at him.

He bowed with clumsy stiffness then stumbled quickly out of the room before Joze could order him shanked or shot. Or worse.

Word was Jozadak Kane can kill a man by crushing his skull in his bare hands. Slowly, or quickly. Depended on the range of his anger.

Joze got to his feet and moved to the inlaid rosewood teacart to pour himself another drink.

A hum of conversation wound through the room.

Linc was talking with Diego Vegas, aka Romeo.

High, sharp cheekbones, full lips with a splotch of black hair on Diego's chin matching the short black hair, shaved on the sides and longer on top, the gluttonous horny man went after anything in a skirt.

Then Linc looked up at Joze and asked, "What is your plan, *fy bráithre,* my brother?" He watched his best friend he considered his brother, add a lemon twist to his scotch neat.

Joze took a sip then set the glass down. "I have to know my enemies to control them." He rolled up the long sleeves of his black shirt baring those brawny forearms covered with thick, dark golden hair and picked up his drink. A gold Piguet Tourbillon Diamond watch glimmered at his wrist as he moved.

Stuffing a hand in his pocket, he paced across the room to stand in front of the window. Idly gazing out it for a moment at the water ruffled by a brisk wind, he turned back to address Linc. With a shrewd glint, he said, "Have Van set up an apartment for me in Dustin, near the Seraphim."

A tawny brow arched over a bronze eye, Linc replied, "How many of us are coming with you, I'll have Van prepare-"

Shaking his head, Joze said, "*Na*, I'm going alone. I don't want to be recognized and if anyone happens to spot one of you they'll know I'm around."

Protesting, "Joze, *bráith*," Calvin 'Tank' Nabendu, rubbed his shiny bald pate then scratched his chin through his beard with hefty fingers. Tats shifted all over his coffee brown arms as he moved, gold flashed from multiple earrings. "That's not safe. You need backup. Falcon DeMarco has soldiers out there everywhere, he would love to catch you alone."

"Yeah," said the shortest of the team at 6'2", Bruno Scarpa's shoulder length, arrow-straight black hair, he combed straight off his forehead was tucked behind his ears.

The only one of the men with a serious girlfriend, always dressed in a white business shirt and tie, Bruno added, "And Boss, you sure as hell know he would take great pleasure in torturing you for a long time before killing you."

Nodding curtly, the curly hair shuffling with his movements, Linc agreed, "Let us at least bunk nearby."

"*Na,*" Joze repeated coolly.

Linc stood up, smoothed his jeans down that had shifted up while he sat. "We won't get in your way, Joze. But, you put the entire business in jeopardy if something happens to you. Stop thinking like the Lone Ranger. You are responsible for a lot of people and a lot of jobs, and a lot of money."

Linc trod across the grey carpet to the small fridge and took out a bottle of water. Twisting off the top, he put the clear bottle to his lips and chugged a quarter of it.

"You'll never know we're there," Sloan offered. He made up for his light skin and freckles with a rock hard, buffed body. The deep cleft in his chin was clearly visible in his stubble. He and Linc worked out doing MMA even more than Joze did, although none of them had ever beaten Joze in a fight. Sloan kept his long hair tied back in a ponytail.

"Geeze, all right, you sound like a bunch of whiny old ladies, *ci dynes*. Fine." Joze frowned, set his glass down and tucked both hands in the pockets of his black jeans. "Just keep clear, stay inside, no booze, no women." Grabbing his cocktail again, he grimaced at the group.

He eyed each of his team, Linc, Diego, Sloan, Bruno, Calvin. They were his compatriots when they were all in Ace Ops 17th Warfare Combat Unit, Advanced Tactical Infiltration.

It was a miracle they all managed to come out pretty much in one piece. Their loyalty to one another was indelible.

Joze scowled at the triumphant grin spread on Linc's face.

"Whatever, asshole," Joze muttered, tossing back the rest of his drink. "Let's get this show on the road."

Chapter Two

"**C**ome on, Dinah, move your butt. I need that wine now!" From behind the bar, Sam Lansky barked out a shout to the young woman still downstairs to hurry it up.

Resting his forearms on the counter, Sam leered at the barmaid in front of him. "I'll have that wine out pronto for you, Sharmain, baby."

"Gawd," the sexy barmaid huffed, plopping a hand with long blue nails on her round hip. Flipping back stiff, curly blonde hair, she complained, "That stupid girl is as slow as she is ugly."

"Aw honey, not everyone can be as gorgeous as you." Sam reached out a long hairy arm to touch Sharmain's hand with tapered knobby fingers.

Moving her hand just out of reach of the 35-year-old bartender with the narrow shoulders and thinning hair, Sharmain Santarosa sighed like she carried a heavy burden.

She was scarcely able to squelch her lip curling at the gaunt bartender who grew his sideburns exceptionally long to compensate for his loss of hair. Looking down at her breasts, her favorite things in the whole world, Sharmain tugged down on the already low-cut, cleavage baring uniform to expose more flesh.

All the barmaids wore tight, violet, spandex-like scoop neck tops, cropped to just barely cover their bosoms, and soft motion short-shorts with a low-riding black leather belt with roller buckles. The barmaids were hired specifically for their looks. And, the sleazier the better.

Food was available in the Seraphim Saloon. Besides the main room that was filled with an array of tables covered with white tablecloths, there was a separate barroom where smoking, cigarettes as well as cigars were allowed.

The kitchen was to the very back of the saloon. Storage rooms, a separate room for the staff to hang in, and another small dining area trailed down the end of a short hallway. Saturday night, the building was packed to the gills with hungry, thirsty patrons.

People crowded all the way around the square bar counter. Glasses clinking, boisterous drunks mixed with couples whispering in each other's ears, chairs scraping on the oak floor, the room was big and noisy.

Antique white and beige brick walls soaked in some of the noise. Windows lined the front. Lime green lamps hung from the ceiling, violet tinted glass vases held candles in the middle of the white clothed tables.

Violet lighting shone on liquor bottles stacked on shelves. The bottles glistened like multicolored jewels in every conceivable color, blue, amber, red, purple.

Sharmain prided herself on out of the entire staff, having the biggest breasts money could buy and she loved to show them off. It was like being the biggest Hoot at Hooters.

A grimace scrunched her heavily made up face as the bar-back/cleaner/busser, Dinah, came up the stairs with a bottle of wine.

Sharmain snatched the bottle out of the smaller woman's hand with a huff, scratching the girl's hand with her long nails, which was likely no accident.

"About time, slow ass. You're as pokey and stupid as that hunchback retard. How you got hired with that plain face and," her snarky gaze raked Dinah's body in the big shirt and loose pants.

Her sharp nose in the hair, Sharmain continued her disparaging belittling, "With that God awful figure, heaven knows. And don't get me started on that shitty brown hair and those ridiculous, huge tinted glasses."

Dinah wiped under her glasses at the dust on her tired eyes. Even if she had the energy to snipe back at Sharmain, she wouldn't.

Sighing with dramatic flair, Sharmain sniffed, "You can't even carry on a conversation for cripe's sake. I guess that's why they keep you in the back scenes and not out front with us hot bitches. I'd say you must have slept with someone to get the job but, ick," she sneered as she spun and flitted away, "there's no way any guy with eyeballs would fuck you!"

That last remark brought a flush of pink to Dinah's round cheeks.

"Hey, Dinah," Rubal Sacket said, "don't let that haughty bitch get to you, she's just testy because the only guy she hasn't slept with and she really wants, that construction owner, Lennie Boston, wants nothing to do with her slutty self. Right Jimmy?"

Standing in the doorway to the back of the bar counter scratching his armpit, Rubal smirked at the tall guy hunched over beside him. The hunchback tugged his knit beanie down lower and nodded with a goofy grin.

Dinah pushed back her scruffy shoulder length hair and shrugged with indifference. "I don't care, Rubal, really." She sidestepped Rubal's octopus hand reaching for her bottom and smiled at Jimmy.

"Jimmy, can you please get me a box of that wine Sharmain ordered. I managed to drag the box to the stairs. I tried, but I can't carry the whole box up the stairs."

The big guy with the goofy look on his face nodded emphatically. "Yeah, Dinah, shuh." As the tall guy with the bent back loped to the stairs, tugging his beanie down harder past his ears, he inclined his head watching Rubal try to make another pass at Dinah.

She slapped the hand away that was trying to make its way around the front of her shirt.

Jimmy hurried off, his boots making plopping sounds as he lumbered down the stairs to the wine cellar.

9

Dinah raced to the dirty table to clean it but she wasn't quick enough.

Margie stood with her hands on her ample hips glowering at her. "Can ya speed it up any, plain Jane? You're costing me money, a snail moves faster than you. I'll be damned if I give you any portion of my tips tonight, I don't care what the rules are."

Margie figured if she herself cleaned only one table out of all she waited on then she was entitled to not have to tip the bussers at all.

A party of six at a nearby table laughed at the brunette's mocking of Dinah while ogling Margie's full hourglass figure squeezed into her two sizes too small uniform.

Margie carefully dressed to expose her ample assets so that her butt and bust spilled out all over. She didn't squawk at the frequent pinch or fondle, it meant more money at the end of the night.

It worked. Getting the desired effect, several of the men leered at her. A couple patted her huge bouncing rear as she flitted over to them. The blowsy girl teased and chatted with the party while Dinah finished clearing and cleaned then reset the table that Margie was actually supposed to help her with.

Music played in the background; people talked over it. Occasional bursts of laughter floated above the din of chatter and plates clattering into bus pans.

Hours later, after the bar closed, barmaids Sharmain, Margie, Brenda, Jessica, and Marsha were out back in the semi-darkness hanging with two of the bartenders, Jeff and Gregg.

Rubal, a bar-back, tagged along. They were smoking cigarettes and sucking on beer and cocktails while the girls counted their tips.

Jimmy loped out the back door with the trash. After he dumped it he meandered over to the group.

"Hey, guys," he greeted. His back rounded, he peered up at the young people with a lopsided grin.

Everyone ignored him except for Rubal and Gregg.

Tossing his head to shift his baby fine, sandy hair out of his face, Rubal said, "Dude, want a smoke?" His narrow chin covered with sparse light whiskers bobbed, he smiled at Jimmy with crooked yellow teeth and held out his pack of cigarettes.

A big grin split Jimmy's face. "Yeah." He joined the group sitting on patio chairs, drinking and smoking in the twilight.

Cars intermittently drove past the side street next to the saloon.

A few minutes later Dinah exited the back door with empty liquor boxes. She dumped them in the recycling dumpster. Wiping her hands on her slacks she headed back into the saloon.

Sam the bartender came out lighting his cigarette, he bee-lined for Sharmain. Sitting down beside her he held out a bottle of tequila. He said, "Here hon, let me freshen your drink."

She passed him her glass and he filled it to the brim. Spilling a little, she giggled while slurping the pungent overflow. Sam yakked in her ear for a good solid ten minutes.

It was almost dark but the area was fairly well lit. The air was still warm from the day's sun. A few wispy clouds wafted in front of the cool silver moon.

Bored, Sharmain got up and wandered over to Jimmy. His shoulders slumped, he rested his elbows on his knees. The barmaid stood in front of him, a cloud of strong designer perfume enveloped her.

His mouth hanging open, Jimmy gawked at her from her thighs up to her big breasts.

"You like what you see, retard?" She bent over so he could see down the front of her top.

He adamantly nodded his head. "Yuh." His brown eyes were glued to her bosom.

Bending over, Sharmain grabbed the back of his head and rubbed his face in her cleavage. Laughing like a drunken hyena, she shoved his head back and blew smoke in his face. "You'd like some of that, wouldn't ya, Jimmy?"

She bent over again and wiggled her breasts in his face. He timidly reached out a large calloused hand to touch her but she backed away waggling a finger at him. "No, no my stupid boy, lookie but no touchie." She blew more smoke in his face.

11

Then Margie and the other girls got up and jeered at Jimmy, all blowing smoke in his face. The men chided him calling him retard and idiot, brainless hulk and stupid.

Jimmy just stared at them with wide dark eyes, his mouth hanging open. "I'ma, uh, I'm not a retard,"

That made them all laugh louder.

"Yeah ya are, you big dufus. Can't tell if it's just your retard voice or you have some kinda freaky guttural accent," Jessica said, on one side of him. She gave him a little shove, on the other side Sharmain shoved him back until he was jostled back and forth like a ping pong ball.

The group laughed at him, mocking him until he looked about to cry.

"Hey!" Dinah stormed over, her face red with anger. "Stop it. Stop that. Leave him alone."

Sharmain turned her attention to the girl in the baggy clothes. Throwing back a few hearty gulps of her drink, she sneered, "What are you, you ugly bitch, his babysitter?"

Jessica chortled, "Yeah, you could turn around and we wouldn't be able to tell your back from your front!"

Gregg mocked, "Is it time for the big boy to get his diaper changed?" Everyone laughed raucously, slapping each other on the back and clinking glasses together.

"You gonna take him in a back room, plain Jane, and suck him off? Teach him how to be a man?" Jeff snickered snidely behind a black goatee, big ears stuck out of the side of his straight black hair.

"He's a big guy, must have a big dick," he sneered with a nasty leer. "You'll like that, babe, he'll fill you right up. Probably be the first time for you, huh?"

Blushing again, Dinah muttered, "Oh grow up." Holding her hand out to Jimmy, she said, "Come on, Jimmy, leave the lushes to their jokes, you can help me finish up."

She took Jimmy's hand and tugged him to his big feet then led him back to the saloon leaving the gang's mean laughter outside.

Some time later, Dinah and Jimmy were straightening up the back room where the help ate dinner. Jimmy kept staring at her mouth.

She asked him with a grin, "Do I have mustard on my face?"

Tugging down on his beanie, his brow furrowed with confusion, he muttered, "Mustard? I don't…"

Setting down her cleaning rag, she smiled kindly. "I mean, you keep staring at my mouth, is something wrong with it?"

He looked sheepish, shook his head and stuck his big hands in his back pockets. "*Na*, it's just, your lips are really small but they are, like, you know, like my ma says, uh, pl- ah, plush." He appeared proud of remembering the word.

"Yeah, sexy huh?" Rubal said, coming into the room. "Such hot plump lips on such a plain girl. It's too bad honey, maybe if you wore some makeup- or like lose the glasses and do something with that hair, wear some decent clothes. A guy can't tell what you look like under all that loose bulk and big glasses."

"Sure," she murmured, turned away and went back to cleaning.

Rubal said craftily to Jimmy, "There's something about her, but with those huge tinted glasses and plain hair, those shitty clothes, it's hard to tell."

Blinking behind long, fine bangs of sandy hair, Rubal nudged Jimmy with his elbow and a leer. "But there's something there. Maybe we can get her naked and then we could see what it is, huh?" He playfully poked Jimmy again with his elbow.

Jimmy looked at Rubal his eyeballs almost crossed with bewilderment. "Huh?"

Rubal laughed. "What, bro? Your beanie too tight? You ain't had a girl yet?" He grinned indecently, the light whiskers sparkled catching the amber glow from a table lamp.

"Oh yeah, you're too mentally dented to get it up and know what to do with it once you did!" He clapped Jimmy on the back.

"No worries. I gotta hit the road now, but some late night when she's here alone," he leaned in and whispered conspiratorially, "we'll snag her in the back room. You hold her down, I'll show you how to do it, okay?"

13

"B-but that's like- like rape, ain't it, Rubal? She go to the cops if we did it."

Rubal shook his head, the straight hair swished around his head. "Naw, she ain't gonna complain, probly be thrilled a guy finally gave it to her, ya know? Besides, we'll just threaten her with great bodily harm if she says she's gonna report us. She's such a little thing, be easy to scare her into submission."

Jimmy stared blankly at him with his mouth hanging open.

"It's okay, dude, stick with me, I'll take care of ya," Rubal said in a bragging tone. "Or maybe you prefer Sharmain with her big fake tits and hefty ass?"

A scowl pulled at Jimmy's dumb face, he shook his head. "Ugh, she too fat and hard. She sexes with everyone. Don't like it when she puts her boobs in my face. Ya know, plastic like a mannequin?" His mouth pulled in crookedly, he said, "Dinah, she soft and pretty."

Rubal laughed showing his crooked teeth stained with tobacco. "Yeah. I bet she's soft and pretty on the inside too. And one night," he nudged Jimmy with his elbow, "you and me are gonna find out. She's a nobody, there's no one she can complain to if we take a piece of her. Ya know? I bet she's a virgin, tight and tender."

He nudged Jimmy again with a smirk. "Anyway, that Sharmain's been with so many men you'd need a net to keep from falling in!" He laughed crassly at Jimmy's perplexed expression.

"Never mind, big guy. I gotta go, catch ya later." He slapped him on the back and split.

Leaving the room he called over his shoulder, "I got the front door locked on my way out."

Chapter Three

The building was pin drop quiet. Everyone had gone home except Dinah who was cleaning up out front and Jimmy mopping the back kitchen.

Dinah went to turn off the outside light and check the door to make sure it was locked when it suddenly pushed open hard and fast.

Four armed men rushed her-

A tall, hard looking man grabbed Dinah, and a shorter, heavier man slammed the door closed and locked it.

Surprised, Dinah screamed bloody murder and tried to fight off the man holding her.

"Calm down, little sugar," the tall guy holding her ordered, grinning, fully aware he radiated menace. "We're just gonna shake down the place."

One of the thieves was at the vault hidden in the bar under the sink.

Short heavy guy stood looking around, he spotted her purse. "Hey great, I bet you got a nice cell phone." He stalked over grabbing up her purse. He opened it and dumped the contents out on a table.

"Leave that alone, stop, let me go!" Dinah thrashed her petite body, trying to break loose from the man holding her. He only laughed and tightened his grip so shockingly painful she gasped.

"Holy hell she's a goddamned cop!" The man rifling through her belongings cursed holding up a badge.

The men all turned to stare at her.

"Crap, Wally." Heavy guy said to the man holding Dinah, "We need to snuff her quick, ditch the body."

Wally shook Dinah so hard her head snapped back and forth. His mean eyes narrowed at her. "Why are you working as a bar-back if you're a cop?"

At her stunned silence Wally pinched her arms with his tight grip and demanded, "You undercover?" A slow smile slid over his face.

Wally was a big muscled man, his moustache rode down past his mouth and circled his chin. His light brown hair was short but grungy. "That's it, isn't it, you're fucking undercover."

Recognizing Wally as the guy who delivered soda to the saloon, Dinah kept her mouth shut. She was in big, dire trouble. Four men, and she was unarmed. Things did not look good for her to get safely out of the desperate situation. Her terrified brain spun frantically as she tried to seek a way to escape.

Wally's toady brown eyes studied her. "Why the hell would you be undercover here in this shit-assed saloon?"

The man at the vault muttered, "Drugs, you idiot. She's likely trying to take down dealers." He spun the dial on the vault. Seeming to know the combination, the take down appeared to be an inside job.

"Hey, Dinah, these you friend's?" Jimmy asked with a slight lisp. He was standing in the doorway from the kitchen, his long body hunched over. A dopey grin made a crooked line across his face, his mouth hung open as usual. "Are they police people too?"

Dinah screamed, "Run Jimmy! Run!"

Wally's wicked slap made her head snap to the left with a cry of pain.

In her face, Wally barked, "Shut up you cop bitch!" He roughly pinned her arms behind her back.

The other three men pointed their guns at Jimmy. One of them ordered him, "You, get over here."

Her voice hoarse with terror, Dinah screamed again at the mentally challenged young man, "Jimmy run! Run away outside!"

One of the men's vitriolic bark added to the noisy chaos in the room, "Goddammit, Wally, control that bitch!"

Wally maneuvered Dinah so her back was against his chest. Holding her wrists with one hand, he clamped the other over her mouth. He said to one of the men, "Just shoot him, Kelvin."

Kelvin was long and rangy. "Wait, come here bro," he said to Jimmy. "I recognize him. He's that retard that cleans up and helps behind the bar. He's harmless. He don't keep nothin' in his brain for more'n a few seconds. C'mere, what's your name, oh yeah, it's Jimmy. Come on over, Jimmy."

His grin pleased, tugging on his beanie, Jimmy shuffled out of the doorway into the room. "Are we playing? What game we playing? Cops and Robbers? Cowboys and Indians?" he asked eagerly like a young child.

Pointing his gun at him, Kelvin said, "We're playing give me your phone and money."

Jimmy blinked confused then grinned again. "Okay." He pulled three crumpled one-dollar bills out of his pocket and set them on the table. Mournfully he said, "I don't got no phone, Daddy won't let me, says I keep losing it."

Laughing, Kelvin scooped up the few dollars stuffing them in his pocket. "It's all right bro, you're a good guy." He patted Jimmy on the back.

Jimmy beamed at him like he had given him a crown. "You good man." He shyly ducked his head and seemed to stand a little straighter than before, his shoulders a bit more hefty.

"All right, let's get a move on," the man at the vault said. He was stuffing bills into a bag. "Take her out back and shoot her. We'll dump her body on the way back."

Struggling in Wally's arms, Dinah's face drained of all color.

Wally smirked at Dinah, his eyes rolling over her figure. "Can't tell what you look like with those loose clothes, but a chick's a chick, even if she's fat, flat, or a cop."

17

"Yeah," Kelvin agreed with a lewd grin. "He's right. Bring her, we can take turns with her on the long ride home. Close to home is Longbow Bridge. We can break her neck and toss her in the river. Be months if she's even ever found."

"What about him?" The fourth guy jerked his head at Jimmy.

Shrugging, Kelvin replied, "Ah, he's too stupid to even remember his last name much less us. Leave him. He'll take the blame for the robbery and her going missing. No one will believe him about us. Guy won't be able to describe four men accurately the twenty-thousand times the cops will ask him during their interrogation. Right?"

Kelvin said to Jimmy, "You stay here, we're gonna play hide-and-seek with the girl. Count to 100 then come look for us, okay?"

"Uh, okay." Jimmy grinned, seeming to grow even taller, broader.

Wally started dragging Dinah to the hall to go out through a rear room.

She kicked and screamed, her arms flailed trying to hit him to let her loose. He just snickered at her futile efforts and dragged her towards the back room.

Kelvin barked, "Hit her already, Wal, knock her the fuck out so she don't scream."

Wally grinned his acquiescence at Dinah. "You need to be silenced hon before you bring the neighborhood down on us." As he walked past Jimmy, he pulled back his fist to knock her out-

Suddenly, Jimmy leaped in the air- his legs whipped like scissors kicking Wally in the head twice with steel-toed boots.

Wally dropped Dinah who fell to the floor, then Wally crumpled down beside her out cold.

The other three thugs stared frozen for a shocked second. Then, as they sprung to life, Jimmy raced over, bashed his foot so hard in Kelvin's stomach he stumbled back crashing into a wall.

Before the next two men could blink, Jimmy twirled and struck out again with his steeled boot slamming straight into the heavy man's throat crushing his windpipe, then he spun and smashed his fist into the fourth guy's jaw so hard its shattering was audible.

The fourth guy dropped like a sack of potatoes, but Kelvin gathered his wits and came running at him.

Just as Kelvin got to Jimmy, Jimmy stepped aside and as Kelvin, moving too fast to stop hurtled awkwardly past him, Jimmy slammed down on the back of Kelvin's head with both fists, it sounded like his neck snapped.

Kelvin grunted, staggered a few steps then slumped to the floor. Jimmy crouched beside him and pulled the dollar bills out that Kelvin had taken from him and stuffed them back into his own pocket.

The man Jimmy had kicked in the throat was on his hands and knees holding his neck and gagging, struggling to draw a full breath. Jimmy jammed his knee into his face. As he toppled over, Jimmy stomped on his head.

Flat on the floor now, the man didn't move.

Jimmy trod over to the unconscious Wally and viciously kicked him in the head with the steel-toed boot. He looked over at Dinah's horrified gasp.

Jimmy's expression filled with revulsion for her, he said, "That was for you, for the slap. You're welcome, *cachau plismyn-* fucking cop."

Turning from her, Jimmy stood scanning the carnage, then he quickly raced behind the bar, returned with a roll of duct tape and taped all the unconscious/and/or/deceased thieves' wrists together behind their backs. Then, as he had done at the end of his shift every day since working there, he wiped down everywhere he had touched.

When done, he turned his attention to Dinah.

She was still sitting on the floor where Wally had dropped her, her face a mask of terror and shock and confusion.

Jimmy stomped over to her, bent and grabbed her arm jerking her to her feet. His face a fierce scowl he accused, "You're the undercover looking for me."

Dinah's jaw dropped, her wide eyes stared at him behind her tinted glasses. She gawked up at him, way up, over 6 feet 4 and continuing up. She babbled, "You- you're-"

The timid, mentally challenged hunchback was gone. Reeking of strength and confidence, Jimmy bowed arrogantly and announced, "Jozadak Kane, at your service."

He swiped his beanie off his head, the white-blond plumage crested out. "And you're the fucking cop on my tail here to dig up dirt to send me to prison. I shoulda known they'd sneak in a little girl to mislead me. Son of a bitch." He shook his head, angry at himself for falling for their trick.

Shocked, Dinah blanched. Blinking rapidly at him in stupefaction, she tried to back away but he held her arm.

"Come on," he said, his fury at her deceit rising. "We're getting out of here before someone else comes. They might have a driver or a lookout posted outside."

Yanking his knit hat back on, hiding the shock of blond hair, he twined his fingers around her arm like a steel clamp.

As he dragged her past the unconscious men, he saw a green hue tint her skin as she quickly looked away from the bloody and broken bodies.

"Are- are they dead?" she stammered, too stunned to fight his grip on her.

He grabbed up her badge and ID off the table and stuffed them in his pocket. Long-legging it through the room he shrugged, and replied, "Don't know, don't care."

Joze hauled her down the hall then into the back room. Once there, his face red with rage he shoved Dinah against a brick wall.

"Mister-"

"Shut the fuck up, bitch," he spouted. Spinning her around to face the wall, he took her wrists and pressed her palms and forearms flat against the bricks beside her head.

"Please, wait-" A frantic sob cut from her dry throat.

"I said shut up, *geneth*, girl. Don't move. Do what I tell you and I won't kill you right now." He spread his big toughened hand on her slender back to hold her, then nudged her feet apart with his boot. He ran both hands down her back and then down her sides to her waist.

Dinah yelped and tried to fight him, struggled to roll away from him and the wall.

He put his hand on her head and pushed the side of her face against the wall. Restraining her so it was impossible for her to move even a finger, he looked away from her small but very plump trembling lips forced to pout out from her head being squashed against the wall and continued to frisk her.

Joze leaned his torso against her back to keep her immobile then pushed both hands up her loose shirt. Feeling her flat belly, he ran his hands up her ribs to her breasts. His frisking slowed, feeling the exceptionally tight and thick bra she evidently wore to disguise her figure.

In a panic she started fighting again, twisting, pushing at the wall, her breath barely able to squeeze out of her throat constricted with fear.

"The more you struggle, little bitch cop, the longer this will take," he growled at her. His hands still cupping her breasts, he was shocked at how good she felt, a sudden burning sensation scorched his loins. A moan escaped him, which made him madder.

What the hell? He's had a lot of women in his lifetime, his reaction to touching her, even through the thick bra totally unsettled him.

Between those pouty lips and lush tits, he shook his head stymied at the feeling that struck him, he'd never felt such an urgent searing reaction to a woman before. His pants had grown suddenly uncomfortable. Without thinking, he pressed his arousal against her ass.

Pissed, he snarled in her ear, "This is what we do to fucking *plismyn*, cops, we fuck them before we kill them."

"Ji- Jimmy," her voice tight and shaking, she said, "you're not this kind of person, you're a gentle-"

His mouth next to her ear, his accent coming out heavy, he commanded viciously, "*Shut. Up.* I am not dumb Jimmy. I am Jozadak Dekar Kane, as you fucking well know, head of Chianina Enterprises."

21

Through clenched teeth he grated in a low, quiet snarl, "And like the name Chianina, a bull, I am not gentle, or kind, or nice."

"You mean you're head of a criminal syndicate, a Welsh mafia," she croaked through her throat clutched in fear.

His erection pounding at his jeans, the thought came to punish her, for being a cop, the cop sent to screw him, and for shocking and confusing him by feeling so good in his hands. Those puffy lips and swaying ass had already kept him awake many nights.

Keeping her hands braced against the wall, Joze could hear her trying to gulp back tears.

He stroked his hands back down her ribs over her waist, *what a damned tiny waist*, sticking his fingers inside the waistband of her pants, he moved them around the waist feeling for any hidden weapons.

Freaking out again, she jerked and twisted her body trying to get out from under him, but he kept her immobile, pressed against the wall.

His mouth still next to her ear, his voice grated harshly, "Don't worry, I'm only looking for weapons. Contrary to what I said, I would not sully my dick in your filthy cop pussy."

Crouching, he ran his hands over her hips and down each leg and ankle. Standing back up, he grasped her arm and swung her around, pushing her spine against the wall.

Even through the tinted glasses he could tell her eyes were brimming with tears. Her chested heaved and hitched with the struggle to stifle her sobs.

He snatched her glasses off and studied them. "Plain glass," he snorted and hurled them across the room.

Looking at her face, he said with a deep growl, "I knew there was something wrong with a woman who went to extreme lengths to hide her beauty. Even with that shitty disguise any red blooded male could see you had something going on."

His gaze went to her trembling lips, then up to see her blinking rapidly to hold back her tears.

With stiff, unemotional coldness, making a statement, not a compliment, deep anger chomping his voice, he said gruffly, "Those amazing eyes could be seen even behind those tinted glasses, at least for anyone who bothered to look."

He gripped her jaw, tilting her head up to stare at them. "They're kinda like amethyst quartz, blue-ish, with a tint of like a violet. No wonder you kept them hidden, you would have stood out like a fucking sore thumb with those jewel eyes."

Ashamed of the tears gleaming in them, Dinah lowered her eyes. She made to move from the wall but he gave her a push back against the bricks and spread his hand over her chest holding her secure.

Dark color furled over his chiseled face. With barely suppressed rage, he ground out, "Don't fucking move, cop, until I say you can."

She kept her head down as his gaze traveled her body like he could see through her clothes. His eyes burned right through them so intensely, she shivered.

He said quietly, "I'm betting, doll, there's more curvy action than I could feel going on under those frumpy duds."

Her lips parted confused, then her body turned rigid at his implication.

Laughing harshly without mirth, he said, "I don't have the time right now to strip you." Still clutching her arm, he tugged her ID out of his pocket.

Holding it up to read it, he looked at her and frowned. "*Shyt*, Dinah isn't even your real name." Glancing back at the ID, he said, "Is it, Glorie Lee Toby?" Stuffing the ID back in his pocket, he looked at her.

His eyes narrowed and he reached out to her. She flinched, turning her head expecting his fist to slam into her. She covered her face with her hands.

Irately, he pushed her hands away and grasped her chin. Turning her face forward, he glared at her. Her cheek was still pink from the man's slap, but there was a mark there now too. Indicating the cut on the side of her face he snapped, "Did I do that?"

She kept her eyes averted, she had obviously been wounded when he shoved her face against the bricks.

Trying to wrench her chin out of his grasp, Glorie frantically put her hands on his chest to push him away. Tears of fright welled in her desperate eyes. Realizing who held her in his grip, she was right to be terrified.

He looked down at her small slim hands pushing against his hard block of a chest. It was like a bunny pushing at an ox. Unfortunately, the warmth of her palms stoked the flames of lust he was already struggling to tamp.

Aggravated at the erotic feelings she stirred in him, nasty and crude, he mocked her, "What kind of fucking cop cries like a *bach babi,* a little baby?"

Her eyebrows suddenly slashed down as she glared at him with a flash of anger.

Still holding her chin he asked, "Who has eyes that crazy color?" He shoved her chin up forcing her to look at him. "Are you wearing colored contacts?"

When she didn't answer him, he slid a finger across one of his own eyes and held out a brown dot on his fingertip, and said with a mock, "Like these?"   .

Watching Glorie's brow furrow as she stared at the contact, he slipped out the other one and shoved them in his pocket then waited until she raised her eyes to his.

When she did, she reacted as he expected. Her lids opened so wide the whites around her irises were visible. Her plush lips parted, and deeper fear infiltrated her own pretty orbs. She tried to twist out of his strong grasp but her struggles were useless.

The electric blue sliced at her like twin lasers. Still trying to hold him back from her, her palms shaking against his shirt, the wall at her back, Glorie shrunk from him. He was so close; his powerful body enveloped her with his harsh masculine scent.

His attention moved to her hair. He released her chin to reach out and touch it. She pulled her head away from his reaching hand.

Smirking at her vain attempts to stop anything he chose to do to her, Joze touched her hair. Frowning, he clutched a handful of it and yanked her wig right off.

Her hands left his chest and went to her hair to stop the flaming curls from tumbling down around her shoulders and down her back.

Impulsively, he caught a bright curl. Rubbing it between his fingers, he murmured, "Sunrise has nothing on you, babe."

Studying the lock, he thought, *damned if I've ever seen hair that color before, like the part of a candle right between the yellow and the beginning of the hot orange part.* He sniffed it. It was *tirf-* fresh, fiery, luscious. He stuffed her wig in his back pocket.

His hands occupied, she suddenly bolted. Running as fast as she could, Glorie made for the hall.

She got about six steps away when he threw his arm around her waist jerking her to a hard stop. When he lifted her up in the air, she let out a piercing shriek then flailed at him, hitting and kicking out.

"Goddammit, cop," he cursed a string of vitriolic words in several languages. He had a set of handcuffs stashed in his boot.

Setting her on her feet, he swung her around so her back was to him. Bending over, he quickly snagged the cuffs. Pulling her arms behind her back, he snapped them on her wrists.

Heaving with panicked hitching breaths, Glorie cried, "Please, don't-"

Ignoring the stream of frightened tears flowing out of those amethyst eyes, he tied a cloth around her mouth.

Then he wound one hand around her arm and the other over the front of her neck, and said without emotion, "You were the one sent to find me. A fucking skirt." He looked her up and down, smirked with a grunt. "They covered you up so you wouldn't draw attention."

Fearful of his intent, she dropped her head.

He stuck his hand in her hair. Clutching a handful, he wrenched her head up and got in her face. "Huh," his snort angry, his gaze resentfully swept her face. "I thought you were so kind and sweet every time you stood up for me. You did that deliberately so I wouldn't suspect you as the cop?"

She looked down. He jerked her head so she had to look up at him. One dark brow arched puzzled, he wondered, "But you didn't know who I was until now."

25

Shaking his head, a corner of his lip pulled in. "You guys are good I'll give you that. I was expecting a male trying to track me down, not a..." he held her head up by her hair.

Completely vulnerable with her hands cuffed behind her back, she visibly trembled.

He sneered, "*Ie*, yeah, not a frightened little girl."

Joze jerked her hard towards the door and barked roughly, "Let's go, cop." He bent and scooped her up, hauling her over his shoulder.

Chapter Four

Joze carried her outside to his truck, set her down, opened the driver's door, and ordered, "Get in and slide over."

Balking at his command, Glorie turned away from him, her terrified gaze searching for a way to escape, someone to come to her aid.

His voice low with fury and impatience, he grated through clenched teeth, "I said get the fuck in the truck, *gast*, bitch." Then he realized as petite as she was, with her hands behind her back she wouldn't be able to get up the high running board.

He slid his hands under her, lifted her up over the high step and shoved her into the truck. Sticking a long leg in, he gave her a little push with his hip to move her in further along the bench seat then he slid in next to her.

She squirmed to the furthest corner of the passenger side and huddled against the door.

Joze reached over her- she cringed away thinking he was going to strike her, but he only pulled her seatbelt strap across her and locked it. He fired up the truck and pulled out of the lot, quickly hitting the main road.

A black scowl hardened his face like it was made of hostile granite. Keeping his eyes on the road, Joze drove a few miles before glancing over at her.

She tried to scrunch into the corner, hard to do with her hands cuffed behind her. Over the gag, her jewel-like eyes stared at him like he was a serial killer about to jump her and stab her a hundred times.

His eyes lowered, with her arms pulled back, the loose shirt tightened. Even under the tight, thick bra, her breasts strained against the shirt, jiggling with each rocking movement of the truck.

Seeing the direction of his gaze, she tried to turn from his view but she was trapped with the cuffs and the seatbelt. She turned her head away from him to face the side window.

Shifting his gaze back to the front, not wanting to get stopped by the police, Joze kept to the speed limit.

For miles, Glorie was sniffing and gulping so hard next to him he finally couldn't stand it.

Pulling over, he put the truck in park and reached in front of her to open the glove box.

Her eyes widened at the gun in a holster he pulled out. He hooked the holster on then grabbed her arms turning her, so her back was towards him. He moved her around easily with his brute strength, like she weighed nothing more than a doll.

The sudden rigidity of her spine told him she thought he was going to shoot her in the back of the head.

Instead, he unlocked the handcuffs and took them off, looped them over the back of his belt, then removed her gag.

His tone laced with promised violence he threatened her, "Don't try anything or I'd just as soon kill you and dump your body in a damned swamp."

Wiping at her eyes, she mumbled, "You're going to anyway." Glorie rubbed hard at the tears with her palms trying to stop their flow.

Joze looked at her then away without a word. He shifted the truck into drive and once again hit the road.

After a few miles, she put her hand on the door handle-

His arm snaked over in a flash, stabbing his hand in her hair. Wrapping it around his big fist, he snarled, "We are going 55 mph, you will die if you try to jump out. And if you try and you can't get the door open quick enough, I will fucking break your arm for trying. So go ahead, try it."

Not daring to look at him, she moved her shaking hand to her lap. His furious tough voice was frightening enough.

He gave her a small shove as he released her hair, moved his furious gaze back on the road and headed towards the expressway.

After hours of driving, Glorie kicked off her shoes and curled up in a ball. Her legs up on the seat, she wrapped her arms around her knees and fell asleep with her back against the door and her head on her knees.

Joze liked the air cool, but he saw goose bumps on her arms. Pulling his jacket off the back of his seat, he laid it over her. He didn't need the little bitch cop getting sick on him before he figured out what to do with her.

He drove for half a day before stopping at burger place.

"Hey, cop." He gave her arm a nudge. Resting his left arm on the wheel he watched her long lashes, a bit darker than her flaming curls flutter.

Her lids opened slowly over those remarkable eyes. Obviously disoriented for a moment, her body froze, then she turned slowly to face him.

Observing her under hooded lids, Joze saw her pupils flare in fright, her arms tightened in protection around her knees. The jacket slipped off her. She swallowed so hard he could hear her.

He handed her wig to her.

She stared at it without moving. Thrusting it in her hands, he ordered, "Put it on."

He waited while she struggled to stuff her full curls into the brown wig.

"Look at me," he commanded. She turned to him. He tugged the bangs down over her brows. He leaned in front of her and opened the glove box. Pulling out sunglasses, he handed them to her. "Put these on."

Joze waited until she had the glasses on. They were his so they were big enough to cover half her head.

Satisfied she was unrecognizable again, he said, "We're going inside that restaurant. After I make sure the restroom is clear, you will go in. When you come out, we're going to order food and sit and eat it. I need a break from behind that wheel."

His brows lowered, anger sparked in his blue eyes. "If I suspect you so much as look at someone, try to talk to anyone, pass a note, trust me," he clutched her chin, bringing her face within inches of his and threatened, "I'll kill you and the person you try to contact. Tell me you understand."

Trying to blink back her fear, Glorie nodded.

He shook her. "Out loud, cop."

She swallowed hard, rasped barely audible, "I, uh, understand you."

He stared hard at her for a moment, then he let her go and opened the door and got out and waited for her to shuffle across the seat to the door.

Standing aside, he gripped her upper arm, helping her slide out of the truck and down the high running board then closed the door and locked the truck.

Twining his thick fingers around her slender arm, her head barely reached his shoulder, he ushered her inside the fast food restaurant. They went straight to the ladies room.

"All right. You go in and come right back out to tell me if anyone else is in there." He opened the door, with his hand over her head he held it open while she walked under his arm to go inside.

Letting the door close, he waited while she went in. In seconds she came right out.

He asked, "Is there anyone else in there?"

She shook her head.

"Okay, go in. I'll check after you come out, so don't try to leave any kind of message. You will only endanger an innocent party. You clear?" He waited while she nodded then opened the door for her again. When she went back inside, he stood like a guard in front of the door.

In a few minutes the door opened, he grasped it holding it open for her then walked her up to the counter. He didn't bother checking the restroom for a message, she wasn't gone but for a few minutes and she had nothing to write with. At the counter he asked her, "What do you want to eat?"

Her hand on her stomach, she murmured politely, "Nothing, I couldn't eat a thing."

Joze frowned down at her. He knew she hadn't eaten since the day before. He had heard her mention to Rubal that the saloon had been so busy all day starting with crack of the dawn prepping, she hadn't had a moment to eat.

He ordered them both burgers, fries, sodas and two bottles of water then took her to a booth.

"Get in and slide over." He waited while she sat on the red vinyl seat and moved over before sitting beside her.

A big guy, his powerful shoulders took up three quarters of the seat. Glorie pressed herself against the wall to get as far away from him as possible.

He unwrapped his burger and took two huge bites then shoved several French fries in his mouth before he noticed she hadn't moved. She sat staring at the food he'd placed in front of her.

He ordered her, "Eat, cop."

She didn't move a muscle.

Letting out a labored sigh, Joze said, "Glorie, I'm not going to be a happy guy if I have to tell you twice to do something. Now, I'm not dragging a starving, dehydrated woman all over town, so," he leaned into her face, and shouted beneath his breath, "*fucking eat.*"

The words tumbling tremulously over her tongue, without looking at him, Glorie said quietly, "You can leave me somewhere along the road, by the time I could get to a phone you would be long gone."

"*Ie,* yeah, sure. You'd blab to the first *plismyn,* cop you saw how I took out those robbers, if not dead, at the very least they all will have some recovery time in the hospital."

The word he said, ie for yes, sounded to Glorie like 'ee-eh'. Now she looked at him, but his eyes were so cold and cruel she quickly looked away. "It was self-defense, Jim- um, besides, when they realize we are missing they will figure it out."

"Ah, but they will know me as Jimmy Jones. They would never be able to find a person who doesn't exist. Trust me, I was ultra careful to never leave a print or DNA. The ID and SS# I used for the hiring were false, and I was careful not to leave a print on the application form."

He smirked at her. "And, any descriptions of me? A hunchback of indeterminable height and weight with brown hair, brown eyes."

Smiling, he hunched over, and let his mouth hang open in a stupid stupor like he'd done the entire time he'd worked at the saloon. "They won't have a clue that Jimmy Jones is really Jozadak Kane."

He shoved in a few more fries, chewed them while peering at her under hooded eyes. "But you, sweetheart, you know who I am. Now. Don't you?" His lip turned up in an unpleasant sneer. The sneer quickly turned into a scowl. "Eat, goddammit," he demanded.

Grabbing up his soda, he shook it to loosen the ice noisily and gulped some.

Glorie's lip trembled, she made a gesture towards her burger but didn't unwrap it.

"Okay, fine, Glorie Lee Toby. I told you, I ain't hauling around a sick cop." He put his mouth near her ear and said quietly, "See that old lady over there?"

He nodded towards an elderly woman sitting alone at a table. "Do you think she can take my big cock?"

Glorie choked. The threat of Joze Kane attacking and raping the old lady, paled the pink out of her round cheeks.

Joze picked up her burger, unwrapped it and handed it to her.

She took it, nibbled a bite. Every time she set the hamburger down he inclined his head towards the elderly woman. He made her drink all of her bottled water before touching the soda.

Watching her struggle to stuff down the burger into her roiling stomach, Joze said, "I don't get it. Either you're a helluva lot older than you look, or, *shyt*, I don't know. You are too young to be undercover. It's clear as a bell that you are tremendously inexperienced, hell, they didn't even give you a fucking gun leaving you vastly vulnerable."

Turning sideways in his seat to face Glorie, his gaze stroked over her. "Tell me, little cop, how the hell did you get this assignment?"

Glorie set her food down, chewed then swallowed the meat past the lump in her throat. She considered what she should say. Maybe if she was open and chatty she could win him over and he'd let her go.

Wiping her fingers daintily on the paper napkin, she said, "I only just got hired. I was a civilian doing cybercrime surveillance. I was just about to go through the academy when a…detective came into my division and summoned me. He, uh, told me I was to go undercover, immediately. They swore me in, gave me a badge and sent me here."

Chowing down the last of his fries, Joze licked the ketchup off his fingers, then started on her fries knowing she wasn't going to eat them. "Why did they take such a green, delicate," his gaze slid facetiously down her body, "*bach gethen*, little girl, to do such a fucking dangerous job?"

She took a sip of cola. "They wanted to go after…uh, you, quickly. All the pros they had, my…handler thought you might already know. He said you could have placed a mole in the department. He thought that my…greenness would actually benefit in that you would look right through me."

Shrugging slender shoulders, she said, "You would never be suspicious of the homely," her lip turned up wryly, "young woman, a wallflower blending unnoticed in the background. You would be so interested in the beautiful barmaids out front you'd never give a nondescript woman like me any notice."

His snort dry, he said drolly, "Don't kid yourself honey. Even in that disguise most men saw through it. Saw that graceful sensuality that-" he broke off, quickly slugged down his soda.

Playing with the straw in her soda, she said, "It worked."

Joze sat back against the seat and studied her. "No one hit on you, cop, because you kept a wall up and stayed as far in the background as you could get." He laughed short. "Except Rubal. *Cachau pigio*, fucking prick wanted me to help him rape you in the back room."

He smiled at the drop of her jaw and shocked disbelief flashing from her eyes. "Honey, a man can get tired of those tawdry plastic dolls in the bar real quick. You, you're a whole different ballgame."

She didn't understand what he meant, and she didn't want to know so she didn't ask.

When they were done, he picked up both sodas, refilled them then ushered her back to the truck. Holding the door for her, he clasped her arm to help her up the high step and handed in her soda.

Joze didn't follow her inside. He closed the door and locked it, then went around the front. Leaning a hip against the hood, he pulled out his phone and lit a cigarette.

He talked for a few minutes, all the time staring at her through the window.

She'd put the soda in a cup holder then curled up again in the corner of passenger side, kicked her shoes off, pulled her feet up on the seat and protectively wrapped her arms around her knees.

His lips twisted bemused that she still thought she could do anything to stop him from doing anything he wanted to her.

He filled Linc in on what had happened, then he told Linc to leave an anonymous call to the cops advising that Rubal Sacket was the inside guy associated with the robbers.

After ending the call, Joze hopped in the truck then they drove for hours, occasionally stopping for food and so they could relieve themselves.

Not quite dawn yet, Joze pulled into a hotel parking lot. Turning off the vehicle, he said, "Keep the wig on, and put the sunglasses back on."

At her look, he said, "I don't care if it looks strange having dark glasses on at night. Just do as I say."

34

When she followed his instructions, he exited the truck then leaned back inside. He said brusquely to her, "Come on," and grasped her arm to help her down.

Outside the door, Joze said under his breath, "Again, if you say a word, or look funny at anyone," he lifted his shirt showing her the gun. Her eyes popped at the weapon then rose to his cold eyes, his threat was real.

They went inside. He told her to stay over to the side near a wall and study tourist pamphlets so she wasn't as noticeable, and he strode up to the counter and got a room.

He took her to the room and stuck the key card in, opened the door, motioned for her to go in then put the security lock on when he closed the door.

Glorie stood frozen staring at the room. It had double beds. She let out a held breath.

"You can go use the bathroom, take a shower if you want. This is an inside room, there is no window for escape in the bathroom, but you will keep the door open an inch."

At her red face he said, "Take it or leave it. I have no desire, cop, to see you naked. So relax." He turned from her.

She stood for a minute, unsure, then she went into the bathroom.

Hearing the shower run, Joze stared at the bathroom door. She'd followed his instructions and left the door, well not really open but not closed completely either. He told the truth that he wouldn't hassle her, but he lied about not having the desire to see her naked.

A few minutes after the shower shut off, the bathroom door opened slowly. Her cheeks flushed with embarrassed color, she kept her eyes lowered as she came out dressed back in her clothes. The flaming curls were wet. She combed through them with her fingers.

"Come over here," Joze ordered, his voice held a husky rasp. He waited while she went very slowly to him.

He pointed to one of the beds. "Get in and lie down."

Peeping nervously up at him through her lashes, she did as he said.

Towering over her, Joze said, "Give me your hand." She held her hand out to him. He took it and snapped his handcuffs to her wrist then to the lamp that was attached to the nightstand.

Her eyes never left him as he trod to the window and looked out.

After a long perusal, he closed the curtains tight. Without looking at Glorie, he went to bathroom and took a shower.

Ten minutes passed then he came out and went to the other bed. He removed his gun and put it under his pillow. Then he set his phone, keys, wallet, and a few other things on the nightstand. He left the knives on his person.

Without a word, he shut off the light then laid on top of the covers fully clothed as she was. However, she had slipped beneath the sheet and blanket.

Like in the truck, he listened to her sniffing and hiccupping, trying to hide her sobbing breaths until she fell asleep. He figured she was assuming he was going to kill her when they reached their destination and it would be futile to try to escape him.

In that last assumption, she would be right. He was too big, too fast, too strong, too lethal.

The morning had passed by the time Joze woke up. He swung his legs over the side of the mattress and got up.

Glancing over at Glorie in the room still dark from the heavy curtain, she appeared to be asleep.

Taking his gun from under his pillow, he shoved it back into the holster at the back of his waist, tugged his shirt over it and put all the other items into his pockets. He made not a sound as he left the room.

When he returned, it looked like she was still asleep.

His footsteps were soundless as he trod across the carpet to Glorie's bed. Joze stared down at her.

Long lashes curled on high, round pink cheeks. Brilliant curls spiraled around her pillow. Not a beautiful girl in the classic sense, her mouth was plump but small and her eyes were big, yet her looks were crazy startling, and way more interesting than the cookie cutters he normally saw.

She was vulnerable and sexy at the same time even in the loose clothes. A sharp twinge struck his groin.

Ignoring his penis' attempt to get his attention, he leaned closer to her.

She had a few light freckles sprinkled across her small not quite turned up nose. There was that tiny plump pink mouth, and her small chin a contrast to the rounded cheeks. She looked young, helpless.

He stood up straight with a snap, *and a cop*. She might not look like one, but they come in all shapes, sizes, genders.

She was not at all like the women he was used to, His world attracted lusty, tough, coarse, strong women. This girl was creamy skinned and petite and…nice. He wasn't the only one he'd seen her bravely try to protect from the mean staff at the saloon.

Annoyed with himself for studying her so intently, he roughly shook her arm.

The amethyst eyes opened slowly, then flung wide in confusion. Disorient turned to terror when she saw him looking down at her. She grabbed the sheet and pulled it up her chin.

Leaning over to unlock the cuffs, he could feel her so afraid she was shaking against him.

Tucking the cuffs in his belt he said, "Honey, if I wanted you, and fucking believe that I don't because you make me sick," he sneered, "no flimsy sheet would keep you safe, right?"

Looking up at the tall man with his strapping physique, every threatening part of him was muscled without an ounce of fat. Her eyes just grew bigger and more frightened.

Seeing her so afraid of him, his voice gruff, he said harshly, "Get up, we're leaving. You have 5 minutes in the bathroom."

He pointed at her nightstand. "There's a donut and coffee. I expect you to eat. I don't need to carry around a starving fainting *gethen*. You don't eat and I will grab the first old lady I find and," he grabbed his crotch, promised crudely, "tear her up."

Satisfied at the horrified look on her face, he stood back and said coldly, "Make it snappy."

He drove for several hours then pulled off the side of the road. Shifting towards her in the seat, he said, "Put your hands in your lap and don't move them again until I say you can, or the cuffs go back on."

Staring hard out the windshield, she did as he ordered.

The truck still running in park, he leaned over and wrapped a cloth around Glorie's eyes.

Her mouth opened, she gulped in a deep breath but didn't say anything.

After several more hours, there was the sound of gravel crunching of gravel beneath the tires indicating they'd left the main road.

After a bit, the truck came to a halt.

Chapter Five

"**O**kay, you can move now."

But she didn't. She was too afraid of what she would see.

Making an impatient sound, he reached over her, unbuckled her seatbelt then removed the cloth from her eyes. When he took it off, he felt it damp with her tears.

She rubbed her eyes and blinked to adjust to the light. Looking out the window she could see a large structure like a lodge, with bunches of smaller buildings, and some dorm-like places scattered around the building.

To the back were barns, paddocks and stables. Beyond them spread soft green pastures, and meadows teeming with wildflowers, and way off in the distance blocking the horizon was a fringe of dense forest.

Unseen due to a thrush of trees, near the east side of the house was a steep hill that ultimately dropped sheer to a treacherous waterfall. It helped protect the property from sneak attacks from the rear of the property.

Joze exited the truck then waited for her to slide over. Putting his hands around her waist, he lifted her out, setting her on her feet.

Holding her arm, he walked her up the gravel driveway to the house.

There were numerous cars scattered around the area. Horses' whinnies broke the silence of the balmy day. The front door to the large building was open. He pushed through the screen door and brought her inside. Immediately a short round woman scurried over to them.

"Master Joze!" she exclaimed in a Hispanic accent. "You're finally home!" She threw her tubby body at him and hugged him.

If her situation weren't so dire, Glorie would have been amused at the short stout woman hugging the lean abdomen of the very tall, hard muscled man.

Surprisingly, Joze hugged the woman back. "Ah, Maria. *Ie*, yes, I'm home. I hope that's paella I smell cooking." He stepped back from her.

Looking at Glorie, Maria's grin puffed up her round face. Clapping her hands together, she declared with great cheer, "So, you have brought back a beautiful bride with you?"

Both Glorie and Joze winced.

"*Na*," Joze said quickly. "She is, uh, I'll explain later. Right now I need you to take her into the room that adjoins mine, get her clothes off her and bring them to me. Underwear, everything, her shoes included."

Both women looked aghast at him.

"Señor Joze! What on earth-" Maria protested.

The blush drained from Glorie's face.

He frowned at both of them. "Maria, you know I don't like to have to repeat my orders or have them questioned."

Shocked, Maria nodded awkwardly. "Of course, Master Joze. Um," her gaze flicked to Glorie's mortified face, she asked, "what will she put on?"

Joze contemplated Glorie's petite figure. "After you bring me her clothes, see if Julia has something to loan her if she's still here. She's the closest to her size. Now go." He motioned with his hands for them to go.

Maria said kindly to Glorie, "Come with me, señorita."

Glorie had no choice but to go with her.

Maria led the young police officer down a long hall. Joze followed them at a slower pace.

They passed a large living room where half a dozen people were hanging out. They stared curiously at Glorie as she went by.

They moved past numerous rooms before Maria stopped.

She brought Glorie through a bedroom then through an adjoining door that led into another bedroom.

It was plain, decorated with cream walls and pale blue carpet. It contained a bed, dresser, nightstand, a small table and a couple of chairs.

"Wait right here, miss." Maria scurried out of the room and came back quickly carrying a robe.

"Maria," both women looked over at his deep voice, he stood just outside the doorway. "You watch her. I mean it. Don't take your eyes off her."

Her face pooling into a puzzled frown, Marie closed the door almost in Joze's face.

"Um," the maid said awkwardly, "I guess, the master said, uh," she trailed off at the frightened apprehensive look on Glorie's face.

"It's okay, Maria. I know we have to do as he says." Glorie could tell although Maria hugged him like he was a son, she also had strict respect for Joze as a man, as a boss.

Having no desire for this forty-something woman to suffer Joze's wrath for not following his orders, she unbuttoned her blouse, drew it off and handed it to Maria. Then her pants, socks, bra, panties, last she handed her the shoes she wore.

As fast as she could, Glorie pulled on the robe and tied it closed. It was big, it swamped her small figure.

"I will return shortly." Maria opened the bedroom door and hurried out. Glorie could see Joze leaning a hip against a wall, his arms crossed, knit hat still covering his hair, waiting.

It took a while before Maria returned with a pair of jeans and a pale blue blouse with pearl buttons. "Here miss," she said, handing the clothes to Glorie. She also had a pair of sheer pink panties and matching bra.

Glorie dressed quickly.

Maria nodded with approval. "Yes, Julia is small and skinny, you fill out her clothes very nicely. Your figure is much more," she broke off at the red flooding Glorie's face. "I see that you are very shy, miss."

She smiled kindly at Glorie. "Here, miss, she gave me shoes and socks too. The hiking boots are hardly worn, she's always buying new clothes, shoes," she sighed but with affection, "that girl, what a spendthrift!"

Then Maria stepped outside of the room and handed Glorie's clothes to Joze.

Taking them, he said, "Do not leave this room, either of you." He closed the door.

Seeing Maria's calm pleasant expression, Glorie said, "You don't seem to be afraid of him?"

Shaking her head, wisps from her bun fluttered around Maria's round face. "Of course not, miss. I've known him most of his life."

"But- but he's a- a gangster, a killer, he's a criminal!"

Maria frowned darkly at Glorie. "He has a family business passed down from his father. Mathius was a hard cruel man. He molded Mr. Joze. Beat him brutally almost daily, pushed him, forced him into the family business.

"Mathius Kane thought Mr. Joze was the only one of his children smart enough, strong enough, to take over the business. His three brothers were free to find work as mercenaries after all four left the military, and his little sister does as she pleases."

Taken aback a bit, Glorie said, "That sounds, dreadful. But, it doesn't change that he is a- murderer, a racketeer."

Maria's lips pursed. "He has never been charged with murder, and he has struggled to turn the businesses into legitimate enterprises. He couldn't do that until his father passed which was only this past year."

"Nonetheless, Maria, he is still a criminal."

Maria eyed her with suspicion. "You sound like a police officer."

Glorie's face stiffened, she replied coolly, "I am a police officer."

A smirk pulled up one side of Maria's mouth. She looked Glorie up and down. "Please, miss, you are too young and too fragile to be an officer. Besides, Master Joze would never bring the police into his house. He was brought up to distrust and hate the police. He's known so many corrupt officers they all disgust him."

Her lips compressed, Glorie glared at the maid.

Maria's eyes widened. "You tell the truth? You are a policewoman? I cannot believe it."

The door opened. Joze poked his head in. "Maria, you may leave." He glanced at Glorie, his face expressionless, he said, "You stay here. The door will be locked."

Seeing Maria's distressed look at Glorie, he ordered, "Now Maria."

The maid patted Glorie's shoulder. "Everything will be all right, miss." She left the room and without another look at Glorie, Joze closed the door. The lock clicked.

Joze retrieved a hammer, nails and a couple of pieces of wood about 18 inches by 3 inches. He hammered them across the window of the room Glorie was in. A person could still see out but would not be able to get out.

Then he went to his truck and hopped in. He drove a distance away before parking.

Climbing out of the vehicle, Joze took Glorie's clothes to a campsite and burned them. Then he took the ashes, put them in a plastic bag, shoved some rocks in the bag, got back in the truck, drove a few more miles then threw the bag off a bridge into a rolling river.

Back at the house, a group had gathered, no doubt the word about Glorie had spread. Joze went inside.

Linc came right over to him. "Anything else happen since we talked?"

Sticking his hands in his pockets, Joze shook his head. They waited until the rest of his team joined them then he told the entire story in detail.

Rifling his fingers through his beard stubble, Sloan said, puzzled, "Why didn't you let those men take her, they would have silenced her and ended your problem."

Joze didn't respond. He looked out the window.

The spacious room behind him was comfortable with beige walls and dark brown rugs. Big cushiony chairs in different prints along with numerous tables scattered around them filled the room, and several sofas lined the walls.

A half dozen men helped themselves to the bar set up over by the kitchen. Women, scantily clad, lounged around on the furniture like it was a harem except also occupied by tough men.

"Joze? Why did you bring her here of all places? Why didn't you let those men take her?" Bruno asked. He kept sliding his phone out of his pocket hoping to see a text from his girlfriend, Melissa.

Seeing the cell was blank, he shoved it back in his pocket, and with irritation stiffening his fingers, he combed them through his long, straight black hair.

Joze pulled his hands from his pockets and crossed his arms over his chest stacked with slabs of rock hard muscles. "It's better to know who my enemy is, and where she is, then wait for another one that I don't know to replace her."

A loud laugh burst from Linc, his amber curls bouncing. "*Ie*, right. Bullshit, Joze. You can't fool me. You couldn't leave a woman, even a cop, to be gang-raped and murdered. Right?"

He smirked at his friend's annoyed expression. Then, one curly brow drew down over one of his triumphant bronze colored eyes. Linc said slyly, "I bet she's a looker, *bráithre*, am I right?"

"*Cachau bant, pen pidyn*, fuck off, dickhead. I'm hungry, is dinner ready?" Joze glanced around the room ignoring the women that displayed themselves wantonly, vying for his attention, and he searched for a maid.

He spotted Maria scuttling out of the kitchen towards him. With his friends chuckling at him, he scowled and asked, "Maria, is dinner ready?"

She nodded, her normal cheerful face pensive. "*Si*, everyone can go into the dining room."

Joze nodded at Sloan. "Tell everyone to go on in."

He waited until the room started clearing then he said quietly to the housekeeper, "Bring her a plate, Maria, and a lot of water. And whatever else she asks for. Make sure the door stays locked. Don't turn your back to her."

He looked around for one of his men, then called Maria again just as she started for the kitchen, "Maria."

The older plump woman turned, her twinkling dark eyes smiled at him, one brow waited high for his instruction.

A side of his mouth turned up. "Find something for her to sleep in. A nightgown or something. Make sure she has any..." Joze never felt embarrassment, but a tinge of pink lit his severe cheeks. "Uh, women things she needs, and you know, a toothbrush to replace the crappy hotel one, and a comb."

Scowling at her teasing wink, Joze saw the man he was looking for just walking in. Joze called him over.

The tall, lanky man with dark blond hair smiled at Joze. "You're back, Boss," he said redundantly.

"*Ie*. Listen, Van, you've probably heard I brought a woman back with me."

Van nodded and winked. "You've never brought one of your women into this house. You fool around a little here, but you've never taken a woman into your bed here. She must be special."

Sighing, Joze briefly explained about Glorie.

Van's brows drew down further and further as he talked.

When he got done, Joze said, "I have a job for you. I want you to be the *plismyn*, uh cop's guard. I want you to have eyes on her all the time unless I say otherwise."

Van's yellow eyebrows rose, he said, "Of course I'll do whatever you say, but why me?"

The side of Joze's lip curved up. "Because you are not an essential personnel, you're tough, and I know you are the only male here that would not be susceptible to her wiles to be tricked, or want to jump her bones."

His mouth pulled back in a smirk. "I see. So I get this job because I'm gay?"

"Yup. When you see her you'll understand. So, she's in that back bedroom, the one that adjoins mine. Get yourself something to eat then go park in my bedroom door. *Iawn*, all right?"

Van nodded. "Yes sir, no prob." He swung around and headed for the kitchen.

Letting out a held breath, Joze went into the dining room. He could smell the paella from where he was, and he could hear the animated voices ringing down the hall.

He joined the people at the long table, but only half listened to conversations. His attention was glued to the room at the end of the hall.

A woman on his left did everything she could to engage him in conversation, or anything else he wanted, however, she was nothing but an annoying fly buzzing around his head.

He pictured the little cop roaming around the room seeking an escape. A small smile curved his harsh lips until he then pictured her stepping into the shower. The warm water spraying her naked body-

Joze tore his imagination away and addressed his paella. Thoughts like that were not good for him, or anyone else.

It took everything he had to put out of his mind the way she'd felt when he'd pressed up against her, his hands roaming her body, how soft she felt, the scent of her- again- he shook his head and reached for his drink.

He'd need a lot of liquor tonight to banish the filthy cop from his mind. A lot.

Chapter Six

Towards the end of dinner, Jake Jenkins came in through the kitchen door. He hesitated only briefly in the doorway before he quickly spotted Joze amongst the 20 plus men and women sitting around the long oblong table.

Jake caught Joze's eye, then looked over at Linc then back to Joze. Joze stood up, as did Linc, Joze glanced at Calvin, Sloan, Diego and Bruno, they all rose.

Conversation stopped as the seven men filed out of the room. They made their way down one of the halls to the study.

Joze pushed open the French doors to the room decorated in masculine browns and blues, scattered with easy chairs and numerous small tables. A few had a book or newspaper left on them.

A round table with wooden chairs also cushioned circling it stood off center. A stone fireplace took up the far end of the room, and sliding glass doors opened to the pasture where the horses were let out in the early morning.

When the men had made themselves comfortable at the table, Joze folded his hands together and rested his forearms on the cherry wood. "So, what's going on, Jake?" he asked the gangly man with a long nose and sharp chin. Fine light hair wisped over his eyes.

Jake dragged his long knobby fingers down the front of his face. Light brown eyes the same color as his hair darted around the table at the other men then settled back on Joze.

Several lamps were on, the light brightened Joze's white-blond hair even more than usual, it made him look other-worldly, like a tough angel.

Jake cleared his throat. Adam's apple bobbed sharply, he said, "Yeah, Boss, it's Greer."

Joze rolled his eyes. What was it with his people that he had to drag information out of them? "And, Jenkins, what did Samson Greer do?" he prodded the lanky guy.

Muttering, "Yeah, well," Jake pulled at his long nose. "His men broke into a few of the, uh, your business offices."

He took a deep trebly breath then went on, "They couldn't get to anything important, the computers and stuff, but they tore the rooms up just to be assholes." He watched and waited for Joze's reaction, preparing himself. Joze had a violent temper.

Joze pushed to his feet and stalked out of the room. The five men of his top echelon got up wordlessly and followed him out.

Jake sat paralyzed at the table, blinking, panting like he'd held his breath for an hour and licked his dry lips. He'd been terrified to give Joze the bad news.

Grabbing his black leather trench coat and his keys, Joze strode out the door.

By the time he climbed behind the wheel of his truck, Linc, Bruno, and Calvin were jumping in.

Diego and Sloan scrambled in Diego's truck and were right behind Joze as he raced out down the gravel road, tires spitting gravel and dust behind them.

When they got to the city the street lights were on and most of the windows in the buildings were dark.

A few modern steel and window skyscrapers steepled across the night sky, but most buildings were one to three floors made of brick and plaster, more rustic and antiquated like the western town it was.

Both trucks parked.

Joze got out and strode around the back of his truck and unlocked the chrome toolbox that was bolted to the bed of the truck.

Once he opened it, the men took out gloves, crowbars, hammers, shotguns, and other variegated weapons. Joze closed and locked the box.

They all trod down the back alley to the back of Samson Greer's main office building. Greer was a rival of Joze's as well as Falcon DeMarco.

While Linc went and cut the alarm, being the most massive of all of the men, Calvin, built like a bulldozer, hooked the crowbar around the bars over one of the windows. It took all of his strength with grunts and groans, his shaved brown head sweating, but he'd done this before. He grinned when he peeled down the last bar.

At 6'2" the smallest of the men, Bruno tapped the wooden bottom of the window with a hammer until it loosened then he and Sloan pushed it up and Bruno climbed through.

They only waited a few minutes for him to make his way around to the door to let them in.

Their footsteps barely registered on the carpeted stairs.

Using the hammer and pliers, Bruno pried the door to Samson's office off. They set it neatly to the side, leaning against the wall, then they all traipsed in.

Joze went through the webbing of offices and hallways to Samson's opulent office.

Diego came in behind him with a metal-detecting device, he walked around the room holding it up until it beeped. Moving a picture, he grinned at the vault. It took him very few seconds to break into it. He pulled out the computer and handed it to Joze.

Joze carried it to Samson's desk, set it down, pulled his fancy chair up to his lavish, gold and marble desk and fired it up. He inserted a USB that had a program that hacked passwords.

Amidst the pounding and hammering, smashing and shattering going on around him and down the hall, Joze browsed through several documents, opened a few and studied them.

After a bit of scrutiny, he slammed the lid down, picked the laptop up and stuffed it under his arm then strode from the office.

By the time he reached the stairs to leave, his men were in a line behind him.

They moved swiftly and silently back to their vehicles, tossed the tools and gloves back into the box then hopped in and drove off into the dark.

Back at the ranch, Calvin, Diego, Bruno and Sloan took off for their own rooms.

Linc followed Joze back to the study.

Once Joze set the laptop on the round table, fired it up again he sat down in front of it.

Linc pulled out a chair and straddled it. He rested his burly forearms on the back of the chair and set his chin on his wrist.

"How long's it going to take you to transfer his accounts to yours?" Linc eyed the ashtray Joze pulled close to him never looking away from the computer.

Frowning, Linc scratched at the side of his temple, pushing back some of the curls over his ear. "Joze, *bráith*, you've gotta quit that shit, man," he said, watching Joze light a cigarette and set it in the ashtray.

"*Ie*, sure. You want to open a window, Sarg?" Joze tucked the end of the cigarette in a corner of his mouth and kept tapping at the keys until he found what he wanted.

Shaking his head, Linc got up, pushed one of the sliding doors to the side to let in fresh air then went back and sat down.

Answering his question, Joze pulled the cigarette out holding it while he exhaled the smoke then said, "Probably just a couple of hours."

"Huh. So," Linc grinned slyly. "Why are you working here instead of at your desk in your room?"

Joze ignored him, his face an impassive mask, he scanned the monitor.

A tinkle of a snicker trickled from deep in Linc's rough chest. "Which one is it, Joze, you afraid you can't resist the temptation, to kill her, or fuck her?"

His fingers stopped moving for a second before Joze bent his head over the laptop and kept searching without responding to Linc's niggle.

Linc kept him company, they chatted here and there while Joze worked.

A few hours and his task was completed. Joze sat back and stretched.

Linc said, "You want a scotch to celebrate?"

Yawning, Joze shook his head and pulled his black shirt down from his stretch. "*Na*, I think I'll just turn in."

Smirking again, Linc said, "Worried the booze will lower your willpower and you'll break down the adjoining door and take her?"

"Goddammit, Linc," Joze cursed and rose quickly to his feet with annoyance. "Get off it. She's just a fucking *gast plismyn*, bitch cop." Stubbing out the cigarette, he closed the laptop and tucked it under his arm.

"Uh, huh," Linc needled him, "so why on God's green earth did you bring her here? It's exactly what she was looking for, where you live, to dig up shit on you, bro."

Struggling to keep his scowl at bay, Joze muttered, "She doesn't know where we are. I blindfolded her on the way here. Here she'll be under my nose, I can see what use she could be to me." He headed towards the door.

Linc swung his leg around and off the chair to his feet following his friend. "Yeah, sure, that makes fucking sense. Shit sense. Cripes, Joze, all the other bitches and extraneous men here you don't think she'll find out where she is in like," he snapped his fingers, "a skinny minute?"

Over his shoulder, Joze grumbled, "Just shut up already, bro, when the hell did you become such a fucking chatty Kathy?" He stalked through the ranch to his room with Linc's snickers in his ears.

Joze's bedroom was large enough to hold a king-sized bed, a mahogany armoire with matching dressers and nightstands, a big desk took up a corner of his room with cabinets and bookcases.

A door opened into an all white bathroom with whirlpool tub. Another door in the middle of the wall led to the adjoining room Glorie was in.

He locked Samson Greer's computer in his own vault in the walk-in closet and hopped in the shower. Thank God there was a shower in his room and also one in the adjoining one. He and the cop should be able to avoid each other easily enough.

Standing under the hot water beating down on him, Joze thought about her. His surprise and disgust at discovering she was a cop still shocked and disgruntled him. Who would have figured that mousy yet brave little chick at the saloon would turn into a fucking femme fatale cop.

Worse, the *gast* wasn't even aware of her allure. The bitch seemed green, like she was plucked from the Midwest countryside and suddenly plunked down in the middle of the big city.

Ah shyt, he couldn't believe his dick was growing hard. He twisted the knobs to make the water as icy as he could take it.

After getting out of the unsatisfying shower, Joze dried off, pulled on a pair of boxers and climbed between the cool crisp sheets.

The lights off, he dropped a forearm over his eyes. He was so exhausted, he figured he'd drop off in less than a second. Then his mind strolled off on its own.

He was too keenly aware of the little beauty on the other side of the door. A thin wall, a slight door separated them, he could get through either of them with little effort, then he could get her- he threw himself over on his side and pulled his pillow over his head.

Goddamn bitch, huh, witch *-dewines* was more like it. A conniving, sneaky, flame-haired, big crystal-eyed cop witch, with the hottest softest supplest tits he'd felt in forever. He *needed* to *see* them, feel them without the constriction of that thick bra- goddammit!

He punched his pillow and slammed his head back down on it.

Chapter Seven

The next morning, Joze woke just before sunrise.

It was predicted to be a cooler day so he dressed in black jeans and a dark blue, long-sleeved thermal.

After tying his farm boots, he trod over to the door between his room and the attached one *she* slept in.

His ear to the door, not hearing any rustle of movement, he left his room and made his way to the kitchen calling Van on the way there to come and guard the door.

Maria and another maid, Greta, a young woman built with all angular planes and a blood-hound face, were already bustling around bringing breakfast supplies from the fridge to the counter.

"*Bore da*, ladies," Joze greeted, snagging a banana off the basket of fruit on the tiled island.

Greta kept her eyes lowered from the boss-man. She was terrified of the big hard man with the freaky electric blue eyes that eerily turned black when he was angry, and the extremely light hair. His vicious temper was notorious.

But Maria smiled and said cheerfully, "Good morning to you too, Master Joze. Breakfast should be ready in less than thirty minutes. There are only a few peoples around today."

"*Iawn*. Sorry, I forget, I meant okay." Peeling the banana, Joze went out the kitchen door, tromping though the hazy, dew-laden grass to the paddocks. He could see although it was still twilight, Daniel had already let the horses out to graze.

Out in the pen in front of the three-sided shed, the only ones awake, a cria, a baby alpaca stood behind his dam, mama, peering between her legs as Joze strode by.

The dam's nervous hum turned to soft clicks when she saw it was him. He stopped for a second, gave her a bite of banana and scratched her head. He bent to pet the cria, but the shy critter shrunk away from him.

"Ah, that beautiful *gwyn*, white fur, little guy, you'll make beautiful fleece." Joze gave the dam another pat then shuffled off to where he could see Daniel fixing a chain link fence.

Wearing construction gloves, Daniel Kane was twisting wire with pliers. He didn't look up when his nephew approached. He muttered, "*Bore da.*"

"*De*," Joze grunted in reply. "Why are you doing this when the north stable needs repair?"

Daniel, a man still hard as iron in his late sixties, wiped his forehead with the back of his glove and kept working. "*Drwg mab*, son, this is more important. There is too big of a gap here, the juvenile alpaca got out the other day, the barn can wait."

His light beige hair was still thick but slivered with grey. A lock flopped over one blue eye that he rolled up to Joze. Seeing the younger man's face stiffen, Daniel sighed and stuck the pliers in his back pocket.

Joze frowned at the sigh. "Daniel, just because you have your years of experience doesn't mean you always know best."

"*Ie*, sure, whatever." He pulled his gloves off as he walked away to repair the barn.

Nothing annoyed Joze more than when his orders were questioned or not followed. Daniel, and Linc were about the only ones he let get away with it. He stood scanning the land.

The metal on the barns' roofs gleamed in the rising sun breaking through the early morning clouds. Horses whinnied happily chasing each other in the pasture stirring up flies that glistened in the mist.

More alpacas came out to welcome the cool daybreak.

His hands in his pockets, Joze wandered around for a while checking out the pens and stables before heading back to the big house.

Off to either side of the house were dorm-like barracks for some of his business staff as well as ranch hands. He nodded at one of the hands that was emerging from a barrack and waving a greeting to him.

When Joze stepped inside the house, stopping just inside the mudroom, the warmth of the kitchen and toast cooking assailed him. It was a comfortable feeling. He didn't feel that way often, he stood momentarily and savored it.

Van strolled into the doorway. He inclined his rectangle narrow head at him, said with a short smile, "Hey, Boss. What do you want to do with the girl?"

People were drifting into the dining room.

A corner of Joze's mouth pulled in. Good question. A lot of things. But he said, "Just go fetch her, bring her to the table."

Van bowed his fair head slightly and took off on long lanky legs down the hall.

By the time Van returned with Glorie, the rest of the people were sitting at the oblong table, and Greta and another woman were setting platters of eggs, toast, bacon, fruit, and biscuits and gravy on the table. Coffee was being poured. A glass of orange juice sat beside each plate.

Everyone looked up with abject curiosity at the young woman as she entered the dining area.

Sitting at the table, Joze pulled out the empty chair beside him, but didn't look up from his plate of steaming eggs.

Maria hustled off to the kitchen and Van brought Glorie and indicated to her to sit on the chair next to Joze.

Without looking at her, Joze could see her balk. He felt Van's unsure gaze on him. Was he to force her to sit?

Joze angled his head slightly at her. Toughness shot through his voice, he said coldly, "Sit down, or I'll make you sit. Your choice."

Van set his hand gently on her shoulder to give her a little guiding push.

Glorie gingerly sat down. Not wanting to make eye contact with the criminals present, she lowered her eyes. As an officer, she should be trying to memorize faces to identify later, if there was to be a later…but right now she felt too vulnerable, too overwhelmed. Her future hung in uncertainty.

Van pushed her chair in. She put her hands in her lap and other than the uncontrollable trembling from her body, she didn't move.

Seeing her frozen, Van scooped a spoonful of eggs on her plate, and laid down a piece of toast and a few slices of bacon, then he went to take his own seat.

She just stared down at her hands, ignoring the plate.

Joze shot a dark gaze at the rest of the people at the table to stop staring at her.

Several ranch hands, some women who had stayed over with a few of the hands, along with some of his soldiers tore their curious eyes away from Glorie and conversation started up again haltingly at first. Soon the room was rife with talking. A few had hangovers and just ate quietly drinking gallons of coffee.

His breakfast almost gone, Joze looked down at Glorie's untouched plate. He bowed his head so only she could hear him. "Cop, we've been here before. I don't give a *cachau shyt, plismyn gast*," hearing the words coming out of his mouth, he reverted back to English.

Stifling his sigh, he said, "I don't give a fucking shit, cop bitch, if your stomach is upset with nerves, when I have a plate of food placed in front of you, you will eat." And he rattled off a slew of angry words.

Stinging red flooded her face. She didn't understand the foreign words he said, but it was obvious he cursed at her.

His eyes piercing his threat at the girl's head, Joze could see Linc staring implacably at him then at Glorie then back at him. Joze turned slightly to him, a brow arched.

Linc mouthed, '*Meddwol*' with a sly smirk across the table at him.

His skin darkened, Joze glared impassively at his friend.

Linc had called her, intoxicating.

56

Crossly, Joze thought, *ie, ydy, yeah, she is, if you like that type.*
Personally, soft and sweet is not his type. He looked at her, she just
stared at her food, hands folded in her lap.

Word had spread. They all knew about her. Everyone kept
sneaking quick glances at Glorie.

Besides the hatred of her being a cop, the women glared with
resentment and jealousy, they pondered in whispers, why did Joze
allow the woman, a danger to him, sit at their table, and right next
to him?

The men slid sly peeks murmuring how drop dead hot the babe
was, for a cop that is.

His mouth near her ear, Joze said with quiet menace, "Do not
make me tell you again, *geneth*, girl," he sat back in his chair and
buttered a piece of toast.

Glorie hesitantly picked up her fork, cut a bit of egg, stabbed it,
slid it into her mouth, chewed with difficulty then forced it down her
throat. She picked up her coffee cup and washed down the food.

"You want that *du*, uh, black?" Joze asked her looking at her
coffee.

She didn't answer, just set the cup down and picked up a piece
of bacon and nibbled on the end of it.

Joze swallowed his irritation at her not answering him. But, she
was eating, that's all he cared about. He could see the headlines now,
"Mob fiend kidnaps young, helpless, female cop and starves her to
death."

As they finished their breakfast, one-by-one people left the
table to go either to their rooms or some to their jobs in the city.

Glorie had managed to stuff down about a quarter of her
breakfast.

Getting to his feet, Joze said, "Come with me, cop," and waited.

When she didn't move, he grasped the back of her chair and
pulled it back. "Get up."

Glorie set her hands on the table and gracefully rose to her feet.

Impatient and annoyed now, Joze grabbed her arm and drew her
with him out of the dining area and into the living room.

He'd set up cleaning equipment for his weapons on a table. Releasing her, he bent under the table, picked up a case and set it on the table.

Glorie stood in front of a twin set of sliding glass doors, staring pensively out the glass.

"Don't even think about it, cop. You run, you won't get a dozen yards before I catch you." The blue of his eyes clouded with dark threat, he threatened, "And make you regret it." He pointed to a chair and ordered, "Sit there."

He waited while she stepped with a slight feminine sway of a surprisingly heart-shaped ass, that was suddenly visible in the borrowed jeans, over to the cushioned chair he gestured to.

Glorie was petite, but she had generous curves, the girl who loaned her the clothes was bonier. The jeans fit Glorie's slender legs and shapely ass snugly, the cap-sleeved top of the pale blue was looser.

Julie liked to hide her small breasts in bigger tops. The blouse almost, but not quite hid Glorie's curvier attributes.

Realizing his gaze was drifting over to those perfect breasts, Joze scowled, muttered a few curse words under his breath then went to his worktable and pulled out oil, rags, brushes and a few guns.

He started to relax. Cleaning his guns was meditative to him. It helped distract him while he was awaiting news regarding his businesses. He glanced over at Glorie sitting rigidly on the edge of the chair, her eyes glued to him.

"Tell me, little cop, how does your family feel about their soft, delicate, shy young daughter being a cop? I say shy, not timid, because you are bold when defending someone. So, what do they say?"

His head shifted slightly towards her.

She lowered her eyes, her skin pinked, she said nothing.

"Hmm, well then, a pretty *geneth*, uh, girl, like you must have a boyfriend, a husband maybe?" Watching her through his thick lashes, he observed her reactions without appearing to actually be looking at her. What he saw took him aback.

The color leeched instantly from her face, the big eyes widened then clinched in pain as she lowered them. She didn't open her mouth. Huh. Something bad went on there. None of his business. He tried again.

"So, then, what about your handler? You have to have someone that's in the background pulling your strings. Tell me about this *pigio*."

At her puzzled look, he interpreted, "Prick. Tell me about this manly *pigio* who would send a little girl, a newborn lamb into the rapacious wolves' den." A wry, lopsided grin pulled up the side of his harsh mouth.

She bit her lip, but remained silent.

"Yeah, you won't tell me about him, will you? You'd be afraid I'd go after him." Under his bemused scrutiny, she blushed slightly at his accurate assumption.

Shaking his head, he said, "I'm not used to a woman who doesn't yak nonstop." Actually, this was highly unusual; he didn't normally talk with women, except his mother and sister.

To Joze, other than family, women pretty much had only one use. And after he used them, he left them and went on about his business. He deliberately chose women who wouldn't cling to him. Those that tried to, he cut dead. Figuratively. He peered over at Glorie.

She licked her lips then bit the bottom one again, her eyes staring blankly at the floor.

With a shrug of his big shoulders, Joze turned to his task. He worked deftly, and silently for a while, vexed at his overly keen awareness of the frightened woman perched on the chair watching him. His interest in her vexed him; he could not fathom why he was asking questions about her life. He certainly didn't care a whim about the beautiful cop.

In fact, since he might have to eventually dispose of her, it was better the less he knew. No connections, no feelings, no guilt. Right. He needed to make that his mantra.

"*Cachau!*" cursing, he threw down a wrench. He was getting nowhere trying to take apart one of the guns. It was too tight. He needed a different wrench.

Stalking out of the room, he pointed at Glorie and said roughly, "Don't you fucking move a muscle."

She looked so scared he doubted she would even breathe while he was gone. He figured he'd cowed her, she'd be too frightened to run.

As soon as he stepped back into the room he knew she was gone.

His eyes cut to the glass doors, they were still closed. She could still be in the house, but he was pretty sure she'd made a run for it.

He hurried to the doors, pushed one open and stepped out.

Outside, he took the time to quickly scan the area.

There- He could see her running towards the thatch of trees to the east.

She would be thinking she could be hidden quicker, shrouded in the dense woods.

"Stupid *gast-*" he spat.

The fool was heading for the most perilous area in that part of the woods.

Chapter Eight

Racing after her, his legs twice as long and ten times stronger than hers, Joze caught up with her with little effort.

He darted around a tree until he was standing right in front of her.

"Oh!" Glorie gasped. She was running too fast to stop- she plowed right into him- she hit him so hard the breath was knocked out of her.

Ricocheting off his brick wall of a chest, she stumbled backwards. As she fell, Joze leaped forward and caught her arm.

Jerking her straight up, his grip like steel, infuriated Joze shook her roughly, and yelled, "You stupid bitch, I fucking told you not to run."

Gasping for air, Glorie choked in short breaths, her knees buckled. Joze rolled his arm around her shoulders and held her taut until she gulped in deeper breaths and stood steadily on her feet.

At that point, Joze twined his long fingers tightly around her upper arm and started dragging her out of the woods, back across the lawn and into the house.

Inside, he turned his dark furious face to her and gave her a little push. "I told you not to move. I told you not to run. I told you that you would regret it if you tried. Do you remember?" Vehemence slew from the violent, electric eyes.

She turned from the dangerously ferocious man and took a step back towards the open glass door. Exclaiming breathlessly, "I don't have to- to do anything you say. You're a- a thug," Glorie inched to the door.

Already a big guy, Joze swelled in his fury. His tanned skin darkened, his pupils flared more and more until they ate up the blue irises turning them into black discs radiating pure rage at Glorie.

Snarling, "You fucking bitch, you listen to me," he took a giant step towards her and snatched up her arm. He roughly yanked her back to him.

"Let go of me you- you beast, you- hoodlum-" Glorie struck out with her free hand, but he captured it and held it.

Livid eyes as black as licorice dissected her slender stature, her fearful but angry face. Joze growled, "Hoodlum? Beast? *Da*, you got it, bitch cop. I'll show you what a fucking bad guy I truly am."

Squeezing her arm painfully, Joze ignored the pain strike her frightened face and dragged her out of the room and down the hall. Enraged, he kicked his bedroom door open and shoved her inside.

Glorie stumbled trying to catch her balance. She gawked with terrible fear when she saw him slam the door closed and lock it.

He took a step towards her, she backed away.

His grin unpleasant, Joze said, "You got nothing to say, cop? No insults for me now? What's the matter, cat got your tongue?" He reached out for her; she stepped out of his reach.

"Don't touch me you- you- you horrible criminal!" Glorie turned to run into the bathroom, Joze threw out an arm, wrapped it around her waist to stop her, then swung her up in his arms and stomped to his bed.

Dropping her on the mattress, Joze crouched to untie his boots, never taking his eyes off her. Glorie struggled to sit up with her palms bracing behind her. The big amethyst eyes wide with terror, she scooted away from him.

Kicking off his boots, Joze unbuttoned his shirt. Smirking meanly he said, "There's nowhere to go, *bach geneth*, little girl." He moved to the bed.

As she scrambled backwards towards the other side of the bed, he grabbed her leg to stop her.

In a panic, Glorie kicked at him, trying to get away. Landing a kick on his jaw, he stopped smirking and his face turned hard with fury.

He wrapped his hands around her thighs and yanked her back to the middle of the bed, and snapped her shoes off throwing them to the floor.

Brows drawn hard down over the now blistering pitch black eyes, he said harshly through grit teeth, "I will show you, cop, what happens when you don't do as I say, when you try to hurt me."

Sliding his knee on the bed, he moved to her, grabbed the borrowed blouse and ripped it open.

Glorie gasped, and flailed her hands at him. He pushed her down on her back and grasped the top of her jeans with both strong hands, jerking the top button open.

"Stop!" Glorie screamed. Heaving her body, she grappled at his hands, trying to fight him off.

But Joze was twice her size, an ex-marine, a trained MMA competitor, he boxed and kick-boxed for fun, she was a mere rabbit fighting off a crazed wolf.

Joze viciously tore open her jeans and jerked them roughly down her legs along with her panties. He dropped a leg over one of hers pinning her to the bed and unbuckled his belt then undid his pants.

He started to shrug off his unbuttoned shirt but Glorie shoved at him, punching at him, twisting frantically to get out from under his big hard body.

He moved between her legs and staked her hands over her head. He looked with glazed enraged eyes down at the terrified woman under him. His gaze fell to her heaving chest.

Her breasts rose and fell, rounding over the pink satin bra with each panicked breath she took. He didn't look further down to see her nude lower body.

Using his knees to aggressively push her legs apart, he reached down and unzipped his pants, took his ramrod shaft out and pressed it to her core, against her female opening.

She gasped, big frantic gulps of air, tears burst and rolled down her cheeks.

Joze took one of her hands and forced it around his thick shaft. He growled menacingly, "You feel this, cop? You see I am for real, what I say I mean? That I will punish you for disobeying me?"

Her sharp inhales cut with cries, Glorie struggled to stop him, but her efforts were ineffective.

Joze wrapped his big hand over her slender one around his shaft and forced her hand to rub up and down on it. It was already like iron, he pushed it harder towards her opening. "Answer me, cop, or I swear I'm taking you right now. Answer me!"

Her breaths scraping with squeaks and sobs, Glorie shook out the words in a husky cry, "*Yes*," shuddering sobs wracked from her chest.

Joze pressed his powerful chest against her soft breasts, using his weight to control her. He stared at her terrified eyes, watching her weep.

Releasing her hand, he grasped her jaw. Holding it tightly, he lowered his head. He kissed her hard, then let off softly. With a sharp glance at her, he moved off her trapped body and rolled over the side of the bed to his feet.

She immediately drew her legs up and to the side to hide her nudity. He had deliberately not looked at her sex, or touched it, knowing it would have been near impossible for him to stop himself from plunging into her if he did.

But Joze couldn't prevent himself from staring down at her sharply rising and falling breasts partially exposed from the open blouse.

Gaping at her breasts, his manhood still out, he wrapped his fist around it, pumped it a few times then catching his sense back, he struggled to get a grip on his control.

The petite woman with the big terrified eyes had managed to do what no other person ever had, bent his steel hold on his self-control.

And he had wielded his superior strength and male sex organ on her to punish her. What a man.

With painful difficulty, he stuffed his erection back in his pants. Zipping up and buckling his belt, he buttoned then pushed his shirt back into his black jeans all while watching her lying so vulnerable and crying.

Her light flaming hair fanned out on the mattress around her head. She turned her face to the side refusing to look at him, her slim shaking fingers doing up the buttons still there on her shirt. Big tears rolled out of her crystalline eyes and down her round cheeks.

When he didn't come near her, Glorie pulled up her panties and jeans and fixed them.

When she was done, he suddenly bent over, grabbed her upper arms and lifted her out of the bed and onto her feet. "Look at me, cop," he commanded.

Glorie stared at the floor between them. "I- I-" she stammered, "don't want to look at your despicable face."

His growl audible, Joze pushed her against the wall, grasped her chin forcing her to look up at him. "You've got brass balls, cop," he shook her chin.

Her tears slipped from her face onto his hand. He pinched her chin until she raised her emboldened eyes. His raging black pupils were shrinking back to expose more of the piercing blue.

Other than beating her, he didn't know how else to threaten her. If he hadn't gotten to her when he had, she would have fallen down that steep hill to the falls and she would have definitely died.

The land all around them could be treacherous, he couldn't have her running around out there all by herself, for cripe's sake.

Doing what he'd just done to her was way over the line. But he said anyway, "Take my threat to heart, honey, you do what I say, when I say, and you will not try to run again, or I swear to *Duw*, to God, I will follow through next time and I will fuck you bloody, then beat you into the cold dark earth."

Her hands behind her pressed against the wall, Glorie said quietly through her tears, "You said you had no desire to be with a...policewoman." She sniffed. "The only way you can get your way is to use your masculine strength to overpower someone weaker than you."

A cold smile curving his full, chiseled lips, Joze reached down and took her hand and held it up. "That's somewhat true, sweetheart."

He gently formed her fingers into a fist, then held his own fist up beside hers, comparing them. "See how mine is bigger, cop?"

Tugging at her hand to no avail, Glorie's lips pursed in a frown but she made no response.

Holding her chin again, he gazed callously into her eyes, and said, "That makes me in charge."

"You are an arrogant pig, nothing but a big bully," she mumbled, glaring fiercely at him. Clearly she was afraid of him, but he was controlling her through his strength, and that made her angry.

His head dropped, he shook it, then he gripped her jaw harder. With a wry grin, he said, "Like that, your sassy mouth," his eyes fell to her mouth. "A sassy beautiful mouth, honey, a deadly combination." He suddenly captured her lips, kissing her rough and hard and punishing.

His tongue thrusting wildly inside her mouth like he'd wanted to do with his cock, then, he gentled, his lips nipped at hers tasting the full plumpness of them, his hungry tongue soft and searching, stroked sensuously inside her mouth.

He still grasped her chin, but his touch lightened, his thumb rubbed her jaw. His hand on her back so hot it scorched, lessened his clenching possession.

Even as her body betrayed her, responding to his change from ruthless to gentle passion, Glorie struggled, trying to wrench her mouth from his, but he held her easily with his muscled arms.

Then, just as suddenly as he grabbed her, he released her. His chest heaving, heart pounding, Joze looked at her, he could see his reflection in the amethyst, he looked as dizzy with passion as she did.

But she licked her lips and forcefully stifled the heat in her eyes.

He growled his warning, "Do you understand now, honey, that if you screw with me, I will screw you. That clear?"

Her mouth firmed mutinously.

"Ah, you try me, cop." He pinched her chin again and shook her, demanding, "Answer me, woman."

A tiny, "Yes, I got you," slid out with more tears.

He brushed gently at the tears with the back of his fingers.

"Get yourself together," he ordered, then strode from the room without another word.

Chapter Nine

Glorie was left locked in the small room. The room adjoining Joze's was apparently designed for parents with a new baby.

Later in the evening, there was a knock at her door before it was unlocked and opened.

Van stuck his head in. "Hey," he grinned and asked, "you hungry?" His lips pulled in with sympathy. "Uh, of course you aren't with that shaky stomach of yours. Come on, the boss said to bring you to dinner." He stepped into the room.

Glorie was sitting at a small desk reading a book someone had left there. She smiled amiably at Van. He'd been nothing but kind and nice to her.

"Thanks, but I'll just stay here. I'm not in the mood for food...or people. They just stare...unpleasantly at me," her mouth twisted wryly, *like they want to assault me.*

Van crossed his arms, smiled shortly. "Sweetie, the boss didn't send me to *ask* you to come to dinner. He doesn't ask," he ran his palms through the sides of his dark blond hair, and said, "he orders."

"Really, Van-"

He moved closer to her. "Glorie, you put both of our well-being in jeopardy. You refuse to come, and, well, he will certainly come and give you a visit. And me as well. I'm not into getting beaten this evening, are you?"

Her mouth pulled back in doubt. "Come on, really, Van, he certainly would not beat you, not over something as trivial as whether or not I come to the dinner table."

Van nodded. "Trust me, sweetie. He can go ballistic over a lot less. Don't do this to us. Please." He smiled with his brows raised, his hand held out to her.

Letting out a breath, Glorie rolled her eyes and got up with a huff. "Fine."

With a big smile, Van took her hand, tucked it in his arm and ushered her out of the room and through the hall. Just before they reached the dining area, Maria stepped out of the kitchen.

"Hello, Miss Glorie, I hope you like Brunswick stew!" The maid smiled at Glorie then said to Van, "Van, as long as you're here, can you carry that big stew pot into the dining room for me?"

Van looked unsure, his eyes cut with uncertainty to Glorie. "Well, uh, I don't think-"

"Go on, Van," Glorie reassured him, touching him on the arm. "I will stay right here. I swear to you I will not flee. Not when it could cause trouble for you."

Her pretty smile was hard to resist, even for a gay man. "Uh, okay, Glorie. Please," he turned serious, "please don't get me in trouble, or yourself, please let me trust you."

A sadness filtered across her face. She replied softly, "I promise, Van. I will not run."

"All right. Don't move. I'll be right back." With a kind smile, he drew a knuckle down her soft cheek and followed Maria out of the room.

Glorie let out a breath. She couldn't believe she'd been kidnapped by a deranged, mafia-like brutal madman and she was promising one of his cohorts that she wouldn't run for her life- so that he wouldn't get a beating.

But, she sighed, she did promise him. She thought moving just a few feet to look out a window wouldn't hurt.

Taking in the land surrounding the structure, the soft green pasture, the earthy paddocks, she smiled at the horses dodging the man Daniel. Van had pointed out Joze's uncle to her earlier, as he tried to corral them to go into the stables.

She didn't hear someone approach her until a hand settled on her shoulder. "Oh!" She jumped and turned around. A man she hadn't met grinned amicably at her.

"Hey, sorry, I didn't mean to startle you, sweetheart." He stood back a foot from her. "I'm Bruce, I haven't met you yet but I saw you at your first night at dinner." He held out a hand for her to shake.

Glorie looked down at his proffered hand then up to the cheerful smiling man with oily black hair and grey eyes. It would be rude not to, so Glorie shook his hand then took a wary step back from him.

She was being held against her will in a ranch of a well-known gangster and his associates, soldiers and enforcers, she'd be a fool to trust anyone. She glanced anxiously over his shoulder looking for Van.

"Calm down, honey, I won't hurt you." Bruce sidled up closer to her and lifted a curl off her shoulder. "Wow, what an amazing fucking color, like a burning flame." Twining the curl around his finger, he gazed at her face.

He remarked, "You are damned pretty, honey, those eyes could drag a man straight to the bedroom, which," he moved within a few inches of her, smiled down at her breasts, "sounds like a damned good idea, doncha think?"

"Uh," Glorie protested. Grabbing her hair, she tugged it from his grasp and backed away from him. "I uh, please leave me alone, Mr. Kane will be angry,"

"Ha, isn't that cute, *Mr. Kane*, he's Boss to the rest of us, honey. Now, let's get back to you and me," he reached for her, she backed away until she came flush with the wall.

Her eyes darted around the hall praying for Van to hurry back. "Listen, um, Bruce, please step away from me, move back, please."

Glorie wished so badly they had let her attend the Academy before putting her in this undercover assignment. She was woefully inept at protecting herself. Of course, even if most of the occupants of the house weren't twice her size, they were also carrying.

Grinning lewdly, Bruce put one hand on her shoulder holding her against the wall and wrapped the other around the back of her neck to keep her taut as he lowered his mouth onto hers. Her scream muffled into his throat; she brought up her hands to push at him.

Annoyed that the bitch would consider fighting him, Bruce squeezed the back of her neck hard enough to draw tears. "Now, you just hold still, sweetheart, I just want to get to know you a little. *Mr. Kane* is hardly possessive of his women, or any women. Come on now, give me a kiss," he pressed his mouth on hers hard enough her head banged into the wall.

Glorie pushed her head aside to avoid his mouth. Dazed from the bash, Glorie closed her eyes and pressed her hands over them.

"See now, babe, calm down, we can have a nice party together," his voice as oily as his hair, Bruce put his hands around her waist them skimmed them up-

"Stop!" Her eyes still closed fighting the dizziness from the banged head, Glorie grabbed his wrists trying to hold his hands down.

"Fucking bitch-" Angry at her resistance, Bruce shoved her hands away and grasped the top of her blouse and yanked it apart.

Opening her mouth to scream, Glorie shoved at him with all her might but he slammed her back against the wall with a crunch.

"I'm not going to fight with you, bitch," Bruce snarled. "I'll just fucking slug you, knock you out and take you to my room. So, let's skip the pain and the drama and come peacefully with me."

He grabbed her open blouse clutching the material with his fist and jerked her towards him. Holding her blouse, he stuck his other hand in her hair clenching it, yanked her head back and brutally crushed her lips.

Glorie punched at him, squirmed, struggled, it was no use. He was hurting her, his mouth smashed hard on hers, his fist so tight on her shirt his knuckles pressed painfully into her breasts. He was pulling hair out of her head he clutched it so tightly, pulling her head back so hard she feared her neck would snap.

"Motherfucker!" Joze's enraged voice broke through the dizzy haze that threatened to suffocate Glorie's brain into a faint.

His trench coat swinging around his ankles, Joze grabbed Bruce's collar wrenching him loose from her.

As Joze pulled Bruce back, he bashed his fist into his stomach. Bruce doubled over with a wailed gag. Joze slammed his other fist into his jaw sending him flying into the wall across the hall where he hit it hard, staggered, but stayed standing.

"What the hell, Boss? The bitch is yours? I didn't hear you lay claim." Bruce rubbed his jaw, opened and stretched his mouth to take the shock out. "You fucked her, let the rest of have a shot." His eyes slid like snakes over at Glorie who stood frozen, stunned, afraid.

What if Joze did just that? Handed her over to the other men? She shivered. She'd had set all her fear on Joze, she hadn't considered other horrendous things that could happen to her. She started shaking uncontrollably all over.

Laced with unleashed fury, his tone a grating bane, Joze derided, "I don't fuck cops."

Hearing Glorie's teeth chattering in her terror, he turned, throwing a quick glance at her. Surprisingly he asked, "Are you all right?" He sucked in a deep breath laboring to mute the rage in his heavily accented voice.

She just stared at him with wide petrified eyes, her body shaking so badly she could hardly stand. Seeing her distress, Joze turned back to Bruce. He stomped several long steps to Bruce and power-housed his iron fist into his face again. Bruce's head cracked against the wall and bounced.

While Bruce shook the stars from his head, Joze clenched his fists. His accent making his words hard to understand, he snarled fiercely, "Touch her again, Doyle, and die."

Bruce's gaze sprang up to Joze's as he wiped the blood from his mouth.

Joze said, "Don't doubt me, Doyle. Now, get the hell out of here before I fucking kill you right now." He wanted to, but he wouldn't do it in front of Glorie, she already looked about to pass out.

Restraining himself with effort, a vein pulsing at his temple, Joze stood glowering at the other man with his arms bowed, fists tight, cordons of muscles pumped across his thick wall of shoulders.

His hand on his face, as he stumbled past her, Bruce glared with surly anger at Glorie like this was all her fault.

Seeing Glorie shrink from him, moving in front of her, Joze raised his fist, and took a step at Bruce, but Bruce jumped and scurried off as fast as his ruptured gut would let him.

Joze turned to Glorie, unaware his eyes blazed with insane wrath, the pupils had overtaken the blue, fiery black discs thundered at her.

The violence between the men and now aimed at her was too much. Acute terror struck her face like a whip, Glorie swooned against the wall.

"Glorie!" Joze rushed to her and quickly strung his arm under her shoulders to hold her up.

She was so afraid of him, his savage violence, she hysterically struck out at him. Joze pulled her against his chest and wrapped his arms around her, holding her so she couldn't move.

He could feel her heart pounding, her breathing frantic. Holding her with one arm he stroked her hair, then her back. "Shh, shh, little one, it's okay, I won't hurt you, I promise. It's okay." He soothed into her ear, "Bruce is gone, you're safe. I swear, no one will hurt you."

Vivid visions of him attacking her on his bed only a short time ago flashed in his mind like a guilty sword, Joze swallowed hard. He had been trying to teach her a lesson, to not disobey him, to not try to run. Short of beating her, he didn't know what else would be severe enough, frightening enough to make an impression on her.

Do iawn, yeah, he had made an impression all right.

What an ass. If he were her he would have already tried to run, only a coward wouldn't take the chance. He knew she wasn't a coward. She'd constantly stood up for others at the saloon, including him and he was twice her size.

He snorted to himself. As the mentally challenged Jimmy he hadn't needed her protection, but she didn't know that then. But now her fear was so stark, her body vibrated against his. "Come on, Glorie, calm down," he whispered softly, gently petting her.

People were starting to walk by the hallway. A couple stopped and rubbernecked the pair.

To the couple, down the end of the hall, it was a sight, the tall fearsome man in the black leather trench coat, the shock of platinum hair, like a vampire he was bent over the petite girl with the locks of bright curls rolling down her back.

Feeling their attention, Joze hid Glorie with his big body and slightly turned his head towards them, his glare a black lance blazed up the hall at them, so fierce and frightening, the couple blanched and quickly moved off.

Glorie's knees buckled, causing her head to drop back, her blouse slipped apart. He glanced down, then his eyes darkened again. "What the fuck, Glorie, no wonder that *pigio* was all over you, you're fucking half-dressed, your tits are hanging out all over the place-"

Holding her head in her hands, Glorie looked down and gasped. Bruce had forced her blouse completely open, her breasts were half exposed in the pink satin bra she'd been loaned.

The déjà vu of going through the same thing with Joze as Bruce made her head pound, she feebly tried to pull the ends together. "I-I didn't," she stammered weakly, tears gathering, "he- he-"

"Wait," Joze ordered holding her hands back.

Frightened of him again, he stared so lustfully at her breasts, Glorie whimpered and pushed at him.

"No, stop, *bach babi*, let me see," Joze gently pulled her hands away, tearing his eyes away from her luscious breasts heaving and mounding so lushly over the satin bra, he saw the bruises on her chest from Bruce's rough knuckles.

"*Fy Duw*, my God, Glorie," Joze's voice strained, he cradled the back of her neck with his hand and pushed aside the lapels of her blouse to see them more clearly.

Not realizing his intent, frightened again of him assaulting her, Glorie fought him in a blind panic crying, "Please don't-"

"Damn," Joze ground. Frowning, he captured her hands to stop them before she hurt her tender hands on the granite planes of his body.

"It's okay, *babi*," he spoke softly. "I see that he hurt you, shh." Seeing her eyes rolling dizzily back in her head, he scooped her up in his arms and strode down the hall to his room. He passed through to her room where he carefully set her on her bed.

She immediately sat up, then moaned with her hand to her head.

Joze sat down quickly beside her. "What is it, Glorie?" He wanted to hold her, help her, but she was clearly afraid of his touch so he kept his hands on his legs.

Wincing, she gingerly dabbed at the back of her head with her fingertips. "He uh, I got pushed back and hit my head on the wall. I feel a little dizzy is all." Her lids drooped over her bright eyes.

Joze felt the wrath build back up. He would go give Bruce another visit later, the fucking *pigio*. And that son-of-a bitch Van. Where the hell did he go to leave her alone? Wait 'til he got his hands on-

"Master Joze." Maria was in the doorway, her face wrought with worry. She came hesitantly into the room, her eyes on Glorie. "Is she all right?"

Not answering her, Joze delicately touched the back of Glorie's head. She cringed from him but he held her still with his hand on her shoulder. "It's *iawn*, ah, okay, I won't hurt you, I just want to see how seriously you're injured."

He gently felt the lump on the back of her head, blanching at her wince. Checking her eyes, he asked, "Are you feeling nauseous?"

Her voice small, she said, "No."

He gently brushed her hair off her face and behind her shoulders. "You have to let me know right away if you feel nauseous or more lightheaded than you are now. I think you'll be all right. If you appear to have a concussion I'll take you to the hospital."

Her surprised eyes swung up at him in disbelief.

Joze looked over at Maria wringing her hands. "Maria, help her clean up and get into bed. Afterwards I want you to bring her some tea and aspirin, and a dinner plate."

At the sour look on Maria's face he growled, "What? What's the problem?"

"Miss Julie took back her nightgown, apparently her boyfriend made some kind of rude crack about how he'd like to see Miss Glorie in it-" she broke off at the angry color flushing Joze's face.

"Um, anyway, my clothes are all in the laundry, not that the little miss," she smiled fondly at Glorie, "wouldn't swim in them, and," she sighed, "the other ladies refuse to help. Bruno's girl isn't around this week, I know she would help out."

Joze frowned blankly at Maria, thinking. He hadn't realized he'd tucked Glorie against his chest and had laid her head on his shoulder, his hand still soothingly rubbing her back.

She finally relaxed, melting into him. His groin stirred, he felt a funny feeling somewhere else too, but stuffed it. "All right, go get one of my pajama tops. Not the bottoms, they would be way too long."

Maria's brows dashed up to her hairline. Her eyes narrowed at him. Although Joze fooled around with some of the shameless women that hung around, he never had women over in his room and she would swear it would annoy him to see a woman in his clothes.

"Maria," Joze broke her out of her revelry, "go." He pulled Glorie closer, patting her head, combing her curls with his fingers.

Shrugging, Maria left and returned quite quickly with one of his pajama tops, white with blue pinstripes.

Joze stood up with Glorie in his arms then rested her to sit against the headboard. Then he stepped back.

Her eyes were closed. The bruises from Bruce were visible over her cleavage. He could hardly throttle Bruce; after all, Joze himself had cut her cheek when he callously shoved her face against the brick wall at the saloon.

Joze shivered at the memory. His stomach turned seeing the cut still slightly visible on her cheek, realizing he had brutalized a defenseless young woman. Sure she was a cop, but in name only. She'd never done the training, never worked in the field.

And Bruce hadn't done anything to Glorie Joze himself hadn't. They were both fucking animals. Joze needed to get a grip. He hadn't brought her here to abuse her. Still, he was going to go visit Bruce when he left her room.

"All right." He moved towards the door. "I'll leave you to it, Maria, just help her clean up and get into my…uh…pajamas. I mean, do you need my help? If you do-"

"*Si, si*, you are not needed, shoo, I will take care of her. I do not need you to help undress the child. Go on then," she motioned at him to go as she hurried to Glorie.

Joze hesitated in the doorway. His voice tight with some strange emotion, he said, "Uh, tuck her in, okay, Maria?" He wanted the girl to have some semblance of security. A heavy blanket should help, he supposed.

Over her shoulder, Maria, murmured, "Uh huh," as she helped Glorie get to her feet.

Chapter Ten

Hours later Joze was awakened.

Was that someone screaming? He cocked an ear, there it was again, it was coming from the attached room.

"*Shyt.*" He rolled out of bed, jerked on his jeans, grabbed his shirt off the back of a chair and ran through the adjoining room. Dragging the shirt on, he hurried over to her bed.

Glorie was alternating screaming and crying and thrashing like a wild woman in her bed as if she was trying to get away or fight someone off.

Joze dropped down on the mattress and grasped her shoulder. "Glorie, what the hell is wrong, are you in pain?" In the dark he could see her eyes were shut tight, she kept thrashing and shrieking.

Murmuring, "Oh, honey," he realized she was sound asleep. She was having a nightmare.

As he reached for her, she screamed, "Please don't hurt me! No more, *please*," her voice was strained, hoarse from her screams.

Joze dragged her up and into his arms. She lashed out, hitting and struggling, he wrapped his arms tightly around her.

Suddenly Linc and Calvin barged into the room. "What the hell are you doing to her, Joze?" Linc barked, dismayed and heated.

"Stop bro! Let go of her!" Calvin shouted.

Scowling at his friends, Joze cuddled Glorie in his arms and said, "Get your minds out of the gutter, boyos, I'm not raping her, she's having a nightmare, she's asleep."

Glorie let out a pained gasp and begged, "Please don't do it any more, *it hurts so much…*"

"Okay, Glorie, hush now, no one is hurting you." Joze held her tightly enough so she couldn't harm herself thrashing against him, but gently so he didn't hurt her. He stroked her hair, murmured softly in her ear.

He quieted her like he would an unbroken horse. He shot a glance at the two men gawking at him. "I got this, you guys can take off." Then he turned his attention to the hysterical girl in his arms. Finally, she seemed to be calming, her body jerked and thrashed less.

Linc and Calvin watched them for a moment, then shared a look and left the room, closing the door quietly behind them.

Her body stilling, Glorie's eyes suddenly popped open. Seeing him so close to her, holding her, she started to scream and strike out.

Joze curled his arms tighter around her, he whispered softly, "Calm down, Glorie, I'm not attacking you. I just came in, you were having a bad dream. You were screaming."

Her breathing wheezed, rough and harsh and erratic, her eyes wild with fright, she looked at him bewildered.

He pushed her gently back down on her pillow, lightly holding her hands down. "I'm not going to hurt you, Glorie, I'm going to let go of you now so you see it's all right." He released her hands.

She brought them up to cross protectively over the front of her body. Her frantic eyes still wild with fear gaped at him, the tangled flaming hair curled over the pillow. Sucking in huge gulping breaths, her eyes darting back and forth, she started to calm a little.

When her breathing grew slower and deeper, his hands benignly in his lap, Joze said, "Tell me, Glorie, what was it about?"

The fright back in them, her eyes flashed to him. Her lips parted, she licked them. Seeing him stare at her mouth, she pulled her lips into a compressed line. "Um," her voice shook, she looked away from him, her fingers kneaded the sheet. "I uh, don't remember…"

His brows drew down in a frown, he could always read people. She was being evasive. She knew what the dream was about but wasn't going to tell him. He wondered why not.

Hell, he remonstrated himself. A mob boss, he was holding her, a police officer captive, he'd molested her, and another man had also molested her in his own home. And Joze wondered why his little prisoner refused to open up to him? She had every right to be terrified of him and everyone else around them.

"*Iawn*, okay. Well, you seem fine now, I'll leave-" he stood up but she flung out a hand and grabbed his shirt.

She cried with hysteria strangling her voice, "No! Please, he's," her eyes flew around the dark room in a panic. "He's here, he's hiding! Don't leave me alone with him, Mr. Kane, *please*."

His brow quirking at her calling him mister, he frowned, glancing around the room. "Glorie, there is no one here." He made to start to leave again but she held onto his shirt.

"Please, he- he's hiding! If you leave he'll get me!" Her eyes wide on him with pleading, her skin was flushed, she clenched his shirt in her hands.

Speaking to her as if she were a child, Joze said quietly, "Okay, okay, Glorie, calm down. Who is hiding?"

"Him- him- I can't tell." She covered her eyes with one hand, still clutching his shirt with the other. Hiccups of frantic breaths cut out of her constricted lungs.

She peered over her arm, trying to see in the dark. "He's here, I know he is. He's hiding, when you leave, he'll-" a shiver violently shook her entire body. Clearly still half asleep in the throes of her nightmare, she was projecting her dream as she woke more and struggled to shake it off.

"All right, Glorie, calm down. I will check the room out, okay?"

Glorie climbed up on her knees, pulled the sheet up to her chin like a shield. "Please, can you please, Mr. Kane?"

He smiled. "Sure, honey, if you stop calling me Mr. Kane. That was my old man, I'm Joze."

She didn't say anything, just kept her big crystal eyes trained on him with fearful faith.

As he started to move, she cried, "Be careful, Mr. Kane," she warned. "He's dangerous, very, very dangerous. Be careful."

Amused over her sudden concern for his safety, he said, "I'll be careful."

Joze left her and went to the bathroom and turned on the light. He stepped inside to look in the shower, then leaving the light on to comfort her, he closed the door but left it open a fraction.

Crossing the room to the closet, he opened it wide, waggled his hand back and forth inside so she could see it was empty. Then he went to the window and looked out through the two, three-inch wide boards he'd nailed from the outside to prevent her from using the window for escape.

Kneeling on the bed, she sat back on her heels raptly watching his every move.

He came back over to the bed, crouched down and lifted up the bottom of the blanket to peer under the frame.

Standing up, without a trace of mockery, he smiled reassuring at her. "See, room is clear. No bogey-man. Now, you snuggle down, go back to sleep-" he turned to leave when she reached out and grabbed his hand.

"Stay with me, please." She raised beseeching, childlike eyes at him. "I'm afraid to go back to sleep, he'll come back as soon as you're gone." She moved over on the bed and patted the mattress beside her. Still like a child, she said, "Sleep with me." The nightmare was making her regress to her most vulnerable younger years.

At first Joze was stunned. Then he realized she really meant *sleep* with her, as in snoozing. Muttering, "Uh," he looked down at her wearing only his pajama top, and panties. At least he hoped she was wearing them. He suppressed a quiver at the thought she might be commando under-

"Please don't leave me, Mr. Kane."

Frowning at her formality, it made it clear to him she did not have sex on her mind. *Shyt*, he didn't know if he had the forbearance to do this without climbing all over her, and in her.

Really, lying next to a half-naked hot chick in bed? He could barely make out her silhouette in the dark. The bit of light that there was from the window and bathroom made her skin creamy, the blue-violet eyes gleamed, still rife with tears.

She had been so afraid of him earlier when he was assaulting her like a dog. He remembered how her body had quaked under his, her breasts heaving in panic against the weight of his chest.

He shook his head recalling her shame and mortification of him stripping her and threatening her with…rape. Yet now, as scared of him as she had been, whatever was in her dreams had a more terrifying grip on her that she was begging him to be in her bed, protecting her.

Okay, this is a first. To literally sleep with a woman without having sex? The idea would never have entered his chauvinistic brain before.

Damn. "Okay, honey, scoot over." He lifted the blanket. She grinned gratefully through her tears and squirmed over to give him room.

With a deep sigh, Joze crawled in next to her wearing his jeans and his unbuttoned shirt, and drew the sheet and blanket over them.

"Thank you, Mr. Kane."

Before he could blink, she set her palm down smack dab on the mat of dark hair in the middle of his bare chest. His groin hitched. *Shyt.*

Her body still quivered with fear, he realized she was cuddling up next to him because she was afraid. Afraid of something so horrendous she would prefer to have him, a murdering gangster, in her bed, than be alone with whatever monster she perceived was out to get her.

He soothed, "It's okay, little cop, go to sleep. I won't let anyone hurt you." He stroked her back.

As her body relaxed, his grew harder. Her curvy little body warm against him in his pajama top and panties, curled up with her tits on his chest and a leg against his thigh. Holding his breath he muttered, "I should get a goddamned medal for this."

With a hard-on that could give a sledgehammer a run for its money, Joze managed to doze on and off.

He woke as the dark clouds of the night were thinning and dawn approached. The full moon a huge silver dollar in the black sky shone through the window.

Oh, hell, he was crushed up tight against Glorie's back, freaking spooning her.

His hand was under her top, his palm against the smooth warm skin of her belly. Of its own volition, his hand was moving upwards. Taking a deep breath, he kept it still. Recognizing that if he kept his hand there it was either going to move up to her breasts or down into her panties, he carefully pulled his hand out.

His hard-on that had finally diminished with sleep was now straining at his jeans. His eyes closed, he thought, *I only need to unzip my pants, pull down her panties and I can take her from behind. Shove my throbbing cock into her tender body before she even becomes fully awake.*

"Oh *cachau*, fuck," he groaned. He was certainly no saint, and only had so much willpower. Pushing gently away from her, Joze carefully rolled off the bed.

Standing still, he looked down, seeing her face finally tranquil, soft and pale in the moonlight.

She looked so sweet and vulnerable, and damned sad. He covered her with the sheet and blanket, kissed her softly on the forehead and left the room.

After taking a shower as cold as he could make it, Joze dressed in jeans and a flannel shirt, shoved his work boots on and strolled to the kitchen. It was still early; no one else was up yet.

Grabbing an apple, he paused, then grabbed a few more, and went out the kitchen door.

Striding through the crystal-laden grass, wet with cool dew, he traipsed past the snoozing alpacas then on past the chicken coop. He could hear a mild bit of clucking and feather ruffling.

He found Daniel already at the back of the north barn, hammer in his pocket and nails in his mouth. No matter how early Joze got up, his uncle was already out and about, hard at work.

Although Joze came up behind him without making a sound, as he neared the older man, Daniel mumbled through the nails clenched in his teeth, "*Bore da*, Joze."

Nodding, Joze agreed, "*Oes,* yes it is." Lumbering up to him, Joze asked pleasantly, "How's it going?"

Daniel shrugged one buff shoulder and replied, "*Da, iawn,* good, all right." Taking a nail out of his mouth, Daniel placed it on a weather-treated board and hammered it in expertly with three taps.

He glanced over his shoulder at Joze then took out another nail. "I still think the fence should be mended first,"

Joze stuffed his hands in his pockets with a frown. "We already talked about this, I want this done first."

"Huh." Daniel shrugged his shoulder again. "I guess we all have to learn from our mistakes."

"Daniel," Joze warned with a low pissed growl.

"Humph." The older man grumbled. "Speaking of mistakes," he ignored Joze's lowering brows and deepening frown and said, "that *geneth*, the girl. The cop with the *fflamio blew,* the flaming hair."

Joze's brows straightened defensively to a severe heavy line over his eyes that were quickly darkening. "What about her?"

Daniel hammered the nail in, then turned to face his nephew. "What the hell were you thinking, son?" He admonished him harshly, "Kidnapping a law enforcement officer? You of all people? Do you have a death wish?"

"Ah." Joze's shoulders hunched, he glared at the ground. "I had to. At the time, there were four fucking thugs robbing the saloon, she was alone and helpless. They were carting her off to gang-rape then kill her. What did you expect me to do? Leave her there and sneak out the back to save my own skin?"

"Huh." The older guy grunted. "You said you dispatched them, might have left them for dead. What danger was she in?"

They stood under the dark sky that was slowly brightening. Birds started rustling, a breeze swept along the top fringe of the grass.

Joze rolled a shoulder in annoyance. He said coldly, "I don't know if any or all of them were dead. I didn't know who they were, if they had confederates, if I left her there were there more outside waiting? I had to make a quick decision. Besides, she was stalking me, Daniel, planning to get some trash on me to get a conviction."

"Ah," Daniel murmured, nodding with a wry pull to his mouth. "So, you thought it best to bring the lioness to the den to make it easier for her?"

Joze's mouth quirked at Glorie being called a lion. More like a kitten with tiny claws. "Whatever, Daniel, what's done is done."

"Uh huh." Daniel's mouth curled drily. "Then why is she still here? Why didn't you just drop her on the road somewhere and carry on to here without bringing a cop witness into your home?"

Sniffing back his irritation, Joze grunted but didn't answer. His hands still in his pockets, he gazed back over at the horses meandering around the pasture. Above them strips of orange and violet streaked the horizon as dawn broke.

"I want to show her the farm."

A hard smirk, Daniel scratched his square jaw, the unshaven morning bristles scraping under his calloused fingers. "Why? You want to prove to her what a nice guy you really are? What do you care what she thinks?"

Scowling, "Shut up, old man," Joze growled and stalked away from him. He could feel Daniel's eyes piercing his back, amused at Joze's annoyance at his words.

Joze stopped to eat one of the apples he brought, then fed the others to the horses that wandered over to him.

Wiping the apple juice on his pants, he trod back to the house. Lights were springing on, people were awakening.

Stepping through the screen door of the mudroom, he made his way to the dining area. As he reached the room, he heard voices.

Standing in the threshold, he saw Glorie at the table, with Van on one side of her and Kurt Quinto on the other. They were laughing and joking, she was giggling. An unfamiliar irritating flush ran through Joze's body, heating his brain.

His eyes narrowed at Kurt's arm draped around the back of Glorie's chair. The guy had brought his chair so close to hers, he was almost straddling her. A half empty plate sat in front of Glorie. At least she was finally eating better.

Maria jolted him from behind with a loud cheerful, "Good morning, Master Joze," and strode past him with a platter of waffles and sausages. She carried them to the table and set them down amongst cheers from the people surrounding the table.

A few ranch hands, plus Linc, Sloan, and two slatternly women they had picked up last night that looked the worst for wear, were seated at the table.

No doubt Linc and Sloan planned on another hit before they hustled the girls away. A blonde and a brunette, both hung-over with harsh faces, makeup smeared, rat's nest hair and grumpy expressions. Still wearing the scandalous, sleazy outfits from last night, the women were slugging back mugs of steaming coffee.

Joze's attention flickered back to Glorie.

Her fresh scrubbed face was shiny, pink cheeks rounded with her smiles, the remarkable jewel eyes bright. Her plush, heart-shaped lips curved up, white teeth glistened behind them. She was so different from the women he was used to. Joze felt a tug at his loins.

She didn't look up when he pulled out a chair and sat down.

Maria scurried back with a fresh mug of coffee for him.

He forked several waffles off the platter onto his plate, dropped a glob of butter on the waffles then poured a generous heaping of maple syrup over then.

Without tasting the flavorful waffles, Joze's eyes narrowed at Kurt. He had his hand on the back of Glorie's chair and was rubbing her nape with his thumb. She was oblivious to his touch as she was laughing at something Van said.

Joze watched as her merry eyes on Van, Kurt leaned over and, *fuck me*, looked down the front of her blouse.

Scraping back his chair, the grating sound brought everyone's attention. Joze carefully did not look at Glorie, he wasn't sure he wanted to see her uncensored expression as she recalled last night.

Dropping his napkin over his half-eaten breakfast, he waited a few beats then said to her, "Go wash up, Glorie, and come back."

His chest gave a sharp twinge at the sudden fearful look crossing her no longer smiling face.

Pressing his lips together to bite back the scowl, he said tersely, "Go."

Chapter Eleven

A soft look of hurt flicked across her face at his cold, abrupt order. She smiled at Kurt and said graciously, "Please excuse me."

A fleeting glance at Joze, Kurt said to Glorie, "Will I see you later?"

She gracefully pushed her chair back and got to her feet. "Oh, I don't know." Smiling at him, she set a slim hand on his big shoulder and said, "I enjoyed our chat," and walked towards the hall their rooms were in, with Van behind her.

Van glanced back over his shoulder with a barely concealed frown at Joze's highhandedness. Joze gave him a hard look that said 'mind your own business.'

Van brought her back in ten minutes.

His brow lowered over one knife-like blue eye, Joze said to him, "You can take off for a while."

When Van hesitated, looking slightly concerned from him to Glorie and back to him, annoyed, Joze said with a chilled command, "Go." He was astounded when Van leaned over and lightly kissed Glorie on the forehead.

"I'll see ya later, Gloworm." Ignoring Joze's look of disapproval, Van stuck his hands in his pockets and whistled off down the hall to the front door.

Sighing out the tenseness in his shoulders, Joze said to Glorie, "Come on, I'll show you the ranch." He was rewarded when her apprehensive expression broke into an unsure smile.

Knowing she wore borrowed jeans and a T-shirt and had little else, he dropped his windbreaker over her shoulders, and with his hand at her lower back, he walked her to the door, held it open for her to pass through then followed her out.

The sun was still making its way up the horizon so it was on the cool side. A sharp breeze ruffled their hair.

Once outside, Joze dropped his hand from her back. He tried to match his long strides with her shorter steps.

He took her first to the stables.

Inside, it was warmer from the heat of the animals, and smelled like dry straw and pungent hay, earthy soil and dusty wood. Hooves stomped, tails swished. A few snorts greeted the pair.

Joze led her to his steed. Running his hand down the horse's nose, Joze said proudly, "This is Montraya. He is a Calabrese."

Patting his nose, Joze drew his strong hand down the horse's muscular neck, over his prominent withers then over his long, sloping shoulders.

Montraya had a broad, deep chest, and a straight back, his legs were also quite muscular with strong tendons. The fiercely strong, chocolate chestnut with flaxen mane and tail, and the man, strong with platinum hair, could be as one.

"He's beautiful," Glorie said in awe but did not go near the horse.

With a slight frown, Joze studied her stance. Her hands were clasped in front of her, she stood a little stiffly. He asked, "Have you never been on a horse before?"

A trace of pink darkened her cheeks. Her eyes on the mammoth animal, she shook her head.

His lips pursed, Joze held out his hand to her and said gently, "Come here."

Glorie looked up at the huge steed then to Joze's hand. Her lips parted with reservation, but then when Joze kept his hand out she shyly set hers in it.

Joze's mouth was full yet masculine, a rare smile softened his chiseled lips. The sharp blue eyes tempered into a dusky mellowness. He slowly pulled her closer to the horse.

"It's *iawn, bach babi,* he will not hurt you." Letting go of her hand, Joze ran his big hand down the horse's long nose again, "Montraya does not bite. He likes this."

Glorie's nervous eyes flicked from man to beast.

"Come." Joze held his palm out to her again.

When she tentatively put her hand in his, he slowly raised it to stroke whisper soft down the length of the horse's nose.

Montraya snorted and threw his head back. Glorie let out a little squeal snatching her hand away.

Joze laughed. "It's all right, *babi,* he is saying *bore da,* good morning to you."

"Uh huh." She eyed the stallion warily.

The horse's big, melting dark eyes probed her. A fringe of long lashes darker than his light mane, like his master's, swept around the liquid orbs. He suddenly gave Glorie's arm a little nudge.

"Oh!" She backed away.

Joze chuckled again, a deep warm rumble in his chest. "He's just saying hi, honey."

She moved back into the shelter of Joze's body, he set a hand on her shoulder. "Go ahead, pet him again."

It took a minute, but then she slowly drew her hand down the horse's nose, and again.

Trusting the horse a little more, she moved closer to him.

His chest feeling oddly barren when she moved away, Joze watched Glorie study the steed, so immense next to her delicate petite form.

After a few moments, Joze said, "Come on, I'll show you the chickens and the alpacas."

"Alpacas?" Her brows jolted up with curious surprise. "What do they do?"

He took her hand walking her out of the dim, warm barn into the sunlight and cool, fresh air. "They are raised for their fleece."

He grinned at her perplexed expression. "They are really quite friendly and very family oriented. They can also be quite skittish," *like someone else I know.* "They like to hang in clusters." He took her to the alpaca pen and watched her reaction.

Her eyes widened in interested wonder as she cautiously approached the fence.

Several of the animals loped over to her, which made her stop in her tracks. Staring at them, she said, "They're like llamas?"

Nodding, Joze came to stand beside her. He held his hand out and one of the juveniles came right to him and stuffed his nose in his hand, then rubbed his face in it.

That brought a ring of laughter from Glorie. She gingerly stepped closer and slowly held her hand out. He shifted from Joze to check out the new human. Without restraint, he nuzzled her hand, she petted him.

"He's so soft, Mr. Kane."

Frowning at her still formal use of his name, Joze said, "His fleece is better to make clothes out of than the llamas. Llamas have a tougher fiber. This guy's name is Buster."

He watched Glorie interact happily with the animals for a bit before breaking her away to see the rest of the ranch.

After feeding the chickens, Glorie squealed in delight as the baby chicks scuttled and hopped and peeped around her.

Joze smiled at her child-like glee. His hands in his pockets, he watched her chase the chicks around the pen.

Crouching to scoop up a tiny yellow fur ball in her hand, she petted it with a fingertip. It peeped at her making her laugh. She held it in her palm and showed it to Joze. "Isn't he so cute?"

"He is an adorable *babi*, like you."

Brushing the top of the chick's head, she asked, "What does that, uh, bahbee you say mean?"

His lip twitching at the way she butchered the accent of the word, Joze replied, "It means baby." He smiled and told her, "But he is a *melyn babi*, a yellow baby. You are a *melys babi*, a sweet baby. "

"Oh, hey," Glorie giggled as the baby chick jumped from her palm to the floor.

"Let's move on." Joze took her hand leading her out of the coop and across the expanse of fresh green grass.

He kept her away from the dangerous east side of the ranch where she had fled from him.

Strolling across the thick blades, they came upon Daniel. Glorie caught Joze's frown.

Daniel stood up from the wire he was twining with pliers. His deep blue eyes fanned with wrinkles unabashedly perused Glorie from head to toe, bringing a slight pink blush to her cheeks.

"Daniel, this is Miss Toby. Glorie." Joze nodded to the girl, his eyes dark on the foreman. "This is Daniel Kane, my uncle."

Daniel dragged his fingers through his hair trying to neaten it. He nodded politely to Glorie. "Pleasure," he commented with a short smile.

"Daniel," Joze said, "we talked about this, fixing the barn before the fence."

"*Ie*, we did. The barn is secure enough for now, this fence is more important," Daniel replied to Joze, his eyes on Glorie.

She could feel the tension between the two husky men. Daniel with his weathered tanned skin, beige hair and stubble. Joze with his intense blue eyes obviously annoyed at the foreman.

Joze mirrored Daniel, raking his fingers through his white-blond hair.

His teeth clenching, Joze tried to stay patient. "Daniel, I appreciate your years of experience over mine, but you will do things my way."

Daniel's eyes flicked to Joze and back to Glorie. He looked at her curls coiling down her back. "*Fflamio ter*," he said in Welsh, his eyes narrowed at her, "*ydy glas geneth, gwyry.*"

Glaring angrily at Daniel for avoiding the argument, Joze muttered, "*Ie*, her hair is bright flaming, *ydy*, true she is young, I don't know about the virgin part."

He bit his tongue at Glorie's gasp. He had inadvertently repeated Daniel's comments in English. Scrubbing his hand down his face, Joze said curtly, "The barn, Daniel. Do the barn first."

Appalled, Glorie cried, "How dare you talk about me like that!" Color flooding her face she turned away. Her back rigid with embarrassment she strode angrily from the men.

"*Shyt*, way to go, Uncle." Joze scowled at him watching Glorie stalk across the grass. "You better not have pissed her off enough that she tries to make another run for it."

Daniel crossed his arms with a smug shrug. "Humph. You're the one who spoke in English, son."

Glorie's angry exit did nothing to diminish the sexy sway of her hips. A crafty glint glittering in his eye, Daniel remarked, "She does have a fine little-"

"Watch it, Daniel," with a pissed grunt, Joze shot his uncle a dirty look. Daniel stared back innocently at him.

Turning his back on his uncle, Joze hurried after Glorie. "Wait up, Glorie," he snagged her hand when he caught up with her.

Walking beside her, the argument with his uncle over his orders steamed Joze, made him stalk faster.

His angry strides slowed as he noticed her panting beside him to keep up. Still holding her hand, he said, "Sorry, it's just, men talk stupid sometimes," he ran his other hand through his hair in agitation.

Calming down with the quick pace, Glorie asked, "Why do you not consider his recommendations? You agreed he had years of ranching experience and you, how much have you had?"

His mouth pulled in. He didn't look at her. "I just bought the ranch a year ago." He shook his head with annoyance. "It doesn't matter. He is my manager, I am the boss. He does what I say."

Glorie was quiet as they walked back to the house. Then she asked, "How do you know him?"

Joze bumped one shoulder. "I told you, he is my uncle. He came over from the old country to help me run the," he broke off, the less information he gave her about him and his family the better. "Never mind."

Her perplexed brow furrowed, she started, "Mr. Kane," Joze grunted with irritation at her continued formality, "you obviously love this ranch. Why don't you stop your illegal enterprises and just live off the ranch? Raise your horses, sell your fleece-" she broke off at the darkening of his skin, the hardening of his eyes.

"It's none of your business, Glorie. Don't talk of it again," his voice etched with anger closed the topic.

A flurry of activity caught his attention. Linc was rushing towards them with Van and Bruno at his heels.

"What is it?" Joze asked.

Linc spoke quickly, "A few of DeMarco's men jumped some of our boys. For no fucking reason. They ambushed them, they're in the hospital." His eyes dusted briefly on Glorie's puzzled face before returning to Joze.

"Van," Joze said darkly, "take her to her room, stay inside with her, lock the door." Disregarding Glorie's sudden look of trepidation, Joze asked Van, "You packing?"

Van lifted his shirt to show his gun.

"Okay. Grab extra ammo, and your knife. Clear the other women out to the safe house in the back, including Maria, even if she squawks, carry her if need be." He lightly touched Glorie's cheek before turning to Linc and Bruno, "Let's go."

As Van tugged Glorie towards the house, the other three men bolted for their trucks.

Shortly after Van and Glorie got inside they could hear gravel spewing and engines roaring down the road.

It was almost morning before Glorie was awakened by the sounds of truck engines, closing doors and male voices. She crawled out of bed and hurried to the window.

Peering through the two slats Joze had put up to keep her in, she gasped in shock when she saw Joze and a group of his men striding across the driveway to the house.

Joze carried a shotgun in his hands, hands that were raw, cut and bleeding. His face was landscaped with more cuts and bruises, rips and blood stained his shirt and jeans.

She peered through the dark, lit only by outside lamps; the other men looked just as ruthless, violent and bloody as him.

Behind her, Van clasped her shoulders drawing her from the window. "Come on, sweetheart, he would not want you to see that."

"But, Van, they're injured, they-"

"Yeah, hush now and get back into bed." Van guided her back to her bed and waited while she climbed under the covers. But she wouldn't lie down.

"Van, what-"

He shook his head. "Don't ask, Gloworm, no one is going to tell you. Let it go." His hands on his hips, he glared at her but with a smile and told her, "Go on then, lay back down. I'm going to check them out and I'll be back."

He moved towards the door then turned back. "Don't go near the window," he said, his voice terse, "he won't like that you saw what you did. It would be best if you don't mention it to him." He went out the door.

Van was gone thirty minutes before he returned to her room. Slipping in quietly in case she was asleep, he groaned when he saw her still sitting up, eyes like blue-violet lighthouses glowing through the dark at him.

Without a word to her, Van lay back down on the couch near the door and pulled the blanket over him.

The next day, most of the men quickly avoided her when she appeared. But they strutted like macho gladiators, the women hung on them like they were gods.

Van had explained to her about the ranch. Half of Joze's soldiers-employees lived at the ranch in the dorms, some in the big house, the rest resided in the city.

Ranch hands also stayed in the barracks, and a flock of women, groupies, whores basically, flit around from man to man like gadflies.

Rolling his eyes with disgust, Van told her the men were mostly indiscriminate, sleeping with any and all of the women that hung at the ranch. However, Joze only saw women in the city, quick flings, he never slept with a woman at the ranch. He didn't shit where he slept. Van sighed when he had to explain to Glorie what that meant.

The next few days Glorie saw little of the soldiers, and only glimpses of Joze.

He briefly looked at her, blinked impassively before turning away.

Van took her outside so she could hang with Daniel for a change of pace and some fresh air.

Glorie knew she was carefully watched. Daniel acted like he kept a lazy eye on her, but she noticed whenever she moved more than a few feet from him, his lids drew down in a squint and the lines around his mouth tightened.

Like now. Something scurrying through the grass caught her eye. Without thinking, she chased after the tiny grey rodent with brown and white stripes.

When she neared the woods in her pursuit, Daniel called out sharply, "Glorie!"

She came to a reluctant stop watching the creature scamper away. Sighing, how the heck did she end up a prisoner of a gangster on a ranch in the middle of nowhere?

Smoothing back her runaway curls, Glorie turned around and started back to the foreman. She didn't know if he would have run after her and physically dragged her back. She peeked up at him through a hedge of thick lashes, she was pretty sure he would.

He stood laconically watching her return to him.

Pink stinging her cheeks, hoping to avoid the reprimand she expected, she asked, "What was that, Daniel? It was so cute."

His eyes stern, he said calmly, "It was a *gwenci*, a weasel, like a chipmunk." His brow creased, the corners of his eyes sharpened.

"*Melys babi*, you must be careful. *Blaids*, wolves, like coyotes and bobcats run in the wilderness. You could be taken in a flash," he snapped his fingers, "and be gone forever, a furry animal with big teeth's dinner.'

Glorie smiled sadly at him. "It's okay, Daniel, I know it's not the coyotes you fear harming me."

Daniel leaned on his shovel, rested his arm on the top and his chin on his hand. "*Gethen melys*, sweet girl, it is not for me to discuss my nephew's actions with you or anyone else. He is a good man with a bad reputation."

Glorie coughed out an elegant snort. "Come on, Daniel, I saw them return the other night. They were all bruised and bloody, and happy. They had gone out to fight. A good man doesn't go looking for trouble."

Daniel's enigmatic gaze studied her. "*Ie, gethen*, true, but a good man protects and avenges his own. He didn't go looking for trouble, it had come to him. One of his rival...uh...associates, attacked several of Joze's men, unprovoked, and injured them pretty badly. Just to be assholes, begging your pardon."

"There, you see, if he didn't-"

"If he lets it go, Falcon DeMarco will run roughshod over him, destroy his businesses and hurt his people down to the innocent women and children. Joze does what he has to. His enterprises employ a lot of people. He is responsible to keep the food on their families' tables."

Daniel took a deep heavy breath. He'd said more than he's spoken in a long time, and more than he had planned to.

"I see. And a good man- kidnaps, and- and- assaults women?" Her voice rose strident in her embarrassment.

He thrust his head at her, a disturbed cast of incredulity blustered in his blue eyes. "He hurt you?"

Her lips parted, she held the back of her hand over her mouth. She shook her head. Curls bounced around her back. "N- not really, not exactly."

She was clearly distraught. Daniel said softly, "He didn't...rape...you, Glorie?"

"He – he," she broke off, shaking her head. What would you call frisking her and stripping half her clothes off her and putting his naked male part against her female core- her head moved back and forth.

97

She could in no way verbalize what Joze had done to her. Her cheeks flamed, she covered them with her hands, her mortified eyes dropped to the ground.

Daniel scrutinized her with an incisive stare. At the very least his nephew had manhandled her and scared the hell out of her. Joze had some explaining to do to him. Those actions sounded more like his own brother, Joze's father's indecent behavior.

Joze did not have the reputation of harming women. He protected them. Daniel's accent thickening his words, he said sadly, *"Mae'n flin gen I, gethen melys."*

Glorie was astute enough to hear his tone and understand he was saying he was sorry for what had happened, and was happening to her.

Her lips pulled in. "It's not your fault, Daniel." Swiping at a sliding tear she said hopefully, "Perhaps you could help me-"

He smiled grimly. *"Na.* He is my nephew. He will do what's best, he is in charge."

At the crestfallen pull of her eyes and mouth, Daniel said quietly, "Be assured, Glorie, if he does hurt you, if he does…force you…I'm positive he would not, but if he did, I will end it. You have my word."

She knew he wouldn't go against his nephew, but she did see his strength and sincerity, if he thought she was in any real danger he would get her out.

Her smile weak, tremulous, she nodded. "Thank you. I appreciate you just listening to me. I know you are loyal to Mr. Kane. As you should be, he is your blood."

He looked her hard in the eyes, then said gruffly, "Here, take this spade and see if you can pull up those weeds near the back of the house there," he motioned with his head. "Maybe you'd like to grow some flowers, or vegetables there. I can teach you."

Understanding his deliberate changing the subject, Glorie smiled wanly at him. "Really, Daniel, do you think I will be here long enough for that?"

Seeing the uncomfortable lift of his chin, Glorie smiled kindly, "It's okay, I would love to grow some tomatoes, maybe cucumbers. Will you show me how?"

A brief grin tugged up his weathered lips. He nodded, "*Ie.*" He gestured to the house, "Go on now, go get those weeds, *melys gethen.*"

At her look he translated, "Sweet girl. Our dialect is harder to understand than normal, we put words together differently than is standard, it's hard for others to pick it up," then he turned back to his work.

Chapter Twelve

A few days passed, Glorie was feeling more and more uncomfortable. She could feel Joze's eyes on her. When she looked at him, his blue orbs were inscrutable, and he always looked away without speaking to her. It was giving her the willies.

She changed into some clothes one of the women finally offered her so she could wear something while her clothes were being washed. The door to her room was open, as was Joze's.

Glorie could hear voices outside her door. Dressed in the borrowed small silk shorts and top, after tying her white sneakers, she peeked out of Joze's room and saw Van leaning against the wall with his back to her talking with one of the ranch hands.

It was the first time someone didn't have eyes directly on her. She lightly closed the door and hurried into her room where she closed that door too. She moved quickly to her bedroom window and pushed it up. The two slats were still blocking the way.

She gave each one a sharp hit with her palm and they fell out. While working in her vegetable garden near the window, she had used the trowel Daniel had given her to pry the nails out of the wood.

Pulling a chair over, her body starting to shake with nerves, Glorie climbed up on it, pushed a leg through the window then carefully jumped the few feet to the ground.

Not knowing how long it would be before someone discovered she was gone, she ran straight for the closest block of woods.

In the living room, a bunch of the guys and a few women were hanging around.

Deep in thought, his mind on Glorie, Joze drummed his fingers on his chair arm while occasionally swatting away the annoying fingers of the blonde who kept trying to run them through the top of his wavy hair.

Suddenly a man shouted, "Joze, bro! Your bitch cop is heading for that steep drop off."

Joze's head shot up. "What?" He jumped to his feet and ran to the window.

He saw her just as she disappeared into the crop of trees. "What the fuck-" he could see Van hanging in the hall chewing the fat with a ranch hand.

Joze sprinted out the door with Linc and Sloan right on his tail.

Sloan blurted as they ran, "She won't know the hill suddenly drops off and she'll go tumbling, she won't know the falls are there until it's too late. She goes over the falls Joze, she'll bite it-"

"I know, Sloan. Get some guys, meet me at the crest," Joze ordered as he dashed to his truck.

He had the ignition turned on before his butt hit the seat.

Throwing it in gear, he tore around the yard, slowing as he reached the side of the house, he stopped briefly as several guys climbed in, then he raced for the hill.

Glorie was running as fast as she could down an inclining hill, ducking branches, dodging holes, trying not to stumble over exposed roots, when suddenly the ground just dropped out from under her-

The hill beneath her emptied to an almost sheer drop.

Her feet hit loose dirt then she fell on her face and started tumbling out of control down the hill, rolling and bumping, bashing over rocks, stabbed by sharp bushes as she plummeted.

Frantically, she tried to grab at roots and rocks to slow her descent but she was plunging too fast.

****

Joze drove at breakneck speed down a winding road to the side of the hill until he slammed on the breaks and leapt out of the truck. He was parked on a flatter part of the hill, ten yards or so below from where Glorie was plunging down the sheer section.

Carrying a rope wound around his arm, he raced over to a sturdy, towering tree and threw the rope over a high thick branch. He swiftly tied one end of the rope under his arms, and then the other end to his truck then ran to the side of the hill.

Joze scanned the land until he spotted her.

Across the span of the hill and rapidly descending to where Joze stood, Glorie was tumbling like a rag doll out of control down the steep ravine.

His heart clenched, the way her limbs flung loosely, she already looked dead.

Linc yelled, "Joze! No!" Just as Joze ran and leaped off the side of the hill like a damned Tarzan.

His body arced out from the tree, out over the hill; he snatched one of Glorie's flying arms just as she was hurtling over the cliff to drop like a rock down into the raging waterfall.

Clutching her arm, he threw his other arm around her, catching her tight against his body, then wrapped both arms around her as the rope swung them back like a pendulum.

As they swung back to land, his men were there with their hands out, grabbing them both, trying to hold them from hurling back out over the cliff as the rope tried to pendulum back out.

Slamming into Calvin, Joze grunted, "Oof!" and held tight to Glorie like she was a caught football and he was on the run.

Hitting Calvin was like crashing into a mountain, but Joze didn't let go of Glorie, and Calvin didn't let go of Joze. The swinging rope was pulling the three of them back over the cliff-

"Shit, Joze, what the hell-" Panting, Linc cursed at him as he threw his arms around Joze's body, struggling to hold him from being dragged back out by gravity-

Sloan and Bruno grabbed Joze's legs in a desperate bid to hold him and Glorie from being hauled back over the ravine.

Diego raced up and threw himself on top of Calvin who still held onto Joze like a linebacker, knocking them to the ground.

Joze rolled with Glorie held tight against him to protect her from the crash.

Stretching with his arms out, Linc was able to grab the rope and hold it from swinging back out, the other men fell on Joze and Glorie, pressing them on the ground with their weight.

Finally, everyone stopped dragging back to the crevasse.

They all lay for a few heart beating, breathtaking moments. Heavy breathing filled the air. No one spoke until they were all able to catch their breaths. The first to muster, Linc untied the rope from Joze.

Then, Joze struggled to sit up holding Glorie in his lap. He pushed her thick curls off her face to see how she was.

"Fucking A, Joze, what the hell were you thinking?" Linc reproached him as he helped the couple to sit up.

Loud panting and cursing still reverberated around them.

Seeing Glorie's eyes closed, her head draped back over Joze's arm, Calvin asked anxiously, "Is she-"

Joze put two fingers to her pulse, then lowered his ear to her parted lips. He gazed down at her, her eyes were still closed. "She's breathing," he said. A collective sigh of relief rolled through the group.

Forking his fingers through his curly hair, Linc scowled his fright at seeing Joze hurl himself off the damned cliff. "Come on, let's get her back to the house," he groused. Swallowing the tension Linc muttered, "What a goddamned stupid stunt, bro."

He and the other guys helped Joze straggle to his feet, still clutching Glorie in his arms. The battered, unconscious girl was bloody from head to toe.

As he walked to his truck, Joze gazed down at her. Seeing for the first time what she was wearing. Tiny, thin silky shorts and matching top. He could see she wore no bra. The shorts as well as the top had tears and holes from her fall, the small piece of ragged top left a lot of her chest exposed.

Draped over his arm caused her breasts to press hard against the strands of material still holding together by threads.

He shook his head and held her up tight against his chest, and mumbled, "What the hell happened to that thick cotton bra you had?" Oh yeah, he'd burned it.

He had to work at carrying her without touching the side of her breast and having to fight an unwanted erection. Now was not the time to be feeling lusty.

Linc opened the door to the passenger side of the truck, Joze slid in still holding Glorie. He sat back settling her to rest against his chest.

Linc drove, Calvin and Bruno climbed in the back with Bruno complaining that Calvin 'the Tank' took up more than his share of the seat. The other men scrambled into other vehicles and they all drove back to the ranch in tandem.

Once inside the house, Joze carried the still unconscious Glorie down the hall to his room.

Passing through the adjoining door to her room, he carefully set her down on her bed. Taking in her cuts and bruises, his eyes were drawn to the shredded clothing exposing more fair flesh than covering it.

Her round breasts molded against what was left of the light material, her tiny nipples poked through the silky top. The slender legs were curled to the side.

He flashed to when he had stripped her, threatened her with rape if she didn't obey him, the guilt inflamed his skin. His pants were already tight from carrying her, they were growing unbearable now.

He left her to find Maria. The tubby lady was already scurrying down the hall towards him, her face white with concern.

"Master Joze! Is she okay? Are you okay? What happened?"

Joze scrubbed his hands down his face and nodded weakly. "*Ie,* she is all right. She's battered up pretty good. I want you to get maybe Greta to help you to bathe her. She's got blood all over her. When you're done, wrap her in a towel, put her back on her bed and come and get me."

Her salt and pepper brows rose in objection. "Nude? You will see to her, nude? Master Joze, I don't think-"

"Do not question me. Just do it." Something caught his eye. "Where did that nightlight come from?"

Maria smiled, crossing her arms over her ample stomach. "Master Linc got it for her. To ease the nightmares. She has them frequently."

"What?" Joze looked at the maid. "I only know about the one. What are you talking about?"

Maria shrugged. "You are out late many nights. Van is guarding the door and he hears her. He goes in and wakens her. I guess the men talk amongst themselves."

Troubled at what the maid said, Joze went outside to smoke a cigarette while he was waiting.

The screen door slammed and he heard footsteps on the gravel coming to him.

"Joze."

He didn't respond, he'd known it was Linc. He took a puff then blew the smoke out and said, "I don't want to argue, Linc. I'm tired and I need a drink." His back against the wall, he braced one of his boots against it and tucked one hand in his pocket.

Linc grunted. "I'm saying it anyway." He leaned against the side of the house next to his friend. Watching the smoke spiral he said, "That was the stupidest, most fucking insane thing I've ever seen in my life, you asshole."

Joze smiled, he could hear the anger, caring, and relief in Linc's voice. "*Ie*, you're right, can't argue with that, *fy bráithre*, my brother," he sucked on the cigarette, inhaled deeply, slowly blew out the smoke.

"Yeah, well, geez, Joze, you took ten years off my life with that damned stunt." Linc snuck a quick glance at him. A reluctant grin tugged at his lip. "But if any motherfucker could do it, it would be you."

Exhaling a cloud of smoke, Joze grinned. "True that."

Linc's expression turned serious. "Joze-"

"Don't."

"Someone has to. What the hell are you going to do with her? You kidnapped a cop and you're holding her against her will. *Why?*" Linc swiveled his head towards Joze. "Do you even know why?"

Finishing the cigarette, Joze dropped it on the ground and ground it out with his boot. "I've made it clear that I do not want to talk about it. Even with you, *fy ffrind*," his closest friend. He tapered one eye at Linc. "You bought her a nightlight."

Looking a bit uncomfortable, Linc grinned weakly. "She has a hard time with those nightmares. I feel bad about the times Van doesn't hear her to go wake her. The next morning you can see the purple shadows under her eyes from, I guess she doesn't really get any sleep.

"Between Van and me, we think something happened to her, something so horrendous she can't get away from it, and she still thinks it has the ability to come after her."

Joze crossed his arms over his chest. "Does she talk about it?"

Linc shook his head. "*Na*, she claims she doesn't remember what she dreamt. I don't believe her."

"Yeah, I don't either."

"It's…heartbreaking, Joze, to see her like that. So scared, hysterical with terror. I mean she's just this sweet little female, cop or no, it's hard to stand by helpless to help her."

Greta poked her head out the door. "We're uh, ready, sir." Her eyes downcast, both men scared the wits out of her. Big and tough, they were always doing that fighting stuff in the yard, the MMA business. She didn't understand men's need to hit each other.

"Later," Joze tossed over his shoulder to Linc and went inside following Greta down the hall to his room. He went through to Glorie's room.

She was lying with her head on a pillow. Maria was fussing around her. "How is she?" he asked going up to the bed. Glorie lay still, her face pale as the moon, eyes closed.

"Oh," Maria wrung her hands and told him, "she woke briefly while we helped her bathe but she's fallen, I don't know, I think she's asleep, not unconscious. Van told me she hasn't slept at all the past few nights."

Joze's brows rose, he hadn't known, then they lowered in anger. "Where is Van by the way? Why wasn't he with her?"

"Um…" Maria didn't want to say.

He shook his head. "Never mind, I will get with him later." His eyes drew up to the open window with the chair in front of it.

Shaking his head again, he grinned grimly. She'd gotten the slates off, industrious little woman. He turned his attention to the sleeping beauty on the bed, naked except for the towel wrapped around her.

Maria had set swabs and alcohol, bandages and antibiotic cream on the nightstand.

The two maids stood silently watching their fierce, vicious leader tenderly wipe and dab at Glorie's scraps and cuts. Their faces scrunched when Glorie whimpered or groaned at Joze's touch.

He was as careful as he could be. As large as his hands were, he was as gentle as if he dressed a butterfly.

When he was done, he sat for a moment watching her sleep. Touching her warm silky skin, knowing she wore nothing under the towel, his eyes traced around her body hesitating at the swell of her breasts over the top of the towel.

Keenly aware of the two maids watching him, he leaned over, drew his knuckles softly down the side of her face and stood up.

"I'll be back in a minute," he said. "Dress her."

Maria frowned. "I only have a pair of shrunk sweatpants and shirt of mine, the other ladies won't…"

"Fine. Put them on her."

He returned in ten minutes. "She's still asleep?"

Maria nodded. "*Si.*" Her face wrinkled with concern. "As soon as you left, I think she had a bad dream." At Joze's concerned look she said swiftly, "It is over, I think she is peaceful now."

"*Iawn*, okay." Joze moved in front of Maria and surprised her when he scooped Glorie up in his arms.

"Master Joze! What are you-"

107

He swept past her out of the two rooms and down the hall. Glorie's wet curls dampened his shirt, he held her high and tight to his chest as he calmly entered the living room.

He sat down on one of the sofas and settled Glorie half on the sofa cushion and half on his lap. He nestled her head against his shoulder and smoothed her hair.

The other men scattered around the room watched him with dismay. One said sarcastically, "Hey, wattup, bro, she your new fuckin' pet *pussy* cat?"

Joze's glare was blank and oddly ominous at the same time. The man visibly shrank back into his chair.

Looking down at her, Joze inaudibly murmured, "As long as I have my hands on her she can't run." He didn't want to chain her to her bed, and he certainly could not trust anyone to keep a sure eye on her.

Since he didn't dare climb into bed with her to watch her there, he did the next best thing and brought her out here with him. He liked the feeling of her nestled safely on his lap.

He glanced around the room at the men who quickly hid their astonished expressions. He said curtly, "Get on with it."

Looking at Sloan, Joze said, "You were going to tell us what you got when you hacked into Greer's *shyt*,"

Watching Joze absently stroking Glorie, Sloan shrugged and said, "As you basically found when you briefly skimmed them, the accounts were valid, you cleanly transferred his funds to our accounts." He stopped talking, his gaze following Joze's hypnotic strokes.

"And?" Joze prompted, his eyes on Glorie's sleeping face.

The other men, twelve in all, shifted and grunted while waiting.

Sloan said, "I was able to access most of his other businesses, Joze," he grinned proudly, "you totally destroyed him."

Tommie Martin said cheerfully, "Yeah, teach that and any other motherfucker to mess with Joze Fucking Kane."

Diego added, "The damage he did to your offices was extensive. The remodelers are working on them now. It can all be fixed. Thank

God they didn't get to your bigger establishments, like the strip clubs and-"

"Yeah, yeah, I got it." Joze cut him off. Feeling Glorie stirring in his lap, he ordered, "Everyone, go take ten."

Taking a break, a few men went outside to smoke, some into the kitchen to make a sandwich, several went to the bar and poured hefty drinks, others hit the bathrooms.

His head bent, Joze watched Glorie's eyes flutter then open.

She smiled sweetly up at him and whispered, "Hi."

He smiled back, but his wasn't as sweet. "Hey."

Glancing around, Glorie saw that she was lying in his lap and started to sit up. He held her still.

"What am I-" Bewildered as to how she got there, she suddenly winced in pain. Holding her hands up, her eyes widened at bandages on her arms.

"My- my arms, my back," she winced again, said with confusion, "everything hurts." Narrowing her eyes at him in suspicion, she stiffened, shifting away from him.

His face darkened with a frown. His strong jaw covered with evening stubble firmed, the blue eyes turned dusky.

"I did not harm you, Glorie. You ran. You ran from…here. There's a steep hill with a break off you didn't know about, you fell down the hill. We found you." He didn't go into details of his Tarzan rescue.

"I had some of the women help clean you up and dress you. I treated your wounds as best I could." He watched confusion flow over her face. She looked down at her body, then back up to him.

He grasped her chin gently making her look at him. The black of his pupils enlarged taking over the blue. "You ran, Glorie, you almost died. Why did you run?"

Tears collected in her eyes, she wiped at them. "You're going to kill me anyway, what's the difference?"

"Glorie, I…" he trailed off, what could he say?

"You have been glaring at me all week. Your eyes were hard and cold, you've been even more distant than usual with me. I- I got scared. I thought that…it was time, that you were going to…" She sucked in a deep shuddering breath, let it out slowly. She squirmed in his lap but he held her still, both arms wrapped around her.

"*Babi*, I…ah…" should he reassure her? His mouth opened again but he said nothing, still holding her against his chest.

Squeezing her, he complained, "You are too thin. I insist that you eat more. I will speak to Maria tomorrow about your meals." He cupped her chin and insisted with a hard demand, "You will do as I say."

"Why? The thinner I am the less you have to bury." She pulled from his grasp and moved off his lap, off the couch, and headed for her bedroom. Joze stared after her.

Van was in the doorway, Joze nodded to him to follow her.

Chapter Thirteen

It was several days before Glorie was recovered enough to leave her room. Van and Maria had been her only company, except for occasional visits by Daniel, Linc and Calvin.

Glorie was eager to get to the horses. Before her erroneous ascent down the ravine, Daniel had showed her a mare about to foal.

After she gobbled down a quick piece of toast and a bite of bacon for her lunch, she rushed outside oblivious to Van's complaints that she hadn't eaten enough and was fostering Joze's wrath for not following his orders.

Van watched her until he saw she was under Daniel's careful eye.

"Hey, Daniel," Glorie greeted him cheerfully as she approached the older man.

Daniel was working on restructuring the barn. He set his hammer down when Glorie reached him. "Hey yourself, *gethen*. I heard you had a bit of an adventure." Censure was in his tone.

"Um," Glorie bunched her lips. "It wasn't exactly planned. I hadn't meant to cascade down a darn ravine." She picked at a healing scab on her arm.

Grunting his disapproval at her ill-advised deed, he said, "Where did you think you were going, running willy-nilly into the forest? Didn't Joze tell you how dangerous the woods are?" His brow rose then fell with ire.

When he'd heard what had happened, the weathered skin had instantly lost the dark tan color, turning his face sheet white. Not only fear for the young woman had lanced him, but the escapade that his nephew had instituted to rescue her had punched the air from his lungs. Two deaths so narrowly missed.

He hadn't found it humorous when the men teased Joze all week by calling him Tarzan.

"Yes, well, he did. But," Glorie lowered her head, then raised it, squinting up at the older man. "Daniel, I am being held prisoner. I thought he, ah, Joze, was about to kill me. He'd been acting so cold to me lately, I thought, well," she trailed off, and looked away.

Pushing back hair flowing from the breeze into her face, she said, "I took my chances. In my mind, I was facing death either way. I couldn't just sit there and let him," her face scrunched, "kill me. I couldn't put up a fight. He's too big, too strong, he has weapons, and- and people. My only chance was to hide in the forest and hope I could find my way to civilization."

Daniel studied the young woman. Her chin in her heart-shaped face was lifted with determination. "Glorie girl," he said, "other than a few misplaced attempts at frightening you into submission, has my nephew really harmed you? Yes-" he said quickly as she opened her mouth.

"He has taken you captive, that is wrong, no way around his excuses why he did it. However, other than that and his trying to scare you, has he laid an injurious hand on you?"

Her lips bunched again, her lids lowered in consternation. Glorie replied, "No, he hasn't. But he-"

"Glorie," Daniel cut her off. "He risked his life to save you. You had to have heard what he did? Reckless to say the least, but," a tinge of pride lit the old man's eyes. "He put his life on the line, did an outlandish rescue, and you were saved. How do you reconcile that with the rest of it?"

Glorie was silent for a moment. Of course those same thoughts had been chasing around inside her head ever since Joze had snatched her and imprisoned her here. He hasn't hurt her. In fact, he insists she eats, he's held her gently while talking her out of her nightmares.

He even checked out the room and stayed the night with her that time she'd asked. The side of her mouth nicked up at the memory.

Joze must have thought she was such a cowardly ninny child acting that way. Still, he had done as she'd asked. Even so much as slept with her, with his clothes on, and hadn't even tried to make a pass at her. Her brows daggered down in a slight scowl. Perhaps he wasn't attracted to her.

Regardless that he said he despised cops and wouldn't want to screw one, he was still a red-blooded man lying beside a young woman all night, it would only be normal if he'd had sexual urges towards her. But, he had been a kind gentleman, he hadn't even mocked her for her perverse, unexplained fear.

But, nevertheless, he would not let her leave, and that was wrong. Kidnapping, no matter the initial reasons, that he had feared the thugs at the saloon would harm her, it was wrong now that he kept her imprisoned.

Then again, she pondered, the thought of actually leaving, going home. A shudder rippled across her shoulders, why did that make her feel...lost?

Glorie had been stunned when Van had told her of Joze's brazen, brave rescue effort. She knew how terrified she'd been rolling uncontrollably down that hill, fearful of what the end result would be. The thought that Joze had flung himself out to the same danger, well, shivers had roiled up and down her body for hours when she'd learned of his daring deed.

The men had been yodeling on about it for days. They were impressed with Joze's wild Tarzan idea of how he planned the rescue, and the extreme, selfless bravery in carrying it out.

If the circumstances were different, Joze would be her hero. He certainly was in the eyes of his men. And women. After the incident, the groupies poured over him everywhere he went. Clung to him like tics on a buck.

Daniel broke into her revelry, "Come on, *gethen*, let's go check out that foal."

Glorie blinked at him. Her perplexing thoughts chased away at the desire to see the new baby. Smiling, she eagerly followed the strong man as he led the way to the stable.

Chapter Fourteen

A few days later, after dinner was done, a crowd of people hung around the living room, drinking and joking, loud music played, a few of the men and women danced.

Joze slouched in a chair with a drink in his hand. A woman hung over him from behind, pawing at his arms, gushing about how big and bulging his biceps were.

Another woman, half drunk, was sitting on his lap, her back against his chest, legs splayed over his. His hand was up her shirt. He absently fondled her breast while he wondered for the hundredth time where the hell Glorie was. She hadn't been at dinner.

Diego had assured him she was fine. He'd checked on her periodically. She was at the stables with Daniel and Van watching over her.

Just as he gazed impatiently again at the door, he was about to get up and go look for her when he saw her come in.

She was laughing at something Kurt Quinto said as she made her way through the crowd. What the hell- why was Kurt with her? Joze glared at Diego, who shrugged with his palms up.

Looking back at Kurt, Glorie's eyes caught Joze's and connected. Then her gaze slid down to where he was unenthusiastically feeling up the woman on his lap while another draped over him.

Appalled disgust struck her face; she whipped her head around and said something to Kurt.

"Hey, bro, that wee cop of yours is rocking hot," a ranch hand sitting near Joze crowed, ogling Glorie's bouncing breasts and then her ass as she hurried out of the room. "Nice fucking tits, and an ass that screams mama-"

Joze leaned over and slapped him hard in the head. "Put your eyes back in your head, asshole." He got to his feet so fast the girl on his lap landed on the floor.

She didn't utter a complaint, just sat there until her friend came around from behind Joze's chair and pulled her to her feet.

Joze was already pushing through the crowd. By the time he crossed the room he could see Glorie already halfway down the hall, Kurt dropped his arm around her.

Seeing red, Joze barked out, "Quinto!"

Kurt turned around holding Glorie. She looked like she was trying to disengage his arm. Hugging her tighter, Kurt waited until Joze reached them.

"You got something to do?" Joze barked at him again, the black creeping into his eyes. His jaw was rigid. He didn't look at Glorie.

"Nah, we were just gonna go play cards. Van went to get us some drinks-"

"Get lost," Joze told him brusquely, then he turned his gaze to Glorie. He cringed inside. She was glaring at him, looking down that little nose at him like he had been rolling in mud with the pigs.

"Listen, Joze, man, you obviously have your own entertainment going on in the other room, I mean, we saw your action," Kurt wiggled a brow with a sly grin. He said, "So, if you don't mind, we are gonna-" he lowered his hand from around Glorie's shoulder to her waist and squeezed it. He ignored her hand pushing at his side.

"I do mind." Joze's eyes went from black discs to mere slits. He said coldly, "Don't make me tell you again, get your hands off her, *man*, and get lost. Now."

Kurt tried to stand his ground.

Joze set his hands on his hips, curling his long fingers over his lean hipbones. The rigid planes of his face like cleaved steel, the hall lights glinted off them. His eyes had all but disappeared into malevolent slits.

Kurt slowly dropped his hand and Glorie moved slightly away from him. "All right, Boss. You win, this time. But all's fair in love and war, right?"

He turned to Glorie and said, "Catch ya later, beautiful." Before she could react, he caught her chin and kissed her quickly on the lips. At Joze's menacing growl, he let her go, bowed to her, then sauntered off down the hall.

"What the hell do you think you're doing?" Joze blustered at Glorie.

Her mouth parted, brows like boomerangs arched over her eyes. "I beg your pardon?"

Joze scowled, his hands gripping his hips hard in his jealous anger. He snapped angrily, "You know what I mean. You were going off to- to fuck with that asshole?"

"Oh!" An affronted gasp tore out of her. Then those arched brows drew down like fireplace pokers, she exclaimed, "How dare you! Who do you think you are talking to me like that? You have no right to tell me who I can- can, uh," flames of anger and embarrassment shot up her face. "Not that I was, or would- oh!" She crunched her hands into tight fists and narrowed her eyes at him.

His arm snaked out and he gripped her jaw like a clamp, pulled her face up to his. "I dare because, for now, I own you." His smile hard at her aghast expression, he said, "I will tell you whom you can and can't fuck."

Her face grew so red she looked about to burst. "Do not talk to me like that, and let go of me right now!"

He smiled crudely down at her, his face inches from hers. "I'll talk to you any way I want." His face firmed, his voice caustic and angry, he asserted, "You will not have such public displays of affection like that and you will not-"

"Oh!" she cried again. Jerking out of his grip she stepped back. Red darkened her fair skin, her amethyst eyes ground ire at him. "How dare you talk to me like that? When you- the degrading way you behaved out there. You should be ashamed of yourself treating that woman like that! Your hands all over her in public, you have no respect for her, or for yourself. You are a disgrace!"

Taken aback at first, Joze was surprised, then he had the grace to look slightly abashed.

He told her, "Honey, those girls throw themselves at, on and under us all the damned time. They're like groupies, they'd drop on their backs and spread their legs in the middle of the living room floor and let us fuck them in front of everyone if we'd let them."

"Huh. I see. So that makes it okay to- to grope, take advantage of a poor drunken woman who hardly knows where she is, but you put the brakes on actually- uh," her face flamed again, she slammed her hands on her hips.

Her face twisted in a grimace, she said, "Actually, I'm surprised after the way you, uh, assaulted me, that you didn't force yourself on her in the middle of the Persian rug."

Now he did look a shade guilty. Fighting off the feelings of shame, he snapped, "Enough of this talk."

He cleared his throat then said calmly, "You are right. Just because it's freely offered doesn't mean I have to take advantage of it, especially when I had absolutely zero desire or interest to touch her, doesn't mean I should."

She looked confused. "I don't understand. Then why did you?"

He shrugged indifferently. "I was bored." *And focused on wondering where you were and what you were doing.* "I'm so used them hounding me it's almost not even a second thought to," *shyt*, she was making him feel ashamed and dirty. She was kinda right.

Joze shook his head and stated, "Never mind, like I said, this subject is closed. We were talking about you. How you will conduct yourself-"

"What!" Her hands on her hips, the crystal eyes narrowed to tiny glowing streaks. "You're back to telling me what I can and can't do? Well, you are not-"

Joze grabbed her so swiftly he knocked the breath out of her. He cupped both sides of her face and covered her mouth with his silencing her protests.

118

He hadn't meant to do it, then he hadn't meant to do it so hard, so rough, but as soon as his lips met hers, and he pushed them apart, and tasted her, he no longer could remember what he wasn't going to do.

Joze was lost in the kiss, her lips so tender, he could feel her inexperience; it made him hotter. If he could, he would devour her mouth, her tongue, her teeth, then move down her body. The room was spinning, his erection was immediate and he couldn't help but press it against her. They might as well both be uncomfortable.

He was aloft, his brain a crazy fog of desire, it took a moment before he realized she was pushing at him. Disoriented, his eyes a blind glaze, Joze was breathing so hard, she seemed a beautiful rippling fair ribbon in his hands.

"Mr. Kane," she gasped, panting for air, "what, why did you…"

A bucket of cold water doused him. Mr. Kane. What the hell? He gripped her upper arms, his teeth clenched, he growled angrily, "Glorie, you will stop calling-"

Her voice now small and afraid, she murmured, "You're hurting me," and tried to twist out of his grasp.

He blinked, mouth dropped open. He shook his head to clear the lust and the anger, first of seeing that bastard Quinto with his damned hands on her, and now she acts like Joze is his father or something. *Fuck.* Forcing his fingers to unwind one at a time, he released her.

She stepped back rubbing her arms. Great. Now he was a woman abuser. It keeps getting better. He dragged his sleeve across his confused forehead.

Letting out a long breath, the rough edge to his voice indicated how much the kiss had affected him, he said gruffly, "*Iawn,* uh, okay, Glorie, let's uh, take it down a notch. Let's take a breather, gather our wits, go back to the living room and have a drink to calm down."

Glorie glanced down the hall to the crowded room of people drinking and getting more boisterous. "Uh, I don't think that's a good idea. I think I'll just go to bed." She started towards her room but he caught up her arm.

"No. I don't want you to go to bed with things so fraught, you're clearly upset. You already have nightmares-" he broke off, she got all uppity and clammed up before whenever he tried to press her about her bad dreams.

He let go of her arm, making his voice softer, he urged, "Please, Glorie, humor me. You're right about my behavior. I am, ah, I feel bad about my boorish conduct." He smiled inside at the look of distress on her face as he made his expression sadder and more shameful. He knew feeding on her tender heart would do it.

"I'm not a nice guy. I treat females crassly, and I shouldn't have, ah, kissed you just now. Let's chill for a minute. It would make me feel better if you, ah, forgive me for my misogynist behavior, and you calm down before you hit the sack. What do you say?"

Her eyes flit back and forth looking at his eyes as if searching for the sincerity in his words. Apparently convinced, or at least she wanted to alleviate the tension, she agreed, "Okay, Mr. Kane, if that's what you want."

Goddammit, he picked up her hand and tucked it in his arm. He said quietly, "What I want, Glorie, is for you to stop calling me Mr. Kane. I told you it makes me feel like my father. It's bad enough I look like him." He patted her hand. "Do you think you can do that?"

She started, "This situation," her lips pressed, she glanced at him. He was staring earnestly at her.

"I mean, you are keeping me here against my will. I don't feel we can be on..." She contemplated, then said, "Friendly terms. You've said some horrible, hateful things to me, called me nasty names, and you won't let me go home. I don't know what you expect from me."

He nodded, agreed, "*Ie.* But, not to blow my own horn, I did save your life in a dangerous feat. That should at least give me a couple of brownie points?" A lopsided grin coaxed at her to give him a chance to equalize the fact that he'd abducted her.

Glorie cocked her head with a tiny smile. "I wouldn't have needed saving if you hadn't seized me in the first place."

He reminded her, "If I hadn't abducted you, been there in the first place, you might be dead right now." They both grimaced at the reminder of that deadly day at the saloon.

She returned, "But," the smile grew but with slight accusation, "if you hadn't been there, I wouldn't have been sent there to begin with to spy on you, so it all never would have happened."

With his own critical smile, Joze explained his actions, "Hey, I didn't make your idiot handler send you on a fool's mission. I knew the cops were trying to sic someone on me, put them undercover. I just set up the situation so they could. Keep your enemies closer and all that.

"As long as I knew the cops were watching me, I could watch them, and thereby keep my head low. If I had them in my sights, they couldn't catch me at what they would describe as nefarious exploits."

"Very clever," she said with sarcasm, "aren't you the bright criminal?"

His smile fell. "Listen, Glorie, I've never been brought up on charges. There's just cops making assumptions, wanting to get that big promotion off my back, my arrest. They're just searching for a conviction, setting up traps they hope I'll fall into."

His lips twisting sadly, he said, "And it's pretty lousy of you to just jump on the bandwagon, *assume* that I'm dirty. Makes me feel really shitty, like I'm not a person, a decent human being without even having been found guilty in a trial or anything." His expression turned crestfallen, he sounded miserable. His bottom lip pushed out, and can you say 'woeful puppy dog eyes?'

And it worked. Glorie's soft heart jumped in. "Oh, I didn't mean to hurt your feelings, uh…"

He filled in, "Joze."

"Um, Joze," she repeated. Her lips bunched, her eyes grew warm and apologetic.

His smile returned. Before she could harp on the fact that he had in truth abducted her and was keeping her prisoner, he said, "How about we call a truce for now? At least pretend to be friends?"

"But, uh, Joze, nothing changes the fact that you are holding me against my will."

Joze shoved his hands in his pockets, his shoulders hunched. "Hell, Glorie," his voice gruff, he stretched his neck. "I..." he paused.

Then he said, "For now, I just think everyone, you, me, are safer just to leave things as they are. So, for now, can we call a truce? I won't molest women that I don't want to molest, even if they're dropped in my lap," his grin was devilish. "And I'll try to keep my hands off the ones I do. What do you say?"

Glorie leaned back from him, not sure what he was agreeing to. But his grin was so boyish and engaging, a complete turnabout for the cold ruthless gangster. Her brows knit, then she agreed, "Ah, I guess, okay."

"So let's-"

"Boss!" His face white as a sheet, Van hurried down the hall to them with a glass of water in his hand. Once again, somehow Van had taken his eyes off Glorie and troubled had ensued.

The look alone on Joze's face told Van this could be his last day on earth.

Chapter Fifteen

Joze rounded on Van. "Where the hell were you? You left her alone for every Tom Dick and asshole to screw with. And she could have run again."

Van faltered, "Uh, I got her a glass of water. We worked hard, and-"

"It took you twenty fucking minutes to get a lousy glass of water?" Joze barked at him.

When Van's mouth moved but no words came out, Joze's voice dropped low, he said, "I asked you, where the hell have you been?"

Van's eyes blinked nervously. "Uh, well, that is, Kurt asked me to, uh, give him a few minutes alone with her. I was outside. I was watching to make sure she didn't hightail it out. He, uh…"

Van swallowed several times before going on, "Kurt likes her. He said you always keep her so wrapped up tight he hasn't had the opportunity to…get to know her better. So…"

Frowning, Glorie broke in, "Hey, uh, I'm standing right here, you can stop referring to me as 'her' and talk to me directly-"

Joze glanced at Glorie, said shortly, "I am not talking to you, I am talking to your supposed guard." Dismissing her affronted expression, he put his attention back on Van.

It was obvious Joze was struggling with his temper, his fists clenched, his neck taut, mouth grit with strain. "So," he said with deceptive quietness, "you thought it was okay to leave her alone with Don Juan. Did it occur to you he might not have her best interests at heart?"

Glorie stood awkwardly between the two men. She was prepared to hold them off if they came to blows. But then Joze coiled his hands over her shoulders and set her aside as if she were a child. He was livid and he didn't want her to get hurt accidentally.

Van's face had drained of color, but now it flushed back in. He stammered, "No, I mean, Kurt said he really likes her, and- and he wouldn't harm her. Geez, Boss, everyone knows by now that you would kill anyone who hurt her. He just wanted a little private time with her, to maybe build a relationship..." Van trailed off at Joze's gravely furious expression.

A vein ticked at his temple, his mouth was set like cement. With icy contempt, Joze said softly, "You need to get the hell out of my sight, right now. I'll talk to you later."

Van hesitated, Joze snapped, "*Get out.*" He didn't watch the guard as he flapped his lips uselessly then turned and hauled ass down the hall.

Joze's eyes turned in Glorie's direction and narrowed. "What were you doing outside so late anyway?"

Blinking from the scene that she feared would be explosive, Glorie had to gather her wits.

Then her face lit up. "Oh my gosh, Mister- uh, Joze, it was the most exciting thing in the world! The cow Marybelle had her calf. They let me watch and pet her while they struggled to calm her." Her eyes glowed like brilliant torches. "It was amazing," she crowed.

Scowling his displeasure, he groused, "What? Marybelle calved and they didn't come and get me? They know I wanted to-"

Glorie said, "Oh, I mentioned to Daniel you might want to see it, but he said you didn't care about the ranch as long as everyone did their job and it functioned properly."

She toned down her glee seeing his scowl darken. "So, um, anyway, it was amazing. I've never seen a live birth before. I can't wait for the next one."

Shoulders hunched, Joze sullenly jammed his hands in his pockets and glared at the floor. He and his uncle needed to talk. His lips pulled in, he exhaled, blowing them out.

Dragging one of his hands out, he scraped his fingers over the shaved side of his head then raked them through the top of his wavy hair. His eyes calmed back down to dusky blue, he rolled them up to Glorie. He said, "Come back to the party."

Incredulous, she piped, "Are you kidding? No way. Look at me." She gestured to her jeans and T-shirt.

Not seeing the problem. Sure, she looked scorching in the snug jeans and tight T, her breasts molded against the tight cotton begging to be palmed.

Joze cleared his throat; he could deal with her looking so hot as long as she was in his company, under his protection. "What? What's the matter with what you're wearing?"

Her snort was soft and ladylike. "Really? There are tons of gorgeous sexy women in there dressed to the nines, and I-" shaking her head, she said, "I don't think so," and she started to head to her room.

He grabbed her wrist to stop her. "Glorie, trust me, you have it way over those plastic bitches."

Frowning at his language, she stared at his hand clutching her wrist.

With a grunt, he let go and stuck his hands back in his pockets. Glaring at her from under his brow he grumbled, "I want you there. Van is not here now to watch you. Come on," without letting her object, he took her hand and brought her to the party.

If she went to bed now the disharmony would stay between them. Joze hoped a little social time together would lessen some of her acrimony for him. Not that it wasn't well deserved, but nonetheless, he didn't want her to hate him.

Picking his way through the crowd, as he neared one of the sofas he looked at a man sitting on one end of one of the couches.

The man catching his look, smiled, and got up and went and found another seat.

Joze brought Glorie over and told her to sit down on the cushion the man had vacated. Then he turned to where he'd been sitting before, near the couch, one of the women he had been dallying with was slouched in it.

"Deidre," Joze said, "get up. Go get yourself some coffee." He waited but the woman leered drunkenly at him.

"How bout I get *this* for you?" She slurred, lifting up her blouse. Her tight skirt had ridden up to the very tops of her thighs. She wasn't wearing a bra. Shuffling to the end of the seat she shook her boobs at Joze. "Come an' get 'em, slugger. I've been waiting all night for my chance with you, baby."

His ears burned. Even without looking at her, he knew Glorie would be unable to hide the shock on her face. He could feel her start to get to her feet and move towards the woman, great, she wanted to help her.

Off his shoulder, he said, "Sit down, Glorie." Then he turned to Deidre with a sigh. As a stripper, like many of the women there, she wasn't showing him, or anyone in the room anything she hadn't flaunted many times before.

Joze caught Linc's eye. As Linc made his way over, Joze bent and tugged Deidre's blouse down. "Come on, honey, we're going to get you a little coffee and then you can sleep it off."

Deidre coyly tilted her head at him. Gazing through blurry eyeballs, she leaned over and put her hand on Joze's chest and stroked it down fast before he could stop her.

She clutched his man's package and exclaimed, "*Gawd*, Joze honey, you are as big as you look! Take me, take me to your room, I want you so badly," her whine slurred as she licked her lips and squeezed.

"Fuck, Deidre-" Joze snatched her wrist, jerking her hand off him. Normally it wouldn't have bothered him all that much even though he had absolutely no interest in her, even with her hand on his private parts it stirred no desire in him.

What bothered him was that Glorie sat there witnessing it. She just got done telling him what an immoral scumbag he was.

126

"Yeah," Deidre said, her inebriated words unintelligible, pulling her blouse back up to bare herself to him, "you want it too. Come on, baby, take me to your-"

Joze very gently grasped her blouse and pulled it back down. Then he took her hand and carefully pulled her to her unsteady feet.

"Oh baby," she slurred, falling against him. She threw her arms around his neck and tried to kiss him with sloppy results.

Joze held her upper arms, keeping her off him, then Linc arrived. Joze handed her to him.

"Come on, sweetie," Linc said, sounding like a big brother, "let's get you fixed up."

"Ohh," Deidre moaned, crossing her blurry eyes at Linc. "I want Joze, but," she snuggled up to him, "you're pretty hot too. You've got the cutest curly hair."

Linc smiled at her, holding her carefully so she wouldn't stumble and winked at Joze. "My girl Kristi is going to help me get some coffee into you."

He half-carried, half walked Deidre towards a friendly looking pretty girl with long brown hair. Kristi took one arm and Linc held her other, between the two, they ushered her out to one of the dorms to let her sleep off her buzz.

With a big expelled breath, Joze turned awkwardly to Glorie, expecting a look of disgust for him on her face. But her expression was blank. There was no contempt, no judgment, no emotion whatsoever. "Uh, you want something to drink, Glorie?"

She shrugged one slender shoulder. "I guess. A soda would be okay."

Joze forked his fingers through the top of his wavy hair and let out another deep exhale. "All right." Then he narrowed his eyes at her.

Her hands were folded primly in her lap, and she crossed her ankles. His stomach pitched at the thinness of her arms and legs. Even the high rounded cheeks looked like they had thinned.

"Did you eat dinner?" His voice came out harshly accusing. Van had told him every time she had that nightmare she couldn't eat the next day. And she had it frequently.

Glorie's lips pulled in, her mouth firmed. "I was busy."

The woman sitting next to Glorie looked from her to Joze to her, like a nosey Ping-Pong ball.

His mouth opened, then he shut it. This was not the place or time for an argument. He turned on his heel and went to get them both a drink.

When he returned, the woman who had been sitting next to Glorie had gone and one of his soldiers, not one of his close team, had sat down next to her. His arm was stretched across the sofa, behind her.

Joze glared at the man's arm, but he wasn't paying any attention to Joze. He was half-turned in his chair facing Glorie. In fact, he had boxed her in against the corner of the couch.

"Here," Joze said handing the soda to Glorie, he sat down in his chair with a big glass of scotch, his eyes on Guy Whaler, the man sitting next to her.

Diego plopped down near Joze. "Hey, bro, you chose a woman yet?" His dark eyes flashed around the room checking out the ladies.

Joze looked over at his friend. Diego was a good-looking man, he was a player and the women loved him. He kept his dark hair slicked and short, his cheekbones were high and sharp, and under his full lips he had a splotch of hair on his chin.

As Joze and the other men, their close friends, Linc, Calvin, Sloan and Bruno, Diego worked out, he loved sparring MMA with the boys. His buff body showed his dedication to the gym.

"*Na.* You know I don't do the talent that hangs around here." Joze resisted looking back over at Glorie. He could hear her and Guy talking, but he couldn't make out their words. Scowling, he wondered if someone had hung a sign over Glorie's head that said, 'available, come get me.'

His grin sly, Diego bumped his dark eyebrows towards Glorie. "Uh huh, and it seems since you dragged little miss cop here, you haven't tasted the talents of any woman anywhere."

Joze shrugged and took a big swig of his scotch.

"So," Diego leaned over conspiratorially, said snidely, "you drilling the cop? I can't say I blame you, she's a hot looking bitch."

Joze cut a wrathful look at Diego. "Shut up, asshole."

Diego laughed, sat back and crossed his legs. "I see how it is. You want her but you're telling yourself you don't. Just do her, bro, the blue balls aren't worth the mental tennis."

Diego drank down half his bourbon and soda. His eyes continuously darted around the room.

Before Joze could deny his words, Diego licked his lips. "Now, tonight, I'm inclined to take that brunette there, the one over by the window. They're both from the strip club but haven't been here before. I like the fuller figure."

He indicated a blowsy woman talking with a slim blonde. "Hell, I'm digging those huge tits and her even bigger ass." His gaze flicked to the blonde then back to the brunette. "Yeah, I think I'll do her first, then tomorrow the blonde. Oh yeah," he took a big swallow.

Diego went on, "Of course," and smiled at them, they were glancing back at him and tilting their heads with coy smiles. "If they're willing to both do tonight at the same time, I'm up for that."

His conceited, macho sexist prattle was bugging Joze, and that bugged him. Normally he was just as callous and loose as Diego. But he hadn't been feeling it lately. Today with the girls all over him bored him, and annoyed him. It had actually gotten old a while ago, he was just recognizing it now.

With Glorie here, any residual temptation to be with another woman had disappeared to zilch. She was killing him for ever desiring another female but her.

"You aren't worried someone will spill about the cop?" Diego asked.

Joze turned his black gaze to his friend. The look in his eyes was sufficient to make Diego grin. No one snitched on the Chianina organization. They knew they wouldn't make it from the police station to protective custody if they did.

Diego's attention switched back to the two women who were both now smirking at him.

Joze glanced over at Dave Matthews.

Dave's eyes had lit up as his wife entered the room. Joze had always thought that love crap was stupid. Trapping a man with one woman forever? That's just not normal.

He watched Ginger cross the room towards her husband; the two only had eyes for each other. Dave always chased off any other women who came onto him.

Dave stood up when Ginger reached him. She had worked late, Joze had noticed all evening Dave had kept glancing at his watch with a furrowed brow. But now, his face aglow, love radiated off the man's face.

He wound his arms around his wife and kissed her as intensely as he had the very first time. Joze couldn't believe it. They'd been married for five years.

Without a glance at anyone in the room, their arms around each other, the couple left the room. There was no doubt where they were going and what they were going to do. They had their own home a few miles away.

Now *that* was disgusting, Joze thought using Glorie's words. Except, the pit of his stomach pinched, a twinge of rare envy pricked, then that fell away leaving an empty feeling in his gut.

He watched the couple touching each other until they were gone. Pursing his lips, he took a sip of scotch and glanced over at Glorie.

That asshole Guy had moved as close to her as he could get. His arm around the back of the sofa had lowered and was almost curled around her shoulders.

He had a hand on her knee, effectively hedging her in. Guy's mouth was near her ear. He lifted some of her curls, whispered something then put his lips on her neck. Glorie's face blew up like a red balloon.

His face darkening, Joze started to get up when a woman dropped herself in his lap. He sputtered, "Goddammit Valerie, what the hell-"

"Oh don't be so nasty, Joze. I've missed you." The redhead twined her hands behind his neck trying to pull his head down for a kiss.

"Geez, Val, knock it off." Joze clinched her arms to pull them off him.

"Aw, baby, you haven't been around the club for a while, I've been patiently waiting my turn with you." Like ivy, she twined around him again, rubbing her chest against his.

To think he used to enjoy this blatant salacious behavior, or had fooled himself into thinking he did. He grabbed her arms again and with more aggressive force, pulled them off.

His voice reflecting his anger, he growled at her, "Valerie. I am not interested. You have three seconds to get off my lap before I toss your synthetic body out the door." His pupils completely covering the blue irises, he looked like the very devil and as pissed as him.

Valerie was shocked at his anger, it seethed out of him like fierce heat. "Geez, okay already. Boy, what the hell got into you?" She slid off his lap, straightened her skintight tiny skirt, then sashayed off to find someone more willing.

Joze glared down at the empty glass in his hand. Then he heard Glorie's voice sounding slightly anxious.

Guy had taken her soda from her and was now forcing a drink into her hands and encouraging her to keep taking sips.

She did to appease him, but the alcohol was starting to make her feel uncomfortable, and hot. Using both hands to hold the fairly large glass she didn't have a free one to push away his hand that was creeping up her leg.

"Uh, I need to get up, Guy," Glorie murmured, trying to nudge away from him.

The arm around the back of her slid down, he sifted his hand into her hair to hold the back of her neck. "How about just a little kiss, then I'll walk you to the bathroom, okay?" He forced her head to turn and face him while his other hand continued its journey up her thigh.

"No, I," Glorie protested. Squirming away from him, she shoved herself to the edge of the couch to stand up. But Guy put both hands on her waist and pulled her back almost spilling her drink.

Another hand reached down and plucked the glass out of her hand and set it on the table beside the couch. "Come on, Glorie." Joze held his hand out to her.

Guy scratched the top of his black spiky hair, his black fringed hazel eyes peered up at the intrusion. "Hey, Boss," he greeted Joze cheerfully, "she's okay, I've got her."

Guy wrapped his arms around her waist and pulled her back against his chest then nuzzled his face in her hair. "Damn you're soft, honey," he inhaled deeply, "and you smell so good." He nestled his nose deeper, moving his mouth closer to her neck.

"Get up, Glorie," Joze ordered, his voice dug lower, rougher, a warning.

She tried to move, but Guy held her tightly. "Come on, Boss," he said to Joze. "We're having fun." His mouth now on her neck, motioning with his hand, he mumbled, "There are lots of lovelies out there for you to fuck. This one's mine."

He moved his hand to Glorie's shoulder, nudging her to turn around towards him and pulled her closer. When her breasts squashed up against his chest, he looked down at them, a bold leer brightened his eyes, he literally licked his lips.

His voice like a block of ice, Joze's voice so dark and low it scared the people sitting nearby that weren't even involved. "Let go of her, Guy, before I take your arm and rip it off and tie it around your neck and fucking strangle you with it."

Guy was about to brush him off when the hairs on his arms stood up. The quiet of Joze's tone, the granite set of his jaw and the black eyes barely visible under low lids like a shark's unnerved him. His boss was well known for his deadly brawling.

He opened his arms and squinted up at Joze. "Yeah, sure. You laying claim, Boss?"

That was the second time another man asked him that. The house was littered with horndogs. Joze hooked Glorie's arm and drew her to her feet. "*Na*," he replied tersely.

Holding Glorie's upper arm, as they started to walk her away, he heard Guy's snort, "Good. Cause I will."

Joze glanced back and saw the calculating roguish smirk crawling over Guy's face.

Joze's eyes slit so threatening at him, Guy's face withered.

Guy stared at the rigid set to Joze's block of shoulders as the big man turned, and with his hand on Glorie's lower back, led her from the crowded, alcohol drenched, carnal room.

Chapter Sixteen

That night, Joze was awakened by horrible, gut-wrenching cries and blood curdling screams, it sounded like she was being tortured on the rack.

Joze rolled out of his bed and yanked his jeans on as he hurried to the adjoining door. Throwing it open he rushed in and to her side.

Glorie was screaming and physically, desperately fighting something in her dream.

Throwing her hands out, she cried, "Please- stop, you're killing me, it hurts, the blood, God the blood, help me, please, someone help me!"

Sitting down on the bed, Joze bundled her into his arms, securing her gently but tightly against his chest like a careful straitjacket.

"Glorie, *bach babi*, wake up, wake up, you're dreaming, shh," he cooed in her ear, stroking her. But she kept screaming and thrashing.

Alarmed that she was going to hurt herself or have a heart attack from sheer terror, Joze held her upper arms and shook her.

He said loudly, "Wake up, Glorie!" It sickened him to see her head flail back and forth, but he kept shaking her, calling for her to wake up.

Her breathing was so wretchedly rasping, Joze worried she'd slip into a panic attack and stop breathing before he could wake her.

He grasped her jaw hard, and shouted, "Glorie, wake up!"

She froze for just a second, then she gulped her breaths and hiccupped, her eyes flickered. Joze could see the delirium clouding them as she struggled to wake.

His voice lowered to a gentle whisper, "Glorie, *babi*," he soothed, "you were dreaming. It wasn't real. You're here, you're safe." He held her in one supported arm and stroked her face, watching as she came to, her eyes wobbled then steadied on him.

"Joze?"

"*Ie*, you were dreaming. You're here with me." His mouth pulled in wryly, that might not make her feel any safer.

Her frantic eyes travelled his face as if trying to determine if he was a danger to her or not.

It took an effort, but Joze willed his face to relax into a mild, calm, nonthreatening veneer. He felt the tension in her body, slowly, inch by shuddering inch drain out of her.

She closed her eyes. Long lashes curled over the normally rosy cheeks but were now pale and translucent as teardrops.

Joze huddled her against him and rocked with her until the ragged breaths eased and she fell limp in his arms. They stayed like that for a few long moments as she calmed.

When she stirred, then moved away from him, he dropped his arms. Her eyes lifted to his, then they quickly lowered, but not before he saw the shame and embarrassment in them.

Joze curled a finger under her chin and raised it. He told her, "Glorie, you have nothing to be ashamed or embarrassed about. You had a bad dream."

Her eyes flit from him to the room, then lowered again.

He let go of her chin but slipped his large hand over her willowy shoulder and lightly massaged it. His voice firm, he insisted, "You must tell me what it is about. Let me help you." He waited, but her eyes stayed lowered.

Her lip quivering, she pushed away from him. "I'm fine…" she took a ragged breath. "It was, as you said, just a bad dream." She wiped at her eyes and moved further away from Joze. "You can go back to bed now, I'm fine. Thank you for- uh, thank you." She wouldn't look at him.

He reached for her to make her, then let his hand fall, he could see she had brought a wall down covering her emotions. To try to force her to talk would only be more stressful for her.

Joze studied her, his mouth pressed thoughtfully. He was sure she knew what the dream was about. He wasn't even going to ask her if she remembered the dream. She did. The terror hadn't completely cleared from her jeweled eyes, but she wasn't talking.

Something devastating happened to her, and it still had its grievous claws in her. It was *bullshyt* that he had to sit and watch her suffering in agony and not be able to help her.

"Glorie-"

She wiped furiously at her eyes. "Please, I'm fine. Please leave."

Joze turned more towards her, she shrunk away from him. "Listen, Glorie, I stayed with you the last time, I can-"

"No!" Sobs caught in her throat. "Please," she croaked, "go away."

"All right," he sighed. "Do you want me to check the room out for you? Make sure no one is here?"

She froze. Pulling her knees up, she wrapped her arms around them and set her head on them facing away from him so he couldn't see her cry. "No."

Joze stood up. "I'm going to leave the adjoining door open, *babi*, just call out if you want- or need me. *Iawn?* Uh, I mean, okay?"

His answer was a raw broken breath. He put out his hand to stroke her head, then lowered it without touching her and quietly left the room.

****

Later in the early afternoon, Glorie came into the dining room with Van at her side. They took seats at the oblong table for lunch, far down from where Joze and Daniel sat.

Uncle and nephew were in deep discussion and didn't notice them come in. A handful of ranch hands were present chowing down on sandwiches and potato salad. A few of the business' staff, the soldiers, were there, as well as several women that most of the men were flirting with.

Joze and his uncle were arguing, their fierce whispers carried down the table.

His grizzled face tight with frustration, Daniel said, "Joze, son, it's expensive now, but vinyl siding on the house will save money in the long run.

Joze glowered at him, irritation stiffened his face. "*Na*, it costs too much and you get stuck with the same color forever." He repeated, "*Na*," then took a big bite of his sandwich, chewing vigorously.

Daniel shrugged his ire away and said mildly, "You will save money in the long run, you won't have to keep painting forever or worry about tenting for termites or-"

"Daniel," Joze warned.

His uncle shrugged again, ignoring Joze's intimating look. "Whatever, son, suit yourself." He put his rough calloused hands on the table and pushed to his feet. Without another word he trod out the door letting the screen door bang shut behind him.

Setting the sandwich down on a plate, Joze muttered after him, "I am not your son." He pushed the plate away and picked up his coffee.

Glaring at the mug, his eyes drifted to the end of the table where Glorie sat. He took a sip of coffee, scrutinizing her over the rim of the mug. Her eyes were dark smudges of weariness, and something else he couldn't read. Seeing the tiny bit of sandwich she took made his mouth compress.

Glorie had cut off a piece of a sandwich and handed the rest to Van. Then she stood up.

Stuffing Glorie's sandwich in his mouth and grabbing up his own, Van snagged a soda can off the table, the pair walked to the door.

Joze's brows flew up practically right off the top of his head. *What the hell was she wearing?* His head swung around ogling her as did every other man at the table.

Someone had apparently loaned her a very tiny pair of shorts and a tinier half-shirt.

When she neared the door, Guy Whaler entered the room. The second he spotted her, he bee-lined straight to her. "Hey precious, damn but you look sweet!" His eyes seemed to engrave her body from head to toe like he wanted to take portions of her and eat her up- without using utensils.

Glorie's smile was weary from lack of sleep but polite. She tried to keep up with Van to the door but the tall guard had long legs and left her several feet behind.

Guy took the opportunity to settle his arm around her shoulders and give her a big squeezing hugged greeting.

She tried to quicken her pace, but he held her back and slid his hand to her lower back forcing her to curve around to face him.

"Hey, sugar, how about I take you-"

Joze's impatient voice tinged with ire crossed the room. "Guy, go out and help Daniel with the fence."

Guy paused, then he tugged Glorie a little closer to him pretending he hadn't heard the order.

Like an animal's warning of attack, from deep in his chest, Joze's growl like a serrated knife sawed through the suddenly tense room, he hissed, *"Now."*

Everyone hushed and sat waiting with bated breath to see what was going to happen. Joze looked about to splinter like bomb shards and blow Guy into pieces.

Guy shrugged. Then grinned. "Sure, okay Boss." He moved his hand up to Glorie's neck and whispered, "Catch ya later sweet thing," he brushed her hair off her shoulder and lowered his head to kiss her but she turned her face and his lips landed on her cheek. Tucking his hands in his pockets he strolled out of the room.

Joze's harsh eyes moved to Glorie, he said, "Come over here."

She looked about to argue with him, but the blue eyes had turned black, his brows drawn down hard like daggers, the harsh mouth ground into a barbarous line.

One-by-one everyone at the table quietly left the room.

Glorie moved towards him coming to stand an arm's length away. Her expression perplexed. He looked so mad, she hadn't even said a word to him, what could he be angry about?

Grinding furiously, he said to her, "You go the fuck back in your room and change your clothes."

Surprised and even more confused, she looked down at the shorts and shirt Bruno's girlfriend Melissa loaned her. "I don't understand, I'm going to go finish digging up the dirt for the vegetable garden-"

His hand slammed the table, glasses jumped. His glare spiking her with ever mounting anger, he said in a whispered shout, "I don't care if you're going to a fucking party at Princess Anne's, you go change your clothes right the fuck now."

Maria walked in from the kitchen and turned around and walked right back out.

"But why? I only have the borrowed pair of jeans and shirt, I washed them before bed last night but they're still wet. No one else will loan me anything except Melissa loaned me these shorts and top and I-" she frowned at him.

"What do you care what I wear? You're not my father or husband, even if you were that doesn't give you the right to tell me what I can or cannot wear I am an adult-"

He leaned towards her slightly, snaked his arm out and clamped his hand roughly around her arm.

At her surprised yelp, he pulled her over and down close to him, her hair showered like raining flames between them.

He grasped her jaw hard and snarled in her face, "You'll do as I say, Glorie, I don't have to have a reason." He drew her face closer, eyes like angry ink pinpoints, he said, "Do not ever argue with me again. No one fucking argues with me."

The shock lessening, Glorie glared defiantly back at him. "Uh huh," she muttered clearly, "maybe someone should."

One brow arched at her, his face darkened with anger, but his gaze was curious. "What is that supposed to mean?" He released her but his eyes were on her lips like they were pink cheese and he was a hungry mouse.

She glanced towards the door as if looking for an escape, then shifted her wary gaze back to him. Gathering her hair up in both hands she moved it to tumble down her back and said with a shrug, "You never listen to anyone and that costs you time and money."

Watching as the tiny shirt crept up with her movements exposing the bottom swells of her breasts, his forehead furrowed in surprised puzzlement. "The hell you say."

"Yes." Her eyes cut to the side at him, she inched away a fraction.

Glaring at him she said, "Daniel has ten times the years of experience running this place than you, but whenever he suggests something, like putting up a fence with that plexi-stuff, instead of the wire that rusts and injures the animals causing some to die and others requiring expensive vet fees, therefore costing you money, you curse at him to shut up or mind his own business.

"Or, like just now you were discussing putting siding on the house, that makes so much more sense money-wise as well as it will save on future costs and labor." She set her hands on her hips and chided him, "He loves you like a son and you treat him like he's a paid slave."

Joze glowered at her scolding him. Then he stammered, "He...I..." his brows ridged with stiff anger, but his eyes flickered as he considered her words. His gaze turned thoughtfully out the window.

He was quiet for a moment. Then he turned his attention back to her. The pondering look disappeared as his scrutiny was drawn back to her shapely legs in the tiny shorts then up to her chest. The half-shirt was tight and outlined her breasts like plastic wrap. His face darkened again.

"I said that you need to change your damned clothes." He glared at the top. "Your tits are practically naked, you even have a bra on?"

Her face turned beet red shocked at him speaking like that to her. She looked down at the shirt. "I- uh, my uh, undergarments are wet too and no one would-"

"I know, no one would loan you anything. With tits like yours you wouldn't fit in anyone's anyway." His eyes were glued to her breasts. She crossed her arms over them in discomfiture.

Her lip pulled in at what she perceived as an insult. She said with an affronted sniff, "I'm sorry I'm not up to par with your lady friends, but like I said, what do you care what I wear? You think I look awful then don't look at me. Your language is very crude, you are not a gentleman."

She pivoted to turn and leave but he grabbed her arm and pulled her back around to face him.

Angry, Joze groused, "Stop fucking arguing with me. If I see you dressed like that again I will assume you like being nude and I will strip you naked in front of everyone and see how you like that. Get me? How's that for crude?"

Her eyes widened mortified, then her lids lowered half-mast over them. Chewing her bottom lip, she didn't say anything.

Vexed with her nonresponse, he shook her arm. "I asked you if you-"

She snatched her arm out of his grasp, her nose in the air she said haughtily, "Yes, I heard you, everyone ten miles away heard you."

"Goddammit Glorie," cursing a string of foreign invectives, Joze dragged a hand through his hair making it stand up in spikes.

"Come with me." He shoved from the table and started walking, then stopped when he saw she wasn't going with him.

He said, "Glorie," and took a grating breath, "I swear to *Duw*, you disobey me again you will regret it. Now," he said through clenched teeth, "come with me." He snatched her wrist and hauled her down the hall to his room.

As they neared the door, suddenly afraid of the punishment he planned to mete out, she dug her heels in.

Sighing, he was still annoyed but his irritation was lessening. "I am not going to harm you, do as I say, come in."

He drew her into his room ignoring that she was suddenly all rigid and nervous.

When they were inside, he went and opened a drawer in his dresser. Rummaging through the drawer he muttered, "I hate when women fucking wear my fucking clothes." He pulled out a T-shirt and tossed it to her. "Put that on. It's the smallest one I have."

Glorie stood staring at the shirt in her hands.

"Go change in my bathroom, Glorie, *now* for Pete's sake." Damn but the girl worked his every nerve. And he could not take another second of seeing her in that wet dream of an outfit.

She scurried into the bathroom.

Two minutes later she emerged.

He was pushing his shirts back in the drawer and closing it. He looked up at her; his eyes went straight to her breasts. Rubbing his eyes he complained, "Geez Glorie, without a fucking bra your tits are-"

Red with embarrassment and getting angry, Glorie said, "Would you stop talking about my breasts!"

She crossed her arms over her chest, wrapping her hands around to her back. "I can't help it if I don't look as nice as the other girls, just," she waved a hand, "don't look at me."

He snorted, "Uh huh. Honey, your tits are extraordinary compared to the other broads here. If you parade around in my shirt like that without, uh, support, every man here will be trying to cop a feel."

His own erection was straining against his pants. He resisted the urge to adjust them in front of her. Yet, she seemed so green he doubted she would notice it. His gaze slid down the rest of her. The shirt went just past her thighs, barely covering the miniscule shorts.

"Wait," he said, and opened another drawer. In a minute he took out a pair of boxer shorts. "Here. Put these on." He pushed them into her hands.

Her mouth opened, eyes wide with embarrassment, she stared at them. "Uh, but these are men's, uh, things," her blush deepened. "I can't, uh wear, these."

His hands on his hips, he asked with a frown, "Why not? What's the difference?"

Her chest rose with her deep inhale. "I mean, they're like, you know, underwear. Men's." She kept her head down, but her eyes rolled up to him waiting for him to lambast her.

"So?"

Her frown deepened, she mirrored him with her hands on her hips. "How would you like it if you had nothing to wear and I gave you a pair of my pink satin panties?"

The side of his lip curled up in a leer. "I couldn't wear them, they wouldn't fit, but I wouldn't mind seeing you in them."

Her eyes swung to his. Uncertain if he was joking or not, she said nothing.

Picturing her in the pink panties, now he *really* had to adjust his pants or he would be in considerable discomfort. He tried to do it discreetly.

He said, "Honey, just go put that little shirt you had on under my T it'll work like a bra, and put my boxers on over those shorts. At least you'll cover up those fucking tits. I can see your nipples through the shirt, and the boxers will at least cover your cooch and your ass when you bend over."

Mortified, her face turned so red it burned, she covered her face with her hands. "Joze, the way you talk, I mean, gosh, you're so- so vulgar," her words chopped off in her embarrassment.

His brows rose, high dark crescents over his eyes, the angry black pupils had fled back to normal and his irises were blue again. A corner of his mouth pulled in. "Oh, really?"

He studied her red face and eyes lowered in discomfort. "I forget Glorie, that you're not like the women I'm used to. I'll, uh, see if I can curb it a little. Now, go put those clothes on, I have things to do."

Scooting towards the bathroom, she pulled the hem of his shirt up to remove it and put the other one on under it.

His gaze followed her round bottom swaying in the tiny tight shorts until she disappeared behind the door. For some reason it didn't bother him seeing her in his clothes like it did with other women. She was…it was kind of- hot. *Shyt.*

Letting out a held breath, he tugged at his pants and paced around his room to dissipate some of his sexual energy before she came back out.

Chapter Seventeen

"Okay, Daniel huffed, "that's good enough for the day." He gave the horse a last brush.

Patting the steed on the rump, Daniel put up the grooming equipment and watched Glorie sweep out the end of the empty stall.

When she was done, he took the broom from her and put it up with the other stable tools. He wiped his forehead with a rag, stuffed it in his back jean's pocket and smiled at her, his eyes crinkled in his tanned face.

"You're *gethen da*, Glorie, a good girl," he praised her. "A hard worker and a genuinely nice person." He saw her eyes go from perky to bleak in a nanosecond.

His forehead furrowed, sorry that whatever he'd said made her sad. "What is it, honey?"

She pasted on a cheerful half smile over her dismal expression. "Nothing, Daniel." Fidgeting with the bottom of the over-sized shirt Joze had insisted she wear, she mumbled, "It's just…"

"What?" He came closer to stand in front of her. Rolling up the fallen sleeves of his flannel shirt, he waited while she thought about if she should say anything or not.

"Um, I know it's not your fault I'm here. I accepted the job they gave me and circumstances happened…" she filtered off, looked up and him then down at the floor.

"But, I have family, I have a sister that will be worried. I mean, she knows I'm undercover so she wouldn't expect to hear from me frequently. But it's been a few weeks, and what happened at the saloon, had to get to the press, or at the very least the police. I hate that she would think that I was- I was, um, dead." Her voice grew so quiet he almost didn't hear her last words.

She raised sad eyes to Daniel who mirrored her downcast expression. "Do you know, can you tell me how, long Mr. Kane plans to keep me here? If he plans to…" she couldn't make herself say the word kill.

The older man looked uncomfortable. He could not, would not get involved in his nephew's business. Except, unless, he felt she was truly in danger, he would step up and get her out.

"Ah, *melys gethen*, I don't know his plans. As I've promised you before, if I see you are in danger, I will step in and get you out of here. But, I've never seen or heard of Joze ever laying a hand on a woman in his life, so I'm doubting he would hurt you, regardless if you're a cop."

"But, Daniel, don't you see, he's kidnapped me, a police officer, and is holding me against my will. He can't undo that. He only has two choices, go to prison for this, or…make me disappear."

It was a struggle, but she kept the tears stinging the backs of her eyes at bay. "He's always threatening me, yesterday he said he would strip me nude in front of everyone."

Daniel's mouth twitched, pissed at the sight of the girl so scared and embarrassed. "Honey, has he yet carried through with any threat he has given you?"

Her face stiffened into a serious expression as she thought. "No, but, that doesn't mean he won't."

He smiled, his tanned face wrinkling. "As they say, his bark is worse than his bite. At least where you are concerned. Honey, I hear from Van when you have nightmares he runs in to wake and calm you. A man planning on hurting a woman does not do that."

She stared at the ground thinking about how Joze holds her carefully in his arms while she is in the terrible throes of her nightmare. In confused contemplation, she absently hung up some tools.

Daniel grasped the bit in the horse's mouth and walked the steed back into the cleaned stable. Removing the bit he closed the gate to keep the horse penned in.

He returned to Glorie and after putting the bit up he indicated for her to leave the stables with him.

Outside, the air was sweet and fresh, they strolled back to the big house. Before they reached it, Daniel stopped.

He touched Glorie's arm lightly. "Glorie, I know he has no plans to go to prison, and I'm positive he won't…uh, dispose of you. He'll think of something. In the meantime, I will speak to him about letting you contact your sister."

"Really?"

Daniel smiled slightly. Like his harsh nephew, neither man smiled broadly or often. "He has siblings; he would know what they would be going through if it were him. He'll understand. *Iawn?*" He gave her a little chip on the chin with his knuckle.

She nodded with a small smile. "Okay." Daniel could not guarantee her anything and she knew it. But he was kind and compassionate and she appreciated it. She stood on tiptoe and kissed his cheek. "Thank you Daniel, you're a very nice man."

The older man never thought he would ever blush in his lifetime, but apparently there's always a first time. "Uh, *iawn* then. Why don't you go inside and get cleaned up, I believe Van is in the living room."

Glorie glanced around the yard. Most of the cars that were normally there were gone, only a few were still scattered around the yard. "Where is everyone?"

Daniel looked around the area at her gesture. "Ah." This was one part of Joze's inherited family business he truly disliked. Keeping his frown from declaring his feelings, he said lightly, "They've gone to the strip club."

"Oh…a strip club? You mean nudity and dancing girls?"

Daniel ducked his head with a chuckle. "*Ie*, pretty much like that. Now," he gave her a shooing motion, "you go scoot on inside and clean up. Get Van afterwards and have him bring you back outside, the day is too nice to end it inside the house."

They parted company and Glorie hurried inside to do as he bid.

When she came back out still damp from a quick shower and changed into her now dry jeans and a blouse, she was combing her hair as she went into the living room. It was empty.

"Huh. Where is Van?" She checked the house but it was vacant.

Then she wandered outside and saw the last of the men, including Van, climbing into their vehicles and driving off.

She looked around. There was no one in sight. Did they forget about her? Should she take the opportunity to run? What if it was a trick and an excuse for Joze to catch her and really punish her like he'd always threatened?

In a quandary, she wandered around a bit but seeing no one, she went over to where some of the horses were still outside.

Unsure of what to do, other than missing her sister, Glorie realized she actually liked staying at the ranch. If not being held prisoner and fearing her future, she would be enjoying her time here.

She loved the animals, caring for them, cleaning the barns, working with Daniel, strolling through the fragrant wildflowers. The fresh air, meadows filled with acres of green grass, smell of things growing, she would actually miss the place.

Looking forward to seeing the blooms of her gardening springing up, she couldn't wait to taste the fresh tomatoes and cucumbers she hoped were growing beneath the soil.

And, she was learning a lot about cooking the times Maria let her help her in the kitchen. She felt as if Maria and Van, and even Daniel were friends.

Now Joze, her feelings about him were mired in mixed emotions and confusion. As much as she was repelled by his vulgar language, crass behavior, his criminal dealings, fear of his violent nature, she was starting to get a weird little tingle every time when she saw him.

She sat down on the grass near the meadow in front of a wooden fence, plucked some pretty flowers and watched the horses frolic.

The single donkey on the farm was out teasing the horses. Chops would sneak up behind them, pretend he was going to bite them then run off with the horse chasing him for a minute. It was funny, she laughed out loud at his antics.

Even from the little distance away she heard the screen door bang shut. She looked over.

Wearing a suit and tie, his hands in his trouser pockets, Joze was strolling peacefully towards her. She didn't suppress her surprise.

"I thought everyone went to the strip club? Are you leaving soon?" she asked him when he reached her.

He stood gazing down at her.

Her legs crossed tailor style, long wet hair curling around her back, the lowering sun bringing out the flames in the burnished locks. She looked up at him.

He smiled slightly like she was an adorable child. Then he dropped down beside her, crossing his legs like she had.

Joze studied her expression. "*Na*, I'm not going." Did she look happy about that? Or sad? Or indifferent?

She said surprised, "Why not? Isn't that what men like? Naked women all around, dancing, and uh, whatever it is that they do there?"

He shrugged. "I own the club. Mostly it's a hassle for me to go there. If I don't immediately choose one, or two," he shrugged again, "or so, women as soon as I walk in, then I have to fight the strippers, barmaids and customers off the whole time I'm there." His gaze steady on hers he watched for her reaction.

She cocked her head curiously at him. "So, when you say chose, one or two, whatever, does that mean to talk to or dance with?"

A chuckled choked out at him. What an innocent she was. "*Na*, Glorie, I mean to have sex with, for that evening."

Her breath cut in shocked, her mouth hung open. "To- to, you mean you have sex with a different woman every time you go there, or- or more than one?"

149

It had never bothered him too much before; it was the way of the life he had. But she looked so appalled that he felt the back of his neck burn.

He had decided to tell her about it because he wanted her to know everything about him, he didn't want any secrets to come and bite them in the ass later down the road.

Trying to comprehend his world, she took in his expensive suit and silk tie, the blond hair perfectly combed, close shave although a dark shadow showed on his strong jaw. He looked like his part, like the leader of a wealthy mob, or gang, or the king of the vampires.

She shook her head. "So, so, why aren't you going then?"

His gaze heated, penetrating the cooling evening air, it slid down then back up her body to light on her baffled eyes. "I don't have the interest."

Her head still tilted, she pondered what his comment meant.

Then she turned her head straight and smiled compassionately at him. In total innocent sincerity she said, "Okay. I understand. You have one of those…uh…you know, guy problems." She blushed a little and tapped his knee in commiseration. "I'm sorry. Have you seen a doctor?"

His eyes popped, he almost choked. "Are you fucking kidding me?"

Ignoring her frown at his curse, he pushed back a flop of light hair and glared in astonishment at her. "Don't you remember when I brought you here, Glorie? When you tried to run…you know, us in my bed?"

Her face flushed instantly when she remembered him tearing off her clothes and his iron hard erection pounding against her. Clearing her throat she murmured, "So then why aren't you going to the club tonight?"

His gaze flickered around her face, skimming over her eyes, her pouty mouth, the fresh complexion. "I didn't go because I don't have the…desire to be with any of the women."

She said with innocent sympathy, "Uh, well, I…uh…I guess things change. I'm sorry you can't uh, you know, perform now, you should really see a doctor about-"

"What?" He couldn't believe what he was hearing.

Dark color flooded his face. Irately he said, "There is nothing wrong with me," he suddenly grasped her head, cupping her cheeks tightly with both hands, dropping his mouth hard on hers, he rained a deeply rough kiss on her flooded with irritation and lust.

Startled, she pulled away with a look of pity. Setting a gentle hand on his leg, she said softly, "You don't have to try to convince me, Joze, just be honest with yourself about your problem."

"Goddammit Glorie!" Blowing up, he ripped his tie undone, shrugged off his jacket and tossed it on the grass, then he shoved her down on her back on the jacket and before she could react, he climbed right on top of her.

Moving quickly between her legs, he shoved them apart and thrust his erection already as rigid as an iron rod against her core. "Does this feel like I have a problem?"

He had knocked the air of her. Trying to catch her breath she pushed at his chest, it was like a solid wall pressing down on her. Trying to squirm out from under him, she huffed, "Joze-"

Stung with a lust-filled pique, he clamped his mouth on hers, forced her lips open and plunged his tongue inside. Capturing her mouth with abandoned ferociousness, he yanked his shirt out of his trousers and jerked at his belt to unbuckle it.

When he started to pull the zipper down, Glorie went into a full-fledged panic. She fought him with everything she had, hitting his powerful chest with her small slim hands and trying to buck him off her.

He was over twice her size and weight, muscled from head to toe, military and martial arts trained, it was like a duckling fighting a ruthless hungry grizzly.

Having to stifle his desire for her daily and now being taunted by her that he can't perform, Joze went crazy out of control, his savage kiss sealing her mouth, she couldn't scream.

He grabbed her wrists pinning them to the ground, grinding the length of his solid ridge against her core, he reached between them to grapple at her jeans.

Crying into his mouth, she begged, "Stop, please, don't hurt me!"

Joze halted. It was the words of her nightmare. Breathing deeply to steel himself, his body was vibrating with desire. He strained to gather his control.

Pulling his head back, panting like he'd run a mile, he could hear her panicked gulps for air.

Her parted lips were already red and swollen from his assault, her chest hitched with shallow breaths. Yet, even as terrified as she was, her lids fell heavy over impassioned eyes thick with the sultry need he'd swiftly built in her before the fear took over.

Unmoving, Joze just stared at her. His eyes on her damp red lips, her panicked breaths parting them. He looked at the amethyst eyes glimmering with what he was positive was desire. His groin quivered, she wasn't immune to him, but she was afraid. Of him.

Balanced on his forearms on either side of her, his legs between hers spreading them, he felt her struggling against him. His head dropped, the blond waves on top of his head brushed her face.

His cock was pounding; he knew she had to feel it throbbing against her. He bet a hundred to one if he slid his hand down inside those satin panties she'd be wet, she would be ready, he shook his head. *Na*, she wouldn't. She might be wet for him, but she wasn't ready. Not by a long shot.

He looked at her again, Fright had warred with the passion and it won. The flame of desire had sparkled then went out of her young eyes. *Duw*, he needed to stop treating her like one of the groupies.

Letting out a long, hard breath, Joze moved to sit up then pulled her up with him. "I swear to *Duw*, to God, you push me, Glorie," huffing, he raked his fingers through his hair making deep furrows in the thick blond waves.

Sitting there with her so close was not going to help him calm down. He climbed to his feet and helped her to stand. But then, he saw lingering wisps of passion in the jewel-like eyes and he was bulldozed- slammed with a shock of lust.

Without warning, he bent and slid his hands under her butt, and picked her so she was forced to straddle him. Slapping his mouth over hers to stifle her objections, he carried her to the fence.

Sitting her on the wood beam, he pushed his hips between her legs. He wrapped his strong arm around her back to balance her. Still kissing her, he plucked at the buttons on her blouse despite her struggles.

When he had all the buttons undone, he shoved the lapels apart and drew from her lips with a heated breath to stare at her breasts mounded perfectly round and pale and soft over the bra. He wrapped his big hands around her waist and drank her in.

Then he lowered his head to her enticing cleavage. Putting his mouth between her breasts, he kissed her flesh and felt her shiver against his lips. He moved to each mound, kissed then sucked her supple flesh, and was rewarded with a moan he almost couldn't hear ooze from her chest.

Joze lifted his head to look at her, and covered one plump breast with his big hand.

She was breathing hard but it seemed she couldn't catch her breath to speak.

Feeling her rising panic, he moved his hand up to loosely clutch her neck, then cradled her jaw while he soaked in her beauty. His blue eyes shone black, the lusted enlarged pupils glowed insane with desire at her.

"*Sws mi, fy babi, cariad,* kiss me, my baby, sweetheart," he purred and lowered his mouth just as fiercely but not as roughly on hers and pushed at her blouse to move it off her shoulders.

Hands rough from outside labor stroked over the silky skin of her bare shoulders. Her slenderness felt so soft and feminine under his palms, his roaming fingertips skimmed from her neck to her arms.

His arousal boiling over, he squeezed her upper arms. Intensifying his kiss, he started to push the blouse completely off.

"Joze," her voice a cried whisper against his foraging mouth, "please don't…"

He stopped. His crazed eyes flitting back and forth at her frightened orbs, he watched as tears gathered in them. He dropped his head, and set his hands on the fence beam on either side of her hips, his shoulders hunched.

Taking a few calming deep breaths, Joze raised his head, grasped the lapels of her blouse and pulled them together. She was clutching his shoulders to hold her balance.

Silently he buttoned her blouse. Raising his eyes to see the clarity in hers hazy with innocent confusion, a feeling like a hand gripped his groin and squeezed his maleness, so sharp a stab, a wash of desire cascaded over him drawing him again to kiss those lush lips.

But, he knew if he touched her again nothing would make him stop this time.

He was a gangster who took what he wanted, not a gentleman. But, this was Glorie, his Glorie. Last thing he wanted to do was frighten her, force her. His ruthless actions would only make her want to run from him again.

He needed to move slowly, carefully, solicitously tend her like she lovingly tended her garden. Cinching his hands around her waist, he lifted her up from the fence and set her down on her feet.

Watching her tuck her shirt in, he said gruffly, "Go on inside."

She hesitated, afraid of his anger.

"Go," he said, turning his broad back to her.

Without another word or glance at him, she scuttled across the lawn leaving him.

Joze pulled out a pack of cigarettes, lit one, tucked it between his teeth and buckled his belt, bent and picked up his jacket

He leaned against the fence smoking, watching the horses graze and the sun set.

Chapter Eighteen

The next morning, Joze asked Bruno to get his girlfriend.

He was packing up a briefcase in the study when Bruno and Melissa came in.

Melissa was a very cute young woman. In her early twenties, she had long brown hair almost to her lower back, light brown eyes with a golden hue, and freckles all over her cheeks and nose that she complained about but Bruno thought were girlishly hot.

"Hey, Joze," Bruno greeted him, ushering Melissa into the study.

"Hey," Joze responded, snapping the briefcase closed. Joze seldom smiled. He smiled when he was ruining a rival's business, when he was riding his horse, when he saw his siblings, especially his little sister. Otherwise, his smiles were mere forced grimaces because he was expected to give a pleasant response.

Melissa was such a friendly peppy woman that she was one of the few Joze would proffer a little more than half a smile to.

She was also one of the few other than his close male friends that wasn't afraid of him. Even the women who threw themselves at Joze did that because they feared him, therefore expecting an exciting, rough, even violent sexual encounter.

"How you doing, Mel?" Joze gave her that half, almost warm smile.

She grinned a mouthful of white teeth at him, the freckles stretched across her fair skin. "I'm good, Joze, thanks for asking." She quirked a curious brow at him. "Why did you ask to see me, Joze, we all know you're not big on small talk," she grinned.

He took no offense at her teasing. A side of his mouth twitched up. "*Ie*, I need a favor."

Now her face crinkled quizzically. "What can I possibly do for the big Jozadak Kane?"

His smile was a stroke warmer. "It's actually for the cop. The girl."

Her brown brows knit, her eyes flit to Bruno and back to Joze.

Bruno leaned a hip against a table and was combing his long slick black hair straight back then pushed it behind his ears. He shrugged at her; he didn't know what Joze wanted.

She asked, "You mean Glorie?"

Joze nodded. "*Ie*. I need a favor for her."

Melissa crossed her arms over her pert body, said with a half-teasing half scolding grin, "You could start doing her a favor by not calling her the cop or the girl."

His electric blue eyes flashed to Bruno who was smirking at him. His gaze swept back to Melissa, her arms crossed, she tapped a foot, forehead raised, waiting. He chuckled. "Yeah, okay. *Ie*, I need a favor for *Glorie*."

"That's better. She is such a sweetheart, what can I do for her?"

Joze pulled out his wallet and took out a credit card and handed it to her. "She needs some clothes. I need you to get her some pants, jeans, blouses, sweaters, shoes, socks, a jacket, uh, underwear. You need to go in her room and check her size. She'll be in the far pasture with Daniel and Van until later and I want this done as soon as possible."

Melissa stared at him with her mouth hanging open. "Clothes? You want me to buy her clothes?"

Joze nodded. "*Ie*."

"Uh, but, why don't you take her to the store-"

"I don't want her leaving the ranch. Especially to a busy public place. Just do this for me, I'll appreciate it. Buy yourself an expensive pair of shoes as payment." His eyelids half covered his eyes so only a bit of blue blur peered at her. He was wearing a suit and tie, and he had on a fedora that partially covered his shock of light hair.

Her mouth still open, Melissa looked down at the card in her hand, to Bruno then back to Joze. "Well, uh, sure. Can you jot down what and how many of each you want so I don't have to guess?"

His lips pursed, Joze said, "Sure." He grabbed a piece of paper off the table and a pen out of his inside jacket pocket and wrote down what he wanted.

He studied the list for a moment, then said while writing, "Get a nice dress too, something appropriate for the club, but," his eyes narrowed at Melissa, "nothing too sexy, she doesn't need to be showing her *shyt* to every fucking man around." He jotted down some more on the paper missing the look that passed between Melissa and Bruno.

"Uh," he mumbled, thinking, "so I guess heels too, and, whatever else you women need. You know, personal girl stuff, and a brush, hair bows, you know, stuff. I don't think she likes makeup or perfume." He muttered, "*Duw diolch,* thank God."

When he was done, Joze handed the paper to Melissa. "I think that's it. You think of anything else, just get it; you don't need to ask me. I don't care about the cost. *Iawn*? Uh, okay?"

Melissa tucked the paper into her jean's pocket and smiled warmly. "Sure, Joze, no prob."

"All right. I have to go, Linc and Calvin are probably already out front waiting for me. Catch you guys later-" Joze swooped up the briefcase, gave them both a curt nod and swept from the room.

Melissa giggled and Bruno chuckled. Waving the card she said, "What the heck is this all about?"

Bruno just shrugged with his palms up like he had no idea. He and only the close members of Joze's team knew the true story of why Glorie was there.

The rest of the employees and ranch hands and various girls that floated in and out were not told that she'd been kidnapped and was being held against her will.

They had been told that Glorie suffered from flights of fancy and to not believe her if she happened to be alone with them, which Joze tried to avoid, and she gave them the song and dance that she'd been kidnapped. They were encouraged to believe the beautiful Glorie suffered from mental illness. That made the women wary, the males didn't care. A hot body was a hot body.

Joze climbed into the driver's seat of the sleek, black on black Bentley Bentayga SUV.

With four huge, bull muscled men, they needed all the room and 600 plus horsepower they could get.

Linc rode shotgun and by the time Joze had the vehicle powered up and was about to throw it in drive, Calvin and Sloan who joined them at the last minute climbed in the roomy back.

The shiny SUV sped down the driveway spewing gravel and dust behind it. The gravel road rolled for miles through dense forest until it merged onto a blacktop road.

The tarred road at the end of the long, winding, private driveway was only two-lanes. They followed it for many more miles passing few residences, then houses started multiplying as they reached a busier thoroughfare and eventually hit the expressway.

Exiting the expressway after a few miles, coasting through the small city, Joze stopped at one of his businesses and dropped off Linc who would run the books and check on operations.

At the next building, ten stories, big for the city, he dropped off Sloan and Calvin then went on to another of his numerous enterprises.

Smaller at six stories but twice as lavish, he parked in the underground garage and rode the elevator to the penthouse.

The elevator doors opened to an airy room.

The plush carpet a light shade of peach, the front desk was peach and white marble. Large, clean as a whistle windows sparkled all the way down the reception area to the offices spreading to the left and right.

A young woman sitting at the desk rose as soon as she saw it was Joze.

With a squeal, she pulled down the lemon-yellow bandage dress and tripped over to him in 9-inch wedge heels with her arms out. "Mr. Kane!" She gushed throwing her arms around him.

He stepped back, grasped her wrists and put space between them. He didn't want her rich perfume wafting off him all day. Especially after he got back to the ranch.

The neon pink lips drew down in a coy pout, she fluffed her frozen blonde hair off her shoulders and batted her false eyelashes at him.

"Mr. Kane, you haven't been here for over two weeks, I've missed you."

"Ah, Janine-"

"We've missed you too!" More squeals and a half a dozen girls of different shapes, sizes and colors rushed out and up to Joze.

He held up his palms for them to back off. "Come on, girls, I'm busy and I'm in a hurry." The dark sunglasses hid his annoyance.

He shifted his tie back into place and tugged his black Armani suit with the faint blue pin-striping back down neatly and dashed his hands over his hair. He strode down the hall towards his office leaving the group of girls whining in his wake.

Sheri sighed, "He is the epitome of freakin' gorgeous."

Lara's hand flapped at her face fanning away her sexual tension. "Oh yeah, he's shit-spicken fine in that suit that fits those broad shoulders and lean waist to a damned T. And those strong muscular legs showcased in those snug trousers, uh," she waved at her face harder.

Janine groaned, "But I think he's even hotter in the black leather trench coat he wears with the black pants and shirt and those hot motorcycle kick ass boots. I can just feel his fangs biting into my neck," she sighed dramatically.

"Iyee, honey," Jodie exclaimed, "that blond mane, those alien blue eyes, when they turn so spooky black, I just want to drop to the floor and scream, 'take me!' He's so-so violent, so scary, makes me wet wet wet!"

Suddenly blanching, "Oh dear," Janine moaned. She called out, "Mr. Kane! Wait there's a man waiting for you in your-"

Too late, he was already down the hall and pulling open the door to his office.

Each office he had in each business looked different. Modeled dependent on the type of business and style of business it was.

This one had a front of glass doors and windows at the back. The same peach carpet was inside, but his furniture was steel and black leather. There was not a lot in this office; everything important was in his computers secured at the ranch. But he met appointments here and discussed deals.

He'd had plenty of sex on the desk, and on the leather sofa and under his desk. Well, she had been kneeling in front of it actually-his lips hardened at the memories. *Duw* he was such an immoral dog. Half the time he made himself sick with his loose behavior.

He liked to fuck and fight, he was not a lover and a fighter, lovers were kind and caring, he was neither. But, the past year of carnal behavior was weighing heavy on his mind. He was becoming his vicious brutal father.

Joze had accepted the quick easy sex because it was there, in his face. Even if he wasn't that into the broad, since she was throwing it at him he figured he should take it. But now, he was holding a mirror up to himself, and he did not like what he was seeing.

A male slut who didn't care about the women he was with, just took what he wanted and left. He didn't leave them hanging by any means, he gave them pleasure too, but he never completely thawed with any of them. It had just become habit to take what was in front of him. He couldn't remember the last time he'd really gotten true pleasure from sleeping with a woman.

Well, actual sleeping with a woman, as in overnight, was against his rules. Once he got what he wanted he left. Thinking of sleeping all night with a woman brought the night of Glorie's nightmare back to mind.

Shyt, the thought of lying beside her with her in his thin pajama top and panties, her tits on his chest and trying to keep his erection from touching her, scaring her, right now brought his arousal on fast.

Re-arranging his pants, he opened the door.

A man was standing at his window.

What the hell was Janine thinking letting someone, anyone into his office without him being there? Such a fucking violation of his rules, that bitch was so fired.

As he stepped inside, the man turned to face him.

"What can I do for you, officer?" Joze asked with a suggestion of a sneer.

The man's brows rounded with surprise. "Mr. Kane. Do I have a cop smell or something?"

His mouth a wry curve, Joze closed the door behind him and moved into the room.

The sun streamed through the slightly tinted window lighting the back of the policeman's short, wheat-brown hair.

He looked a good ten years older than Joze. Faint lines streaked from the corners of his eyes and around his mouth. His pale blue eyes were as harsh and cold and ruthless as Joze's. But there was something else in them, something Joze didn't like but couldn't put his finger on. Maybe a thread of cruelty lurked in the back.

Not answering his question, Joze smiled unfriendly. "I asked, what can I do for you?"

The officer in a plain brown suit coat and jeans sat his hip on the edge of Joze's desk. His mouth turned up in a sardonic arch. "You don't want to know my name, ask who I am?"

Joze unbuttoned the button on his suit jacket and stuck a finger in his tie pulling it slightly looser. "I asked you what are you doing here. You can answer my question of get the fuck out of my office and out of my building."

The cop spat out a hard laugh. "So it's true. The word is that you are a cold son-of-a-bitch." Pushing his suit coat back he set his hands on his hips and shook his head. "All right." His eyes tapered, slicing frigid animosity at Joze. "Where the hell is Dinah Coleman?"

A good poker player, Joze's face stayed an impassive mask. Then he asked, his voice deadly calm, "Who are you?"

The man chuckled. "There it is. You're a tough one aren't you, Kane?" His gaze sharpened even more. It rolled up Joze's long legs then over the suit pants hanging just slightly below his lean hips, up over his taut abs barely hidden under the white shirt, and up to his thick chest to his huge shoulders.

He looked at Joze's strange lighter than platinum blond hair showing under the fedora, then settled on the enigmatic blue eyes that were bizarrely turning black as his shiny pupils enlarged.

The man announced, "I am Detective Luc Bolton. Glorie's handler." He could have sworn he saw a brow twitch, a hint of color leave Joze's skin then it came back darker.

"I thought you just asked about a Dinah somebody?"

Bolton blinked. Then his skin flushed. Caught so quickly in his deception, he felt stupid. "Yeah, well, let's not pretend you don't know who Glorie is. I must credit with your connections and big IQ, plus the fact that her ID and badge are missing along with the girl, that you have figured out who she is."

"Why are you here?" His face a stone rock, Joze's voice had dropped so low it was barely audible; his eyes were now solid black discs.

Bolton's expression turned serious, hard, his eyes narrowed at Joze. He moved his ass off the desk and stood up straight.

"I am here because I want to know where Glorie is. I know you aren't a witless man. I'm not going to play games. She was sent in undercover to get shit on you. A few weeks ago there was a-disturbance at the saloon she was working in, where I heard you were prone to hang out."

He moved within a few feet of Joze. He wasn't as tall or built as big and strong as Joze, but he wasn't a small man by any means.

"Apparently, a group of assholes tried to rob the place, someone," his gaze hit Joze up and down in clear accusation, "gave them a hurting. Three of the four are still in the hospital, and will probably be there for a very long time, the fourth had crawled out of the hospital and down the street and disappeared."

Keeping the smile off his face, Joze said, "Oh? They're all alive?"

Bolton stared silently at Joze for a moment. "Their description of their attacker was a single man that had been acting as a...mentally challenged weakling, that had previously walked hunched over. But that night, he had stood up, possibly over six and a half feet up and burst into a fighting machine. Easily, in the blink of an eye he took out all four men without getting a scratch himself."

Joze sniffed, looked bored. "And you're telling me this intriguing story because?"

That pissed off the cop, his mouth hardened to match his permanently hard pale eyes. His brows scrunched down half covering the pale blue.

He said, "Because, after some persuasion, one of the robbers admitted that there was a girl there, a young woman, he said they were planning on taking her with them, to," his eyes darted away, then down with a hint of guilt. "Rape and then kill her. But when they came to, the paramedics were there and the tall guy and the girl were gone."

Joze let out a loud bored sigh. "Again, Bolton, why are you telling me all this?"

Glowering pure revile at Joze, Bolton didn't bother disguising his hate for him. "Glorie is an innocent. She was plucked out of her safe, cyber-stalking job she had only just begun, and without," his eyes dropped again, "academy training, or any kind of defense training or police experience at all, she was sent to work undercover, to, as I said, get dirt on you." He sighed and paced a few steps.

Joze remaining silent, calmly watching him.

Bolton scowled. "The shit of it is, is that she's gone. I know you took her. What I don't know is if you have her still, or...you've already murdered her." He stopped in front of Joze with a direct glare at him.

"The thing is, she has family that need to know what the truth is. I'm here to ask you, where is Glorie?"

A small, nasty smile raised the corners of Joze's mouth into points of wrath. "The thing, cop, what I think is, is that you don't give a shit about this defenseless young woman you threw into the wolf's cage like a lamb for slaughter, what you're worried about is your own skin."

His face glazed over, icy with zero emotion, Joze went on, "I think you took it upon yourself to snatch this girl and toss her into this undercover job because you thought her very greenness would be a perfect disguise. I think, your superiors don't know about it. That you did it without permission because you knew it would have been denied. Or you didn't tell the entire truth of it to your superiors."

Like a poker player, Joze studied Bolton's expression. A tint of red colored the detective's neck, a vein throbbed at his temple. Joze knew he'd nailed it.

Bolton's scowl screwed up the rugged planes of his face. "I know you figured she'd have tracers on her, Kane, she did. They only traced for a few hours then they stopped. That meant either you found them and destroyed them, or," he hesitated, "you put her deep in the earth or the water where they wouldn't work."

"So," Joze said, pacing a small circle around Bolton ignoring his comment, "you need to get this helpless young woman back before anyone realizes what you did and that she is missing. Or," his fierce gaze struck Bolton head-on, "you need to come up with some kind of cover up story if she's dead."

He stopped so suddenly, Bolton took a step back. "Am I right?"

Bolton's chest exposed his sudden anxiousness by rapidly rising and falling. Blinking while trying to think, he licked his lips, then got a hold of himself.

"The underground of it is none of your concern, Kane, just tell me if she's dead or alive." He tried to strengthen his voice into a threat, but he knew he'd failed at the smirk on Joze's face.

Like Joze would ever admit to murder. Right. He wasn't born on the wrong side of stupid. Joze trod to the door and opened it. "All I'm telling you, cop, is get the fuck out of my building, and don't come back without a warrant."

"Kane, come on, she has family." Bolton didn't move, his voice showing the strain of keeping the lid on his actions, getting found out. He'd thought it a great idea at the time, if it had worked, if she had gotten shit on Kane, he would be a hero, maybe get promoted, but now that she'd gone missing, it had blown up in his face.

"Just, ah," Bolton's face red with anger and frustration, he said, "I'm not asking you to, ah, confess to murder. Just give me a hint as to her status and I'll hit the road. That's all I'm asking, man, just a fucking hint." His palms rose in a slight plea.

The unyielding closed look in the gaze Joze sent him was the only answer Bolton was getting.

Bolton walked slowly to the door. Stepping past Joze he said, "Listen, if you have a change of heart, she's just a young-" Joze closed the door in his face.

Joze went over and sat behind his desk. He didn't let the air out of his lungs until he heard the elevator ping and knew the man was gone. He pushed the intercom button on his phone. "Janine, get in here."

In seconds, the cheesy blonde slipped in through the door and sidled up to his desk. She knew she was in trouble. "Listen, Mr. Kane, he-"

His voice as emotionless as steel, Joze asked, "Why did you let him in my office?"

"Uh, geez, Mr. Kane," she hobbled her words anxiously together, "he, uh, had, uh, he said he was a detective. He showed me his badge, he said-"

"What is my rule, Janine?"

Her skin turned white under her spray-on tan. "Uh, uh, no one is ever allowed in your office when you're not here except me and the cleaning people at night. But he-"

"You're fired."

She stood frozen; her hands went to her stomach. "No, please Mr. Kane, please don't..." she looked at the glacier blue eyes and knew it was no use. Hanging her head, she stumbled out of his office.

Joze sat without moving for a while. Then he unlocked his office drawer and pulled out some paperwork he'd been working on last week and laid it out in front of him. He preferred paper initially because he could burn it. Computers left trails everywhere.

He worked for a few hours then locked the papers back up, there wasn't anything terribly vital in them for someone to copy or steal. He turned out the lights in his office and locked the door.

Striding down the hall, he tuned out the stares from the other women. This time they didn't throw themselves at him. Janine's tearful departure had freaked everyone out.

He picked up his car and then the other men and headed back to the ranch.

Joze kept very few secrets from his team, they'd been in the military together, they went way back and were loyal to each other to the end. He told them about Detective Bolton.

"Joze, bro, what are you going to do about her? You need to-"

"Not talking anymore about it. Just giving you all a head's up." He said it so tersely there was no argument.

After a few moments of quiet, the men discussed what they had done while out today until they reached the ranch.

A bunch of people were at the table eating dinner when they came in.

Linc, Calvin and Sloan found seats and sat down.

Joze stood in the doorway, his blank gaze on Guy who was sitting beside Glorie.

Feeling the sudden coldness of Joze's chilling gaze blasting a hole in the side of his head, Guy looked up warily.

There was no mistaking the signal in Joze's votive eyes.

"Uh." Guy got to his feet.

Glorie was speaking with Daniel on her left. Guy dropped a hand on her shoulder and said, "I'll catch ya later, sweetheart."

Taken by surprise, she said, "Oh, okay." Seeing his mouth coming towards her lips she turned, and the kiss landed on her temple.

Guy patted her shoulder, lowered his lids to slits and stared for a brief second at Joze before leaving the room.

Joze dropped his jacket over the back of Guy's vacated chair, untied the knot in his tie and took the empty seat.

He had hardly sat down when Maria came scuttling over with a fresh plate of pork chops, fried potatoes and sautéed greens for him.

"Would you like coffee, Master Joze?" She smiled happily at him. Greta was behind her with a glass of water for him.

"*Ie, ta* Maria, thank you." Joze picked up a paring knife and a fork and looked over at Glorie's plate.

Everyone else's was cleaned up. Hers still had almost a full chop, a spoonful of potatoes that didn't look like they'd been touched, just like the greens.

"Glorie," he said without inflection.

She smiled with apprehensive dubiety. They hadn't parted on good terms yesterday. She didn't know what to make of his ardent kisses and, well, she just didn't know what to say.

"What did you do today?" His voice casual and interested, he cut off a piece of meat and chewed it.

That was unexpected. Glorie shot a quick glance at Daniel who was drinking his coffee. He winked at her.

"Oh, well, I helped Daniel with the repairs he's still doing on the barn, and then we fed the chickens, visited with the alpacas, weeded my, uh, the garden, and groomed some of the horses."

Nodding, Joze shoveled in a forkful of chop and potatoes. Chewing thoroughly, he then sipped the coffee Maria brought him. "I see. Sounds like you worked up quite an appetite. Right, Daniel?"

Wisely, Daniel just grunted, kept eating.

"I don't think-" Glorie frowned, but when Joze turned his enigmatic eyes to her, her mouth closed.

"I seem to recall we have previously discussed your eating habits. I don't know what the problem is that you can't eat like a normal human being." Joze slid greens into his mouth and reached for the basket of warm rolls.

"Son," Daniel growled his irritation.

"Go back to minding your own business, Uncle," Joze said laconically, buttering the bun.

"Mr. Kane!" Glorie gasped, appalled. "That is no way to speak to your uncle. That is disrespectful."

The conversations at the table stalled until Joze's gaze cut around at them.

The crowd wavered back into their chatting, tearing their eyes from the trio.

After taking a bite of the roll, Joze set it on his plate then laid his burly forearm on the table and shifted his chair to face Glorie.

Overshadowing her with his brawny body, he said very quietly, "You want to go to my bedroom and discuss my respect?"

Glorie's eyes blanched at his unconcealed threat.

He continued, his voice soft but the threat clear, "Do you want to go and talk about how you will never reprimand me in public. Again. Ever."

She stared straight at him for a heartbeat then seeing the lethality in his eyes she lowered hers. Her hands folded in her lap; she twisted her agitated fingers until they were white.

Setting his coffee down, Daniel stood up and said to Joze, "I need a minute." He waited while Joze looked from him to Glorie and back.

Joze set his big hand over Glorie's perturbed fidgeting fingers stilling them. He leaned over and said quietly, "It's Joze. Remember that." Then he stood up and followed Daniel outside, the screen door banging closed behind them.

Outside, Joze waited patiently for Daniel to speak.

"Son," Daniel started, "when she has that nightmare, you know she can't eat the next day. Her stomach gets locked up, she can't keep food down."

Joze's face pulled in a dark frown. "She had one last night? I didn't hear her. I've been keeping the door between our rooms open just in case."

Daniel tucked his fingertips in his back pockets. "*Ie*, well, she doesn't always scream, just suffers through them."

Joze's eyes flickered from Daniel to the house. He rocked on his heels. "I didn't know."

"You can tell by the purple shadows under her eyes and her pallid complexion when she's had one." Daniel leveled his gaze straight at Joze. "Son, you don't have to be so harsh with her. She didn't ask to be here."

Nodding, Joze kept rolling on his heels. He slipped a sideways glance at his uncle. "Daniel, I'm sorry. She is right. I shouldn't have spoken to you like that. Sometimes I treat you like one of the hands and I don't mean to. It's just," he sighed, "when I'm around her my brain goes haywire. There's a short circuit. I don't understand it. I guess it's because she's a cop."

Daniel snorted. "*Ie mab*, sure son, that's what it is."

"She's losing weight, Daniel, she could get ill. I am responsible for her. What if she gets so sick? I'd have to take her to the hospital, then," he shook his head. "She needs to eat."

"Joze, yelling at her and threatening her are not going to help. She's already distraught from that goddamned nightmare."

"I know." Joze nodded sharply. "Do you know what it is? Will she tell you?"

Shaking his head, Daniel replied, "*Na*. I've asked, and you know how much I hate prying busy bodies. But she just says she doesn't remember."

"*Ie*, I know." Joze stuck his hands in his pockets, his shoulders hunched.

He squinted, staring off into the far forests. "If she would only tell me, I'm sure I can help her. I think there's something, or someone, she's actively afraid of, that she thinks is going to harm her. That has already hurt her and is going to do it again. She gives me the slightest hint of who it is, and by *Duw*," he clenched his hand in a fist and twisted it. "I will fucking *diwedd*- kill him."

Daniel didn't try to dissuade him. He felt the same way.

"Well," Daniel patted Joze on the back, "for now, she ain't talking. I gotta go check on the horses that are still out." He walked away, leaving Joze standing there contemplating how to get Glorie to open up to him.

His mouth curled drily. Daniel was right, threatening her was not going to do it.

Deciding it would not help her appetite any for him to go back in and sit beside her, he pulled out his cigarettes and went to help Daniel with the horses.

169

Chapter Nineteen

That night, hearing the whimpers and crying, Joze knew she was having the nightmare.

He threw off his blankets, slid to his feet and was reaching for his jeans when he saw her walk through the adjoining door.

He started to say something, but she strode past him going to his door. He had locked it from the inside. Dropping his jeans, Joze padded quietly behind her in his boxers.

She was totally unaware of him as she struggled to open the door.

As he reached her, she hit the lock and wrenched the door open and started walking down the hall.

Following her, Joze saw she was breathing hard and frantically, her hands were up in front of her like she was fighting something.

As he reached for her, she threw open a door, the door to the basement and took a step-

"Fuck, Glorie!" Joze leapt and grabbed her around the waist pulling her back just as she was about to fall down the stairs.

His heart beating like a drum, he closed the door and spun her around.

Her eyes were wide open, wild and unseeing, she flailed at him in a thrashing frenzy, crazed with panic. "No! Please, not again, don't hurt me again, please-"

"Oh *babi*," Joze wrapped his arms around her and the couple sank to the floor.

Holding her, he rocked her, whispering softly in Welsh, then switched to English. Stroking his hand down her back, he murmured, "Wake up, *babi*, you're asleep, Glorie, wake up."

She stopped crying but was still whimpering. He cuddled her into his lap and kept stroking her. "Shh," he said gently in her ear, his hand stroked down until he felt skin.

She was still wearing his pajama top. Wondering why she wasn't wearing the nightgown he'd had Melissa buy for her he found his hand moving over her silky skin to her panties. His hand kept going before his mind registered that it was inside her panties and he was stroking and kneading her bottom.

Jerking his hand back up, he continued speaking quietly to her, until finally her head settled on his shoulder. She felt so soft, his hand skimmed over her back, she was so womanly, slender and supple, and on the edge of skinny. Damn the *gethen* needs to eat.

His sigh heavy, after this nightmare, again it was likely she would not be eating tomorrow.

She was calming, snuggling against him. Before he knew it his hand was moving under the top up the side of her ribs, he stopped when the curve of his hand was under the swell of her breast. His thumb lay between both breasts.

The urge to feel all of her soft womanly curves was overwhelming. His fingers squeezed her in an effort to stop their ascent. Joze looked down at her face. She seemed to be in sound sleep now, the nightmare gone.

"*Shyt*," he muttered, what a scumbag he was, molesting a defenseless woman in her sleep. What a nice guy. In another second he would have her flat on her back and be buried deep inside her, with no acquiescence on her part, and with no protection, since he didn't carry condoms in his boxers.

He had never been this out of control with a woman before. Joze wiped a hand over his brow beading with perspiration. He needed to find out what the hell was bothering her and end it before he lost the last threads of his control and did something stupid, and wrong, or she seriously injured herself.

He rose to his feet with her in his arms and took her back to her bedroom.

When he pulled the sheet and blanket over her, she turned on her side and curled into a loose ball. The fiery hair lay brilliant against the white pillow even in the dark. Semi-dark.

The nightlight Linc had so thoughtfully given her glowed over by the bathroom.

Joze wished he'd thought of it. But then, Linc had compassion, and Joze had been born without the compassionate gene. Leaning over, he strung his long fingers through her satin locks, watched them spring right back into curls when he tugged them straight and let them go.

He stood up. He had no business touching her now that she was sleeping peacefully. Still, he watched her for a few minutes until the hardness in his pants like a throbbing iron rod was about to force him to do something he knew he shouldn't.

Quickly, he pivoted and went back to his own bed.

The next day, Joze had put in two hours in the field with the horses before heading in for breakfast. Everyone was gone.

He ate a plate of eggs and bacon then showered, changed and went for a ride into town. He met with a man interested in buying one of his businesses.

After his meeting he checked on a few other businesses then hit the strip club last. As soon as he walked in the door he was swarmed by women.

Normally he would tap out one or two and they would stay with him until he was done then he would take them into the back room where he'd accept what they offered. When they were done, he'd clean up and go home. Alone. Now, he just didn't have the interest, zero desire whatsoever for any of them.

Elbowing through the crowd and pushing away wandering hands, he kept saying, "Not tonight hon, not now, doll," and kept moving.

He grabbed a bottle of scotch off the bar on the way to his office. He did some work on the computer, had several drinks before closing up and went out the back door to avoid the women.

When he got home, he again entered through a back door to avoid having to talk with anyone and went into the study.

A group of guys were in there playing poker. He joined them for a few hands and drank some more.

He won a few hands and lost a few, tossing in the cards, he said goodnight and wandered through the house, still avoiding conversing with anyone and went to the front door thinking he'd go for a late walk. When he got to the open door, he stopped dead.

Glorie was a few yards from the house in the darkening night. Guy had his arms around her and was kissing her.

Van stood off to the side looking up at the night sky.

When Glorie broke away, Joze turned and went back into the living room. His head was slightly woozy; he'd had a lot to drink. The alcohol was making his brain burn as the picture of Glorie kissing that fuck needled under his skin.

When they came inside, Glorie went straight to the hall to their bedrooms, and Guy went back outside.

Joze stalked over to Van and grabbed his arm. "What the hell, Van, why did you fucking allow that?"

Van was surprised. "What? Those two kissing? So what? You told me to guard her that she doesn't leave the compound or make sure no one hurts her, you didn't say I was to be her fucking chaperone. I guess you're here now my guard duty is over?" Not waiting for Joze's reply he turned from him and went into the kitchen.

Joze stalked angrily down the hall, through his room to hers.

Glorie was in the middle of the room. He stomped over to her and snapped, "If you're going to whore around try not to do it in front of everyone."

She looked like she'd been struck. Blinking back the shock, she said with rising pique. "How dare you- first of all I didn't kiss him, he surprised me, second you have no right to tell me what I can or can't do, and- and- how dare you call me a whore-" she threw out her hand to slap him- his hand whipped out and snatched her wrist in midair. Holding her wrist, he pushed her back against the wall, hard.

Wincing, she gave him an angry look and demanded, "Get your hands off of me you bully. You cannot tell me who I can kiss and who-"

In a fury he raised his hand as if he was going to strike her. She cringed, closing her eyes waiting for the hit.

Instead, he grasped her hands and pinned them beside her head on the wall.

When he didn't strike her, she opened her eyes and struggled against his hold, but he easily kept her pinned.

She sputtered, "You are mean and abusive, and drunk, *Mr. Kane*, let go of me!"

The skin on his face and neck darkened several hues. He bent his face close to hers, smiled in satisfaction when she cowered slightly, turning her head away.

Letting go of her hands, he put one of his around her throat under her jaw forcing her head up so they were eyeball to eyeball. "You will not," he shook her, "*ever* tell me what I can and can't do."

She croaked defiantly, "You smell like a whiskey bottle-"

"That's scotch, *babi*, top shelf," he suddenly covered her mouth with his, brutally taking her lips with unhinging violence. His hand cradled her head, holding it immobile, the other hand swung around her back pulling her tight against his body.

Glorie squirmed against the wall to get away from him but his hold was like steel bars. Driving her lips apart, he thrust his tongue in.

She fought him, but he continued his assault on her lips, boldly searching, roughly exploring- tasting the inside her mouth, tangling with her tongue until she responded.

Feeling her body soften, her heady return of his kiss, Joze reacted. His mouth fired with potent passion, draining, sucking every bit of her response until he was breathing so hard his brain spun dizzy with desire. He broke away panting, gasping for breath.

Her eyes were closed, parted lips swollen and dewy crimson from his assault on them, her chest expanded and fell with fast shallow breaths, the flaming hair a tangle around her head.

He released her and stepped back. Without his support, her legs were rubber. She flattened her palms against the wall to hold herself up while catching her breath.

Overwhelmed with his desire for this woman unnerved him, he needed to do something to stop it. His voice coiled with sarcasm, Joze sneered, "What is a woman who kisses two men within minutes of each other?" Before she could say anything he snapped, "A whore."

Like she'd been struck, aghast and hurt, her mouth dropped open, blood flooded her face. "You- you forced me-"

"Ha," he snorted rudely, "you liked it. There was no hiding your wanton lust, you took to me like a hooker to a 100 dollar bill." His gaze swept her body from toe to head avoiding the horrified expression pinching her face.

This time he let her slap him. His head barely moved at her strike, but the pain of hitting him flashed over her face.

She tried to push away and storm off but he snatched her arms, yanked her back and thrust her again against the wall.

Stunned, her lips parted in fear, he grabbed her face with both hands and devoured her mouth until they were both panting again, then she was hitting his chest with her fists.

He broke off the kiss, put his palms flush against the wall on either side of her waist keeping her fenced in, his grim gaze raking her flushed face.

Holding the back of her hand over her mouth to still the gulping, short cutting breaths, she stared at him dazed with panic and shocked with confusing passion.

"Glorie, I..." Joze watched the pink color seep from her fair skin, the shameful pain in her eyes, the swollen lips tremble. He dropped his head and moved one hand to his side, freeing her.

Emitting a soft cry, her hand still over her mouth she fled the room.

Joze swiped a hand through his hair, scrubbed his shaking fingers like rakes down his stubble.

"Nice, Joze." Leaning a shoulder against the doorframe, Linc observed his friend with a sorry shake of his head. "What the heck is up *fy bráithre,* when you don't know whether you want to hit her or bed her?"

Joze dragged his fingers through his hair making it stand up in tufts. Piercing Linc with a scowl, he snarled, "Fuck you. I sure as hell don't want a fucking cop, a fucking whore in my bed. My dick would likely turn blue."

"Come on, Joze, you only sleep with whores. Glorie's a nice girl, that's why you're so screwed up over her. You want her but you don't know how to deal with a sweet woman. She scares the piss out of you. And, you go absolutely apeshit with jealousy, then you react with anger and violence. She doesn't deserve that."

Scowling, Joze glared at his friend. "I don't sleep with whores in *my* bed, I do it somewhere else. I'm not screwed up over her, I have no interest in the *bach plismyn,* little copper, at all."

Linc's face creased in a mocking smirk, he scrolled his gaze down the front of Joze stopping at his zipper. He nodded at the hard bulge straining at his pants. "Your big head may think that, but your little head wants her." He chuckled derisively.

Joze snorted. "It's not little, *bráith*, you must be thinking of your own tiny dick."

Linc just laughed.

Joze's face still dark with jealous anger and confusion, and unfulfilled desire, said harshly, "Go lock her in her room for me and mind your own business." He stormed out the door pulling out his cigarettes with Linc's laughter ringing in his ears

Chapter Twenty

Joze avoided Glorie all day then went to the strip club with Sloan and Calvin.

Late in the evening, when they stumbled in the door, snickering and staggering, Glorie was standing by the hallway to their bedrooms with Van.

She knew where he'd gone, the other men were talking enviously because they had wanted to go too, but Joze had said no.

Seeing her staring at him, Joze careened over to her, almost toppling on her. She backed up with a disapproving frown marking her face.

He opened his mouth, but she said, "Who's the whore now?" and sashayed her perfect little behind down the hall.

Joze stood staring stupidly after her for a few minutes then he tripped to a chair and flopped in it.

Her glare had been wilting; he had felt himself withering under it. He hadn't slept with anyone, but he wasn't going to tell her that.

She would start that crap again about his 'problem' and he would get mad and have to prove again that there was nothing wrong with his dick. And then, how many times would he be able to pull back, stop himself from finally taking her, with force?

Joze dozed in the chair. When he woke up groggy, the entire day wobbled through his sluggish brain. He struggled to his feet with effort and trod unevenly down the hall. When he got to his room, he fell face down on his bed.

Van had been sleeping on the divan in Joze's room guarding Glorie. He woke when Joze stumbled in and got up and left.

Joze must have only been asleep for a little while when he heard her. He could get as pissed off at her as he wanted, but when he heard her whimpers and cries, his stomach got all twisted. He needed to get to her before the screams started. Those just stole the blood from his heart.

He hurried in; she was already thrashing on the bed.

It was only a few steps to where she lay, he quickly sat down on the bed, the mattress sinking under his weight.

She was flailing, her hands were hitting the wall hard enough to cause bruises or even breakage.

Joze grabbed them and held them down, but being restrained only made her panic more. This led Joze to think she'd been restrained in a terrible way before.

Her chest hitched and jolted, she gulped air, Joze collected her up in his arms, and wrapped them around her, holding her snug enough she couldn't hurt herself but loose enough so she wouldn't feel tightly restrained.

Rocking Glorie, he smoothed the curls out of her face while speaking softly in her ear. "Wake up, *bach babi*, wake up little one," his voice reached her. He could feel the change in her body.

The lashes darker than her fiery hair that was on the edge of blonde fluttered then opened. Her eyes went wide with fright at seeing him, her struggles started anew, but in vain.

He held her like an iron belt. "*Na, babi*, calm down, I swear I won't hurt you. You were having that dream."

The frightened blue orbs spun around the room then back to him. He could see the horror alive and torturous in them.

Joze took her pillows and plumped them against the headboard then lifted her and helped her lean back against them. Then he moved a few inches away from her, giving her space to show her that he meant her no harm.

She stared at him, the pain streaking and gouging in her eyes and tightening her face so it was like a frozen mask of terror. But he sat, not moving, his hands benignly folded in his lap.

Glorie looked at the big strong man with the extraordinary light hair, his electric eyes on her bright even in the dim room.

He sat still for as long as it took her. Her breathing finally settled, the fright diminished somewhat.

When the stark hysteria finally left her face, Joze said, "Enough, Glorie. You will not leave this room until you tell me what has the claws of hell in you."

The fear stirred back into her expression, panicking again, she looked around for an escape.

"*Na, babi*, I swear I won't hurt you. But you have to tell me what happened so I can help you. And if that means keeping you here until you tell me, I will. I know just thinking about it scares you, but I'm here now, nothing, no one, will get to you."

She didn't speak, but she studied his face, the sincerity and strength permeating it, his eyes had turned to a warmer blue.

Seeing her face relax slightly, Joze said gently, "I know I've acted like an animal towards you, but Glorie, I swear, I won't hurt you. I want to help you. Tell me what it is." He could see the emotions flicker across her face then her body shuddered letting out some of her strain with it.

Taking a deep breath, she let it out slowly.

Joze took her hand and held it on her leg.

She looked down at it, dashed at tears that gathered. Staring at their hands she said, "I was, attacked…raped."

His harsh inhale caused her to hesitate, when he said nothing keeping her eyes lowered she kept going.

"He, I was only on my job for a week. I- I come from a very, very small town. From, ah, actually it was a religious settlement. My parents were religious freaks. It was kind of like a cult, I guess. We were kept cocooned from the rest of the world.

"My older sister ran away and moved in with a guy. My folks disowned her. She came and got me, now I'm disowned too." Her gaze tweaked up at him. His expression was inscrutable, no emotion, no judgment.

"I uh, got the job at the police department. They were partially paying for my college if I agreed to attend and complete the academy. I was basically apprenticing at the station, working while attending college. But," she took a shuddering deep breath then said, "he was a policeman. I thought all policemen were good. I mean, why would they be police if they weren't?"

Joze bit back the sardonic turn of his mouth but said nothing.

"So, uh," she continued, her face flushed with red shame, "he showed up at the apartment I shared with my sister at the time. She's married now.

"Anyway, he had engaged me in casual conversation a couple of times, and asked me out. I just wanted to concentrate on getting a career going. I had work and school, no time for dating, so I said no. However, during one of our conversations, he asked if I lived alone. I told him that I lived with my sister but that she was on vacation with her then fiancé."

Glorie paused and peered at Joze, but his face was implacable.

She picked at the blanket. "So, anyway, the next day he was knocking at my door. I let him in. I mean, I kind of knew him, and of course he was a policeman, serve and protect and all. I- thought he was safe." She shook her head in dreaded disbelief that an officer of the law could do something so horrible.

"When he said what he wanted, and I said…no, he, uh- attacked me. He beat me first to subdue me, then he beat me more when I screamed and still fought him. He beat me until I was saturated with blood and barely conscious." She gulped in heavy breaths and wiped at her eyes.

Joze sat stoic, not daring to speak and cause her to stop talking.

"Uh, so anyway," Glorie went on after swallowing a sob. "He- the pain, it was so- I was delirious with pain, I couldn't think. The agony was- was, it was so bad I passed out from it. When I came to, I was at the bottom of the outside hall staircase. I might have fallen, but I think he-" she stopped talking at the strangled sound Joze made.

He leaned to her, thumbed her tears, tucked her hair behind her ears, but he said not a word, he couldn't. He'd detonate, explode right then and there, or vomit with the horror of her words, if he opened his mouth.

"So, uh, my legs were broken, and my arms, the doctor said they had been broken before the fall, and, well, other stuff was...broken. I couldn't move, could barely breathe. Blood was suffocating me, I was drowning in my own blood-"

"Enough!" Joze gushed out gagging. "I can't hear anymore." His deep breath so ragged it scratched on the way out. He couldn't look at her.

Covering both eyes with his hand, he struggled to dispel the picture of her lying bloody, broken... *ahh.*

When he could finally look at Glorie, he saw the shame devouring her.

"*Fy Duw, babi*, this wasn't your fault. I couldn't take anymore because I can't stand to hear how- how- hurt you were, how fucking brutal," he moved up beside her and pulled her into his arms.

When he had calmed *himself* down, he cleared his throat. His voice a harsh rasp, he said, "Tell me, *babi*, what happened next?"

Her body shivered, he held her closer to the warmth of his powerful chest, his huge arms solid security around her.

"I, well, I guess I laid there for, um, a day...or two...until my sister, Shana, returned home and found me," she sighed out her anguish.

Joze fought to keep his liquor down. He blurted, "A day or *two*? You fucking laid there broken and bleeding for a day or *two*?" His breath pumped out of him, *what the fuck-* "You could have died!"

She nodded, wiping a tear off her cheek. "Yes. But I didn't." She choked a rueful snort. "But, there were times during and after and...anyway I wished I had."

His arms tightened around her, hoping she couldn't feel the runaway beating of his enraged heart. "So..." he took a deep breath and asked, "what happened? How much time did he get?"

He felt her stiffen again.

"How many years was he sentenced to?" He lowered his head to see her.

She avoided his gaze.

A frown dragged his features down dark. "Are telling me he isn't in prison?"

She silently shook her head.

Now he did explode, "Why the fuck not!"

She jumped at his vehemence and started to move from him, but he held her. Calming his shaking voice, Joze said quietly, "Tell me, Glorie, why is that bastard not in jail?" Already plans to have some guys get to the man in prison were swarming in his brain.

Her breath could barely get in her lungs, every part of her had gone tight. "I did not tell anyone. The hospital tried to do a rape kit. I refused. I said I fell down the stairs, that it had been an accident."

He was shocked. "But why, Glorie? Why would you allow him to hurt you, almost kill you and get away with it?"

Her lids lowered over her eyes blurring with tears. She said, "I am a police officer. If I told that another officer...raped...me, I would be ridiculed, and pitied, and...I would have to quit."

"Glorie-"

"He told me that there would be those that would believe him, that I had encouraged him, seduced him, wanted him, asked for it. I mean, I let him in. Anyway, he said he'd kill me if I told. He said he could easily get to me before a trial could even think about starting."

Her body shook with terrible body-rattling shudders. "I couldn't, try to understand, don't hate me because I'm...weak, I was, am, so- so afraid." The tears streamed, the sobs gurgled up her throat and shook her chest.

"*Babi, babi,*" he cuddled her into his arms, pulled her head to his chest. "Never, I would never think of you as weak. The opposite is true. I can sort of understand your reasoning. I don't agree with it, but," he took a deep breath, "are you still afraid of him?"

It didn't matter; he was going after the bastard anyway.

He saw the evasive shadow pass over her creamy complexion. He pulled one of the pillowcases off a pillow and handed it to her. "Wipe your tears, honey."

She took it and dashed it at her tears.

His heart twisted at her pain. "Tell me," he commanded, "the rest of it."

It took a few minutes to collect her poise. Wiping at her eyes, she turned the orbs wet and blurry like the blue-violet ocean to him, then she looked away.

"He," she choked down a sob before going on, "he said he would come back for me. When I was going unconscious, he grabbed my- my hair wrapped it around his fist and twisted his hand."

Joze's arm tightened around her.

"While he banged my head on the floor, he said he would be back for me and finish what he'd started. That there was too much fighting and blood for him to, uh, get off. Sexually, I mean. He needed to come back...and finish the job. I don't think he, you know...finished. I was a...virgin, I don't think he could get inside me deep enough..." her head dropped in agonized, mortified, anguish.

Stroking her back, Joze waited quietly for her to continue. His stomach was cramped, his throat constricted with holding in his rage and grief for this beautiful girl.

She pressed the pillowcase against her eyes, took several deep breaths, exhaling them slowly. "So, uh, I had just gotten out of the hospital and back to work, before I was," her pained gaze curled up at him, "you know, sent after you. He started calling me. Said he was coming for me. Said it would be worse the next time."

She wiped at a fresh flow of tears. "That's why I didn't fight going undercover. It would get me away," she sucked down a deep breath and whispered, "hide me." She was so mortified, felt so filthy she couldn't look at him. It was a good thing.

Joze's face grew pulsating dark, the blue irises were swiftly covered by his dilating pupils, so fiercely black they were burning pits of obsidian fire. His body shook with fury.

Already big and buff, his muscles pumped bigger, harder. His shoulders rigid with bunched cords of bursting wrathful strength blocked the rest of the room from Glorie's sight.

Feeling the violent heat radiating off him in waves, she looked up and recoiled, her face struck translucent with her sudden terror of him. To her he was like the hulk when raging out of control.

Her fear of him palpable, he struggled to get his rage under control. "*Babi*," he said, his voice hoarse with the effort to sound calm and quiet, "I won't hurt you. I swear." He softened his hard embrace, holding her like she was made of perishable snowflakes.

Brushing a knuckle down the side of her face, he said with regret, "I know I can be a savage animal. I've treated you badly, Glorie, but, I would never hurt you. You must realize that by now. Please don't fear me."

He slid a finger under her chin and tipped it up so their eyes connected. Tears rolled over her cheeks; he brushed them with his thumb.

Giving her a very light kiss, so soft he barely touched her lips, guilt saturating his voice making it husky, he said, "I know I have been abusive to you. Earlier, I, it was," he sighed.

"There's no excuse. I saw Guy with his fucking paws all over you and it just set off something primal inside of me. If I could explain it to myself I would explain it to you, but," he shrugged with a weak, sorry grin, "I can't."

His gaze fell to her small but full, beautiful lips. He brushed his finger over the bottom one, then the top, enjoying the feel and sight of her pout. "I promise I won't hurt you, *babi*." To himself he snarled a promise, *but I will hurt him.*

She softened against his chest.

Joze leaned back against the fluffy pillows pulling her with him. His arms tightened possessively, protectively around her even as he was stinging with guilt over the way he had ruthlessly frisked her and had assaulted her the night he brought her to the ranch, and when she'd run, and again earlier today.

Dragging his arm over his forehead, then over his eyes as if to stamp out the abuse, and the heinous threat of rape he himself has wrought on her, with deep shame, he hugged her, swearing he would somehow make it up to her.

Petting her head, suppressing the broiling rage under his iron will, he asked quietly, "What is his name?"

She stiffened and pulled from him. Her face turned away and down, she murmured, "I don't want to talk about it anymore."

Refusing to let her move away from him, he cuddled her back against his torso. "It's *iawn*, we won't talk about it. Just tell me his name."

The rigidity returned to her body, she shifted to move from his arms, but he held her.

"I won't hurt you, *fy cariad*, my sweetheart, but your nightmares will never end, you will never feel safe again until this *shyt* is over. I won't sit by helpless and watch you suffer, watch you wilt away from your ever present fear of this bastard. I need to end him, end his hold over you," *and avenge you.*

"Already you hardly eat; the nightmares take away your appetite and your sleep." Struggling to keep the rage from making his hands shake, he stroked her hair. He craved to touch her skin, but sitting in her bed, her in his arms, them both wearing next to nothing, was already playing with fire. He only had so much control.

Still she remained silent.

"Glorie-"

"No," she whispered.

Joze put his big fingers lightly around her jaw and gently lifted it so she would look at him.

Her crystal orbs were flooded with tears. Her plea a hushed whisper, "Don't ask, Joze, please."

His gaze direct and firm, he said, "If you don't tell me his name, I will be forced to go and interrogate every cop in your department until I figure out who it is. Save me, and them, a lot of trouble…and pain. Tell me his name." Unable to stop himself, Joze bent his head and lightly kissed her, his lips pulled gently at hers for only a second.

Blinking back tears, her lips tremulous, she pleaded, "No, no Joze, you can't do that. You can't go do anything to him. Please. It will only make him madder when he eventually gets to me again."

Gulping down her tears with the sobs, she cried, "The first time was bad enough, I almost didn't make it," she wiped at her eyes, "I won't survive the next time-"

Joze roared, "What the fuck! Glorie, there won't be a next time!" Taking the bite off his tone, his arm tensed around her, soft as satin he caressed her face. "That son of a bitch is never going to hurt you again. He will never," he trailed off at the fear glowing in her eyes.

"I will see that he never comes near you again. I will avenge you, Glorie. I will avenge your pain, your shame, and your honor. I swear it on my own honor."

He took a hard deep breath, let it out. "Tell me his name, Glorie, right now."

With a gasping cry, Glorie wrenched from his arms, rolled off the bed and ran into the bathroom, slammed the door shut and locked it.

Joze sat, his fingers as hard as nails he dragged them painfully through his hair, into his scalp. Scrubbing his hands down his face he stared at the bathroom door.

He could with little effort get the door open and go in and get her. But, he sighed, she was scared to death and he didn't want to contribute more to it.

Slowly shuffling off the bed, he trod across the carpet into his own room, leaving the adjoining door open. He wanted to be available if she needed him.

Chapter Twenty-One

The next morning, Joze waited until Glorie came out of her room into his.

A look of surprise lit her face at seeing him. He was always gone before she got up. But he was sitting calmly on a chair, his hands folded patiently in his lap.

Her step faltered.

He had his door to the hallway open so she wouldn't feel trapped. Coming to his feet he said calmly, "I will not press you, not now anyway, Glorie. I won't talk about it if that's your wish." But it was by no means dropped.

The worried stress lining her smooth forehead didn't lessen. His gaze swept her, she was wearing the new jeans and blouse, and hiking boots Melissa had bought.

A soft smile drew his chiseled lips up. Trying to turn the subject to something safer, he asked, "Do the clothes fit okay?" He could tell they did, perfectly. Maybe they were a little too snug for his liking, at least when she was around the other men, but they would do.

A wary half smile, she said quietly, "Yes. Thank you. Melissa said you bought them, for me. Why?"

Joze pictured in his mind the tiny shorts and barely there shirt she'd worn, and said with a shrug, "You need clothes. It's my fault you are here," he frowned, he didn't want to go there. Another subject for them to not talk about.

Forcing a smile, he said, "I thought that after breakfast," and he could ensure she ate, "you might like to work with me and the horses?" *Oh yeah*, bingo, her face lit up like a Christmas tree.

"Really? Do you mean that?" she asked eagerly, moving comfortably towards him.

"*Ie*, there is one small condition," he smiled inside at her frown. "You must eat. You eat enough this morning to satisfy me and I'll take you out to the corrals."

She stared for a brief moment, then relented. "Okay." Hurrying to him she asked, "Right after breakfast?"

Now, he grinned. "*Ie, babi*, I promise."

They strode together down the hall to the dining area.

The hour was late, most everyone was gone, which was fine with Joze.

It took a long time, and with great difficulty, for Glorie to force food down while Joze watched until he was satisfied. It wasn't really enough to please him, but he could tell she was at her end.

He stood up and held his hand down to her. "*Iawn*, let's go."

Relieved, another bite and she would have puked everything she had so painstakingly swallowed, Glorie jumped up.

As they walked out, she asked, "What does *iawn* mean?"

He chuckled at her pronunciation. Grinning down at her, he thought, *Duw* was she cute. "It means something like, okay, all right."

Out in the meadow, quite a distance away from the buildings, Joze showed Glorie how to saddle a horse.

Laughing when she tried to lift his saddle and couldn't, he showed her how to put the bit in, adjust the reins. Then he had her sit off to the side while he worked with the pure white horse with huge dark eyes.

The stallion, Blanco, looked kind of like Joze with his funky blond hair and eyes that changed from electric blue to black discs when he grew angry, or passionate.

While teaching the steed to follow his commands verbal and nonverbal, periodically Joze glanced over at Glorie to see if she was bored.

But she clearly wasn't bored. Her big eyes were wide, watching everything he did with enthrallment.

He was about to call it a day and go get lunch when out of the corner of his eye he caught something moving in the bushes. Without turning his head or acknowledging he saw him, Joze carefully, peripherally watched the man's movements.

Shyt- it was no one he was familiar with, which meant bad news.

The person had gotten through the guarded perimeters. Worse, Joze had to go after him, and he had Glorie with him, and there was no way in hell he was leaving her here alone.

There could be other intruders, and they were too far from the house for him to leave her. He quickly, effortlessly mounted the horse and trotted over to where Glorie was sitting. She stood up when he was near her.

Very quietly, pulling out his cell, he said to her, "Listen, honey, please just trust me and don't balk or argue." He muttered into his phone then slid it into his pocket.

She blinked in puzzlement.

"I need to very quickly haul you up on this horse with me and go after…something. On the count of three I'll reach down and pull you up."

Before she could even think about it, he mumbled, "One, two," on three when he bent over he was surprised that she had raised her arms for him to easily grab her and in one smooth movement drop her in front of him on the horse.

As soon as she was seated, he strung his arm around her, holding her tightly against him and kicked the steed into action.

The white horse didn't even rear, he just bolted across the grass.

Joze directed the animal where he'd seen the man hiding and the horse galloped like the wind straight there.

As they neared, the man panicked and ran from his hiding place.

Joze said in Glorie's ear, "I'm going to jump off. You stay on the horse, hold onto the horn-" He waited until she grasped the horn with both hands, and the horse slowed enough he felt safe leaving her on it, he whipped his leg off the back of the saddle and was running before his feet even hit the ground.

He raced after the man, easily catching up to him.

Joze launched at him and took him down like a sack of potatoes. As soon as they hit the ground, Joze punched him once, the man's head snapped back and he instantly fell unconscious.

Joze reached into a low pocket in his khakis, pulled out a pair of flexi-cuffs, rolled the man on his stomach and cuffed his wrists behind his back. He filtered through the man's pockets relieving him of his wallet, keys and cell.

As soon as he had secured him, Joze sprung to his feet and looked for Glorie.

She was still mounted, the horse had slowed and circled back at Joze's whistle. Glorie's hair flapped like a vibrant flame, if the sunrise was a backdrop, she would have disappeared into it. Her eyes were wide with exhilaration, some fear and some excited energy.

The horse trotted over to him. Joze couldn't take his eyes off Glorie. The blazing hair, her cheeks radiantly pink, full breasts bouncing with the horse's movements.

Joze reached for the loose reins and pulled the horse to a stop. He turned at the sound behind him.

Linc and Calvin were racing towards them on ATV's.

Just before they reached them, Joze dropped the reins and jogged to them. He didn't want Glorie to hear him.

"Hey, you guys all right?" Linc's curly hair bounced around in the breeze, he braked the ATV to a stop. Calvin pulled up beside him.

"*Ie*, we're fine." Joze stood between the two men. He glanced at Glorie. She looked nervous but not overly frightened of sitting alone on the big horse. Her beautiful curls wavered around her in the light wind. He clamped his mouth hard, but he couldn't suppress the smile that lingered.

When he looked back at Linc, he frowned at the knowing, teasing look he gave Joze.

"I was working Blanco when I saw that guy," Joze motioned with his head to the unconscious man lying in the grass on his face with his hands cuffed behind him. "I don't recognize him. I'm going to take Glorie back to the house. You guys do what you need to, to find out why he's here."

Both men nodded in acquiescence. They knew Joze really meant, do *anything* they needed to get answers.

"And, make sure you find out how the hell he got in past the cameras, sensors and guards."

Joze opened the man's wallet and pulled out his ID. Not realizing the horse had moved close to them, he read, "Ian-"

Glorie gasped.

Joze swung around, "*Shyt-*" he didn't want her involved for a number of reasons. Then he saw her face, it was bone white, her eyes were rolling back in her head. He ran to her.

As she swayed in the saddle, he wound his hands around her waist and pulled her down.

Rolling an arm of support around her, Joze cupped her chin, his face wrought with concern. "What is it, Glorie, what's the matter?"

Glorie fought to not faint. Her stomach roiled, she clapped a hand over her eyes. She seemed afraid to look at the unconscious man. Then she peered through quivering fingers.

She dropped her hand to her throat, and gasped with relief, "It's not him." She clutched her stomach like she was about to lose her breakfast.

Joze rolled her into the corner of his arm against his chest and stroked her hair. "What, *babi gethen*, it isn't who?" His gaze darted to Linc and Calvin who were looking on with intense interest.

Glorie clamped her hand over her mouth and tried to tug from him.

He held her tight. "Uh huh. Not until you tell me who you thought-" he saw her eyes were streaked with red, her face turned hot and scarlet, she looked about to either pass out or throw up.

Joze understood immediately. "You think, you thought it was, him, the cop who-"

"Joze!" she cried out, her eyes flashing to Linc and Calvin.

It didn't matter to him, because he would be telling his closest friends what had happened to her, because he planned on avenging her, and maybe more than that.

But, cool as they were, Linc and Calvin slid off their ATV's and casually strode away from the couple and over to the man. They both crouched down beside him, giving Glorie and Joze privacy.

"It's not him," Glorie said with pained relief.

"Honey, are you sure?" Joze kept her in his embrace. He wanted her looking at him while she answered so he'd know she was telling the truth.

Gulping like she was swallowing around a golf ball, she nodded her head. "He, I mean," she wrapped her arms around herself and bundled into the warm strength of Joze. "This man has light hair and is…smaller. Shorter and lighter. He," her body shivered from head to toe, "he was really…big." She closed her eyes trying to shut out the picture of the rapacious beast who had harmed her so catastrophically.

"Ah, but the guy, who hurt you, his name is Ian?"

She turned her face into Joze's chest without answering. But to him that was an answer.

He linked his arms around her, holding her close and safe.

"What's his last name, babe?" he asked, trying to fumble her to face him, but she burrowed further into his chest. It didn't matter. How many Ian's could there be in the police force? Plus, he had a basic description now.

Linc looked over at Joze then pointedly at the passed out man. He wanted Joze to clear Glorie out of there before they started their interrogation.

Joze nodded briefly at him. His arm around her, he walked Glorie to the waiting horse.

His finger tipping her chin up, he asked her, "You okay? Can you ride? I can take you back on one of the ATV's if-"

Glorie shook her head adamantly. "No, Joze, I'm fine. Just being a stupid hysterical female, I want to ride back on the horse." Her eyes down, she waited for him to help her back up on the snowy stallion.

Joze stood and stared at the top of her head wishing he could wipe away the memory of the night that fucker- he squinted into the distance getting a grip on his rising anger.

"Glorie, you are acting perfectly normal for what you've gone through. Now, I'm going to mount, I'll have Linc help you up behind me."

Not waiting for her to speak, he called to Linc, "Hey, Linc, need a hand here." He swung up on the horse.

Linc hustled right over. Lacing his fingers he smiled kindly at her, bent over and said, "Hey Gloworm, you all right?" All of Joze's friends had picked up the nickname Van had called her.

She gave him a huge toothy smile and said, "*Ie, iawn*," and stuck her foot in his twined fingers.

Both Joze and Linc looked at her in surprise.

Joze smiled proudly. "That's my girl."

Linc easily hoisted her up and behind Joze.

Joze twisted his head to her and instructed, "Hold onto me, Glorie, as tight as you want." He leered at her amicably. "I prefer as tight as you can."

She giggled and wrapped her slender arms around his hard abs and threaded her fingers together.

Holding the reins, Joze turned the horse to face the big house. "You guys got this covered?"

Both men now hovering over the unconscious man, Linc waved and Calvin grinned.

"Yeah," Linc said, "you go on and cover what you need to." He laughed as Joze half turned to Glorie to see how she took Linc's sexual jest.

Her face was clear of everything except the joy of being on the horse. He looked back at Linc and winked. Then he lightly kicked the horse.

The horse cantered over the field, Glorie held onto Joze. He was acutely aware of her breasts pressed against his back and rubbing from the horse's jostling movements. It was sweet torture that he wished wouldn't end.

"Faster, Joze," Glorie said in his ear.

His ear buzzed with her voice misting it. "You sure you want to go faster, Glorie?"

"Yes, can he run?"

Joze laughed. "He can gallop, fast. Hold on, *babi*," he kicked the horse, made a clicking sound with his tongue and the horse burst into a beautiful, smooth, swift gallop, flying through the air like Pegasus.

Joze was happy; the added speed caused Glorie to cling even tighter to him, her voluptuous little body rubbing up and down his back with every movement.

Now, if only she'd lower her hands in front of him...

Back at the stables, Daniel emerged from the barns as soon as he heard the horse's hooves pounding the ground. He came out and took the reins from Joze, holding the horse still as Joze slid off.

"I saw Linc and Calvin race hell for leather a few moments ago, something up?"

Joze frowned at him and reached up for Glorie. "Later," he murmured, clutched her waist and pulled her down from the horse. He hesitated, holding her in midair with her body pressed against his, her arms dropped around his neck.

Daniel left them, silently leading the horse into the stable, but a tiny smile worked his weathered face.

His eyes steady on hers, still holding her, Joze said, "You liked riding?"

Her cheeks were bright rosy, her lips curved up in a happy smile, the crystal eyes sparkled. She nodded.

His biceps bulging around her, he held her so her head was slightly above his so she had to look down at him. The brilliant hair curled on his shoulders and against his chest.

Their mouths were slight inches apart. He did it before the thought made it to his brain, his lips closed over hers. His body tingled feeling her respond to him. When he pushed her lips apart and slid his hungry tongue inside, she didn't resist. His arms tightened around her, he still held her in the air, her feet were off the ground.

After a moment she drew back, licking her lips. His eyes followed her tongue swirling around those plush petals. The erection already straining at his pants was now throbbing.

"Joze, please put me down." She didn't say it angry, but a bit breathless.

His arms squeezed harder, not wanting to let her go. He knew he had to; he reluctantly let her slide down his body to her feet. When he saw her cheeks darken he knew she'd felt his erection.

"Glorie," he was surprised to hear his voice raspy, his entire body was throbbing, his throat constricted.

When she rolled those amethyst shiners up at him with a soft smile, he felt his knees buckle. Big, tough, dangerous, Jozadak Kane was unnerved by a slip of a girl.

"How would you, I mean, would you like me to give you riding lessons?" His heart contracted at the great big smile she showered on him.

"Really? Do you mean it?"

He nodded, not able to speak. He cleared his throat, turned his head and coughed. What he wouldn't do to see that smile every day.

"*Ie*, on the days I don't have to go into town for business we can do it right after breakfast." He reddened. "Riding lessons, I mean."

She blushed prettily. "I know."

Chapter Twenty-Two

Later that evening, Joze met with his team in the study. After he told them what the cop had done to Glorie, every one of them instantly enraged, cursed and roared their contempt.

"How can a sick fuck do that to a defenseless, helpless girl. She's practically a child for God's sake." Sloan's hands were balled into angry fists, he paced the room.

They all forgot she was a police officer, they only cared that she was a woman who had been horribly and devastatingly abused.

"When are we going for him?" Calvin wanted to know.

The others nodded, agreeing that they wanted to get their hands, and fists, on the bastard cop immediately.

His hands on his hips, Joze stood in the front of the room.

The volatile violence screamed from each of the men's hard muscled bodies. They were ready to go now and take care of this man.

"I've contacted him, pretending I'm an informant. Linc," he nodded at him, then said, "and Calvin will come with me to the meet."

"Hey, what about us?" Bruno said with aggressive bluster. "Anyone ever did something like that to Melissa," he shuddered, even the thought of her being harmed like that stripped the color from his face, he looked ill.

He brought his clenched fists up to his chest and swore, "I would tear the fucker apart piece by fucking bloody piece." He glared at Joze. "I like Glorie, I want in on this."

Joze shook his head. "*Na*. I don't want too much attention drawn to this. We are too noticeable as it is." His grave grin trolled the room eying each of his men.

They were all monsters well above average height and built like brick shithouses with combat and MMA training.

"Joze," Sloan and Diego said at the same time,

"*Na*."

Calvin asked, "When?"

"Tomorrow at seven." Taking in their dour expressions, Joze said, "If something bad goes down, we're caught, or worse, I can't have all of us in the *shyt*. I need to know that the rest of you are in the clear to keep the businesses going. Especially you, Bruno," he gave the guy with slicked black hair a lopsided grin.

"Melissa is planning on tying that knot around your neck in the fall, and she would kill me if I let anything happen to you."

Bruno scowled but nodded. Then he grinned. "Yeah, can you guys believe I'm biting the big bullet and getting myself balled and chained?"

Sloan slapped him on the back. "Better you than me! The balling fine, but no to the chain"

"I wouldn't mind a hot girl with chains and my balls involved," Diego said wickedly snide.

They all broke out with raucous laughter breaking the gloomy tension.

The next night, Joze gave Van instructions. "Do not let her out of your sight." His glowering gaze speared across the room at the far end at Guy who was licking one of the girls' faces.

"And, do not let him near her. If he gives you flack, get Daniel or Bruno or Sloan. I don't want him within arm's reach of her. Got it?"

"Sure Boss, no prob." Van sneered in Guy's direction. "Dude's a slime-ball. I wouldn't leave her alone with him again anyway, Boss. I'm learning he's dangerous. Don't worry, I can handle him."

"*Ta*, thanks, Van." Joze patted him on the shoulder and hustled outside to hop in the truck to join Linc and Calvin before Glorie got near him.

She would ask where he was going just being the sweet and friendly person that she was, and he knew his expression would give it away. So he slid out when her back was turned.

"Hit it," he said, climbing into the passenger side. Linc threw the Ford 2600 into gear and drove off into the dark.

It took 45 minutes to reach the meeting destination. They parked several blocks away from the warehouse in the bigger busier parking lot of a shopping center.

As soon as they left the truck, the three split in different directions.

Wearing all black, leather trench coat, pants, shirt, boots, Joze tugged the black knit hat down over his light hair and strode furtively, in case the cop was watching him, he wanted to look fairly nervous, as the character he was playing would be.

Slightly hunched over, he darted near the walls of the buildings, staying in the shadows. Over one door was the number 101. He turned the knob, it was unlocked, he gingerly pushed it open.

A few small, round hanging ceiling lights dimly illuminated various sections of the big open room and cast vague shadows.

His footsteps silent, Joze made his way cautiously through the room. Stacks of boxes lined the walls, and between them, pallets had been tossed haphazardly on top of each other in crooked piles.

Avoiding the paint stains and oil spills puddled throughout the cement floor, his voice low, Joze called out, "Hanson? Dude, you here?" He waited a heartbeat, only silence met him.

He was about to call out again when he heard footsteps. They were stealthy, the man thought he was being quiet, sneaky, ambushing him, but Joze spent a few years in heavy covert combat, he could hear a gnat landing on a dog.

Acting like he hadn't heard him, Joze kept moving. "Hanson, man, where the hell are you?"

A hard rod was shoved in his back. He assumed if he could see it that it would be cold hard steel. Like his eyes were right now. His hands went up.

Speaking slowly to mask his accent, Joze stuttered, "Uh, h- hey, whoa there, Hanson, is that you, man?"

With a creepy chuckle behind him, the gun prodded him in the back. A male voice said, "Don't move."

Then Joze felt a hand pat him down. His chest, back, down his legs, even patted the top of his beanie and gave it a squeeze. "Turn around," The man ordered.

His hands still raised, Joze turned slowly. "Hey," he said, acting suspicious but friendly, "you Hanson?" He squinted at the man standing in front of him with the gun aimed at his heart.

He was a big brute. Joze's stomach quailed at the thought of the guy beating the delicate Glorie- he blinked away the thought. He needed to retain his calm pulse, steady his wits.

The man had curly dark brown hair, green eyes, a square-ish face and a broken nose. His mouth pressed hard and punishing. All in all he wasn't bad looking, except for the cruel, pitiless look in his sadistic eyes.

His chest and shoulders were beefy, arms brawny. Joze could tell the guy thought he had it all going on. Strength and brawn, good looks and smarts. He would think he'd gotten the drop on Joze.

Probably thought the girls all wanted him, too, and his ego had busted when Glorie turned him down.

What the cop didn't know was that Calvin and Linc had already slunk around the rest of the building, had gotten inside, and were perched high up, guns trained on him.

Feeling he had everything under control, with a smirk, Hanson lowered the gun. "Yeah, asshole, I'm Hanson." He was dressed in civilian clothes, jeans and a black, pullover sweater with a denim jacket over it. His jaw was covered with dark 5 o'clock shadow making him look dangerous and tough.

Joze crossed his arms and asked, "Officer Ian Hanson?"

"Well, duh, bro, who the fuck else would I be?" The cop jeered, holding the gun at his side.

"Just wanted to make sure I got the right guy." Joze's cold smile would give a snake the quivers. The black was already stealing over the blue irises, he knew the lights would be glinting off them like flint discs. He also knew when Hanson looked into them he would be creeped out at the color and the lethal emptiness in them. Empty of mercy.

Even though he had to tilt his head slightly to look up at Joze, Ian Hanson still thought he was the biggest and baddest of them all.

With the trench coat covering his body from neck to ankle, it was hard to see how Joze was built. It looked like he had broad shoulders and a good-sized chest, but Hanson shrugged to himself, he didn't see him as a threat. Besides, he had the gun.

The stupid beanie just showed Hanson how young and punk Joze was. "So, you dumb fuck, you said you had information for me on the carjackings in the Mulltown area. Spit it out, I ain't got all night."

"You got my dough for the info?" Joze asked regarding their agreement.

Hanson chuckled. "Yeah, sure, got it right here." He patted a flat, clearly empty pocket. "Now gimmie the goods, boy." Obviously his plan was to get the information from Joze then kill him. He would use the info to take down the carjackers, after he robbed them of course, and earn himself another medal.

No longer attempting to hide his accent, Joze said, "*Ie*, sure. But I got a question first. Do ya mind?"

"Eh, what the fuck do I care? Go ahead." Hanson stood relaxed but ready to click into impatience in a heartbeat. "Whadya wanna know, how to beat a ticket or what?"

"*Iawn*. Do you recall a beautiful young cop named Glorie? Glorie Lee Toby?" Joze saw the guilt and conceit flash across the cop's face.

A little off balance, Hanson shrugged nonchalantly. "Yeah, so what?"

The features and planes of Joze's face morphed into solid, unforgiving stone. His eyes were full on onyx now, and he could see the deadly wrath in them was registering on the cop.

"Tell me about that time you were with her. The night you ruthlessly and brutally beat her into oblivion, savagely raped her then tossed her down a flight of stairs to kill her."

Hanson's skin paled. His hand tightened around his gun, his eyes narrowed at Joze. "Who the fuck are you? What do you care about a ripe little cop? I don't have to tell you jack shit."

Joze took an aggressive step towards Hanson. "I said, tell me about it. All of it. I already know most of it, so let me warn you, the first time I detect a lie, my friend behind you will break one of your limbs. And so on. So get started."

Hanson's face shriveled, he didn't want to turn around and look behind him. He could feel the powerful tension from whoever was there. The hard steel was now jabbed into his back.

He lowered his own gun. Then he gathered his balls together, the fucker wanted a story, he'd give him the story. It was no skin off his nose.

Hanson shrugged. "So, who gives a shit. Chick shouldn't be a cop if she doesn't expect to spread it for her fellow officers. Women shouldn't even be cops. They're the weaker sex as I've proven. She wanted to argue about giving it up to me, and I didn't."

"Move on. I don't want to hear your fucking opinions," Joze growled, barely raising his voice above a grated whisper. "Just tell me what happened, what you did to her."

"Sure, whatever. Yeah, I put the moves on her, she declined. She made the mistake of thinking since I was a fellow cop I could be trusted. It was necessary to subdue her with a few, ah, you know, punches and, ah such." His shoulders lifted then lowered.

"To tell you the truth, by the time I was done, she was such a petite, dainty little thing, she was so bloody and broken, I hardly remember the whole rape thing with all the fighting and screaming."

He didn't notice or care about the barest wince Joze stifled, nor did he see the hard flint of murder spark in the now completely black eyes.

"She was so small and tight that even after beating her into pretty much unconsciousness I still couldn't get all the way in…" he hesitated at the lowering of Joze's brows over those freaky eyes, his face turning even more diamond slated hard.

When Joze made no response, Hanson shrugged again and continued, "Yeah, so, when she eventually got out of the hospital I wanted to take her again so I could…uh, finish this time, get all the way inside her and enjoy it. I mean, the way she fought and squirmed, I didn't get a real good feel of those fine tits or that tender little pussy. And that ass, whewee," he let out an obscene whistle. "Well, I planned to take that juicy bit too."

It took everything Joze had to keep still as an iron statue and wait until it was all out.

His voice cocky, Hanson's mouth curled in a sick grin. But the grin faded into an angry snarl. "I looked for her when she recovered, but she stayed out of my reach. Yeah, I told the bitch I'd get her again. Seriously, it's only a matter of time before I find her. This time she won't heal as fast," he grinned arrogantly, smugly.

Hanson didn't notice the steam coming out of Joze's ears, or the threat of violence about to be pronounced upon him, he blithely went on.

"I plan to keep her around for a while when I get a hold of her. She's a fine hot piece. She's already been missing, so no one is going to go looking for her once I grab her and keep her locked down in my place. I have cuffs and know how to use them." He chuckled shaking his head at his joke.

"She's undercover somewhere. When she rises, I'll be there waiting. Yeah, I panicked last time and freaked out, plus I was mad as shit I couldn't complete the act so I tossed her, uh, down a flight of stairs."

He scowled at Joze. "So, what the fuck is all this to you? You waiting in line to do her next? You might as well settle in, son, I plan on keeping her for a good long spell." He elbowed Joze slightly in camaraderie and said, "But if you know where the girl is, it'll be hugely financially beneficial for you to give me her location. Whad'ya say, boy?"

As he talked, Joze's fists clenched into volcanic rocks, his shoulders bunched. Calmly, he said, "I want to kill you, cop, but unfortunately, if she ever learned I took you out, she'd be upset. Even after what you did to her, she wouldn't want you dead because that's the kind of woman, officer that she is. But, I feel I must avenge her, *da cachau pigio,* and prevent you from getting your goddamned savage hands on her again."

Now, Hanson looked taken aback, confusion and trepidation started whittling at his confidence. His brows screwed up, he said, "What the hell are you saying? You're speaking a different language? I don't under-"

"I called you a fucking prick." The emotion crawled up his throat strangling him. Joze couldn't stifle his accent, it only thickened with his wrath and sorrow for what Glorie had endured.

And she had endured it alone, hadn't even told her sister what had really happened. Shana thought Glorie had just accidentally tumbled down the stairs. Glorie was afraid her sister would go after the cop if she had learned what he'd done to her. Then Glorie would have worried that the damned cop would hurt Shana.

His voice rusty harsh from the feelings clawing up his throat, Joze took a deep calming breath but the fury squeezed his lungs. He rasped, "You beat and raped a defenseless woman, what a big man you are, you sick fuck. Now, I'm gonna beat the piss out of you, we'll see how long it takes you to recover from your fucking broken limbs."

Fear pooled in his eyes, but Hanson pretended bravado. "Eh, you want to have trouble with a cop for some little bitch?" He started to raise his gun, then, his eyes narrowed in recognition at Joze. "Hey, you're-"

Joze pulled off his beanie, the white blond hair stuck up, so incongruent with his obsidian-disked eyes like a demon's.

The color drained from the Hanson's face. With growing terror, he stammered, "You- you're fucking Jozadak Kane."

A slow, awful smile spread across Joze's harsh face. "Yeah." He shrugged out of his coat, dropping it and the hat on the floor. Then he methodically rolled up his long sleeves.

"*Ie*. Like I said you fuck, I'm not going to kill you, although when we're done you'll wish we had. Unless you croak from heart failure from the pain or fear, or get an infection from your wounds, then," he rolled one shoulder, "I am relieved of that responsibility.

Comprehension of the danger he was suddenly realizing he was in sucked the color out of Hanson's face. "Hey, but listen, I can take care of you, give you some big cake to take off and leave me alone. I got a lotta dough stashed. You only-"

Joze grinned, which was scarier than his normal harsh expression. "Not anymore you don't. As of an hour ago, we wiped out your secret account." He cracked his knuckles.

"So, as I was saying, I'm going to break a bunch, or actually pretty much all of your bones, and shatter as many internal organs as I can, then my friends here," his mouth stretched into a hateful grin at the shredded look on Hanson's face as he heard Calvin land behind him, joining Linc.

Linc shoved his gun harder in Hanson's back and held out his hand and said, "Give it to me. On second thought, please, fight me bitch, I want to fight you. I might be a little harder to pound on than a tiny female."

Hanson froze. Linc slammed the gun into his back with a fiercely hard jab.

Gulping harshly, Hanson handed him the weapon. His hands up, his voice growing as strident as a little girl's, he cried, "Why-"

Linc and Calvin moved so Hanson could see them.

All three stared at the beleaguered cop with chilling grim smiles.

His words steeped in deadly, unemotional quiet, Joze said, "When I'm done with you," he nodded to his friends, "they are going to do to you what you did to Glorie, you know, getting raped while you're all bloody and beaten and broken, like she was. See how you like being on the receiving end."

He couldn't do the deed himself, he wanted to have some innocent deniability when Glorie heard what happened to the cop. She would immediately suspect Joze.

Beside Hanson, Calvin had a long, thick, iron rod in his hand that he was lightly slapping into his palm.

If possible, Joze's face hardened even more, he said with ridicule, "But they won't be using a pathetic little impotent cock like you did," he glanced at the rod Calvin held then smiled back at Hanson.

Hanson's face peaked stark white, he held his palms out. "No, but wait, why? What do you care about a bitch cop? What does a gangster care-"

Joze kept talking, "And, when we are done, I will tell her that in a year or so, you know, when you're back on your feet and your spleen, liver and kidneys, bones, and ass, are more or less healed, you won't ever go near her, talk to her, even fucking *think* of her ever again, or so help me you fucking prick, I *will* kill you as slowly and agonizing as possible. Is that understood?"

Hanson's mouth opened and closed like malfunctioning elevator door. "But- but- but-"

"Feel free to try to sic your brothers in blue on us, just try it. I have cops so far up the ladder in my pocket you wouldn't get one foot on the rung to go after us. And," Joze winked, "you would be dead before your tippy toe got near the ladder. Hear what I'm saying, *son*? You attempt to bring charges against us, you won't live to see them filed."

Hanson's eyes rounding with terror bounced from man to man and back to Joze. "L-listen, bro, we can talk about this! Wait a second," his voice grew shrill when Calvin slapped the iron bar hard on his own palm with an evil, sadistic smile at the cop.

"So, being the gentleman that I am, I'm going to let you go first," Joze said. "Take your best shot, you sick fuck. It'll be just you and me, Hanson, my friends won't get involved until I'm done. They are covering the second part. Go on." He stuck his chin out begging the man to throw a punch.

Linc and Calvin moved back several feet.

"No, but wait-" Hanson cried then threw a wild punch at Joze which he easily ducked.

Then Joze went wild. Savagely punching, kicking Hanson until the man was cowering on his knees.

Spitting and coughing blood, the cop was begging and crying, "Enough! Please! No more!"

"Stand up you cowardly piece of *shyt*, I'm nowhere near done. Did you stop when Glorie begged you as you battered her and left her lying broken and alone at the bottom of the stairs? Did you show her an iota of mercy as you brutally raped her?"

Joze bent and clutched the cop's collar, jerking him to his feet. "Here's the same mercy you showed her," and he punched him in the gut so hard, he stepped aside as fluid spewed from the cop's mouth with his sharp grunt.

He grabbed Hanson and threw him at the cement wall and hammered on him like a boxer gone psychotic.

When Hanson collapsed to the floor barley conscious, Joze picked him up and started again.

He broke both his arms and legs in several places, and jaw, and every finger. When there was nothing left for him to break, or kick, or pummel, Joze let him drop to the floor like a boneless bloody puddle.

Then he bent and scooped up his jacket and knit hat, and without a word or look to Linc or Calvin, he strode to the door.

Crossing the threshold, he was surprised when he heard Hanson scream, he hadn't thought the fuck still had a breath left in him.

Chapter Twenty-Three

Joze avoided Glorie for a week until the cuts and bruises on his knuckles healed. He didn't want the signs of violence on him when he told Glorie that her fears were finally over.

Nonetheless, Guy managed to come across an obscure article on the web about the attack. Glorie was in the kitchen helping Maria prepare some vegetables.

"I hope my vegetables come out as good as these, Maria," Glorie said, while washing tomatoes in the sink.

Maria was peeling potatoes; her peeler hesitated in the middle of a swipe. She smiled kindly at Glorie. "You think you will still be here when they are ready for harvesting?" She sounded hopeful. Maria has been like a second mom to Glorie.

Holding a plump ripe tomato, Glorie set her hands on the counter. She was considering how she felt about that when Guy strolled into the kitchen.

He reached in front of Maria snatching up a long slice of cucumber she had just prepared and stuck it in his mouth ignoring her frown. "Hey, honeypot," he said to Glorie speaking through the cucumber. That earned another frown from Maria.

"Guy," Glorie remonstrated the good-looking man. "I've asked you not to call me that."

"Ah, honey, but that's what you are, and that is a part of you I am dying to taste-" he reached for her to plant a kiss on her mouth.

Facing the counter, jerking her head from him, Glorie said, "Guy, stop it. Don't talk to me like that."

In answer, he set his hands on either side of her, fencing her against the counter.

"Mr. Guy, you stop that right now, let her go!" Maria's voice was studded with anger. In her agitation, her accent made her words harder to understand, but her tone was clear.

Not looking at the maid, Guy said, "Bug off, Maria, this is none of your concern, right honey?" Leaning the front of his body against Glorie's back, he burrowed his nose into her neck. When she struggled, he laughed and hemmed her in tighter, his chest on her back, his pelvis grinding into her butt.

"If you do not release Miss Glorie immediately," Maria's face turning beet purple, she threatened, "I will go get Master Joze-"

Guy rubbed his chest over Glorie. Moving his arms to hold her immobile, he pushed his erection into her bottom, and said, "Fuck off, Maria,"

"Oh!" Maria threw down her peeler and stormed out the kitchen door.

"Fucking bitch," Guy cursed, stepping back from Glorie. She swung around, livid that he was pawing her.

"Listen, Guy-"

"Yeah, stow it honey. I came to show you something. I got distracted by that sweet ass of yours," he sighed. "C'mere, before Mr. Big Badass comes." He had set his iPad on the table, he picked it up and clicked it on. Then pushed it in her face and said, "Read this."

One eye on him in case he pounced on her again, Glorie took the pad from him and read it.

It was an article about a police officer who had been found on the verge of death, savagely beaten and brutally sodomized. After surviving numerous surgeries, he would be spending a long time recuperating in the hospital rehab center.

The police were seeking witnesses. Muttering through his wired jaw, the victim claims to have amnesia and doesn't recall the incident or the perpetrator, or perpetrators.

Glorie looked up at Guy who had his eyes beaded on the window watching for any sign of Joze. "Guy, I don't understand, why are you showing me this?"

He glanced at her then quickly back out the window. "Read the name, sweetheart." Guy had heard rumors that Joze, Linc and Calvin had left the ranch for a long night a week ago. Joze had come back first and his hands were a bloody mess.

Guy had also secretly eavesdropped on conversations, the name Ian had come up in occurrence with Glorie's. Guy wasn't positive, but he was sure there was a tie-in with this whole thing. He peered back to see her reaction.

Ah ha! The look on her face was priceless. The color seeped out, and the hands that held the pad were shaking like leaves in a storm. She set the pad down and stared at it.

He said with mild sarcasm, "Anyone you know, sweetheart?" Enjoying the sight, knowing the pot was stirring, a reptilian grin crossed his face. This should turn her against Joze, and then Guy could step in comfortably, *oh shit-*

Joze was stalking across the lawn like the fucking angel of death straight for the house. Maria was hurrying yards behind him.

"Gotta go, babe-" Guy grabbed her, kissed her painfully hard on the lips then fled in the opposite direction.

When Joze threw the door open looking like hades in flannel, he saw Glorie, her palm on the table holding up her trembling legs, and her other hand over her mouth.

"Where is he?" Joze roared so loud Glorie jerked.

She turned dazed eyes to him. Her face like a ghost, fear tightened around the corners of her eyes, and thinned her mouth.

Immediately concerned, Joze rushed to her, took her arm and helped her to sit. "What is it? Did that motherfucker hurt you?"

Seeing her cringe at his language, he sat down at the table and took her hand. "I'm sorry, *babi*, it's just he works my every fuck-uh, damned nerve."

Holding her hand, he asked gently, "What happened?" He scanned every inch of her face, her lips looked oddly red against her ashen skin.

Loud and furious again, he shouted, "Did that bastard kiss you?" He started to push to his feet, but she held onto his hand.

Seeing her expression of suspicious distress clear as a book on her white face, his stomach clenched, he sat back down.

"Joze," her voice twittered weakly. She cleared her throat, making her voice stronger, she said, "I was shown an article, about a...beating. I need to know if you had anything to do with it?" She watched him.

Joze had an inscrutable poker face. He never gave anything away. But, she was getting used to him, and she was sure she saw something flicker in his eyes. "Don't lie to me. Please."

He sat back in the chair, his long legs apart. He didn't want to meet her eyes, but he did. Her gaze was unfaltering.

Joze was not a liar. If he didn't want to answer something, he just didn't. But, he wanted her to know he would always be candid with her, that she could trust him, and his word.

His arm stretched across the table, he still held her hand. Resisting the urge to drag his hand over his mouth, it would be a tell that he was worried about how she would take it.

"Joze?"

He sat up and leaned forward, towards her. Squeezing her hand gently he looked her straight in the eyes and said, "Just be comforted, *babi*, that Ian Hanson will never bother you again. You do not have to dream of that fucker coming after you, in real life or in your nightmares." He covered their hands with his other one.

She tugged to free her hand, but he held it. "Joze," her voice shook, "the article said he...was not only beaten almost to death, but he was..." her cheeks pinked, "um, attacked...sexually."

"*Babi*, I can tell you with all honesty, I won't deny the beating, but I did not *personally* do the...sodomy. I swear on my honor." He didn't mention setting up the entire incident with Linc and Calvin.

Glorie started to say something, he spoke over her, "Do not ask me any more about it. I've said all I will on the matter. He will never hurt you ever again. You do not have to fear him. He got what he did to you. Now, the subject is closed." Still leaning forward, he wanted her to see the truth in his sincere gaze.

Her back resting against the chair, Glorie studied him.

His blue eyes were so vibrant she could see herself in them. They appeared clear, but not 100% pure of deceit, she believed he was telling her the truth, to a point.

She felt he was holding something back, certainly not telling her everything. He had sworn to avenge her the night she had told him about…it. Part of her was appalled and sickened at the extent of the violence perpetrated on…her attacker.

But, she sighed, part of her cheered that now Ian knew how she had felt, and that he did not get away with what he'd done to her. And hopefully, he has learned his lesson and no other woman will have to suffer as Glorie had.

Plus, now that he could no longer get to her, couldn't hurt her under Joze's clear threat if he did, maybe the heavy cloud of fear will lift from her and the nightmares will finally end.

Her lids lowered, she peered up at Joze through her lashes. "You, uh, went to a lot of trouble and danger to…avenge me. Why?"

His gaze shifted down, then rose to her angelic face. "Glorie, you should not have to live in fear the rest of your life that, that…person, was going to come after you. He made it so you can't prosecute him, this way the chances of him harming another woman, well, they have lessened." The blue eyes narrowed under lowered lids.

"I will not allow someone to hurt you. He's only still alive because, you…ah, never mind. Now, like I said, we're done with this." Joze sat silent and still, watching her compute the information. The tension in his shoulders diminished when she smiled at him.

"Okay." She went to stand up but he held onto her.

"Joze, I know you're busy outside with the horses and Daniel, and you've let Van go on an errand he really needed, and I'm helping Maria, which," she looked around. The maid was nowhere to be seen.

"The horses, Daniel, and Maria can wait." He let go of her hand but before she could blink he clinched his big hands around her waist, lifted her and set her on his lap.

She squealed, "Joze! What are you doing?"

"What I've wanted to do forever." He lifted her again, turning her to straddle him, and spread his hands across her back.

When her lips parted to protest, he lowered his mouth onto them, silencing her complaint before it could stop him. Her mouth already open, he licked her lips, then the inside of them, stroked her teeth then sought her tongue.

She struggled for about five seconds, then slid her hands over his thick shoulders and around his neck, kissing him back as fervently as he kissed her.

Feeling her heady response, Joze crushed her against his chest. Tilting his head, his hand moved up to cradle her head to hold their lips tighter together. The kiss grew more heated.

When she pulled back to take a breath, Joze kissed her jaw, behind her ear, then he moved his lips to her neck. Licking her, he moaned at her delicious taste, then sealed his mouth on her skin and sucked.

Never feeling the sensations he wrought in her before, Glorie's body tingled like bolts of electricity were striking between her legs. Her head dropped back, he splayed both hands across her back holding her as her spine arched, and he sucked harder.

She couldn't help it, a soft moan escaped, her legs drew up at the intensity of the feeling he was bringing out in her. But, sitting on him as she was, straddling him, her legs could go nowhere, they dropped down uselessly.

At her moan, Joze's loins turned feverish, he sucked her neck, down to her collarbone. Her hands brushed over the shaved sides of his hair then up through the wavy top where she strung her fingers through the thick locks.

"Ah *babi*, so good," he groaned with his lips against her skin. He licked and kissed his way back up her neck.

Her chin tilted up, and he moved his hands to hold her under her arms. His palms pressed against the sides of her breasts, he kissed underneath her chin as her neck arched and her head dropped back further.

Glorie melted like hot butter in his hands. He sprinkled kisses back down her jaw, down her neck, to her breastbone then over the swell of her breasts that weren't covered by her blouse.

He kissed and sucked her flesh as low as he could get. When the button stopped him, he suddenly stood up with her in his arms, a hand under her butt, the other cupping the back of her head.

Her legs clamped around his hips. He scored his mouth across hers, seeking to lick her lips then thrust his tongue back in her mouth, locking them together as he started across the kitchen.

Pulling back, panting hard, her chest heaving, Glorie gushed out, "Joze, wait-"

He tried to cover her mouth again as he kept moving, but she turned her head.

His eyes were so glazed with passion the blue had been completely eaten up by the black. Lids heavy with desire drew down hooded, almost covering the blazing orbs entirely.

"Please, Joze, stop," she begged, keeping her head turned.

His lips went to her neck and he sucked hard, meanwhile, he continued walking towards the hall, towards their bedrooms.

"Joze!" she said louder to get his attention, he was in such a blind trance.

Finally hearing her, he stopped moving. He tried to focus on her face. But his body was burning. He wanted her so badly he couldn't even think.

"Wha- what, *babi*?" he panted, his eyes half-mast on her mouth. His lips started towards hers again but she pulled back.

"Please put me down, Joze." Her voice quaked some, but she inserted firmness into it.

He blinked, and blinked, shaking his head, trying to clear the brain fog she brought on him. His blond hair a thick mess from her ravaging fingers. At her request to put her down, his arms tightened possessively.

His voice croaky, he slurred thickly, "I don't understand, don't you want me, *bach babi*?" He struggled to peer into her face.

In the amethyst eyes, he saw fear, doubt, and passion. The blue hue the fear, the hint of crystal pink the doubt, the violet was definitely the passion. He brought her to the couch and carefully set her on it.

Not wanting her to leave, Joze sat beside her and set his hand very gently on her leg. He cupped her chin, turning her to face him. She kept her lids lowered, but her quivering lips gave away her apprehension.

Firmly but soft, he ordered, "*Babi*, please, look at me."

She did. Shy, nervous, yet the heat of her need fanned to him.

He bent to kiss her, but she turned from him.

"Ah, *babi*, don't be afraid of me. Glorie," he insisted, "look at me." He waited until she did. His hand lightly touched the side of her face, he smiled gently. "Don't be afraid of me, *babi*, I will never hurt you. Never."

She looked at him, then her gaze slid away.

"Glorie, I know what I've done, taking you, keeping you a prisoner here. I felt at the time I needed to take you, for several reasons, none of the least that I didn't know who those men were or if there were others waiting to come in. I didn't know if I'd killed any of them. I couldn't afford for you to tell the police, even though I did what I had to do, and I would do it again."

Her voice small, she said, "I know, Joze. I know you could have easily run out the back of the saloon unseen and left me to my fate." Raising her hand, she slid her fingers through his soft blond mane.

"Even knowing at that point because you heard them read my ID, that I was the hated police," she said, smiling at his curled smile, then she was serious. "You still fought to save me. There was no reason for you to have risked your life to come to my rescue."

He said nothing, she stated the truth.

Then he said, "I took you too, Glorie, because, I knew you were sent undercover to find me out, spy on me, get something prosecutorial. I took you, *Duw*," he scratched the side of his face, then dropped his other hand from her.

He said, "Glorie," his eyes grim with perplexity, "I can't tell you why else I took you, I couldn't at the time, just that," he looked at her, begging her to understand. He was rambling, making no sense. Joze decided to be up front, tell her the truth. Admit it to the both of them.

"I had to take you. I knew if I didn't, I would never see you again. I grabbed you to keep you safe, and to see what you were up to, and," for once in his life he appeared a bit nervous himself, a bit shy, a bit uncertain. "I had already started having feelings for you when I thought you were Dinah."

Her eyes shot to his in stunned surprise. "But Joze, I stayed deliberately in the background, dressed down, hid behind a hat and glasses, you couldn't have-"

He smiled, running a fingertip down the side of her face, sighing at the softness of her skin.

"Glorie, you were so sweet, to everyone. So…real, pure, you were terribly shy, but brave. You stuck up for all of us when you thought we were being abused. Plus," he lifted a curl from her shoulder, rubbed it between his fingers.

"I don't know, Glorie, there was just something, the sway of your hips, the tilt of your head, your scent, *fy Duw*, my God, your scent, *babi*," he leaned over and inhaled it, sighing with contented desire.

"I could never get enough. You never noticed I leaned into you every time you brought something to me? A bottle of wine? Clean glasses to stock? I had to get a whiff of you. And, *babi*, don't get me started on those lips…I was about to rip Rubal in half for even thinking about…" he shuddered.

"Hell, I constantly kept one eye on him in case he got carried away with his hands on you. You never noticed the nights you worked late, alone, I stayed late too. I feared leaving you vulnerable to Rubal's lust. I told you that he planned on assaulting you." As he spoke, Joze lowered his head and lightly pulsed his mouth on hers.

She lifted her head. Opening her mouth to accept his, her lips received his suckling, drawn like a desert to rain. Until she caught herself.

"Joze, I...you are a gangster, I am an officer. You know I can't..." she winced at the pained look crossing his face. "You mentioned keeping me here, when will you release me?"

His eyes turned to black ice, they glowed so eerily at her she trembled and leaned away.

He whispered, "I tried hard, *bach babi*, so hard to fight my attraction to you. I had to keep reminding myself you were a police officer. I was terrible to you the day I took you, and since. I had felt so...betrayed by you being a cop. And worse, the one sent specifically to take me down."

A faint pink shaded her cheeks at the shame Glorie felt for her own deception. She'd been doing her job, nonetheless, it was still deceit. She deceived not only Joze but all of the other people she worked with as well.

Joze went on, "I'm sorry, I can't take it back. But, I realize I can't fight it...especially when I know you feel something...not sure what or how much, but you feel something for me too."

Arms twining around her, he leaned with her, forcing her to lay back with her head on a cushion. Her big blue-violets expanded like wild unsure poppies, she raised her palms to fend him off.

"Ah, *babi*," he murmured. Cupping her face, the curve of his thumb on her jaw, his fingers so long they netted the back of her head.

His thumb stroking her jaw, he whispered, "I can make you want me, Glorie. I can make your body cry for mine, your mouth to scream my name," as his lips conquered hers, he slid a leg between her thighs, settling some of his weight on her, staking her in place.

"Joze," her lips protested even while accepting the pressure of his pushing them open and driving his tongue inside.

He captured her wrists pulling them over her head, his mouth harder, his voracious tongue delving, seeking, burrowing inside, tantalizing her to join with him, making stars pop in their heads. He chased her, tasted her until she acquiesced, reciprocating with breathless burning intensity.

When they were in sync, their mouths a scorching mesh of lips, tongues, breaths, still holding her wrists with one hand, he lowered the other hand from cradling her face, stroking it down her neck, to her collar and unbuttoned several buttons while she was too intoxicated with passion to notice.

Joze shifted so his erection bulged against her core, smiling when he felt her body shudder in response. He dipped a thick finger inside her blouse, inside the top rim of her satiny bra, stroked it around inside, lightly skimming the swell of her breast.

Her body reacted to his sensual touch. Her back arched surging her breast urgently against his hand.

Joze put his hand just under her breast to hold it, then kissed his way down her face, along her neck, to her cleavage. With her arms raised over her head, her breasts were pressed together. He put his mouth between them, kissing, licking them at the same time.

A moan cruised achingly out of her lungs taut with desire. It made his erection jump, then throb as it swelled, pressing harder against her sex. When her hips rose to meet his he about came in his jeans.

"*Babi*," he groaned with his lips on the plump furl of her breast. Finding her nipple with his teeth, he tugged at it, sucking it through the sheer satin bra.

"*Joze*," no longer a protest, now a plea, Glorie writhed against his mouth, his hand, his burning shaft.

Holding her wrists high, he moved his hand to under her back, down to her bottom, curved his palm to cup her hips. Lifting her perfectly rounded ass, another minute of priming and he could pick her up and carry her to his room, get her clothes off her before she had a second to think and say no.

He would ravish her so insanely she'd forget her disdain of him, what he is, and she would want him forever- he heard a noise and froze.

Joze instantly shielded her with his body and carefully raised his head. "*Fuck-*" his team was filing into the room.

Linc suddenly spotted them and held his arm out to stop the others.

"Joze?" Glorie voice soft and saturated with passion, she tried to sit up.

"Wait *babi*," Joze groaned and quickly pulled her blouse together and buttoned it before moving off her to let her up.

Struggling to sit up, Glorie leaned back on her palms, then her face flushed with mortified red as she saw the men standing a few yards away.

Joze swiveled to sit behind her as she scooted to the edge of the couch. His hands combing the back of her hair, just wanting to touch her, he lowered his mouth to her ear and said quietly, "Don't be embarrassed, Glorie, *babi*, don't leave, we can go to my room-"

Glorie squirmed to her feet and fled down the hall.

Sighing with heavy, frustrated aggravation, Joze stood up and jerked at his jeans to stretch them down and over his obvious erection.

Seeing Linc's grin, then Calvin's, the cleft in Sloan's chin deepened with his smirk, Joze scowled.

Bruno's face creased in mirth. Diego's olive skin darkened with his snicker, even Van came up behind them smirking.

Joze's scowl darkened to a look that could kill. "Fuck you, fuck all of you bastards. What the hell are you doing here?" He forked his fingers through his waves of blond locks, more to calm himself than to neaten them. He tugged his flannel shirt down to cover the thickness behind his zipper.

"Uh, you forget we had a meeting scheduled?" Linc asked with a curl to his lopsided grin and an arched tawny brow.

"What?" Joze glanced at his watch. "Aw fuck." He sent a longing look down the hall Glorie had disappeared into.

Shyt, the likelihood of him getting a chance to get near her like they just were, and work her back to the crazy heat she had been wildly in, was damned dim.

She'll have time and distance to get her protective walls back up, and let the shame of allowing him to touch her and her responding so intensely sink in and bog her back down. Drown out what they could be together. Dammit.

His sigh heavy he glared at his friends. "All right, you assholes, let's go." He trod angrily to the opposite hallway to the study, followed like the pied piper by his snickering friends.

Van went the other way to guard Glorie.

Chapter Twenty-Four

Days passed, Glorie avoided Joze like the plague.

The only good thing, he noticed, was she hadn't had a nightmare since the day she learned about what happened to Ian Hanson.

When Joze was out in the field working, Glorie would skip breakfast and with Van on her heels, hurry to the far side of the pasture to be with Daniel. He and the hands always had fences to repair, and farm animals to feed, shear the alpacas, as well as to track down escaped livestock.

The alpacas were fast and sneaky. The ranch hands did some of the feeding and shearing, but they mostly did repairs and cleaning, mowing, maintenance.

The more Glorie avoided him, the angrier Joze grew. It kicked him in the gut that she was obviously at least a little attracted to him, he knew he could win her over if she'd let him in just a hair.

But because she believed him to be this cutthroat ruthless hood, and she was a goody two-shoes cop, she would have nothing to do with him. Not to mention that little thing about him kidnapping her.

He wasn't denying it, but, still, cursing, "Damn," he slammed his fist into his hand. Standing with a few ranch hands putting in new fence posts, Joze could see her flaming curls she'd tied up in a swinging ponytail from across the paddocks out to the pasture where she was with Daniel.

His fingers itched to caress those silky tresses. His dick twitched thinking about what they'd feel like slinking along the length of it.

"Damn," he cursed a few more vile words again under his breath, pushing his mind to something else before he embarrassed himself with a king sized hard-on. It was bad enough his friends teased him mercilessly about falling hard for a woman.

And not just any blasted woman, not the tough broads he was used to, no, she had to be sweet, and she had to be a cop. He didn't need the raunchy ranch hands needling him too.

"Lord almighty, why did you put us in the impossible position?" he groaned silently, dragging his palms over his head then got back to work.

Joze kept his eyes on her all day. Van had instructions to keep him informed of her every move.

After a shower, shave and change of clothes into black jeans and long sleeved, black buttoned-down shirt, he made his way to the dining area where he had told Van to make sure he was sitting next to Glorie.

When he entered the room, the long oblong table was teeming with people laughing and conversing, eating and drinking. It was so noisy and chaotic no one saw him look at Van.

The guard nodded and vacated his chair, which Joze slipped into.

Glorie didn't even know he was there until she turned to say something to Van and paused, startled that her guard had been replaced by the tall, rugged blond, with his icy blue eyes tensed on her.

Pink deepening in her cheeks she quickly turned away, not seeing the rueful tic of his lip.

Very few people would talk to Glorie. The women were mostly jealous, the men were too afraid of Joze's possessive wrath that they resisted even looking in her direction. Except Guy. But he was at the far end of the table, not for lack of trying.

He had made every effort to be sitting next to Glorie but Van had persevered in keeping them apart. Van preferred not to have bloodshed at the dinner table.

Calvin was seated next to Joze. Soon they were in deep conversation.

The cognac-infused beef bourguignon immersed in pearl onions and mushrooms that Maria had prepared to perfection was rapidly consumed. The sauce ladled over flat pasta and sopped up with toasty bread earned its own praise. Everyone gorged themselves.

Except Glorie, who without a fuss, stood up reaching for her plate to take it into the kitchen.

Joze grabbed her wrist without even looking at her and forced her to sit back down.

He turned from Calvin and nodded at her plate. "You barely took enough food to feed a bird and then you ate less than half. You're already too skinny. Damn, Glorie, we've gone over this. Sit down and finish it."

Flustered at his high-handedness, Glorie spurted, "What? What do you care if, or what I eat or how I look?"

Calmly stabbing a piece of beef with a slice of carrot, Joze forked it into his mouth saying, "I don't want to sit here and have to look at a scarecrow every day."

The table was suddenly silent, everyone was watching them.

Her feelings obviously hurt. With a face beaming red, she stood back up again, and said in a whispered huff with a tiny hitch in her voice, "Fine. No one said you had to look at me. I'll just leave and save your eyesight having to gaze on such a scrawny ugly sight."

She turned to leave but Joze grasped her wrist and forced her to sit down again but more roughly. This time he did not let go of her wrist, holding it on the table, he kept eating.

The tension at the table had grown as thick as a thundercloud. One-by-one, the group got up and scattered.

Embarrassed at his manhandling her in front of the others, she groused in a low voice, "Why do you care how I look? I'll cover my face with a scarf if I'm so horrible to look at. Now, leave me alone dammit." She jerked at her hand, but to no avail, he held her like a vice.

Still eating, Joze said calmly, "I never said you were hard on the eyes, honey. I've talked about this before with you. You are no longer having the nightmares, so there is no reason for you not to eat like a normal person."

Using her other hand, Glorie tried to pry his big thick fingers open. "Fine. I will. I just don't feel like it right now." She'd gotten in the habit of getting around on low amounts of fuel. His fingers were like thick nails holding her in place and unbendable.

"You've said that before. Now that you've been avoiding me," he kept going at the shake of her head, "you've been skipping meals to do so. Well, that's done. I want you to put on some weight because we are going into the city tomorrow and you'll need to wear that dress Melissa got for you. I'd like you to have a body to put it in."

At her pained embarrassed expression, he sighed. His gaze briefly stroked from her chest to her legs and back. "Babe, you know you have a smoking body," his gaze lit on her dubious eyes.

"But you are too skinny, you could get sick, and without a healthy foundation, it could lead to serious issues. I don't need cop killer on my résumé. I've already told Maria before to serve you fattening food, but she tells me you only eat tiny portions."

"Then let me go, you won't have to worry about me or how I can hurt your reputation," her sneer sarcastic. Then she sighed sadly and repeated, "Just let me go."

He stalled forking his food, his jaw clenched. He chewed without speaking or looking at her. A vein chugged hard at his temple.

Not responding to her request to free her, swallowing the bite of beef, he leaned in glaring at Glorie and said with a frosty threat, "You will eat what Maria gives you if I have to force feed you myself." He scooped up some pasta, stuffed it in his mouth and chewed then washed it down with a slug of water.

"But- but why are you taking me to the city?" She tried to squash the alarm that rose up her throat, *was he going to drop her body along the way somewhere?*

"I have business deals to do and I will look more trustworthy, respectable, if I have a lady on my arm. Not a slut I picked up for the day, somebody I look serious about. Plus, we're going to my club and I need a block to keep the other women from hassling me while I'm there."

He cocked his head and looked blankly at her. "And that block will be you," he went back to eating.

"I- I don't want to go," her voice a squeak, "it makes no sense."

"I don't have to make sense," he snapped in an angry voice like he was talking to a four year old. "Eat your fucking food."

Looking down at her food but not making a move towards it, she muttered, "Take one of your other- uh, women friends, it's not like you don't have thousands to choose from. They already have the gorgeous bodies you so obviously crave. Leave me here, lock me in my room."

He very slowly and very carefully set down his fork and glared coldly at her. "You will come with me as my date. I can't leave you here alone, you know I can't allow you to escape, so you will be with me." Still holding her wrist, he picked up his coffee and slurped down half of it.

"Why don't you just take another woman, someone you like-"

"Goddammit Glorie," he shouted, pounding his fist on the table, all the plates and glasses jumped, as did Glorie. "I said I'm not taking another fucking woman so quit fucking saying it."

Her eyes downcast she murmured, "I guess you only need a respectable woman, not a respectable mouth."

His teeth clenched, he crushed her wrist with his fingers. Staring down at his plate he said very quietly, "You better damned watch yourself, cop."

Not backing down, Glorie sniffed back a tear and said brashly, "You mistake me for one of your women that wants you, that drapes wantonly across your lap while you feel her up in public."

His eyes swept her up and down and he said sarcastically, "Are you sure?" He smirked at her indignant flush of anger. The corner of his lip twitched seeing she wanted to slap him.

But she had learned she wasn't fast enough to hit him without him stopping her, and the one time he let her, she hurt herself more than him.

She pulled at her hand. "So, take me with you, but not as your date."

His eyes narrowed. "What's the difference if you're my date or not?"

Her eyes narrowed back at him. "Because if we are in a pretend relationship it would entail you having to touch me at times, and," she sniffed, her nose in the air, "I do not want you touching me."

Joze's face darkened. He growled, "Oh," and twisted her wrist, "you prefer to be with Guy?"

She didn't answer him, tried harder to pull her hand free.

He released her, growling angrily, "Well, you will be with me, you will be my date and there will be no more discussion about it. We will have dinner after my meeting, then afterwards I have something to show you."

Ignoring the ripple of alarm in her, he nodded arrogantly at her plate. "When you finish all of that you may leave the table." Then he leaned casually back in his chair, crossed his arms over his chest, stuck his legs out, crossed his ankles and stared at her.

Her mouth dropped open. She went to say something, saw the steel set to his jaw and knew she wasn't going anywhere until he decided she could.

Mumbling under her breath, she said, "You are a domineering, crass bully." With a hateful mutinous look tightening the soft features of her face, she daintily picked up her fork and finished her dinner, all while he drank his coffee and watched her silently under lowered lids.

Chapter Twenty-Five

The next day, Joze stayed near Glorie for breakfast and lunch. They didn't speak, but knowing he was going to enforce it if she didn't, Glorie ate as much as she could. Later, Joze told Van to tell Glorie to be ready to go at five.

Just before five o'clock, Joze went and got the Bentley and brought it around to the front of the house. He got out, leaned against the door, pulled out a pack of cigarettes, tapped one out and lit it.

He hoped to smoke it before Glorie came out and frowned her disapproval at him like she usually did for smoking. He wore black slacks, a black suit coat with no tie, and a blue shirt, leaving the top two buttons undone. He'd changed his Harley boots for dressier ones.

The door opened and Van came out. Joze looked up, his jaw dropped. He already knew Glorie was a beautiful woman, but, his breath caught in his throat.

She was wearing the heels Melissa had chosen which were obviously higher than Glorie was used to because even with her holding onto Van's arm, her steps were unsure, which only made her even fucking sexier.

Tossing the cigarette, Joze made quick long strides to the porch. He hopped up the steps two at a time to reach her.

Van grinned hugely. "You kids have fun," he teased.

With a hint of uncertainty, Glorie replied politely, "Thank you."

Joze said nothing to Van, his tongue was stuck, a lump had lodged in his throat, he just stared at Glorie. Then he held his hand out and waited for her to put hers in it. He let out his breath when she did.

His big paw closed over her delicate fingers, completely encasing them. Helping her down the steps, he didn't see Van's grin at seeing his boss flustered for the first time, ever. Joze felt like a young teen on his very first date.

At the bottom of the steps, Joze held her out to look at her. "*Babi*, you are so beautiful you literally stole my breath."

Blushing slightly, she said, "Maria helped. She did my hair and makeup." Glancing down, her brows furrowed. "I'm not really sure about this dress."

The top of the dress was a sheer design of blush and gold that left her shoulders bare. The sparkly print showed no cleavage but its vague transparency snuggly hugged her breasts, displaying them to the point Joze already had to work to keep his hands to himself.

The skirt of the dress was looser, shimmering gold with the fabric pulled to one side at her tiny waist. The skirt was shorter than he would have liked, he was going to worry every time she sat or bent over.

She was a small woman but her shapely legs looked miles long in the short skirt, the high heels made them appear even longer. Her hair was elegantly swept up leaving one long flaming curl spiraling down along the outside of her breast.

He stood there looking at her for so long, she cleared her throat. "Um. Are we going?"

Blinking out of his revelry, he nodded. His accent thick as a brick, he replied, "*Ie*, of course."

Joze ushered her to the Bentley, opened the door and helped her in. His eyes were on her legs as she pulled them up and inside until he closed her door.

Sliding into the driver's side, he turned the SUV on and headed down the driveway.

At the street, he hesitated. Turning towards her, his gaze swept her from head to toe, connecting with those remarkable eyes of hers.

His voice losing the harsh dominating tone of yesterday, he said "You okay, *babi*? Are you all right with this?"

She smiled. With a soft, whimsical lilt of her glossy pink lips, she said, "Would it matter if I wasn't? You made it clear I had no say in it."

His lips pulled in, he didn't break their connection. "*Babi*, Glorie," he took a breath, let it out slowly, then picked up her hand and held it. "I really, really want you to come with me. Forget what I said about needing a respectable woman on my arm, or to keep the other females away," his eyes lowered then turned back up to hers.

"I want you with me. Not to watch over, but I want to show you what I do. And," he said, lifting her hand, softly kissed it then set it back down on the seat between them. "I want to spend time with you, not you as a prisoner on my farm and me as your captor. Not me as a gangster and you an officer of the law. Just two regular people."

Glorie's eyes travelled all around his face as he spoke. His lips, he had gorgeous yet masculine lips, hard cheekbones, those funky eyes that changed with his emotion turning from electric blue to black when he was enraged, or, she blushed, when he was turned on. They were blue jay blue now, a blend of different shades of electric and warm.

His pupils were already covering more than half of the blue. His white-blond hair was neatly combed back off his forehead. She said, "You are such a Jekyll and Hyde, Joze. Horrible and domineering one minute, then," she lightly traced her fingers down his face, "kind and gentle the next." Her eyes dropped.

Feeling the tingle of her touch all the way down his body to his groin, he smothered the shiver it gave him. With his head lowered, he looked up at her through his dark lashes. The dark fringe a contrast around his blue eyes and light hair.

"Glorie," he waited until she drew her gaze back to his then said, "I've lived a…life that I've had to be hard and cold, sometimes cruel and violent, to exist, and keep others safe. I am trying to learn, to be…a better man. I know you think I'm a bad guy, a criminal. I want the opportunity to show you a different side of me."

She said nothing. He sighed. "If you don't want to go, seriously, I won't force you to."

The couple sat in silence for some time gazing at each other while she considered his words and he held his breath. She said. "Okay."

"Uh, okay what, honey?" He held his breath again.

"Okay. I will go with you." Her eyes dropped shyly, obviously unsure that she wasn't making a big mistake. "You're giving me a choice, I, well, appreciate that, and," she peered up at him, "I am curious about…you."

Jaw tightening, his voice hardened, "Oh, the cop wants to gather dirt on me."

"No," she said, quickly touching his hand. Her smile tentative, she told him, "I want to see the real you. Who you are away from the- uh, other men. Like you said, I want to be just us, you know, one-on-one. I can't say it's purely altruistic, I'm sure there is some police officer in me, albeit that feeling would be minimal considering the little training I had. But, it makes me want to separate the man from the gangster and know more about you. And," she smiled, "it would be nice to not have the tension hanging over us for a minute."

His breath came out in a rush, he wanted to kiss her, but didn't want her to change her mind, so he squeezed her hand.

He said with a smile, "I'm glad." Then, the smile thinned with reluctance, "The only thing, honey, is, I need to protect my people and the ranch. Please don't be angry or offended, but I need to blindfold you. Is that all right with you?" If he kept holding his breath all night he was going to pass out.

Surprised at him actually again *asking* her, Glorie scanned his guileless but tense face. And he said a rare *please*. She smiled at him, where was the mean Mr. Kane? Who replaced him with this gentle, polite man? "Um, okay."

"*Ta*, thank you, *babi*. Here," he pulled out a handkerchief and tied it over her eyes. "It's only until we get to the city."

When they reached the outskirts of a different town than the ranch was in, he took the blindfold off. She rubbed her eyes but didn't comment. He continued down one street after another.

Joze could feel her stiffening as he pulled into the strip club. When he parked, he asked, "What's bothering you, *babi*?"

She sat unmoving, looking out the window at the bright lights that spelled out 'Gentlemen's Club.'

"Glorie?"

"Um, I don't think I can go in there where there's...nude...uh..." she gulped her discomfiture as her cheeks pinked.

"Oh, *babi*, I would never take you inside when there're...shows going on." He grinned lopsided at her. "It's way early. There will be a few people drinking at the bar, and a light late lunch is served. The staff will be setting up. It'll be okay, there's nothing for you to be embarrassed about. Everyone will have their clothes on, I promise." He took her hand and kissed it again.

Watching her scan the establishment, he was sure she was trying to make up her mind if the place was too sordid for her to go in. Then he remembered. "Hey, *babi*, I have something for you. You need something to go with that dress."

Her brows arched with curiosity. "For me?"

His mouth turned up at the corners. "*Ie*, for you. Here." His eyes on hers, Joze pulled a long narrow box out of his inside jacket pocket and opened it. A bracelet lay sparkling inside.

Her fingers spread in front of her mouth, her eyes wide. "I don't..."

"Hold out your hand," Joze said.

He waited, she wasn't sure. "Go on," he urged her.

She lifted her arm with her hand out. He took the bracelet out, set the box on the seat, laid the bracelet on her wrist, locked the clasp closed and waited for her reaction.

She held her arm up and studied the bracelet, her mouth opened in surprised wonder. "It's- it's beautiful, but Joze," the gold with swirls of diamonds and amethysts twinkled and sparkled on her wrist. Her big eyes rolled up to him. "I can't accept this, Joze."

"Of course you can."

"No, I, even though they're not real gems I couldn't-"

"Oh *babi*, those are real. I wouldn't give you anything that couldn't rival those stunning eyes of yours."

"But, I don't understand, why are you giving me this?" She stared at it, twisting her arm like any woman would, watching it glint and sparkle.

"I told you. You needed something to go with that dress." He smiled seeing her admiring the jewelry.

Still staring at it, Glorie said, "You've bought me clothes, but I needed those, but this, no," she shook her head reaching for the clasp, "I can't possibly accept this."

Joze closed his hand around her wrist stopping her. "Accept it because it makes me happy. That's all you need to do."

Before she could take the bracelet off he unhooked his seatbelt, left the SUV and was striding around to open her door.

She didn't move, just looked at the hand he proffered to her. Then, obviously ill at ease, she allowed him to help her out of the vehicle.

Watching Glorie slide those hot gams out of the car, the tips of Joze's ears turned red. "Honey, you look like a parfait, beautiful, sweet and tasty, and I so want to eat you up."

Steadying on her heels, Glorie said shyly, "You look pretty good yourself, Joze." She smoothed a hand down his lapel, complimenting, "Very dashing," she blushed, "and handsome."

She turned towards the building so she didn't see him swallow hard, and his own face flush slightly with the compliment, or his eyes turn dusky with warm blue.

He slid his hand around her waist and walked her across the lot to the front of the building.

The parking area was half-filled with high-end cars. The building didn't look like a seedy sordid crummy structure. It was sleek with steel and black-tinted windows.

There were no pictures advertising scantily clad women, just the tasteful sign that announced, 'Club Llewpart.'

"What does the name mean?" Glorie asked looking around as if she expected naked women to be running in and out of the door. Could she remember the foreign name to tell the police, if, when she was set free? Would she tell? At this point, she was becoming very confused about her job, Joze, and her feelings for him.

"It means Leopard Club. My father named it. His uh, father, my grandfather's nickname was The Leopard," his mouth twisted wryly, "for a variety of reasons. Anyway, I inherited the club along with…um…other businesses."

He opened the door for her to walk through.

Stepping inside, Joze set his hand on her shoulder, then dropped it to her waist, securing her against his side. Every male in the place turned to look at her.

All the women had eyes on Joze, along with quick sneering glances of resentment and downright hostility at Glorie.

Feeling her shiver against him, Joze gently wisped a few loose tendrils over her shoulder then whispered in her ear, "Relax, *babi*, no one is going to hassle you."

Almost instantly a half a dozen women in all kinds of sleazy dress hurried over to gather around Joze. "Honey," a brunette pouted, "you've already chosen for the night? You didn't give one of a chance-"

A blonde put her hand on his chest, slipped two fingers between buttons to his skin and simpered, "What about later, babe, you'll be done with her by then, you'll be free for me." She slanted exotic green eyes at Glorie then dismissed her as if she was nothing more than a piece of lint.

Joze grasped the blonde's wrist and disengaged her from his chest and dropped her hand. "*Na.* I am not going to be free this evening. Or ever. Let me introduce my fiancée," he stopped mid-sentence at Glorie's gasp, which was eclipsed by the other women's screeches and groans, he realized he couldn't say her name.

If it got out, and it wasn't a common, name, they could come after him, and take her… He allowed the women's protesting chatter to cover as he pretended to say Glorie's name. Then he nodded, and quickly moved away pulling her with him.

When they were away from others, shocked, Glorie blurted, "Joze, what were you thinking? Why did you-"

He rolled both arms around her and pulled her close, set his forehead on hers. "Calm down, *babi*, I'm sorry. It just fell out of my mouth. I wanted them to just go away and stay away, it was the first thing that came to my mind without being rude or nasty."

His closeness was taking away some of her breath. His raw, masculine dynamism fanned right over her, making her skin quiver. Glorie rasped, "Why don't you just tell them to leave you alone?"

"I have. The night after I brought you home and I came here to check on business, and constantly since then. They just keep throwing themselves at me. I'm the boss, they will always chase me. Unless, or," he cupped her face with both hands, "until I sell the place." He brushed her lips, then sank in for a deep, devouring kiss.

She almost resisted, then liquesced like warm liquor pouring out hot and sweet against him, allowed him to sweep the inside of her mouth with his tongue, luring her to mate her tongue with his.

After a long, luxurious kiss, Joze drew back, but kept her enclosed in his embrace. He craved to kiss her all night long. Oddly, he could even do that without having sex. His dick was telling him different, but her lips were so sublime he could spend every minute for a solid year kissing her and it wouldn't be enough.

"Joze," her voice came out a hoarse whisper. Clearing it, she made it stronger, "You said, until you sell?"

His hand wound behind her neck, he massaged her skin with his strong fingers, nodding. "Yes. That's why I'm here tonight. There's a group of men interested in buying it."

Her eyes popped. "Really? Why? I mean why are you selling?"

He pulled her mouth back to his. "I'll explain later, over dinner, right now, I need this," he sucked on her lips like he was drowning and she was air.

"Wait, Joze," she protested, pressing her palms against his chest. Then, her fingers curled in, clutching his jacket in her fists. Her head tipped back letting him plunder her mouth until she copied his movements, learning what he wanted, what she liked.

A quiet cough came behind them. "Uh, Mr. Kane, so sorry but," the bartender waited, his eyes averted.

Joze dropped his arms and his eyes, his mouth clenched while he tried to keep his temper intact. He tugged at the lapels on his suit, straightening the jacket, then slid one hand around Glorie's waist. Composed now, he looked at the bartender. "Jules?"

The bartender cleared his throat. "Yes, sir, sorry to uh, interrupt you. However, the vault, I need you to open it. Manager Simmons is not in yet and I need the cash trays."

Joze considered bringing Glorie with him, but the rubber matting had holes all throughout for drainage and she had spiked heels, she'd break her neck, or her shoes. Undoubtedly she'd pitch a fit if he carried her over the mat.

"I'll be right there." Joze turned his back to the bartender and said to Glorie, "I'm sorry, I have to leave you briefly. I should only be a minute. Don't leave this spot, *iawn?*"

He kissed her lightly, ran a knuckle down her cheek and strode off to follow the bartender behind the bar.

An awkward faint smile on her face, Glorie set an arm on the bar and faced the wall behind it. She had no intentions of making eye contact with anyone, heaven forbid-

"Hey there, gorgeous. You here to audition?"

Chapter Twenty-Six

A suave voice beside her caused Glorie to turn.

The man, late thirties, auburn hair shone brightly under the bar lights, blue eyes stroked her body up and down.

She shook her head, said, "No, I uh," what could she say?

The man curved an arm around her on the bar counter boxing her in with a wall at her backside. "Wow," he enthused, his voice silky deep, "you are obviously a dancer with that body and those looks. Huh."

He leaned closer, smiled at her shrinking from him and her cheeks turning pink. Interest lifting his voice, he said, "A shy dancer. Never thought I'd see the day. The contrast, babe, fuckin' cookin.'" He held out his hand and introduced himself, "I'm Blaine Tuppon."

Glorie looked down at his hand and up to his dark blue eyes, unsure what to do. Her gaze darted around the bar looking for Joze, but he was nowhere to be seen.

Not to be rude, she shook his hand and responded meekly, "It's nice to meet you Mr. Tuppon." The thought to tell him who she really was and ask for him to call the police strangely never entered her head. Later, she would ponder on why that was.

His smile deepened, he didn't let go of her hand. "Honey, it's polite to announce your name when being introduced." He waited, cocking a brow at her silence, watching her nervously chew her lip.

"Okay, you are a shy one. It's really quite endearing, and," he leaned in, his mouth next to her ear, "hot." He pulled back watching her blush deepen.

"Listen, sweetheart, I'm in the talks to buy this bar from Jozadak Kane, so, I can handle your audition for him, although," he leaned in and whispered in her ear, "I think I will hire you regardless. So," he trailed a finger down her arm, still holding her hand even though she tugged at it. "Let's you and me hit the back room and you can show me what you got."

Pulling harder at her hand, her nerves shaking, she didn't want to cause a scene in Joze's club. Joze was mafia, heavens knows what this man was affiliated with. Firming her voice, she said, "You um, misunderstand, please let go of my hand," her soft lilt did nothing to dissuade Tuppon.

He moved the arm around her on the bar up to her shoulder and pulled her closer with the hand he still held. "Come on sweetheart, let's go. I'll hire you, I promise, but I want a private show first, then a little you and me time-"

"Why do you have your hands all over my fiancée, Tuppon?"

Joze was there, he heard Glorie's palpable sigh of relief.

But Tuppon didn't release her. "Hey, Kane, what's up?" He smirked. "Nice try," he chucked, "there's no way you of all people is engaged, what a joke." He hugged Glorie to his side. "I'm going to hire this little chickadee. We were just going out back so she can show me how she shakes her stuff."

"If you really want to keep those hands, you will get your paws off her, now." Joze's voice was dead calm, quiet. Cold enough to put a chill on Alaska.

Tuppon heard the undertone of threat. He dropped his hands, stood back and smoothed his hair back with his palms. "All right, Kane, don't get your briefs in a twist. You don't want your toys played with, don't leave them out alone."

"*Ie.*" Joze grasped Glorie's wrist and tugged her under his arm. "See you in the meeting." His gaze was direct with no mistaking his quiet order, and dismissal.

236

"Yeah, sure, see you there." Tuppon dipped his head to Glorie and said with a leering lift of one corner of his mouth, "I meant that promise, honey, I'll hire you. I'm looking forward to your audition." He bowed to her then turned and left them.

"Joze, I'm sorry, I didn't want to cause a scene, please don't be mad," her voice worried, Glorie made to move from him.

Holding onto her, Joze slid a hand under her jaw raising her head to him. "It's not your fault, *babi*, he's right, I shouldn't have left you unattended. You're too beautiful, guys are going to hit hard on you, especially in this type of establishment, and you're too sweet and shy and polite to know how to run them off. I hate that I'm going have to leave you again to go to the meeting."

"I could wait in the car," she offered.

His lips bunched with a shake of his head. "That's not going to happen. You would be even less safe there, like an exotic calico goldfish in a crystal bowl. Every wildcat in town would be scratching at the door."

"Joze, really-"

"Anyway," he hugged her, "we need to talk about how you can run people off without insulting them. But for now," he lowered his head, prodded her lips until they opened like a flower blooming to him and dove in tasting her sweetness.

His heart warmed, as did his dick when she gave back as good as he gave her. Pulling her closer, he rolled both arms around her, relishing her soft lips, her plush tender mouth, willing tongue, her breasts so flush against his chest,

"Ahem," someone behind them coughed, again. "Mr. Kane, we are waiting for you."

Holding her face, his thumbs on her cheeks, Joze sighed against her lips. One day, he would have her alone, with her all hot and willing like this, and no one to fucking interrupt them. The second he gets her heated up someone has to- of course this wasn't the place or time.

But it didn't hurt to get her used to being touched and kissed by him. He rolled his arm around her shoulders and turned to the man.

"*Ie*, I apologize." Joze bowed his head briefly in respect, shaking off the haze of lust.

"Well," the man chuckled, "I can certainly see why you were distracted." He nodded to Glorie and said, "You are very lovely, honey." He glanced at Joze waiting for an introduction. But Joze was frowning at him, his mouth shut tight.

"Uh," the man uttered awkwardly and turned back to Glorie and held his hand out. "How do you do, I am Trent Walker." The handsome, broad shouldered man in a designer suit, dark brown hair swept in waves to the side, deep brown eyes radiated his attraction to her.

Glorie resisted looking at Joze. She licked her lips, which both men watched intently, then took Walker's hand and shook it politely. "Hello, I'm-"

"Reece," Joze interjected quickly, "her name is Reece. Honey," he turned quickly to her before either could respond, and said, "I have to meet with these men now. "I'll," this was what he had dreaded, having to leave her alone in a damned strip club with a bunch of horny men. But the meeting shouldn't be long.

Joze looked around for a woman- there she was, he waved and called out, "Tina."

He caught the attention of a full-figured woman across the bar, fortyish with dark hair and dark eyes.

When Joze waved at her, she came right over and kissed him on the cheek. "Hello, Boss," she said while smiling, taking in the entire length of him, "you look good enough to eat."

Joze grinned. He said to Glorie, "Honey, I'm going to leave you with Tina here while I'm in the meeting. She's one of my managers, she will take good care of you," he said the last with narrowed eyes at Tina making his instruction clear- keep the wolves away.

His arm still around her, Joze bent and gave Glorie a quick kiss then said to Tina, "Take good care of, uh, Reece, for me, Tina."

"Of course, Bossman, anything for you." Tina grinned at him but without the coy coquette of the other women that swooned all over him. Even now, a dozen pairs of female eyes had never left the tall blond man.

"Come on, Reece, let me get you a drink." Tina took Glorie's arm pulling her from Joze's clutches, drawing her away.

"No alcohol, Tina, not until I'm back," Joze called out as the women moved through the small crowd that was building.

Tina waved back at him over her shoulder.

"Here ya go, sweetie, have a seat there." Tina pointed at a table and settled herself on a chair. Awkwardly, Glorie pulled a chair out and sat down.

"What would you like, to drink, Reece? Soda?"

"Uh, is there maybe some sweet tea?" Glorie folded her hands together and set them demurely in her lap.

"Sure thing." Tina waved at a barmaid who hustled right over and took the order.

Tina looked Glorie up and down. "Don't get me wrong, honey, you're gorgeous, but not Mr. Kane's usual type. You look, well, sweet. And there's no cynical glint in your eye, or slutty turn of your pretty lips."

She studied Glorie with blatant curiosity then commented, "Mr. Kane never comes into the club with a girl, why, I mean, why now? Why you?" She grinned, crossed her arms, set them on the table and leaned closer to Glorie.

Glorie scoured her brain trying to think of something to say, but this was all out of her league of experience.

Tina said, "Okay," and smiled amicably. "I admit, I'm nosy. He's treating you with kid gloves, horny ones of course, but I've never seen him act this way before. Never seen him kiss a woman in public, and he can't keep his hands off you. And then there's his concern that you not drink when he's not by your side.

"I saw how mad he was at that Tuppon fellow talking to you. First time I've ever seen the green bug of jealousy bite him." Tina snorted and chuckled at the same time.

Glorie's red face and silence only intrigued the manager that much more. She asked, "What is going on between you two? Seriously, hon, I've never seen him do PDA here. He chooses a woman and he discreetly goes to the back room, uh," Tina looked like she could have bitten her tongue. "I'm sorry, my big mouth, I love slamming my foot in it!" A robust laugh belted out of her.

The barmaid brought the tea, and a bourbon on the rocks for Tina.

Tina took a sip and said, "So, as I was so rudely asking, where did you and Joze meet?"

Glorie almost choked on her tea. She set her glass down and grabbed up a napkin dabbing at her mouth. Her face heated as she struggled to think of what to say. She couldn't tell her the truth- she was saved by the returning barmaid.

"Tina," the girl said, "there was a broken glass incident in the back, Jerry cut himself. He'll live but I think you should see him."

Tina looked from the barmaid to Glorie. "Oh, well, I'm sure you will be just fine. I'll only be gone a minute." She stood up.

Tina's gaze jutted around the room at the leering customers then back to Glorie. "You, uh, probably shouldn't encourage any men that will undoubtedly invade this table before I'm even out of sight." She smiled with a hint of worry.

Tina glanced at the door where Joze had disappeared into. "He's not a jealous or possessive person, but then again, like I said, I've never seen him look at another woman the way he was looking at you, or touch one so tenderly. But, our Mr. Kane can have a nasty temper, hon, you should keep that in mind." She scooted away to the back room.

Feeling like a sore thumb, Glorie glanced around looking for Joze but didn't see him. He must be in one of the back rooms, her lip curled, hopefully not the one where he *visited* with his women, oo, she felt a pang at the thought.

She needed to get away from Joze before she grew too attached to him. Just the act of looking around for the man with the blond hair and broad shoulders made her body suddenly heat up. Her face flamed, her breasts suddenly felt like they were swelling, her nipples hardened.

Her eyes were drawn to the door, should she make a run for it? She was in the city, she could certainly get to the police station.

Her gaze sifted through the room, lighting on the bartender who was staring at her, then her gaze moved to the bouncer at the door who hadn't taken his eyes off of her. Did they have orders to stop her if she fled?

Squeezing the lemon in her tea, she stirred it with the straw mixing the sweet of the sugar with the hint of sour then took a sip. Besides the men at the bar that were blatantly eyeing her, she felt like there were a hundred pairs of eyes lancing right through her. She was so uncomfortable she couldn't stand it.

She flagged the barmaid as she passed. "Miss, can you tell me where the ladies' room is, please?"

"Of course," the young woman replied. Pointing, she said, "Go down that hall past the big room on your right and it's on your left."

"Thank you." Glorie stood up.

"Sure thing." The woman scurried off to serve a drink.

Trying to move with confidence and not breaking a leg in the heels, Glorie kept her eyes straight ahead to not see the unrelenting gazes that followed her. She hoped Joze would not be angry that she went to the restroom.

There were three stages that were dark at the moment. Two had poles on them, the third had silk streamers hanging from the ceiling. The large extensive bar took over the entire west wall. The lights were amber bright, they would probably be lowered later when the shows started.

Square tables so they could be linked for bigger parties and more intimate round tables filled the rest of the room that had two inclined levels for viewing the shows.

Up in the wall in the back there was a place for someone to work the lights and music for the stages. Seeing curtains at the rear of the stages, Glorie assumed behind them were changing rooms and such.

When she reached the hall she let out her held breath.

Finally feeling out of the sight of the crowd, Glorie made her way down the hall.

She passed a few doors on the left but saw the bigger one on the right was a distance down the corridor. She moved as quickly as the spiked heels would let her.

Glorie was almost to the room on the right when she heard someone call out, "Reece!"

She hesitated, that was the name Joze had introduced her with.

Turning around, she saw Trent Walker striding swiftly towards her. Joze must have sent him.

When he reached her, she smiled politely and said, "Mr. Walker, did Joze ask you to get me?"

His mouth quirked. "No, sugar. He's still in the meeting. I told them I needed to use the John. But really," he scooped up her hand, "I came to find you."

Everything lately was bewildering for Glorie. "I- I'm not sure I understand..."

He kissed her hand like he had before, but this time he didn't release her. He moved up to grip her arm and now strong-armed her down the hall.

"Wait, stop, what are you doing?" Panic starting to rise, at first she allowed him to drag her from surprise, but now she dug her heels in.

"Come on, sugar, everyone knows Joze doesn't give a shit about the women he bangs. He won't care who takes his leavings."

He was literally dragging her now. Craning his head in the room on the right, he said, "This will do. We can use this room."

"No! Stop! I'll scream-"

"Ah, hell, don't be that way, sugar." One arm around her like a belt squeezing half her breath out, Trent felt inside for a light switch. He found it, flipped it, then yanked her inside and closed the door.

Glorie backed away from him, her eyes flitting around the room seeking a weapon, another door, anything.

Then with two swift strides he moved to her and lassoed her with his arm.

She opened her mouth to scream, he clamped his hand over it and shoved her across a few feet, slamming her up against the wall.

Trent turned from a polite businessman to a vicious rapist in the crack of a whip.

Muscling her against the wall, his hand scrambled up her dress reaching to grip her panties, his other hand slipped off her mouth, she let out a piercing shriek.

He jammed his hand back over her mouth, holding her shoulder to the wall with his elbow, he got his fingers on the top of her panties.

The door crashed open so hard it hit the wall and bounced back.

Joze had already burst into the room before the door slammed back closed behind him.

"*What the fuck-*" with the roar of a rampaging bull, Joze tore across the room and wrapped his fingers around Trent's neck.

He wrenched him from Glorie, then clawing his fingers like metal wire digging into his neck, he squeezed until Trent collapsed to the floor.

Joze followed him down, still holding his neck, he started bashing Trent's head on the floor.

"Joze!" Glorie screamed, ran over and dropped beside the men. She threw her arms around Joze so he would have to hurt her to break her hold and fling her away.

"Please stop!" she cried, holding onto him for dear life.

"*Duw*, God, Glorie, let go of me!" Joze barked at her, his hands still around Trent's neck. The man was still alive, his legs kicked frantically out at the open air.

"No, let go of him, Joze!" Glorie whispered frantically, her lips against Joze's hard cheek.

Joze forced himself to release the man. Kneeling, he rolled back to sit on his heels and dragged his sleeve across his forehead, panting like a runaway horse.

Then he curled his arm around Glorie and stood up with her.

Catching her chin, he tilted her head up. His gaze steeped with worry at her ashen face, he asked her, "You *iawn*, *babi*? Did he hurt you?"

"No, no, I'm okay," her voice shook as hard as her hands that tugged ineffectively at her skirt trying to pull it back down.

Joze spread a big hand on her back to hold her then he fixed her skirt for her, tugging it back into place.

Ignoring the man with his hands clutching his throat, gasping for air and writhing on the floor, Joze set both hands on her shoulders.

"*Duw, babi*, I was suspicious when that bastard said he was going to the bathroom, I went out after him. I was so fucking freaked when I saw you were gone. The barmaid said you'd gone to the ladies' room, I was heading there when I heard you scream."

Shaking his head, he snarled, "Tina told me she had to leave you alone. Damn, she is so fucking fired."

"No, no, please don't Joze. I couldn't bear it if you did that. It wasn't her fault. It was his." Glaring down at Trent still gagging and gasping, she was unaware she'd curved her body into the corner of Joze's arm for safety.

She looked up at Joze. "He said you wouldn't care if he…uh, had me, that you don't care about your, uh, leftovers."

If Glorie wasn't there Joze would have spit on Walker and given him a swift kick in the kidneys for saying that to her.

"Ah, *babi*, I admit what he said was true. I've been a cold hard dog. But, not you," he pulled her against his chest and stroked her hair. He chuckled, "I haven't had you yet, so you're not really leftovers."

She pulled from him. "That's not funny, Joze."

He tightened his grip. "I'm sorry, honey, you're right. I was just trying to break the tension. I came for you, *babi*. Believe me, it's true, *na*, I would not have gone after another woman. I would figure she chose to be with the other guy and let her go without a second thought. But you," he raked at his hair with a trembling hand and let out a breath.

He said, "Listen," and tenderly sifted a few tendrils of fiery hair out of her eyes. "Do you still want to go to dinner? Before you answer, let me say that I really want to. Please say yes. But," he sighed, "I will understand if you say you want to go home, and we will. Whatever you want."

Home. The word bothered both of them. The ranch wasn't her home.

"Glorie?" he asked, hopefulness clear in his deep voice.

Chapter Twenty-Seven

"Uh, okay. I guess, we can um, go to dinner." She turned her body so she couldn't see the man gasping on the floor.

Joze hardly took his eyes off Trent, not trusting the man to not jump up and attack. Before Joze had stood up he had quickly checked him for weapons.

"*Iawn*, great. *Ta, fy cariad,* thank you, my love. Let's get the hell out of here. There's a back door, we won't have to pass by anyone. I had the bouncer and a couple other employees keeping an eye on you, but they figured you were fine in the ladies room." He smoothed his raked hair down.

"Hell, I should have known a beautiful sweet woman like you would be instant prey. I never should have brought you here." Rolling an arm protectively around her shoulders, he led her around the pummeled Trent Walker, then down the hall and out the door.

They drove in silence, each deep in their own thoughts.

When they had gone a few miles deeper into the city, Joze turned down South Chaparral Avenue. The long commercial Texan street was lined with shops and restaurants and interlaced with bars and businesses.

Joze pulled into the lot of one of the restaurants and parked the car.

After helping Glorie out, they walked hand in hand to the restaurant Corbeille. It was still early, just past six. The sun was starting to saunter down the horizon, the air was dry and warm.

Even though it was early in the evening, the dining room was crowded. Guests sat at white table-clothed tables. Pink tulips draped their long necks out of ivory vases on the tables as well as other places scattered around the room.

Individual candles flickered romantically from crystal ampules near the tulips. Soft, muted music mingled with conversations. Tall, narrow windows let in ambient light.

Cutout stencil partitions in light green separated some areas. To one side, deep cherry wood and glass French doors opened into a noisy bar, spurts of loud voices burst through each time the doors opened.

The other side was the restaurant. The floors were pale walnut planked, pretty but not noise insulating.

Glorie and Joze were seated near the fireplace at the far end of the room where it was slightly more secluded.

Encased in antique, light green wood trimmed with gold, tiny marble stones glistened around the fireplace, reflecting the crackling flames. With the balmier temperatures a faux fire was burning.

Joze pulled out Glorie's chair and then seated himself next to her.

The server appeared at their side with glasses of ice water and a bread basket. The warm bread filtered toasty in the air. A dish of creamy butter was placed on the table along with a separate bowl that contained olive oil infused with spices for dipping.

Joze asked Glorie if she would like a cocktail. Joze already knew she probably didn't. The time they'd worked at the Seraphim Saloon and her time at the ranch, he'd only see her drink soda or sweet tea. She declined. He told the man to send the sommelier to their table to order wine.

As soon as the server departed, Joze picked up Glorie's hand, twined his fingers in hers and set them on the table.

"*Babi*," he said softly. She turned to him with a shy sweet smile. "The flames in the fireplace have nothing on your vibrant hair."

The compliment brought pink to her cheeks, she shyly ducked her head. He curled a finger under her chin, lifted it and kissed her softly, briefly. The same firelight shot brilliant flickers over Joze's light hair.

He sat back regarding her thoughtfully. "Glorie, are you okay after, you know, the club?"

Their hands still entwined, Glorie relaxed back in the white leather cushioned chair. "I," she hesitated, peeped at him through her curly lashes.

His countenance was serious. Lips soft but firm, the distinctive blue eyes dark in the lowly lit room were wide open, earnestly waiting for her response.

Glorie reached to touch the petals of the pink tulip, then set her hand in her lap. She turned her head to him. "I don't know, Joze. I...am very confused. Disoriented. My life is...upside down."

Her eyes were drawn to the bracelet he'd given her. Her pupils flared at the beauty of it on her wrist. "This bracelet, Joze, I can't-"

"We already talked about it. You must keep it. Do you want to hurt my feelings?"

She paused, he waited patiently, intently studying her features.

High round cheekbones, plush lips that put the tulip to shame, the fiery hair a beautiful backdrop for those unique crystal eyes.

He was drawn to kiss her again, but he didn't want to embarrass her or draw undue attention to them. With her flaming hair, and his white-blond locks, they were hardly unnoticeable as it was.

Thankfully, he was well known in the restaurant and the staff protected his notable identity by seating them so they were away from the bigger crowd, and with their backs to most of the rest of the room.

"Tell me why you feel disoriented." He knew why, it was obvious, but he wanted to distract her from giving him the bracelet back. Seeing it on her wrist gave him a feeling of...not ownership, well, maybe. He was finally staking his claim.

He'd always denied it when asked, but, being honest with himself, he had laid claim to her the second he tossed her over his shoulder like a caveman and carried her out of the saloon that night.

She was young and naïve, but she had to be aware of his intense interest in her at this point. Unused to the feelings she stirred in him, and afraid of them, he just kept bungling, handling his behavior with her so badly. He continued to behave like a bully, when really, he just wanted to cherish her.

Glorie glanced at him then away, fiddling with the bracelet. "Joze, I barely got hired as an officer. Then, uh, after, my…recovery from Ian's assault," her lids lowered. "I was back to work only a week or so, then, with no training I was snatched out and foisted to work undercover to, well you know what my mission was. Then," she took a deep breath, "I was attacked by those men in the saloon. Then, you took me," her eyes rolled up to his.

A spasm of guilt pulled his lips in, but he didn't look away from her.

She said quietly, "And, you've kept me prisoner. You've threatened me, cursed me, you threatened to- to rape old ladies the day you took me. I…I don't know what your plan is for me, whether it's to- to free me, keep me, or, kill me. I've been assaulted several times now, not counting the times by you." She peered at him.

His eyes dropped, dark color swept his hard cheeks. He released her hand and folded his together on the table.

Glorie slipped hers down to clasp them in her lap. When he said nothing, she asked in a hushed voice, "Joze?"

He didn't look at her.

Murmuring uneasily, "What…what are you going to do with me?" she watched unreadable emotions flicker across his face. "Joze?"

He leaned over, hands folded, his shoulders hunched, he said quietly, "You must know by now my threats against those women were totally empty, I didn't know how else to make you eat. I was worried you would pass out or get sick. You're so…tender, gracious, nothing like I'm used to, so I don't know how to…treat you properly."

Her gaze stayed steady on him.

"I will never hurt you, Glorie, never." He slipped his fingers under her jaw to hold it up. His mouth very close to hers he murmured, "But I do know what I'd like to do to you," the curve of his lips and the hot glitter in his eyes told Glorie clearly what he meant.

When she blushed and dropped her eyes, he brushed her lips with his then let go of her.

"*Babi*, please believe me when I say that I have no intentions of..." how to say it without being crude as she's accused him of? "Using you. I mean sexually, and then tossing you aside. I want more than that," he paused, watching her face color then pale.

"That's not what I asked, Joze-"

Seeing the waiter making his way over to them, Joze said quietly, "*Babi*, for now, let's just enjoy our evening, and each other. I have somewhere I want to show you after dinner."

Before she could ask any more questions, the waiter was at their table.

They both ordered the Aubergine du Bayou Tèche, eggplant fried with crabmeat, shrimp, and Cajun hollandaise with ham, served with caviar potatoes and seasoned vegetables.

The sommelier approached and handed Joze the wine menu.

After a quick perusal, Joze ordered a bottle of Lirac, Domaine Maby.

"Yes, sir." The sommelier smiled broadly taking the menu from Joze with a polite bow. He said, "Lilac, a full-bodied red, blooming with grenache, mourvèdre, and syrah, and a flavor of red and black fruit on the finish."

Glorie was red-faced and Joze frowned when the sommelier then apologetically asked her for ID.

At her panicked look, Joze stared the sommelier in the eye and said, "She left her purse at home. If there is a problem, please have the manager come and see me."

Without hesitation, the sommelier nodded and said, "Nice choice, sir," and poured a small amount for Joze to taste. After a sip, at Joze's nod, he poured Glorie's then filled Joze's glass.

While pouring, the sommelier informed them, "Lirac is located 10km west of Châteauneuf du Pape on the opposite bank of the

Rhône River. Their grapes are," he kissed his fingertips then flourished them into the air and left to place their order.

Joze raised his glass of wine to Glorie. She picked hers up and they touched glasses.

His voice low and husky, he said, "Maybe we can actually go to that winery, together, some day. I would like to take you there, experience it together."

Her long lashes swept down covering her expression, she said nothing, just took a sip of her wine and set the glass down.

Not wanting to push her, Joze said with a soft smile, "So, *bach babi*, what would you like to talk about?"

She licked her lips, gave him a small smile in return and said, "Tell me about the horses, Joze. What are you training them for?"

A safe topic. Joze grinned and told her about the horses he was breeding, and other aspects of the farm until the waiter served the meal.

When the server left, Joze raised his wineglass and said, "Salute me again, *babi*," he waited until she raised her glass to his.

He clinked them together gently and murmured in a low sexy voice, "To our trip to Europe," he quickly took a sip before she could respond, not sure he wanted to hear what she would say.

She looked him in the eye then dropped her unsure gaze, took a sip and set her glass on the table.

A few minutes later, Glorie speared a shrimp and said, "Joze…"

"Hmmm?" Swallowing a chunk of caviar potato, he took a sip of wine.

"Maria said that you, that your father forced you to take over the businesses. How could he do that?"

Holding the wineglass by the stem, Joze stared at the burgundy liquid shimmering in the candlelight. He took another sip then set the goblet down.

"My father and his father, built the business up, one-by-one, atop one bloody body after another. They travelled back and forth from Wales to America to run the enterprises."

He picked up his fork and tasted some eggplant before continuing. "Although my father wanted me to run the businesses, I was too young at the time, so he had tried to push my older brothers into taking over the day-to-day running of the companies. But, they fled to the military.

"I was the youngest of the boys, I have a little sister around your age. From the minute I was born, my father trained me, uh," he didn't want to go into violent details so he skipped that part. His father's cruel brutality towards him as a child, and a teen, was great training for the rigors of the military.

"Anyway, I also tried to escape to the military. I did several tours. In Wales, and in the U.S. with the Marines. I was part of a special elite team of snipers, and a covert hand-to-hand combat and tactical unit." His eyes blanked as he recalled his time in combat, rescuing hostages, the exhilaration of the danger.

His life was almost cut short more times than he wanted to remember. "So, my father kept contacting me, begging me, telling me lives depended on the enterprises, my mother, my grandmother, my sister, employees and their families, all needed the income."

He sighed, broke off a piece of bread. Picking up his knife, he buttered the bread heavily. "I let him convince me. I quit the service and came home."

Glorie took a small sip of wine. Dabbing her lips on the cloth napkin, "So, then?" she prompted him to continue.

"Ah, shortly after I was learning the ropes, my father died. It all fell into my hands." His eyes darkened, he picked up his wineglass. His father had been viciously murdered, another little snippet he didn't share with Glorie. Gripping the glass so hard it looked about to break, he took a hefty drink before setting it down.

He turned to her, his eyes travelling from the tip of her nose and cheeks slightly awash with pink from the alcohol, to her pretty lips. "Glorie, I didn't ask for this life. But I agreed to do it for my father."

"He's gone now. What is-"

"What's keeping me in the life?" He snorted. "You have no idea the strings that tie and bind with blood and money, and power. A noose that tightens with every twist and turn. It's a big web, everything connects to everything.

251

"I have been able to turn some of the industries legit. Re-funneled the funds so they're not laundered. I don't need the money personally, I have more than enough to keep me very comfortable for the rest of my life." He watched her cut a piece of eggplant and chew it with delight. Finally, she was eating. Praise the lord.

"So, my funds are secured in accounts all over the world. The meeting tonight as I told you earlier was to put a line out, fishing to see what I would need to do to sell the strip club. I don't want to be a part of that life anymore, but I can't just close down a business and put so many people out of work."

This time Glorie sought his hand. She covered it with hers. "That is wonderful, Joze, I am so proud of you."

Joze never thought six little words coming from a petite female, a cop no less, would have such an impact on his heart, and his pride.

Not moving his hand from under hers, he drank some more wine. She lifted her hand off his to pick up her fork. His skin felt cold, bereft, when she moved from him.

Imagining their warmth still on his hand, he watched her slender fingers so gracefully hold her utensils, clasp the wine glass.

He set his elbows on the table and threaded his fingers. Touching his chin to his hands, he said in a low hush, "It's the rivals, *babi*, they are more dangerous than the law to us."

He watched her neatly fork a slice of ham and dab it in the hollandaise sauce, everything she did was done with pretty grace.

Changing the subject, he said, "Daniel mentioned that you have a sister." His lips hardened, he said bitterly, "Shows what a cold-hearted bastard I am, Glorie. I was worried about your handler, or the other police, or even the fuckers that tried to rob the saloon and take you."

He slid a sidelong glance at her and saw her lips quirk. He knew she didn't like his cursing, he was still working on curbing it.

"Anyway, I was concerned about all those factors, never once did I consider family or friends that would be worried for you. Except for maybe a boyfriend, and," he shrugged, "I didn't care about him if he existed."

Glorie turned her heart-shaped face to him. "My sister wouldn't really have known for a while that I was…missing. She knew I was going undercover. But, when Shana doesn't hear from me soon," her brows wrinkled together, "she will be frantic with worry."

She peered at him then away. "We had terrible arguments over my going undercover. Shana was frightened to death something devastating would happen to me." Her lip twisted wryly, "It would seem, she was right.

He frowned with rueful guilt. "So, uh, what about your mom, your parents?"

"My mother was sick. She uh, passed last year. My sister and I only had each other. We lost contact with dad after the folks disowned us, but recently my father sent me a postcard. I think he wants to mend bridges. He is still in the religious commune. But, basically, it's only my sister and I."

"I have a disposable cell. You can call your sister tomorrow."

Her lips parted. "Really? I can?"

He nodded.

She said very softly, "Thank you, Joze."

He felt like *shyt*. That she had to ask his permission to call her sister. He knew it would be a matter of time before he would have to let her go, but he didn't want to think about it now.

They shared dessert of chocolate cake drizzled with raspberry sauce.

Joze paid the bill and by the time they got to the Bentley, the sun had almost set but it still blazed brilliant orange behind the building tops as it sank.

As he drove down the road, Joze said, "I have something I want to show you before we go…home."

Glorie smiled out the side window watching the passing shops. She turned to him. "Where are we going?"

He smiled furtively at her. "You'll see."

Joze drove a few miles then turned into the lot in front of a big, sprawling cement building painted in beige and white.

After parking the car, he went around and helped her out.

She was staring at the building, perplexed, but she saved her questions.

Joze walked her to the glass door, opened it for her to go inside.

There was a lobby and two halls and what appeared to be numerous rooms up and down the halls. A middle-aged woman hurried over when she saw Joze.

"Mr. Kane! What a nice surprise. You weren't expected back until Saturday for the game."

"Joze, Mrs. Sariel, please, just Joze." He nodded to Glorie and started to introduce her, "This is," he paused, then said firmly, "Glorie." He didn't explain their relationship and having good manners, Mrs. Sariel didn't ask.

"Nice to meet you, Glorie. What a pretty name." The older woman's voice was warm and friendly.

"Uh, thank you. I'm pleased to meet you too," Glorie responded with a pleasant smile if still baffled.

"We're going to just wander down the hall and back. Come on, honey." Joze took Glorie's hand, smiled at Mrs. Sariel's very curious look at Glorie and they sauntered towards the hall on the left.

Joze stopped at the first door. They didn't go in, just peered through the glass window.

Inside was a group of young people, ages approximately from 8 to 21, maybe older. Most of them were playing a variety of instruments.

"What-" Glorie started to ask.

"Let me show you then I'll tell you on the way home." Holding her hand, Joze led her to another room.

Inside were youngsters again, these had books in front of them and were staring with interest at a person writing on a blackboard.

The next room contained teens that were singing, surrounded by sound production equipment.

They passed more rooms like those until they got to a big room. It was a gym. Inside there was a basketball game going on, the participants wild and enthusiastic.

The chamber past that one had martial arts, then after that, a group of girls and a few boys doing ballet. Yet another room there were kids painting on canvases and a few working with clay to make pottery.

When they returned to the lobby, two boys around ten tore loose from a young man with them and hurled themselves at Joze. Both boys threw their arms around him and hugged him squealing.

Glorie was shocked to see Joze laugh and hug them back, then ruffle the tops of their heads.

"Mr. Joze! Mr. Joze!" They both yelled, vying for his attention.

Then one hollered out, "I got an A on the first test!"

The other one hopped up and down and shouted, "I got chosen for the tennis team, Mr. Joze!" The boys jumped and bounced around Joze and Glorie.

"Okay," Joze said laughing. "Matt, Roman, this nice lady is Miss Glorie. We'll be back on Saturday to watch the big game, okay?"

Both boys settled for a second and said in unison with practiced demure, "Nice to meet you, Miss Glorie," before they started hopping again.

The young man who had been with them came over. After nodding his greeting to Joze with a grin, he collected the boys and ushered them noisily down the hall.

Matt turned around and yelled, "See you at the game Mr. Joze and Miss Glorie!"

Joze grinned at the bewildered look on Glorie's face. "Come on, let's go." He took her out to the car and bundled her in then climbed in the driver's side and had them quickly on their way.

"All right, Joze, I'm ready, tell me what that was all about?" Her face alight with interest, she turned to face the big man behind the wheel.

His large hands making the wheel look small, so strong they looked like he could crush the metal wheel if he chose to. His long legs bookended the steering wheel.

"It's, ah, one of our, my, charities. It's to keep the kids off the street at night. There's nothing to do in Chie except get into trouble.

A lot of our young people were going from school to jail. Even those in grammar school. I have the means to help." He shrugged as if was nothing. "So I do."

Glorie wordlessly gawked at him.

He glanced back and forth from her to the road and back. A frown drew his brows over his eyes. "Say something, Glorie." Maybe she didn't believe him.

"I…gosh Joze, I'm speechless. That is so awesome." She set her hand on his arm. "Clearly, those children, they love you. It was amazing, Joze, so amazing. I'm," her hand over her heart, she gazed at him with pride and wonderment. This gangster, outlaw, had a heart hidden deep inside of him that was pure gold.

Joze kept his hand firmly on the wheel, he didn't look at her palm on his arm for fear she'd move it. Then she did, setting it back in her lap.

"Glorie, I didn't show you that to brag, or blow my own horn, or whatever, I just…" he glanced at her, "wanted you to not think I was all bad."

"I know." She stared silently out the window.

After a few quiet miles, he asked, "Are you all right? What are you thinking about?"

"I…" she faltered. "I don't really want to share my thoughts right now. Okay?"

His forehead creased. "Of course. Whatever makes you comfortable, *babi*."

When they got to the outskirts of the city, Joze pulled over.

"Oh." Glorie frowned remembering the blindfold. In a way it made her feel safe. If he was going to kill her he wouldn't care if she knew how to find the ranch. She sat still as he tied the kerchief around her eyes.

When he finally pulled into the long winding gravel road to the ranch, he untied the blindfold. "I'm sorry about that, it's just-"

"It's all right, Joze. I understand. Joze, why did you come up with that name you called me at the club?"

He glanced at her as he parked the car and smiled. "Reece. It's really from Rhys. It's sort of like Glory in Welsh."

"Oh. It's kind of...cute." She grinned at him, then yawned delicately behind her slim hand.

His smile peaceful he said, "Let's get you inside and to bed. It's been a long day." He helped her out of the SUV and walked her through the quiet house to their rooms.

Joze stayed with her when they entered her room. "So," he spoke softly, "Melissa said you would need help getting out of that dress. I mean," he uttered quickly, "she said you couldn't reach that zipper on your own. So, I'm going to have to give you a hand, all right?"

Her lips pursed, eyes narrowed. But he had a look of pure innocence, so she nodded. "I guess so."

"Turn around, *babi*." He waited while she shyly turned her back to him. Joze raised his hands, he looked at them, they were shaking. He couldn't believe he wanted to touch her so badly he was shaking.

He took a deep breath then reached for the zipper. Using his finger and thumb, he slowly glided it down her back. When it reached the end, he lightly drew his fingertips down the smooth curve of her bare back. Then he put his hands gently on her shoulders and turned her around to face him.

The room was semi-dark, the full moon hung like a silver ornament in the window.

Joze slowly pulled the front of the dress down to her waist. The cool silvery moonlight pale on her fair skin, he set his hands on her waist, then moved them up to lightly, briefly, palm her breasts over the strapless silky bra. "Glorie," he sighed, "you are so beautiful."

He knelt in front of her to peel the dress completely off her but she held her hand out staying him.

"No, please, don't Joze."

"Glorie, let me worship you, please *babi*, let me pleasure you, show you how good we can be together." He didn't move any further, set his hands on his knees.

Looking up at her, the fire clear in his blue eyes, he said, "I will just bring you pleasure, I won't push myself on you, honey. No, uh, intercourse, just let me show you how good it can feel, my touch, my mouth."

Joze tilted his head back further to see her. His light eyes rapidly darkening with desire, peered up through hooded lids and thick lashes, he waited, hoping.

His stomach clenched when he saw how sad she looked. "Glorie," his voice gentle, he took her hand, "we can become closer, in all ways. I think intimacy will help, do you?"

She shook her head, the flaming curls danced around her shoulders. "No, please, not tonight. That man, Trent, I feel…dirty, and, helpless. I don't like it." She shook her head again, crossed her arms over her chest with her hands on her shoulders.

Joze dropped his head. What an ass he was. Trent Walker had almost raped her tonight, another few minutes and he would have already shoved himself in Glorie.

Walker was ruthless, he hadn't cared how young, or innocent, or unwilling Glorie was. He was just ripping her panties off and was going to brutally fuck her against the wall, and she had been so helpless to stop him.

Joze's stomach quivered, he wiped his forehead. It had been close, too close, and it was his fault for bringing her to that place, and leaving her alone. He needed to give her some martial arts training so she wouldn't be so damned vulnerable.

He stood up with a demurring sigh. "I understand. I'm sorry. I'm a thoughtless brute. I won't hassle you honey."

She didn't move. He couldn't help his hot gaze lingering on her breasts spilling over the silken bra. The meager light spreading soft glows and shadows over them like they were rich luscious moons.

He stared so long, his pupils heated. Glorie moved her arms closer together to cover herself.

"Don't, Glorie, you're just so breathtaking, I can't get enough of looking at you." He put his hands on her waist, then raised one to hold the front of her throat, his thumb caressing her cheek, he leaned in and gently took her lips with his.

When she leaned into him with a tremble, he almost didn't stop. But he knew she would undoubtedly try to stop him when he really started loving her, and he didn't know if at that point he would have the will power he would need to stop, so he slowly stepped away.

"I would like you to come to the basketball game with me next Saturday. I take the kids out for wings and burgers after. Then the next weekend, we can go to dinner at this nice little Italian place, just uh, you and me, it has the best homemade pasta and ciabatta slipper bread in the country. The chianti," he closed his mouth, took a breath, he was rambling. "Anyway, you think about it, okay?"

She didn't respond, he didn't expect her to. His eyes dropped with longing to her breasts, to her tiny waist, up to her glimmering eyes.

Then he pulled the dress back up, she put her hand over the front to hold it, and he walked to the door.

"Good night, Glorie." He stepped through the threshold and closed the door.

Chapter Twenty-Eight

The next morning Joze had already been working outside for an hour before breakfast was served.

After washing up, he entered the dining area and sat down beside Glorie. He was pleased when she smiled her welcome instead of moving stiffly away from him. "I have something for you, *babi*."

"Oh? What is it?" she asked with interest.

He held out his palm and opened it, in the middle of his hand was a phone. "I'm offering a bargain. You eat a good breakfast, and right after we'll call your sister. What do you say?"

Her eyes went from the phone to him, a smile happily curved her lips. She nodded. "It's a deal."

They ate heartily of blueberry-topped waffles, toast and sausages, then when they were done, Joze took her into his study and handed her the phone. "I have to ask you to put it on speaker, honey."

Glorie frowned, she wasn't used to people not trusting her. But, he was being kind, he didn't have to do this at all.

She took the phone with a nod and quickly dialed her sister's number. A huge grin spread across her face when she answered.

She said eagerly, "Shana? It's me, Glorie," and perched on the edge of the couch. Joze set a hip on the cushioned arm next to her.

There was a short silence, then a quick intake of breath, then her sister, her voice deep with a sob of hope, cried, "Glorie, baby, is that you? Are you all right? Where are you, let me come and get you!"

Glorie glanced at Joze before answering.

He folded his hands together in his lap as if to keep himself from touching her. His eyes were gangster cold, he was putting himself in a treacherous position by letting her make this call.

Taking a breath, Glorie said quietly, "Uh, Shana, I'm just fine, I'm not hurt."

"What happened, Glorie? That detective, Luc Bolton, I called him and called him but he is avoiding me. Says he can't talk about it. But then he asks me if I've heard from you! I just knew there was something wrong."

Before Glorie could respond, Shana rushed on, "I went to your unit head, but Lieutenant Birch said all he knew was that you were pulled for undercover. Glorie, it's been weeks, why haven't you called me? Even if you were undercover, I knew you would call me if you could...I've been so worried!"

"I'm so sorry, Shana, to make you worry about me. I'm-"

Joze put his hand over the phone, didn't say anything, just looked at her. Then he moved his hand.

"I am just fine Shana."

"Where are you, sis? I'll come right now and get you!"

Joze put his hand over the phone again and shook his head. He pointed at his watch. He had told her it would be short in case there was a trace on the call.

"Um, I have to go, Shana. Please don't worry."

"No! Wait, Glorie- when will I hear from you again?" Her voice rose in panic.

Glorie cringed at the worry in her sister's voice. Her hand at her throat she glanced at Joze, he nodded his head. She lowered hers and spoke softly, "I'll call again, Shana. Please don't worry, I am fine, I promise, I-"

Joze pointed at his watch again.

"I have to go. Goodbye, Shana, I love you."

As Shana was saying, "I love you too," Joze took the phone from Glorie, clicked it off and slipped it in his pocket.

Glorie turned her head from him so swiftly her hair flew over, covering her face.

He set his hand lightly on her shoulder. "Glorie," he said softly.

"Thank- thank you, Joze. I really appreciate it-" The last words cut off with a choking sob, then she ran from him, down the hall to her room.

He stood staring at the empty hallway.

"You're hurting her, son. You need to let her go." Daniel moved to stand beside Joze. "I don't think she will throw you under the bus. Even if she did, she can't tell them where you live, she doesn't know where we are. Not even what town we're in. At the time, you had a valid reason for taking her. You were rescuing her. Our lawyers would make mincemeat out of any kidnapping case. Just, let her go, and stay low, out of sight until it blows over."

"They can get me at any of the businesses, Daniel, if they want to pick me up. Besides, right now, my Intel tells me that they might think I'm involved with the attempted robbery and battle at the saloon, or with Glorie being missing, but there's no proof. I'm safe, for now." Joze was still staring blankly at the hall as if he thought she might return.

"Ah, so stay away from the establishments for a while. Even so, I don't think she would tell that you kidnapped her. She knows those robbers that day at the saloon were a real threat. You saved her life, at your own peril, and you didn't have to. She knows you took her to protect her."

Joze snorted. "Really? I guess I couldn't have just dropped her off at the local police station after grabbing her, huh?"

"Ah, with their corruption so apparent? Huh." Daniel snorted, an unlit cigarette dangled out of his mouth. Chewing on it, he asked, "So then, she had nothing on you that could have been used to prosecute you. So why did you keep her?"

His tone slightly sarcastic, Joze muttered, "I don't know."

The two men stood in camaraderie smoking and staring blankly out the window.

After some time, "You know," Daniel said, blowing out a flume of smoke. "I called to get a price on putting siding on the house. They can start as early as next week." He slid a nonchalant side-glance at his nephew.

Joze opened his mouth, then shut it. He nodded. "Yeah. Sure, Daniel, that sounds good. Go ahead and get started on it." He was unaware of Daniel's shocked but pleased expression.

With a sad longing gaze down the hall where Glorie had gone, Joze turned and strode through the room and out the door. He went straight to his truck, hopped in, spewing gravel in a cloud behind him as he floored it down the road.

He stayed away a few days. When Glorie asked where he was, everyone said they didn't know.

She knew his team knew, they just weren't telling, although Diego intimated that Joze was on a bender. Yesterday Linc had left and didn't return until morning.

Glorie helped Daniel with repairs, feeding the animals and grooming the horses.

After lunch she went into her room for a nap. She'd gotten up before dawn and had been outside working for hours. No one made her do it, she really enjoyed working on the farm and she was grateful Joze allowed her to do what she wanted. He could have kept her locked in her room.

She passed through Joze's room to get to hers. His bed was still made like it had been for days. He hadn't slept in it. She wondered if he was staying with a woman. Or women. She hated to admit that thought bothered her.

But, she knew what kind of man he was since the beginning. Just because he treated her kindly, protectively, didn't mean he owed her anything. Her mouth turned down glumly, she mustn't forget he took her and was still holding her against her will.

Glorie thought about the night he took her out to dinner. The time at the strip club was horrible. From the women throwing themselves at and on Joze, to Trent Walker's assault on her, she shivered. But later, the elegant dinner, his attentiveness to her, he never even glanced at another woman.

She smiled, then at the rec place later with the children. Who would have thought tough, icy, crude Jozadak Kane would be so heartfelt to do what he does for them. And it wasn't pretend or for show, the children were very familiar with him and they obviously loved him.

What she couldn't figure out was what he wanted with her. He'd made passes, but backed off when she said no. Totally under his control, she was well aware he could take her any time he wanted and no one would do anything to stop him. Since he didn't, she figured he must not be sexually attracted to her. Probably just bored. Huh.

Well there were plenty of other women in and out of this house he could occupy his time with.

Although, since the night of the party when that woman was on his lap and his hand was up her shirt, Glorie shook her head with a grimace at the picture, he hadn't so much as spoken to another women except for Maria.

Glorie looked at the bracelet on her wrist. She hadn't worn it since he gave it to her, but she'd felt drawn to wear it this morning even while working outside, it was like she had a piece of him with her.

When she reached her bed, she was so exhausted, physically, and now mentally with the strain of not knowing, just not knowing her future. Add to that the fact that she kept picturing Joze in bed with other women, what else would he be doing for days?

She didn't pull back the blanket, just flopped down in her jeans and sweater and was asleep almost as her head hit the pillow.

Glorie was sleeping on her side when he came in. The curtain was closed but enough light filtered through to illuminate her.

He kicked off his boots, unbuttoned his shirt, and laid down next to her in his jeans and shirt. He moved close to her, facing her back and ran his palm up her back over her sweater.

She stirred, then stiffened.

"It's just me, Glorie," he whispered, his breath teasing loose wisps of hair over her face.

She squirmed slightly away, but he caught her shoulder holding her still.

"Joze," she said in a voice warding him off.

Stroking her shoulder, he said quietly, "Give me a chance, Glorie, don't push me away." He brushed her hair off her neck then leaned over and pressed his lips on her neck.

She stiffened even more.

He nibbled then gently sucked her soft skin, smiling when he felt her shiver. Moving his mouth to kiss her cheek he slid his hands up under her sweater and caressed her breasts with his big hard hands over the silk bra.

"Joze!" Pushing at his hands she moved away from him. "Don't!"

"Glorie, let me touch you, give me a chance," he begged again, grasping her arms he pulled her back to him. Before she could move away again, he pushed his hand back up under her sweater and cradled her breast, the other hand slid down the front of her to cup her mound over her jeans.

Shoving from him, Glorie squirmed away once more, her chest heaving in anger that he'd probably left another woman's bed before climbing into hers. With a huff, she shunted her curls out of her face with both hands.

Scowling, Joze propped on one elbow behind her and dragged a hand through his hair. "I want you, Glorie, I want to be with you, can't-"

Aggravation heavy in her voice, facing away from him, she said, "You just want me because I'm in close proximity. You can have your choice of a thousand different women, go get one of them. You've obviously been with one or more the last few days." She turned away from him in a snit.

Cursing, he said crossly, "Goddammit, Glorie, I don't want a different woman, I fucking want you. I was not with any women while I was gone. It was just me and a bottle, until Linc came. Then it was me and Linc and another bottle."

He set his hand gently on her shoulder, carefully pushed her over on her back and leaned over her. "I've told you, *babi*, other than that mindless fondling I did with that woman, I have not even thought about another woman much less had sex since I met you."

Somewhat resistant, she still allowed him to push her down. "Why did you leave, Joze, if not to have sex?"

His hand on her shoulder holding her prone, his lip wrinkled at having to tell her his thoughts, what a weak man he was.

"Because I was frustrated, Glorie. I wanted you so badly. But that bastard, Walker," lying down on his side and facing her, Joze braced on his elbow, and traced his finger along her jaw, behind her ear, she shivered.

"He'd thrown you around and was brutal in his attempt to get to you. You were hurt, scared and vulnerable. If I'd stuck around here that night, I might have," he shoved a hand through his hair, "pushed you harder. Done things I would have been ashamed of even if you asked me not to." He touched her lips with his fingers.

So soft, so plump, he sighed deeply. "Seeing how hard it affected you when you spoke with your sister, I realized how terribly I'm hurting you by keeping you with…um, here. I had to get away from you and think about…the future."

Lying on her back gazing up at him, her expression was inscrutable. Her bright eyes traveled his body before returning to his face.

"Glorie, I find I just can't stay away from you, I can't keep my hands off of you. Even a couple of bottles of scotch couldn't wash you out of my brain. I would have been…forceful, maybe, with you if I'd been here the past few days. I stayed away to protect you from me."

"No, Joze, you're a good man. You wouldn't-"

He dropped his hand and his head, his hair brushed her skin. Raising his head he looked at her, knowing his eyes were hardening, he struggled to keep them benign. "No, Glorie, I'm every bit the thug in a three-piece-suit your handler said I was."

His mouth pinched wryly. "I've told you, I'm used to doing what I want, taking what I want. I was afraid I couldn't control myself with you if I'd stayed that night. I wouldn't have stopped when you would have eventually asked me to."

His gaze stroked her face. "I know I'm not good enough by any stretch of the imagination for you, Glorie. But I can't help it. I want to be with you, talk with you, hold you, and, I have to be honest," he shrugged with a feeble grin.

"I want to make love to you so much, not just my balls but my damned skin hurts. I can hardly keep myself from exploding, shattering into a fucking millions pieces." He cringed. "Sorry about the language, *babi*."

She looked up at him in confused wonder. "I don't understand, Joze, you could have satisfied your...sexual need with any other-"

"*Babi*, since we worked at the saloon, even in your disguise I wanted you then. I have felt absolutely nothing for any other female since you came into my sight. Your face just keeps coming into my brain blocking out everyone else. I've told you, I haven't been with another woman since I met you. Granted I'm a criminal, but I don't lie. I don't need to."

Her brows lowered. "Yes you have told me. You were groping that girl at the party-"

Arching his neck, Joze dropped his head back and rolled his eyes. Then he looked down at her. "Honey, I explained that. It was a habit. Women constantly dump themselves on my lap unbidden and expect it. It meant nothing. Since you brought it to my attention I have rebuffed anyone that came near me. The only hands I want on me are yours. The only body I want to touch, is yours."

The sparkle caught his eye, his mouth drew back in a broad grin. "You're wearing my bracelet."

Ignoring his last words, she shook her head, her hands tentatively touching the part of his chest his shirt still covered, she murmured, "I can't be with a man that has sex with or even touches any other woman, whether it means anything or not."

He burst with frustration, "I just said-" He bit his tongue to shut up.

Stroking the side of her face with the pads of his fingertips, he leaned over her. His face a surface of solemn care, he said, "Glorie, haven't I made it clear that I want you, only you. Other than that one time, and after I saw your face when you saw me disrespecting her that way, handling her like that in public, the disgust in your eyes, I realized what an ass I was treating women that way. I haven't done it since.

"And, I won't, even if you tell me you don't want to have anything to do with me. I don't like the guy I was, and I don't want to be him anymore."

His mouth lowered near hers, he said, "I don't ever want to see that disgust for me on your face ever again, *babi*. I can't stay away from you, as hard as I've tried per your wishes." His palm stilled along the side of her face, their eyes connected. "Let me kiss you."

Her crystal orbs perused his blues searching for sincerity.

The intensity of his passion and tenderness for her blazed honest and clear, fully authentic without any trace of subterfuge.

When she didn't say anything, Joze lowered his head just barely brushing her lips with his. When her mouth pulsed against his, his elated rumble rippled in his chest, and he deepened the kiss.

Feeling her more fervent response, Joze slanted his mouth to seal their lips harder together. His tongue searching for hers, tasting her lips, her teeth, skillfully soliciting her to follow and mirror his movements.

He lowered his upper body lightly to feel her lush breasts press against the hard contours of his chest, just barely moving, creating a titillating friction. Not wanting her to freak out, he shifted to keep his burgeoning erection away from her.

A soft pink flushed Glorie's skin, her lungs filled with air faster and shallower, she squirmed again but now it was in heady response to his mouth's seething exploration of hers. He commanded her desire, heating it up with his fiery kisses.

She shyly pushed aside the halves of his unbuttoned shirt and tentatively set her palms against the rough velvet hair covering his virile chest.

Joze moaned at her touch. He braced his forearms on either side of her, bent and kissed her, then trailed butterfly bites and tiny suckles along her neck.

The flats of her dainty hands slid over hard muscle, along cords of strong sinew, she grazed a nipple. His back jolted to a rigid arch,

"*Fy Duw, fy bach cariad*," he hissed, tremors coursed down his body. His impassioned breath fanned her hot neck, he couldn't recall a time he'd been so sensitive before.

She ran just the tips of her fingers across his chest, grazing the other nipple and he about bucked off the bed. His breath sucked in a sharp growl, "*Glorie!*"

She quickly pulled her hands back and asked with alarm, "Are you all right, Joze?"

He took a deep breath, a grunted chuckle tumbled out. "*Ie*, very." He ran his tongue lightly over her lower lip, sucked it gently. Still feeling the traces of the tremors her fingers had elicited, his heart smiled at the dreamy haze filling her pretty eyes. His voice slightly husky, he said, "I love your hands on me, Glorie, don't stop."

"Okay." She seemed to like touching him. Still shyly, she reached for his chest. Under her palms, the warmth of his flesh covering rock-hard pecs flooded through the dark hair, she sifted her fingers in the velvety hair. The locks on his head were blond but the hair everywhere else on his body was dark.

Her hands gently squeezed, pressed, trailed the planes and hollows, with each stroke his shaft jumped, it was harder and harder to keep from rubbing it against her. But he'd be on her in a heartbeat if he did that.

When she dragged her nails very slowly back down from his shoulders to his taut abdomen, he grimaced and shook with the unbelievable sensation, his entire body felt electrified.

Her hands roamed back up his chest to his shoulders where she skimmed them across the cordons of muscles stretched across his broad, thick shoulders, then she splayed her fingers into his hair.

Her fingers felt so good on his scalp, he imagined how her small soft hands would feel wrapped around his cock. *Shyt*- if he kept thinking like that he'd come in his pants.

He pushed aside the unbidden thought of when he'd forced himself on her that day, he had been trying to scare her into submission. He had forced her to hold him then, he remembered how scared she had been.

But that was then and this was now. Now it was all about what she wanted. No force, no fear, just their closeness. His imperceptible movements so slow and light she didn't register that he pushed the hem of her sweater up, past her breasts to her neck.

Cradling the back of her head with one hand while devouring her mouth, the other he spread against the smooth skin of her warm belly.

When she didn't protest his hands on her bare skin, he moved his hand slowly up until he molded his long fingers over the sheer bra to cup her plush breast.

At his caress, he could feel the vibration of her groan against his mouth, her torso writhed under him on the mattress. His body railed to have her writhing like that with him inside her and screaming his name.

Those few days alone with the scotch he had come to the realization that he wanted her, not just her body, but all of her, for as long as she'd let him.

She was so frail and skittish, and considering their circumstances of thug captor and innocent cop victim, he had to move incredibly slowly so she wouldn't feel pressured, or afraid, or guilty afterwards.

Her one and only experience with sex was that devastating rape. He wanted her to be ready, and wanting him, he was prepared to take all the time she needed. And do all it took to make the next time she has sex to be a wonderful thing she'd want to experience, again and again…with him. Only him.

Releasing her breast, Joze stroked his hand around the small of her back pushing his palm down the back of her jeans to feel the plump flesh of her bottom. He squeezed each tempting rounded cheek. She stiffened, he reluctantly loosened his grip until she relaxed again.

Although his bursting erection felt like it was being pulled like a steel rod towards Glorie's female magnetic core, he struggled to keep it from touching her, he moved his hand up her back and unclasped her bra. It was done so slowly and deftly she was scarcely aware of it.

He brushed his palm up the front of her enjoying the sleek suppleness of her skin, over her abdomen, her ribs, up to her bare breast. As he clutched it in his hand, there was a hard knock at the door.

Glorie turned her face from him and pushed at his chest. Groaning as if in pain, Joze said, "Ignore it, baby, kiss me," he moved his hand from her breast to cup her chin, bringing her lips back to his.

Outside the door, Linc yelled, "Joze, it's important!"

Joze rolled in agonized, aggravated frustration to his back and cursed a blue streak in Welsh.

Rolling back, he kissed Glorie gently on her lips, then sighed deeply. "I'll be right back, *babi*, please don't move." But she was already tugging her sweater back down.

Pitching off the bed to his feet, Joze nudged his pounding erection so it wasn't pressing as painfully against his belly and stomped to the door and flung it open. He barked, "What the fuck, Linc."

Linc peered around him seeing Glorie dart into the bathroom. He smirked at Joze's scowl at the closed bathroom door. His grin grew wider seeing Joze's disheveled hair, unbuttoned shirt, his gaze dropped to the hard bulge in his jeans. "Ah, finally making headway with your little cop?"

Joze's scowl blackened, "What did you come here for? Talk quick and then go the hell away."

Linc's expression turned grave. "There's trouble. A few of our boys were jumped, attacked, badly beaten."

His brows slashed down like swords between his eyes, Joze stood in the doorway blocking Linc's view of the room and grumbled, "I'll be right there." He closed the door in Linc's face.

Grabbing up his boots, he went to the bathroom door. Through it he said, "Glorie, I have to go. There's an emergency. When I come back…uh, we can, continue. Okay?"

As he expected, she didn't answer him.

Swallowing his raw frustration, as he crossed the room heading out, he muttered, "Goddammit, just when we're making headway." He passed through their adjoining door to his, which Linc had left open and almost walked right into Van.

"I saw Linc," Van said, taking up guard outside.

"*Ie*, stay with her. You hang in my room, not hers," Joze snarled as he strode past him. At this point, his brain and balls were so imbued with Glorie he didn't trust even a gay man, a good friend, to be alone with her in her bedroom.

When he got to the study the others were there, loading and checking their weapons. "Where? Who?" Joze asked as he pushed aside a moveable bookcase to reveal a vault. He unlocked it and he and the others took out more weapons.

Hooking a double holster over his massive chest, Calvin said, "Jackie, Nick, little Tom and Cash. They were at the warehouse working on the vehicles when they were jumped. The hoods pistol whipped them, asked for drugs and money, then wailed on them when they came up with nothing."

"Who?" Joze repeated, checking his gun to make sure it had a full clip.

"DeMarco's men."

"Let's go." Joze commanded, leading the men out the door.

Chapter Twenty-Nine

Glorie left her room and saw Van right away. "Where did he go?" she asked.

"The team all went out. They'll be gone for…a while." Van was not about to tell her where they were going, to put a hurting on the men that gave Joze's men a beat down. He kept forgetting she was a cop, but he did know she was a woman, and most of them freaked out when there was fighting going on. Well, the nice ones did.

"Okay. I'm going out to work with Daniel."

"All right," Van said, walking with her. "I'll take you to him then I need to go to the store. You'll be good with Daniel. He knows not to let you out of his sight." He winked at her to take the sting out that she was still a prisoner.

When Glorie got to the barns and found Daniel, Van took off to go back to get his car and go to town.

She looked around then said to Daniel, "There is absolutely no one here. The place is totally empty. Even Maria and Greta went to buy fresh vegetables. I don't think I've ever seen it this empty before."

"*Ie*, it's nice. The ranch hands are all off this afternoon too, and the women are at the club." Daniel handed her a rake so they could redistribute the straw on the barn floor.

The pair worked silently but comfortably for an hour in the barn. Then they went outside to the coops to feed the chickens.

Daniel's head cocked and he suddenly held still.

"What is it, Daniel?" Glorie tucked her gloves in her back pocket and wiped her hands on her jeans. She wiped at her forehead with the back of her hand and nudged at hair that had escaped the ponytail and was tickling her face.

Daniel stood with his hand over his eyes scanning the pastures then the houses then the woods.

Suddenly, he shouted, "Run, Glorie!" He grabbed her wrist and dashed with her to the barn-

Bullets whistled past and over their heads, slamming into the wood barn sending chips flying.

Once inside, there was no way to lock the door. Daniel looked around then saw a wheelbarrow and ran to it. He pushed it up against the door, forcing the handle to stay immobile.

Glorie stood in shock with her hands over her mouth.

"Come on, get back," Daniel ordered, reaching for her arm.

"D- Daniel, what is it?"

"Keep your head down!" he shouted. Clapping a hand on her head he shoved it down as a bullet whizzed past stabbing a hole in the barn wall. He grasped her arm and pulled her across the wooden floor, straw flying and cracking under their feet.

They ran to hide behind stacked bales of hay.

Just as they knelt down, a banging hit the door.

It sounded like men were throwing their shoulders against it, trying to force it open.

"Daniel, what's going on?" Glorie whispered.

"Shh." He pulled a gun from his boot and trained it on the door.

The men kept running and slamming their bodies against the door, parts of it were starting to splinter.

A man shouted, "Hey old man, send the girl out. She's all we want. Send her out and we'll let you live!"

"Daniel-" Glorie's gasped, her eyes popping. "What-"

Throwing his arm around her, hugging her tightly to his side, Daniel said, "Hush, honey, don't worry, I won't let anyone hurt you."

More crashing into the door, fingers stuck through some of the splinters trying to pry the wood apart.

The man yelled again, "Old man! Send the fucking girl out if you want to live! You've got thirty seconds. I don't see that flaming hair in 30 then you'll buy it. You've got 25 seconds."

"Get behind me," Daniel ordered, shoving her behind him. His gun was aimed at the door.

There was more frightening thunderous crashing, wood cracking and splintering- then the door finally split open. Two men pushed through, shoving the wheelbarrow out of the way.

"Leave now or I'll start shooting!" Daniel yelled.

"Ha!" One of the men laughed, then he and three more men who burst in behind him started shooting. Bullets flew in all directions, hay and straw shot up all around the barn.

Glorie clamped her hand over her mouth to stifle her scream.

"Last chance old man," one of the men shouted. "Give her up and you live. Come on out sweetie, we won't hurt you. We just want you as leverage for Kane."

Glorie looked at Daniel in question. He put a finger over his mouth for her to keep silent.

It was quiet for a moment, then the man said, "Time's up, old man, now we're gonna kill you and take her anyway. Hit it boys," he ordered.

Gunfire erupted. The men started moving towards them. It was obvious to the thugs where they were hiding, there was nothing else to hide behind in the vast barn.

When they were a few yards away, Daniel jumped up, fired a few rounds then ducked back down.

The men rained hellfire at him.

Daniel pushed Glorie down and kept his body protectively over hers.

The man yelled, "It's over old guy, you're dead fucking meat." The taunting humor was gone, leaving a chilled threat hanging.

They moved closer. Daniel popped up again, fired, but there were too many of them. One of the men's aim was true, and Daniel grunted then slumped to the ground.

"Daniel!" Glorie crouched beside him, blood oozed from a hole in his shirt. She whispered desperately, "Oh Daniel, you're hit!"

The voice holding a mocking note, the man yelled, "Come out sweetie, your hero is dead. Come out now or we will put a hurting on you too and still take you!"

Bending over Daniel, Glorie frantically called his name. His eyes half-closed, he was sprawled leaning against a stack of hay with his gun still in his hand. The blood was now pouring out of his chest when the first man peered around at them.

Blam! Daniel fired and the man went down.

"You motherfucker!" Another man leaped at them- Daniel shot him and he hit the floor, straw and dust spewed from his body slam.

A third man poked out from the other side of the hay, and Glorie swung a shovel at him, hitting him in the head. He grunted and dropped.

Glorie looked over at Daniel.

His head was slumped on his chest. The hand holding the empty gun was on the ground. She ran over and stood in front of him with the shovel raised-

****

Joze and his team found the men who had put the beat down on his men quickly. Nick and the three other men were already at the hospital.

It took little effort or time to take out DeMarco's men. They weren't expecting anyone to find them, so they were already chugging the alcohol and toking on weed, bragging in triumph.

Their reflexes were so slow and sloppy, Joze and his men made quick mincemeat out of them.

Leaving them bruised and broken, Joze stuck a note to one of the men's ripped shirt. It said, "I'm coming for you next, DeMarco."

As they were preparing to leave, one of the beaten men on the floor, speaking through a slit lip, broken jaw and nose, bragged, "You think you got the upper hand, bro," he spat out blood and a tooth, "but DeMarco's got you. He's got your chick."

Joze froze in the doorway. He turned around. "What the fuck are you talking about?"

"He's just messin' with you, Joze, let's go." Calvin caught his arm to leave.

Joze shrugged Calvin off and stomped over to the man and repeated, "What the fuck are you talking about?"

The man had a change of heart, he should have kept his big broken mouth shut. He shook his head and winced at the pain. "Nuthin' I was just, uh, delirious."

Joze hauled off and kicked him in the side of his ribs.

The man shrieked and his body folded together as he cried and gagged.

Joze crouched down, grabbed the man's hair and yanked his head up. Right in his crying face, Joze said, "I'm asking you one more time, it's the last time. Don't answer me and I will beat you to death. Now, what the fuck did you mean?"

Blood poured from every orifice on his head, the man cried, "There- there- DeMarco was told there's a chick at your farm that you got a thing for." He grinned and then groaned.

"And?" Joze slapped him.

Stretching his jaw from the hit, the man told him, "DeMarco didn't believe it because, well, it's you. You're a fucking dog. Women slide through your fingers like raindrops to splat on the ground." He spat out another tooth and choked on the blood rolling down his throat.

"What about this woman, who did he say it was?"

When he didn't answer fast enough, Joze punched him in the gut. "Last chance, tell me, you fuck."

The man coughed, and choked, gagged and gasped for air to move through his broken ribs and collapsed lung. Coughing, he hacked, "Dunno, said she's a beauty with crazy fiery hair. The beat down we gave your boys," he gasped for breath, "it was a distraction."

Joze felt his blood literally freeze in his veins.

Coughing up a lung, the thug huffed, "The word was the ranch would be cleared of people today for different reasons, and if you were drawn out too, they could get in and," he coughed, "take your bitch to fuck with you. When you came for her, DeMarco would be prepared and," he hacked and choked, wheezed, "take you out."

As Joze stood, the color drained from his face. He turned and ran to the door. His team was on his heels.

The drive back to the farm was the most frightening time of his life. What they would do to Glorie if they got her while they waited for Joze to try to find her and then get to her- too much time!

"Don't think about it until we know, Joze," Linc said, his voice dark and deep, he was scared too. He knew what would happen to Glorie if DeMarco got his hands on her.

Joze said nothing, just slammed his foot to the floor and hoped there were no cops out on the same road they were racing down.

****

Suddenly a barrage of bullets rang out, men screamed and cursed, the thumping of bodies sounded hitting the dirt.

Then it was quiet.

Shaking like a leaf, Glorie held the shovel over her head, her arms trembling from holding the weight of it-

"Daniel! Glorie!" a voice shouted.

Her voice tiny, Glorie cried, "Joze?"

He stepped around the hay, took in Daniel passed out, or dead, with Glorie standing over him, shovel raised in her hands like a dainty bear protecting her cub.

"Glorie!" Joze choked, and went for her.

Glorie dropped the shovel with a cry and ran to him.

He threw his arms around her, holding her tight. His mouth in her hair, *"Babi! Babi*, are you all right?"

She nodded as the tears fell.

Assured she was unharmed, releasing her, Joze dropped down beside Daniel.

"Daniel, Daniel, Uncle, man, talk to me!" He tore Daniel's shirt open, peeled his own off in one move, rolled it up in a ball and shoved it on his wound. He yelled, "Linc! Go get a horse- now!"

Calvin and Bruno rushed around the bales of hay. Guns still smoking in their hands, they both blanched seeing Daniel lying with his blood pooling around him. "Joze, is he-"

Pressing the shirt on Daniel's chest, Joze said, "No, help me get him up."

Glorie stepped out of the way as the men hauled Daniel up and carried him to the door. Bodies were spread over the floor of the barn as well as a few outside. The whole place was a bloodbath.

Glorie quailed at the sight. She had come a hair's breath close to being one of them. She hurried after Joze as he strode over the grass.

A minute later and Linc came racing up bareback on a steed to meet them.

The men got Daniel up on the horse. With Linc holding him, he kicked the horse and they shot across the field to the house.

It was quicker to run Daniel to the cars on the horse than running there and getting a car then driving to the barn, getting Daniel and driving back.

At the same time, Bruno and Calvin ran towards the house.

Joze spun around for Glorie but she was standing right behind him.

He said, "*Babi*, I have to go with them. Here," he pulled his gun out and put it in her hands. "The safety," he explained, showing her, "when you shoot, push it up, when not, push it down it locks the trigger so it won't accidentally fire." He pressed her fingers around it when she tried to give it back to him.

"Don't ask questions, don't hesitate, don't shoot to scare or wound. Aim at his chest and shoot to kill. Now, go straight to the house and lock yourself in your room. Don't come out until one of us comes for you." He leaned quickly, kissed her, turned and ran.

He was almost to the house when Linc was pulling around in the SUV, he didn't stop, only slowed.

Joze yanked the door open and jumped in the back with Daniel. Calvin and Bruno were already in the front.

As they tore around the front of the house to the driveway, Sloan and Diego were pulling up. Seeing the racing SUV, they spun around and followed them.

Both vehicles disappeared in a cloud of dust.

Shaking from the horrid last hour, Glorie walked as quickly as she could to the house.

By the time she got there, Van raced squealing into the back yard. The car bounced back and forth he braked hard and sudden. He hopped out and ran to Glorie.

"Van, Daniel-"

"I know, honey, Joze called me to make sure I was on my way. Come on, let's get inside. He said he was sending Sloan and Diego right back." He held his hand out and ordered, "Give me that."

Glorie gratefully handed him the gun. It was so heavy she had a hard time holding it. Van took it and shoved it in the back of his jeans. His own was holstered as usual at his hip.

By the time they were inside, Sloan and Diego had returned.

Sloan called in some help to dispose of the bodies. Then they joined Glorie and Van in the living room, and sat down to wait for word from Joze.

The men paced. Glorie made sandwiches and brought them sodas then looked for something else to keep busy with. She thought she'd go out of her mind with worry for Daniel.

It was hours before Joze called.

Van answered his cell.

Seeing the smile on his face, the others grumbled with relief and relaxed a little.

"Okay," he said into the phone and handed it to Glorie. "Here, Gloworm, he wants to talk to you."

While handing it to her, he said to everyone, "Joze says Daniel should pull through. He's lost a ton of blood of course, but the bullet missed any vital organs or a vein big enough to bleed him out faster. With all those bullets flying thank God it was a miracle he'd only been shot once."

The three men shared a look as Glorie took the phone, since when did Joze EVER speak to a woman on the phone? He never hung around one long enough to get or want her number. But then they all started to talk at the same time about Daniel's health.

Daniel was a very respected and well-liked man. Older than the other men at the ranch, the younger men considered him somewhat of a mentor. He was intelligent and patient, but took no shit and could kick ass as good or better than the rest of them.

Diego said to the others, "They were ambushed. If he had time, Daniel could have gotten him and Glorie placed where they couldn't have gotten to them, he could have held them off until we got back."

Sloan got up to grab a bottle of bourbon to celebrate that Daniel would survive.

Glorie took the phone, and said, "Hello?" Her face split into a thankful smile as she listened.

"That's great news, Joze, I was so worried, when he was shot..." the tears choked her speechless, she just nodded with the phone to her ear.

Van sat down next to her and took the phone back. He said, "Joze, man, she can't really talk, she was pretty worried about Daniel."

He smiled at Glorie. "Yeah, she's all right, we're here with Diego and Sloan." He nodded. Grinning at the others, he said with indulgence, "Of course, man, we will all stay with her until you get back."

He nodded again, then said, "Yeah, the ah," he glanced at Glorie and said under his breath, "packages have been mailed." They had to be careful on the phone. Joze wanted to make sure that the men that attacked Glorie and Daniel had been carefully disposed of.

Van listened another minute then replied, "Sure, all right. Tell Daniel we're all pulling for him. Later."

Sliding the phone into its case on his belt, Van slipped a brotherly arm around Glorie and hugged her. She turned sodden eyes up at him and sighed her nerves out.

"It's okay, Gloworm," Van said affectionately, "all that matters is that Daniel will be all right. Joze said to tell you to stay in the house, don't go out at all, not even to take care of the animals. The guys will do that. I'm to stay with you at all times, and Sloan and Diego will bunk in the living room to keep watch."

She was busy wiping the flowing tears from her cheeks. The entire incident of men shooting at her, threatening her life had thrown her into a maelstrom of terror. Her body was still trembling from the aftershock.

At the time, everything was happening so fast, she'd been too stunned to think. When Daniel had been shot, she thought she'd faint right then and there from the fear that he would not survive. She'd been more worried that one of the thugs was going to shoot the injured Daniel again than she was worried about her own safety.

It was only now that she'd had time to settle that the facts were coming to roost. Those animals had come for her. They'd wanted to take her to use against Joze. Would Joze have come for her if they had taken her?

Well, she realized, all the time that she'd spent with him since he'd rescued her at the saloon, gave her the answer.

Yes, Joze would have come for her, and likely they both would have been killed. Her mind spun with the ramifications of it all. Would this be her life if she chose to stay with him? Glorie laughed to herself, what an assumption. That the great Jozadak Kane would want to make a life with her.

For heaven's sake, the man owned a strip club. The ranch was constantly overrun with women that were there entirely to have sex with any male available. No way would Joze desire to have a monogamous relationship with her. Not that she would even consider it. But-

Van told her, "Joze said he doesn't think the fuckers, sorry Glo, will return. Not when the men sent here don't go back and don't report in. DeMarco will know what happened. Joze has called a bunch of his soldiers to come here anyway as reinforcements. We're safe, honey, Daniel's okay, you can stop crying."

For an answer, Glorie shoved her face into his shoulder and bawled.

Chapter Thirty

Several days passed and Joze was still at the hospital with Daniel. The grizzled older guy had taken a turn for the worse before he started back on the mend.

Linc and Calvin returned to the house but all the men took alternating visits to the hospital. No one would take Glorie to see Daniel because Joze ordered that she stay tucked safely behind the ranch's walls.

At the ranch, the men were taking turns caring for the animals, but the way they complained it sounded to Glorie that they weren't doing the best they could, and she worried the animals could be suffering.

Early in the morning, when Van took a bathroom break, Glorie slipped outside and went first to the horses to let them out to feed in the fenced-in pasture.

She had fed the alpacas and chickens and was grooming the white horse when Van finally found her.

"Geez, Glorie, you trying to get my throat slit? I've been looking all over for you! What they hell-" breaking into inaudible curses, he was furious as he stomped up to her, slamming his hands on his hips.

Dragging the brush over the horse's flanks, Glorie remained calm. "Come on Van, it's been days, there are no more men coming here to attack us. I'm perfectly safe out here. Besides, the team guys are all here."

"Glorie, those thugs weren't here to attack us, they were here to take you. And, if Joze had arrived ten minutes later, you would be gone and Daniel would be dead. You are taking chances that you shouldn't." He was rocking back and forth oddly on his feet.

Sighing with slight impatience, Glorie said, "But he did, and we are both all right. The animals shouldn't suffer because I have to be kept inside. Right baby?" She crooned at the horse as she ran her hand down his nose and gave him a hug.

She hoped when Joze returned he could start her riding lessons again. A confusing lump settled in her throat. When had she started thinking she was going to stay here at the ranch? Was she barreling into Stockholm's Syndrome or…what?

Van opened his mouth but then Sloan wandered up. It was his turn to help groom the horses. He grinned, thrilled when he saw Glorie there because he knew she would have already taken care of the job.

Van said to Sloan, "Listen bro, you're here. I have to go to the bathroom. I'm having, uh, issues, my stomach is upset. Stay with her until I come back, okay?" He took off before Sloan answered him.

Sloan complained, "Aw shit, I was hoping I could get away from farm duty since we all have to pitch in until Daniel returns."

Glorie told him, "Oh, Sloan, really, I'll be fine out here, you can go back to the house." She walked the horse back to his stall and shuttered him in.

Shaking his head, Sloan said, "God no, hon. Joze made it real clear one of us has to be with you at all times. Even now." His eyes narrowed in accusation at her. "You weren't supposed to leave the house. He comes home and sees you out here, there will be hell to pay. You need to go back-" he stopped when he saw Guy strolling towards them.

Greeting them, "Hey kids," his hands in his pockets, Guy said cheerfully, "what's going on?"

"Oh, man, this is perfect!" Sloan chortled with glee. "Dude, you mind staying with her until Van comes back?"

"Uh, wait, Sloan," Glorie started to object.

"It'll be okay, hon, Van will be right back. Guy will take care of you, won't ya bro?" Sloan slapped him on the shoulder and quickly walked away.

"No, Sloan, wait, I can't-" Glorie called out to Sloan but he was already gone. She turned to Guy. "Um, I need to put this equipment up and then we can go back to the house."

"Hey, sugar, no rush on my account. Take your time." Guy looked around until he spotted a generous pile of loose hay.

"You get done, maybe we can make ourselves comfortable and," he sidled closer to her, "you know, get to know each other better. Finally Joze is gone so he won't stick his bossy nose into our business."

He went to put an arm around her. "You look tired, sugar, what do you say we lay down over there in that nice pile of-"

"No! Absolutely not!" Glorie twisted out of his hold. She was determined to not be a victim again of a pushy lascivious man. Not taking any chances by lingering, she left the equipment where it was on the floor of the stable and hurried out the door.

"Come on, honey, you'll like what I can give you, wait up!" Guy jogged to catch up with her.

But Glorie knew if he got his clutches in her, he would not be past forcing himself on her. She moved faster.

She was almost to the house when he caught up and grabbed her arm, swinging her around and right into his arms. When she tried to run, he caught her by the neck and held her back.

"Come on, babe, we're not going to have a lot of opportunities without Joze or his meddlesome team hanging around to interfere. C'mere, let me warm you up with a kiss, then you'll be ready for more," he slammed his mouth on hers. One hand fisted in her hair, and the other on her lower back forcing her body so hard against his, she had no room to fight him.

They barely heard the screen door slam and the guttural fierce growl before Guy was jerked back and Joze's fist connected with his jaw. Joze was on him before he hit the ground.

Wailing on him, Joze rained blow after blow so fast and hard Guy couldn't block him or get a punch in.

"No! Joze, stop!" Glorie screamed.

Her screams brought Linc and Calvin and Bruno.

They blew out of the house and raced over and pulled Joze off Guy, wrangling him back. It was a struggling fight for the three men to hold Joze back from killing Guy.

Joze was huffing and puffing, throwing his body and arms, trying to break loose from his friends' restraints.

Coughing and spitting blood, Guy struggled to his hands and knees.

Glorie stood back with her hand over her mouth. If the men hadn't come, there was little doubt Joze would have killed Guy.

Breathing so heavily his chest pumped like a snorting bull, Joze shrugged at his arms and said, "I'm good."

After a few seconds, his friends tentatively released him.

He wiped the back of his hand over his mouth. Through the sweat dripping in his eyes, Joze watched wobbling Guy work to stand steady on his feet. Blood flowed from his mouth and his nose, his face was swelling like he'd been stung by a hundred bees.

Guy shuffled back from Joze, his eyes flicking to all of the men, expecting an attack from all sides.

Joze took a step towards him with his fists up. Linc grabbed his arm. "Easy bro," he murmured.

If the harrowing lethality in Joze's voice wasn't enough to send chills down a person's spine, the malignant glint in his eyes would make even Satan shake in his hooves. He said to Guy, "Get the fuck out of here," he spat on the ground. "Don't come back."

They all stood stock still as Guy revolved right away and quickly made his way around the house to his car parked out front.

Joze shrugged Linc's hand off him and turned to Glorie.

She shrank from him.

His eyes were pitch black flaring with seething rage. His face dark, jaw clenched, tight fists at his side, he grabbed her arm and started walking with her.

When his men started to follow and Linc said, "Bro, wait a minute, you need to calm-"

Through a grimace that would stop a rampaging elephant, with a twist of his head, Joze rasped, *"Don't,"* and dragged Glorie into the house.

The men stayed outside unsure if they should intervene.

Bruno rocked from one foot to the other, uncertain of what to do. With worry in the tone of his voice, he said, "I've seen Joze pissed, but never like this. He is literally shaking with rage. Do you think he'll hurt her?"

"He's never hurt a woman before in his life," Calvin offered, fairly confident.

Linc muttered, "But he's never cared about a woman like this before."

"Yeah," Calvin agreed. "That jealousy can be a killer. He's never experienced it before, he's going to have a hard time reconciling with it."

Inside, Joze kept dragging Glorie through the kitchen.

Realizing that he was so angry because he thought she wanted Guy's hands and mouth on her, Glorie cried out, "Joze, wait, stop, it wasn't what it looked like, he-"

He barked, *"Shut up,"* so viciously her knees buckled.

"No, Joze, stop," she cried, stumbling across the rug as he roughly pulled her through the living room.

He bent and swept her up in his arms and kept stalking down the hall and to his room.

Kicking the door closed behind him, he set her down and locked it the door. When he turned around she was backing away from him.

She raised her small feminine hands up to hold him off. "Joze, please listen to me-"

Towering over her, his shoulders bunched with anger, he snarled, "I'm fucking done listening to you. I thought you were a real person, good, sweet," he dragged his sleeve over his eyes, wiping away the sweat pouring down.

"It was all fake, you're a hell of an actress I'll give you that. You played me real good, honey. But I'm done with it. Now I'm taking what the fuck I wanted from the first second I saw you. Enough of this patient, caring gentleman *shyt*." He reached for her, but she backed away.

"Please Joze, listen to me, it isn't, I wasn't-"

Intense desire incited the jealous fury blazing in his dark eyes. He reached for her again, snarling, "You want to fuck, I'll give it to you, I'll fuck you raw-"

Crying out, she tried to run, he grabbed her wrist and pushed her backwards until her back hit the hard wooden door.

Flailing her hands at him she, screamed, "No- don't you touch me you monster!"

"Really, *bach gethen*, you think you can say no to me? I'm done with your fucking no's." Wrapping one arm around her back, he clasped her chin with the other. Holding her head taut he lowered his mouth, fusing his lips on hers.

Glorie struggled against him, splaying her hands against his chest she tried to push him away, he just held her tighter, closer.

Joze devoured her mouth with such force her head was bent back. He sought her tongue, stroking it, sucking it with his lips, biting with his teeth. He tasted salt. *Fuck.*

As enraged as he was, he still could not take her tears, they burned right through his anger and raving lust. He let out a loud exasperated exhale.

Still holding her, Joze held her chin in the crescent of his hand and lifted it so their eyes could meet. Hers were so big and filled with fear and tears, his stomach cramped.

"Glorie, I care so much for you, and you fucking around with another man, that's not something I can take." He rubbed his thumb over one rolling tear then the next.

His voice rough with fury and frustration, he said, "I know I don't have the right to claim you, tell you who you can and can't be with. But, what my brain knows, it's not telling the rest of my body, my heart."

Her voice a faint tremble, blinking back tears, Glorie replied weakly, "Joze, I can barely kiss you, and I want you, why would you think I'd want to kiss another man? Look," she waited for him to move back from her a little then she turned her head slightly. She could feel the bruises on her neck Guy had made holding her.

"What-" His mouth dropped open. Joze touched the bruises with his fingertips. "From Guy?"

She nodded, the tears falling.

Joze held her jaw turning her head so he could see them clearly.

"Joze," she gulped back her tears and admitted, "it was my fault it happened. I left the house against your orders, but the animals, they weren't getting proper care. I snuck out on Van. He came for me but he's having ah, stomach issues," she sniffed and wiped her eyes with her palms.

"He left me with Sloan. But then Sloan left me with Guy. I tried to stop Sloan from leaving me alone with Guy, but he doesn't know how…persistent Guy can be. Guy tried to get me to lie down in the stable with him. You can go see, I left the tools where they were to run back here from him."

With her every word, guilt seeped color from Joze's complexion. The black pupils were drawing back, letting the blue show. He moved his hand from her jaw to the back of her head, his other hand stroked her back while she was talking.

He murmured, "Guy was forcing himself on you when I arrived," he stated rather than asked.

At her nod, pain filled his blue orbs, his mouth pinched. "I'm so sorry, Glorie, I'm a jealous fool. I can't bear another man's hands on you, it just makes me nuts."

His voice hushed, he said, "*Babi*, you said you can barely tolerate me kissing you," he tilted her face back up to his, "are you saying you really don't want me to kiss you?" The fear was now in his eyes that he had gone too far with his anger and pushed her away for good.

Glorie smiled tremulously. "Joze, I've had very little experience with men. Ian, that cop that, well, anyway, I'm afraid, I hate to say it, but I'm so afraid of getting hurt again. Of being beaten, and…viciously assaulted. But, if I was going to kiss any man, Joze, it would be you."

Chapter Thirty-One

Joze stared at her for a very long time. Then he bent his head and gently set his mouth on hers. Her automatic response was to stiffen and push at him.

But he didn't back off, just kissed her gently, a soft romantic kiss. Then he prodded her mouth open to accept his tongue to mate with hers. The kiss deepened as Joze felt her becoming aroused.

When her resistance lightened, he moved his mouth from hers to kiss behind her ear, then down along her jaw, then lower to suck and lick her neck, she started melting like hot caramel from the thrilling heat of his mouth. He nibbled her neck, sucking and biting lustfully just on the edge between pleasure and pain.

Her head slanted to the side letting his lips slide over her skin, he sucked so hard he marked her neck like a teenager. His lips and teeth on her neck he murmured, "You taste crazy good, *babi*, I will never get enough of you. *Never.*"

Feeling her skin tugging in his voracious lips, his teeth gently biting, a faint moan slipped through Glorie's lips.

Joze moved his mouth back over hers. Releasing her chin, he set his hand on her waist, the smallness of it covered by his big palm. Digging his fingers in slightly, he pulled her more tightly against him.

Then he moved his hand from her back and slipped it under her blouse. He caressed her side then over her ribs, to slowly but urgently cup her breast over the sheer bra.

She froze and pulled back, but he didn't loosen his tight grip on her.

He whispered against her lips, "Shh, *babi*, don't fight, let me." But fire struck his loins at the feel of her lush flesh, he squeezed her breast with such erotic roughness she cried out. He pushed down his unleashing lust and forced himself to gentle his touch.

Kneading her breast, filling his big hand with her plumpness, he caressed it then lightly pinched her nipple between his finger and thumb before wrapping his long fingers tightly around her other swollen globe.

Joze growled, "You feel so fine in my hands, Glorie, like I've dreamed you would."

When a shocking tingle shook her body so palpable he felt it, she squirmed, pressing against his hands, against his chest, wanting to feel their bodies touching.

Spurred by her body's reaction to his touch, Joze took control of her mouth again. His masculine carved lips nudged her pink petals open. Pushing his tongue in, he led her, teaching her what he wants, learning what she likes.

With a low purring moan, Glorie shivered and oozed into him. Her mouth sizzled under his scorching kiss. Her brain was so buzzed by his sensual ministrations, overwhelmed by new erogenous feelings, she didn't feel him unbuttoning her blouse.

Excruciating tingling and prickling spiking throughout her body sent Glorie reeling into a soaring euphoric high. She just wanted more of what he was making her feel. Winding her hands around his head, she pulled it down to press their lips together as hard as she could.

Joze moved both hands to cradle her face. Kissing her more deeply until they were both breathing heavy in fevered ardor, the sound of their passion filling the room.

He pulled from her lips and kissed down to her collarbone. Continuing down, he nibbled along it, licking and kissing lower to her breasts. He raised his hands to cup them in her silky bra, then bent to kiss her skin.

Taking small bites all over each rounded mound, he tried to push her bra down so he could suckle her, but it was too tight, fitting to her like a second skin.

Glorie's head rolled back with hitching moans, her breasts thrust out filling his hands.

Joze groaned, "Ah *Duw, babi*," he covered her mouth with his again in a rampant heart-trembling kiss, and held one breast while sliding his other hand back down over her ribs, moving slowly over her flat belly, down to the apex of her writhing thighs.

His desire overtaking him, he roughly, almost violently cupped her sex. She twitched, trying to back away from his coarse, roaming hands.

Realizing he was getting too rough with her, moving too fast and losing his control, Joze took a deep breath letting it out slowly. She wasn't a tough whore from the club, she was his sweet *bach babi*. Down the road when she was comfortable with his love making he would introduce more exhilarating, rougher, and possibly kinky endeavors.

He moved his hand from her sex and started to undo her pants, but she jerked her mouth from his, gasping, "No, stop Joze-"

"Glorie," he said with tenderness and patience, "try this with me. If you really want to stop, I will. But give us a chance first, okay?"

He could feel the heat of her desire, her scent steamy and intoxicating to his senses, she wanted to be with him but thanks to that deranged cop she was afraid.

Glorie studied his face. His lips bunched from the strain of holding back from brutally driving into her, but his eyes were fully earnest. Her gaze flowing steady to his, she nodded.

His held breath eased out. With a reassuring smile, he said, "All right, try to shut off your mind and just feel me." He worked the button open on her jeans.

While he pulled her zipper down, he recaptured her lips. Kissing her gently, he murmured, "It's okay, *babi*, I know you're inexperienced. I will be careful, gentle, please trust me," he suddenly scooped her up in his arms and carried her to the bed.

Letting her slide down the length of his body to stand on her tiptoes, he slipped his hands down the inside back of her jeans, and inside her panties to caress her bottom.

The unzipped jeans spread apart barely making room for his big hands. He pulled her against his erection so she could be familiar with him, his erection, his size. "Hot, *babi*, you are so insanely hot." His smile broadened when her hands wound up around his neck to pull his head down to kiss him.

His voice gruff with desire spinning around inside his body, he said, "It is time for us, for this." He grasped the top of her jeans with both hands and pulled them with one swift move down to the floor.

"Joze- wait-" she cried in a panic.

"Shh, baby, let your body do the thinking." He slipped his arms around her and just held her against him and kissed her softly. In his arms, her body quaked with fear and burgeoning desire.

When he felt her calm a bit, he caught the lapel of her open shirt, pulled it off her and dropped it on the floor.

She instinctively started to move away from him, but he rolled his arm around her back holding her, and cradled her face while they kissed.

Feeling her relax again, he stroked his hand behind her and unclasped her bra. The straps slid down her arms. Her shyness took over, she put her hands up to hold the bra from falling off.

Joze spread his legs, his feet planted firmly on the floor and he pulled her into his embrace. Feeling her body so soft and plush against his hard planes of sinew and muscle, his huge biceps pumped and bulged while he stroked her back helping her grow calm again.

Next to her ear, he whispered, "It's only you and me, Glorie. Show me how beautiful you are." He bent back to look at her face.

Scanning the big amethyst eyes flooded with desire, shyness and a shade of trepidation, he viewed the tiny pouty lips slightly parted, but she didn't move.

"Glorie, I know I scare you. I go blind with rage seeing you with another man and I mistreat you. I want to not do that, help me by teaching me your sweetness, and let us both learn how to trust."

Their eyes joined, he stroked her face. "Don't be afraid to make love with me. I want to see your body. I've craved to see it since the first days at the saloon when I'd only see hints of your curves when you'd move just right in those loose clothes." He kissed her softly on the lips. "Please, *babi*."

Searching his blue orbs that were turning inky again with his desire, Glorie saw nothing in them but trust and caring. "Joze, you, ah, after what you know I went through, you were going to force me a minute ago, you were going to...rape me." Her voice trailed off small and hurt.

He scrubbed a hand down his face then through his hair. "I was rough with you, I regret it. But, I swear to you, I would not have done it, I would not ever rape you. Clearly there is something going on between us. It freaked me out seeing you in another man's arms. I, ah, had to show you how much it affected me."

His eyes lowered with a hint of shame. "I was not going to go further than just kiss you, feel your luscious body. However, the taste of your tears stopped me, brought me to awareness how very afraid you were."

Setting his hands on her shoulders, he said, "Glorie, this, caring for a woman, is a new thing for me. I know I act like a crass barbarian sometimes, please be patient with me, help me to learn to be more of a gentle man."

Joze brushed her hair back, letting the curls fall behind her shoulder. "I want a relationship with you. I know this is all...bizarre, my keeping you here like a sociopathic kidnapper and then blathering on about having a relationship. I," he paused, sucked in a breath. "I have to admit I just don't know what to do about it. It all just kind of...happened."

He chuckled then said, "I had planned that after I stopped playing Jimmy at the saloon that I was going to ask you out. You see, that there shows you how serious I am. I've never taken a woman out on a date before. Women to me have always just been mindless sex, everything else like restaurants, sailing, skiing, whatever entertainment I did was with my friends. But you, as Dinah, even then I wanted more with you."

He laughed again at her dubious expression. "Truth, Glorie. I envisioned going dancing, doing picnics, museums, even going to the zoo with you." He dragged his fingers through his hair. "Yeah, hard to believe, I was totally startling myself. Thoughts of hanging with you kept me up nights."

He stroked his fingertips along the curve of her apple round cheek then rested them back on her shoulders and said, "Anyway, in the meantime, I'm hoping you and I can build on, well, whatever is between us. Am I mistaken in thinking you have feelings for me too?"

He dropped his hands from her shoulders, leaving them at his sides.

Glorie let his words ramble through her brain. Then, surprising him, she reached up and started undoing the buttons on his shirt.

He stood motionless watching her. His erection was throbbing beyond belief, but he didn't move or touch her. *Duw* it was insanely erotic watching his shy little cop undressing him. "Can I take that as a yes? Do you care for me, *babi*?"

"Joze," she said, but didn't stop undoing his shirt. "I don't know what I feel. I've never felt like this before. Like I've said, I have pretty much no experience with men. You," she sighed her words as she pushed aside his shirt to see his chest.

Losing her train of thought, Glorie put her palms on his chest, feeling his skin quiver under her hands.

Not thrilled that she didn't answer whether or not she had feelings for him, Joze thought, at least she did say she'd never felt this way before, that means she does have feelings for him. Plus, she has let him cuddle her and kiss her, not often, but still, she hasn't let anyone else.

That bastard Guy forced himself on her. Joze felt a guilty twinge, of course he has too. His thoughts disintegrated as Glorie stroked her hands over his chest.

"You're beautiful, Joze," she admired his body, drawing her hands over every contoured hill and hollow of his chest, sliding her fingers through the thick dark hair. "So strong, so masculine, you make me feel safe." Her fingers trickled up and around his shoulders and down his muscular arms.

A groan shed with a shiver from deep inside him. "I love your hands on me, honey, but for now I need you to stop or this will be a very short lesson."

Joze took the straps of her bra and slid them down her arms and off, this time she let him. He picked her up in his arms, she was only wearing her lacey panties, and laid her on the bed then he rolled down beside her.

She sat right up, her legs curled to the side and shyly covered her naked breasts with her arms and thick wavy locks of hair.

"Joze," she apologized, uncomfortable, troubled that she might disappoint him. "I- I've never been, undressed, in front of, you know, a man. I don't think I can-" seeing his perplexed expression, her eyes dropped in shame. "He, you know, when he attacked me he just tore my clothes to get at-"

Joze sat up too. He gently murmured, "Ah, *babi*." With both hands he brushed her hair to tumble down her back. "I don't want you to ever be afraid to talk about, him, what happened to you. But, I think it's important to not bring him into our bedroom with us. If I had thought it wouldn't make things worse for you, I would have taken his life."

He spoke quickly when she started to speak, "Let's not talk about him when we're about to make love." He bent and kissed her naked shoulder. Her hands still covered her bosom.

"*Na*, honey." Joze grasped her wrists and gently lowered her hands. He leaned back to gaze at her.

His eyes glowing, he mumbled in awe, "You are so beautiful, Glorie, your tits- ah, breasts are the most perfect I've ever seen." He covered her round globes with his big hands.

They both lowered their heads watching him caress them, his long hard fingers clutching and feeling their plumpness, molding them in his hands. It was hot watching her watching his hands fondling her breasts. Joze's erection stirred to rock hard. What amazing breasts, mighty *Duw*, what a heavenly creation God had made with Glorie.

He could play with her chubby breasts forever, but he was feeling his grip on his desire slipping. He didn't want to come now. Reluctantly, he moved his hands off her to shrug out of his shirt.

While shoving it off, he leaned over and kissed her. Tossing the shirt to floor he pulled her close so her breasts were pressed against his broad chest made granite hard through tough farm work and boxing matches with his friends.

Moving slightly so her softness rubbed over the matting of his chest hair, a heavy moan rumbled out of Joze. His erection strained at his pants screaming to get free and get to Glorie.

"You are so hot *babi*, if I could, I'd have you naked all the time." He slid a hand around to stroke down her inwardly arched spine smiling at her shiver. He skimmed his palm over the curve of her lower back then down under her panties to cup her bottom. His movements make her jump, slightly raising her behind.

When he drew his fingertips up the crease of her bottom, she nervously shuddered. "Um, Joze, I uh…"

"Shh, baby, trust me, I won't do anything you're not ready for. I just want to feel every damned inch of you." He frowned and pulled from her.

Holding her upper arms, his gaze serious, he was suddenly unsure.

She raised her misted half-mast eyes up to him in question.

Chapter Thirty-Two

He said quietly, "Glorie, you know that I've wanted you for like forever," his smile small and tender. "Actually since even before that very first time you so bravely defended me thinking I was slow witted. I loved your lips, your sweetness with everyone, but then I saw those stunning eyes and I was a goner."

At first they both smiled at his words. Then they thought about that harrowing day when her life would have been over at the saloon if not for Joze's supreme bravery. He'd been confident that he could take on the four men though they had weapons.

He also had a few hidden armaments himself, but he knew his fighting skills surpassed most, and he could see in a shot the men were amateur thugs. The one fool aiming his gun at Joze was aiming at his head. The chances of the idiot hitting the small target from the distance they were apart was about a million to one.

And, Joze was proficient with weaponry, he had experienced sniper skills. He could gage how the guy's finger was to the side of the trigger, and Joze would be able to tell the second he was about to pull it and be able to move in a snap out of range before the bullet fired from the gun.

Then he would be on the man before the other jerks had their own weapons drawn. Most had them tucked into their back waistbands or belts and their draws would be slow and awkward. Joze could, and did, easily and quickly take them all out.

They were pugnacious bullies that weren't afraid of someone smaller than them, but were inept when it came to hand-to-hand combat with a big man of equal or better strength and ability. And, Joze had speed, surprise, and guile on his side.

Glorie's head cocked to the side as he spoke. She said, "You saved my life, but you were so mean to me, so rough, aggressive, I was as terrified of you as I was of those robbers."

Joze looked away, then when he turned his gaze back to her it was suffused with guilt and regret. "I was gruff and cold to you the day I took you because I was rattled how affected I was by you. That, and I was pissed that you were the cop sent to take me down. It felt like a betrayal."

"We didn't really know each other, Joze, we had no relationship outside of a working one," she reminded him.

"I know. Still, unbeknownst to me, I was already developing feelings for you and it hurt when I realized you were there technically to harm me."

"Joze-"

"Anyway, when we were here and I finally got brave enough to do this," he stroked a finger down the front of her and grinned at her shiver, watching her breasts joggle with her movements, her nipples pucker.

His shaft jumping at the confines of his jeans, he told her, "I've wanted to make love to you so badly my brain hurt."

Glorie's eyes dropped, self-conscious at his bold words.

"The thing is," he went on, "I fear, honey, you're basically a virgin and I have to warn you, it's probably going to hurt, at first, but it will not hurt, after...a while. Your body will stretch naturally to take me."

He looked in her eyes to judge her feelings. In the dimly lit room with her eyes half covered by her lids he couldn't read her.

"So, Glorie, I need to make your body ready to take me. I need to make you wet so it'll be easier and-" he smiled at her blushing cheeks. "Anyway, just enjoy, us, together, *babi*."

He webbed a hand around the back of her head pulling her in for his kiss. Capturing her lips, her legs were curved to the side, he parted them and slid his hand between her slim thighs over her sheer panties to cup her mound, gently this time.

She withdrew from his mouth with an embarrassed hitch, and tried to close her legs,

Joze gently pushed her to lie back down on the bed. When she was stretched out, he stripped her panties down her legs and tossed them aside.

Surprised, she instinctively tried to sit up. Lying down beside her, Joze dropped a leg over hers to hold her down and put his palm on her belly, and kissed her.

Their lips pressing, exploring, gently at first, then with steam, he moved his hand to mold her breast. A husky growl vibrated out of his chest at the supple softness in his hand. He tugged, lightly elongating her nipple, pinching, twisting it until she was squirming deliciously under him.

He moved his hand to her other breast and did the same. Squeezing her flesh, he bent and kissed her warm skin then took her nipple in his mouth, bit it, then sucked it, flicking it with his tongue.

Glorie bucked off the bed with a sharp utterance. His hand went to her belly and he pressed her back down on the mattress. His mouth still suckling her nipple, he moved his hand back up to fondle the other breast.

Her chest expanded, her breathing quickened, moving in and out fast and shallow. Joze looked down at her. Her eyes were closed, lips parted, her face twitched and creased with the carnal feelings he was eliciting in her.

Leaving her nipples, he put his mouth back on hers. She eagerly accepted him. Joze could feel her moving into a hazy, sensual place where if he asked her what her name was she would have to think long about it before answering.

Glorie's arms wound around his neck then she brought her hands down his chest in a long, slow caress. She broke from their kiss to see what his flat nipples tasted like.

302

When her tongue licked one, he shook, cursed, "Damn, Glorie." She bit it and his body jerked. When she started sucking on him he had to stop her.

"*Babi*, when we wear off some of my sick lust for you and I can last longer, we can do other things, like you touching me like that, with your, hands, and...mouth." His skin quivered when she stroked a finger over his nipple, he caught her wrist and moved it off him.

Kissing her hand he said, "But right now, I want to be inside you. And that means only I get to touch you, for now." He covered her mouth with his, pulling her back into an intense heated kiss.

When she was firing up under his lips, he slipped his hand down her naked body to her woman's mound where he moved slowly this time to not shock her. His palm palpated lightly over her core then he drew one finger down her slit. He could feel her body preparing to resist, but she didn't push him away.

He suddenly rolled off the bed. Unbuckling his belt, he gazed down at her.

On her back, she'd drawn her legs up again, curling them to the side in shyness, her arms were up, her palms next to her head. Her hair a fiery cloud curled around her head and over the pillow.

His gaze strolled over her nude body, up her shapely legs, to her breasts, back down to the curve of her bare tush.

"*Fy Duw*," he groaned, yanking the button on his pants open. He pushed the zipper down. His eyes blazing, he growled, "You're a living doll, *babi*, a fucking perfect living doll." In his racing arousal, he almost forgot to grab the condoms out of his wallet.

Joze," she scolded faintly at his cursing. Her shy gaze rolled over his chest, his broad shoulders, the massive arms. Watching him, her lashes fluttered over eyes clouding with growing, smoldering desire.

"Sorry, babe." His eyes on her body, he shoved his jeans and boxers down and kicked them off then quickly climbed back on the bed to lie beside her before she had an instant to feel fright at the size of his thick erection.

Gently pushing her legs back down and straight, he rolled over, pinning her leg with his. He nudged her thighs apart and carefully set his hand back on her core.

She wiggled but he kept his hand there.

"Just relax, honey, just let yourself feel. I won't do anything freaky, I promise." He covered her mouth, bringing her to a softly frenzied kiss and then drew two fingers up the side of her slit, she trembled. He set the pad of one finger on her woman's bud and caressed it.

Her hips jumped at the stroke, he slipped his finger inside her slightly to get her silk. She was wet, he rubbed it over her bud, slowly, languidly then as her hips started rolling with his movements, he moved his fingers faster, caressing her sex harder.

Moans started spilling from her lips. Joze slid his finger inside her, and she stiffened. He pulled it out then pushed the digit back in slowly until he felt her pulsating around it and he could slide it inside her tender sheath as far as he could.

Curling his finger, he searched for her hottest erotic spot. When a stunned sound rushed from her, he stroked it again and again until his hand was soaking

Murmuring, "Joze, I, uh," she ground her hips at his hand, her eyes scrunched in a wince.

"What, *babi*?" he asked while licking her lips and then her neck.

"I...don't know, I feel, uh..."

"Just let go *babi*," he ordered hoarsely. His accent taking over, his voice roughened, desire tightened in his chest, constricting his throat.

Sliding his finger in and out of her fast, he stroked his thumb around her clit until she was breathing so hard he could hear her. Glorie's back bowed, she dug her nails into Joze's back, which made him smile. *Oh yeah, she likes it-*

He lowered his mouth to her breast and suckled her nipple while rubbing her clit and inserting his finger faster and faster- until with a strangled scream, she arched off the bed.

Joze watched her. Glorie's head flopped from side-to-side while she thrust her hips erratically at his hand. Gasping harshly as the orgasm took her over, her face creased with unbearable pleasurable pain.

"Ah, *babi*, you're magnificent," he whispered, kissing her. He continued moving his hand until she shuddered and exhaled as if her bones had melted. She lay panting in a quivering pool on the blanket.

As he watched her body tremble with aftershocks, Joze rolled the condom on and moved between her thighs.

Her legs stiffened, her fingers turned into rigid pegs clutching his shoulders.

"Stay calm, Glorie, stay relaxed, open your legs for me honey," he spoke quietly while nudging her thighs apart. He put the tip of his shaft against her opening and reached down to spread her silk on it.

Voice tight, he said soothingly, "*Iawn*, uh, okay *babi*, I'll go slow," and he pushed just inside her.

He inched in slowly. Her vagina clenched around him, he had to steel himself from coming, from just hammering into her. His mind was already fogging with his body's thrumming pleasure like electric sparks jolting in his shaft and up his loins to his chest where they exploded into his brain.

Glorie was so tight, and small, and he was hard and quite big, she made tiny sounds of distress.

He stopped, letting her get used to him. Her satiny insides milked him, her walls trying to enclose and then expand around him.

"It's okay, beautiful, we're taking it slow. Stay with me," he urged.

When she eased again, he penetrated deeper. It was like pushing a train through a too small tunnel, albeit a soft pulsating one.

Finally, he was buried completely inside her. He stopped again, letting his manhood just throb against her sleek, feminine sheathe that tightly hugged him.

Her back arched slightly, forcing her hips at his, and at the same time he was suddenly clutched by her saturated channel and her violent shiver.

"*Fy Duw*, Glorie!" A harsh rasp groaned deep in his throat as his penis jumped. He pushed up from his elbows to his hands to keep himself from ejaculating.

Becoming aware of how strongly she affected him, Glorie stroked her palms up his shoulders and around his neck.

His arms rigid, biceps pumped from holding himself up and back from coming, his teeth grit with the strain. Lines cut around his eyes, Joze looked down at her.

The amethyst sparkled from under hooded lids, her mouth was turned up in a sexy soft smile. "Kiss me, Joze," she purred, pulling his head down to her sumptuous lips.

His brain dense with swirling lust, Joze lowered to her lips like a blind bee to honey. He bent his elbows to lower back down on his forearms, pressing their bodies together.

Their lips bridged then welded with heat. Joze groaned into her mouth and started boring his aching shaft all the way into her, then drawing slowly out.

He nudged her legs wide and pulled her thighs up so she could wrap them around his hips, then he pumped steadily faster and deeper as they consumed each other.

Joze's body was steaming, vital and throbbing, he moved so he was angled and could stroke her clit with every thrust.

When his rhythm quickened, whimpers and moans sifted up Glorie's throat. Thrill rose higher in him as he observed her while he pushed harder and deeper.

A flush spread across her chest, up her neck into her cheeks. Her lips parted, soft cries fell out of them as she met him thrust for thrust, her fingers tied in his hair.

When he felt her clench his shaft, saw her eyes go wide then flutter and her breathing rushed and keeled strident, he wrapped his hands around her shoulders and plunged deep and fast until he felt her body undulate against his.

With long, hard, gasping moans, her sex rippled along his manhood as it clutched, milking him. With a sharp inhale and taut scream, she shattered against him with his name repeating on her lips, "*Joze, Joze, oh, Joze!*"

Damn, he wanted to enjoy this longer, but she had annihilated his clamp on his control. Joze held her suffocating tight and thundered into her. His own breaths rushing loud and harsh and rapid, he drove until he was so engorged he finally burst. Pumping maniacally until his seed erupted and he cried out her name. He climaxed like an out of control roaring locomotive running off the tracks.

His chest heaving, he could feel her heart battering against his. Joze slowed, arching his spine, his head fell back with an agonized growl as he still felt his seed pummeling out of him with jerking tremors.

He wanted to collapse on Glorie, get as close to her as he could get, be as one, but knew he was too heavy so he dropped to the side.

Still in her, with his leg over hers, his hand possessively clasped her breast. He listened to her breath quieting, the rising of her chest lessen. His lips found her neck, he sucked her soft flesh, then sought her lips and kissed her gently.

When their bodies had calmed, his voice hoarse and hushed, he asked, "*Bach babi? Ta, fy cariad, es chwi iawm?*"

Glorie chuckled, it was a muffled tickle against his face. "Joze, I have no idea what you said."

Sighing contentedly, he cupped her breast, toyed with her nipple and smiled against her cheek. "Ah, sorry, brain buzz. I sort of said, 'Little baby, thank you my love, are you okay?' "

Her giggle delighting him, he prompted, "So…"

She purred, "Yes, it was…"

His heart paused. "It was what, *babi*?" He held his breath, *what if she hated it?* Ah, no worries, he had other ways to burn her up.

When she turned to face him, still semi-hard, he pulled out of her. Glorie put her palm on his face, brushing her thumb across his lips, she leaned in and kissed him. "Joze, it was too incredible to describe."

"Uh, so, does that mean you liked it?"

Smiling dreamily, she murmured, "I feel," then shivered, his eyes fell to her shimmering breasts, "delicious."

"Yeah?" His grin beamed.

"I can't wait to do it again."

"Really! *Ta Duw*, thank you, God," he praised gratefully. Sliding his hands around her hips, he pulled her to him and announced, "I'm ready." His erection twitched, he pushed it against her.

She laughed. "Wait, Joze, I need a minute, I'm kind of...sore."

"*Babi*, I can kiss where you're sore, and lick it, and make it better." He said with a sly leer, "In fact, I am so dying to taste you."

Gazing at him in confusion, she watched his eyes darken, they travelled down to her sex then back up to her face. His smile was a leering lopsided grin.

She got it. Her face burned red. "Joze, I mean, oh my gosh!" She covered her flaming cheeks with her hands.

"Ah, Glorie." Joze put his hand in her hair, tenderly smoothed it off her face and kissed her. "You are the best thing that ever happened to me."

He reluctantly rolled off the bed with a heavy sigh to dispose of the condom.

When he returned, she was stretching like a satisfied slender cat. He quickly joined her, the mattress sinking with his weight.

Lying beside her, Joze pulled her body against his side and settled her head on his chest. Combing his fingers through her hair he said, "You are exclusively my whore now. No more kisses from other men."

She froze in his arms. Then she pushed away to sit up. "You called me a whore?"

Rolling on his back, he dropped an arm over his eyes. "Aw come on honey, it was a figure of speech, doesn't mean anything, come back and lie down with me." He grabbed her wrist to pull her back down.

She snatched her hand away and stumbled to her feet.

He opened his eyes. Looking at her nude body with admiration he enthused, "Honey, you are so fucking exquisitely beautiful you take my breath away."

"Oh, Joze," she gushed with sarcasm, "I bet you tell all your whores that."

Still not getting that he insulted her, Joze said, "Come on, Glorie, I said it was just a figure of speech. Forget it. What I meant was that from now on you will stay with me, in this room, in my bed."

Grabbing up his shirt, she threw it over her head. Yanking it down over her thighs, she slammed her hands on her hips and glared at him. "You think because you pushed me to have sex with you that now it's okay to *order* me what to do? Take away every ounce of my meager independence?"

Snorting, he said smugly, "Huh. I did not push all that much, apparently you did not hear the cries of ecstasy coming from those beautiful lips that I did."

"You manipulated me, you touched me against my will until I was…uh…"

"Out of your mind with pleasure?" his conceited smile did nothing to mar his tough beauty.

He reached for her, catching her arm he pulled her to him. Smug again, Joze said, "You know you wanted it, you want me." He moved to kneel on the edge of the bed. Pulling her close, he pushed the lapels of the shirt aside to press her naked body against his. He looked down at her breasts wedged against the dark hair matting his chest.

Running his hands down her back to clutch her butt he then slid them back up to grasp her breasts. Kissing them both, he sucked on her nipples. He slid his hand down between her thighs, and sighed greedily, "Ah, *babi*, you're wet for me. You're ready now, come here."

She struggled to move away from him.

"Come on, Glorie," he said with anger tingeing his voice. "You can't be mad because I called you my whore. You know I didn't mean that. Get over it. Don't give up our pleasure for a misplaced fucking word."

She put both palms against his chest and pushed from him. "I have to go to the bathroom." Stalking to the door she jerked it open.

Seeing the rigid set of her queenly shoulders it was obvious she was pissed. "Glorie, come on, I said I didn't mean-"

She marched to her room, grabbed her clothes and boots, went back to his bathroom to clean up and change her clothes.

When she was done, she pushed his bathroom window open and slipped it up.

Chapter Thirty-Three

When she didn't come right back, Joze drifted off to sleep.

He didn't stir again until the morning. Waking up to the memory of Glorie's soft curvy body impaled by his thick, hungry manhood, writhing so hot under him last night crying his name, Joze grew hard immediately.

Throwing out a hand, he reached for her, but the bed was empty. And cold. Then he remembered her storming out of the room after his stupid comment. Shaking his head with slight mirth, "Women," he grumbled.

Swinging out of bed, he hit the shower, dressed in black jeans and a dark blue thermal, socks and boots and went to go find her in her room.

"Yeah," he muttered to himself. "I can sweet talk her, soothe her ruffled feathers. Remind her how good it was between us. Women are always so damned sensitive." That's why he always avoided them, just took what he wanted and moved on, quickly.

But, Glorie, he sighed, growing hard at the thought of her in his arms, she was worth everything to him. And he would tell her that as soon as he saw her. Apologize for talking stupid, and show her how much she meant to him.

He opened her door and strode right in. "*Babi*, come on honey, forgive me, I'm sorry I said such a stu-" he stopped in the middle of the room. It was empty.

He looked to her window. He had nailed new boards over it, they were still intact. The morning sky had darkened with thundering black clouds and solid sheets of water cascading from the sky making visibility nil.

After checking her bathroom, he went and checked his. Hearing the roaring crash of thunder, rain and wind rage at the glass, his eyes lit on the window.

The rain was stampeding in, the curtains flapping like wicked flags. Closing the window, he went to look for Van.

Finding him in the dining room finishing breakfast, he said "Van."

The guard looked up with a mouthful of toast, his brows vaulted in question.

"Where is she?"

Speaking through his food, Van mumbled, "Who?"

Joze's forehead furrowed in irritation. "Glorie of course. Who the hell else would I ask about? Where the hell is she?"

Van sipped a glass of orange juice. "I don't know. She was with you, you know, alone, in your bedroom?" One brow arched in a roguish wink.

A twinge of uneasiness started a prick in the pit of his gut. Joze rubbed the length of his jaw, trying to think of where she could be.

"Joze?" Van called, as Joze strode off.

Joze searched the entire building before finally admitting she was, he looked towards the rain beaten window, out there. He unhooked his phone and called Linc.

When he answered, Joze said, "Glorie has taken off. Outside. Alone. I need to go look for her. I'm going to the stables." He didn't wait for Linc to say anything, just tapped the phone off, hooked it back on his belt then hurried to get gear to go out in the storm.

Dressed in rain gear, hat, boots, by the time he reached the stables, Linc, Calvin and Bruno were already there and dressed the same.

Calvin said, "Diego and Sloan are heading here, they'll check that sheer hill where she went the last time, but I don't think she'd go there again."

Linc shouted over the roar of the storm, "Why do you think she's out here? Maybe she left with someone?" His Stetson was tied tight, rain dripped off the brim.

Saddling his horse, Joze shook his head. "No one has been here except us and no one has left. I said something…wrong…ah, to her." Shame for his thoughtless comment darkened his skin.

"Cripes, bro, what did you say that was so bad that a woman would go out in this shit in the fucking wilderness?" Calvin groused as he readied his steed. Throughout the dim stable, horses stomped the hay covered floor and snorted.

"And at night," Bruno added. The men slung their saddles on their mounts and prepared their horses to ride.

"Ah," Joze tightened the stirrups. His voice half muffled against his horse, he muttered, "We sort of, made love, for you know, for the first time," he paused at the whistles and hoots and congrats from his friends. "And then I kind of called her my uh…whore."

Dead silence hit, except for the storm battering around the stable.

"It was, ah, I was trying to make a joke. Kind of."

"You what?" Bruno was stunned. "You said what? Melissa would castrate me with a rusty fork if I said that to her."

"Ah…" Joze slammed his shotgun into the back of his saddle.

"Joze, bro, you said that to that sweet little thing, after finally getting her to give you a chance with her?" Calvin shook his head, water sprayed off the brim of his hat.

"You are an ass," Linc grunted in disgust. He tied his hat tighter as the wind tried to run away with it.

"Fuck, this is why I don't keep a woman, they're hard work," Joze groused as he hoisted up on his horse.

"So, let her go then," Bruno advised, already knowing Joze's response.

"No way in hell." Joze gathered up the reins.

"Let's go," Linc said, mounting his steed, "and pray that she is still alive."

"*Ie.*" Bowing his head against the wrath of the storm, his hand on his Stetson, Joze led the way out of the warmth and dry of the stables, and into the heart of the hammering squall. His heart was kicking like a mule at the thought of Glorie being out in this.

The wooded area surrounding them was perilous enough without the storm's treachery. She had been gone probably since the minute she left his bed last night. His gut cramped.

Linc was right, what a fucker he was. He had taken something so special, what they'd shared had been so beautiful, and he trashed it, ruined it, he had treated her like shit. He hadn't meant to, he just was a crude dick.

He'd finally made headway with her, and he chased her away with his crude words. The worse was, he'd hurt her feelings and that just killed him. He tugged his hat down over his brow, the rain sloughed right off the brim but at least it kept the water out of his eyes.

They split off, separating to follow different trails, scouring the area. Visibility was difficult and limited.

Every hour they met back up again. Then they circled and fanned back out but found no trace of her. Which, considering the fury of the storm, any tracks or trace would have been long washed away.

Joze's phone vibrated, the ring was drowned out by the rain. It was Diego.

"Bro," Diego had to yell to be heard, "unless she fell into the river, she wasn't down the hill."

Joze's heart hammered and thudded with the thought of her in the river. She'd have no chance. No, he wouldn't think that way.

Replying, "*Iawn,*" he took a breath. "All right, you and Sloan take the west, recheck behind us."

The day was passing, if the sun had been out it would be almost set. Joze's hope plummeted with it. Fourteen hours had ticked by since they'd left the house to search.

The men met up again. They stopped to rest, piss and eat a power bar.

Bruno said, "If she manages, somehow, to get out of here, do you think she'll go right to the cops and spill about us right away or would-"

Joze swung his head furiously at him and ground, "I don't give a fuck, I just want her home. Safe."

"Bro," Calvin's voice carried his sad hopelessness over the gale. "We've already gone out way further than she could have gotten on foot. She's either in the river, or an animal-"

"Shut up!" Joze shouted, his stomach turning. "Shut the fuck up," he shoved the last of his power bar in his mouth, took a swig of water from his canteen.

"I am not giving up on-" his head slashed to the right. Something down the side of a ravine caught his eye.

He hurried over and looked down.

At the bottom, he saw a hint of color. Flame. He started down the hill as fast as he could go. His boots slanting in the mud to keep from sliding out of control, he grabbed a hold of tree branches to help keep him from tumbling down.

Linc was right after him. When Bruno and Calvin went to follow, Linc said, "No, stay here. In case we can't get back up."

Joze finally reached the bottom.

Through the sleeting rain and diminished light, he saw a saturated crumple of clothes, and bright hair. He ran to her, dropped to his knees and shouted, "Glorie!"

She didn't move. He scooped his arm under her back and lifted her to look in her face.

"Joze, shit, don't move her, if her back is broken-" Linc sputtered as he reached them.

Joze growled, "It's freezing, she'll die anyway by the time we could get help and get her back to the ranch." He smoothed her soaking hair off her face with his long fingers. "Glorie, *babi*, talk to me!"

Her lashes fluttered before the raindrops forced them closed.

Linc knelt beside Joze. Surprised at his own shaky voice, he asked with dread, "Is she...?"

Joze stood up with her in his arms. "*Na*, barely alive, her pulse is terribly shallow." He started towards the hill but Linc hit his arm.

He gestured with his hand to the east, "That way, down a few hundred feet it's not such a steep incline."

Joze carried Glorie, and Linc kept his hand spread against Joze's back to help him up the hill as the torrential rain bulleted down on them.

Linc took out his phone with his other hand and called Calvin.

"We got her, Cal, we're heading down a ways to the east, about an eighth of a mile, meet us there with the horses."

The two men trudged through the wailing storm, ankle deep in mud, struggling uphill, until they reached the other men.

Joze gingerly handed Glorie to Linc while he mounted his steed then Linc handed her up to him.

Cradling her tightly to his chest, he murmured, "Stay with me, *babi*, stay with me. I love you, don't leave me," tears stung the back of his eyes. *Shyt*, he hadn't cried since he was four and fell off a roof and broke his leg.

He rode as quickly as he felt was safe for her.

When they reached the house, Diego, Sloan and Van were there to meet them.

Joze handed Glorie down to Van who started walking quickly to the house.

Leaving his horse to the care of the others, Joze jogged after Van.

"Give her to me," Joze's voice was hard and unforgiving, he knew it was wrong to blame Van for her fleeing, it was his own fault. But his choked up heart wasn't acting right.

"Joze," Van balked, looking down at the woman in his arms. He felt like he'd let her down. "God, Joze, she-" Her face was bruised, her eyes closed, she was frozen and soaked to the bone.

"Give her to me," Joze demanded holding his arms out. Van handed her to him.

Cuddled up against his chest, Joze quickly brought Glorie inside and to his room. By the time he got there, Maria was flustered and fretting behind him.

"Master Joze, I put a blanket on the couch. Set her there. We can change her, get her dry, then put her in bed."

His brain charged with panic and dread, Joze could hardly think, so he did as Maria instructed. He set Glorie down on the couch.

Maria came bustling over with more blankets, towels and clothes. "Here, I will undress her-"

"No, I've got it. Go make some hot tea, get a heating pad, more than one if we have them."

"But, she-"

"Go!" Joze barked.

She glanced at Glorie lying so still, so pale her skin was translucent. Without a word, Maria turned and dashed out of the room.

Joze shrugged out of his jacket, tossing it and his hat aside, untied and kicked off his muddy boots. He took her boots off, and her wet socks. His hands shaking with nerves, he lifted her, pulling off the crappy thin little jacket she'd worn as protection against the fucking gale.

"*Fy Duw, babi*, you need someone to look after you." Of course, he thought, if he hadn't taken her, held her against her will, fucked her then insulted her, she wouldn't be in this situation.

Dropping the sodden jacket, he unbuckled her belt, unbuttoned her pants and pulled them and her panties off. Keeping his eyes from the apex that had given him such joy only a day ago, he toweled her lower extremities then laid a blanket over her.

Then he unbuttoned her blouse, lifted her, in his huge strong arms she weighed but a feather. He slipped off the soaked shirt dropping it on the floor. He fought it, but her beautiful breasts in the transparent sheer bra made him hard.

Keeping his eyes on her face, he unclasped the wet bra dropped it and quickly toweled her dry then pulled the blanket up over her to her chin.

After wrapping her hair in a towel, leaning over her, he petted her face. "*Babi*, can you hear me?" He set the side of his face on her chest, it hardly rose, he moved his ear to her mouth, her breath was so faint.

"Motherfucker," he cursed, the backs of his eyes stinging again. Grabbing the sweatshirt Maria had brought, Joze lifted her again and it was a struggle, but he got it over her naked torso. Taking a deep breath, he reached for the pants, then saw the dry panties, he shook his head, he couldn't, but he needed to get a grip.

He moved the blanket, took the panties and slid them awkwardly up her slender shapely bare legs, and over her sex. Now that was something new, putting clothes on a woman instead of taking them off. It was much harder. Especially with how badly he desired this woman.

Sweat dripped in his eyes from the struggle to not get turned on, not that it worked. He could kick himself, she needed his care, not his lust.

As quickly as he could, he pulled the pants on her then lifted her in his arms and carried her to his bed. He laid her down and covered her with the sheet and blanket. He set his hand on her head. She was cold. Very cold. Like a block of ice.

"Maria!" he shouted just as she came hurrying in with three heating pads under her arm and a small tray with hot tea steaming out of a small pot and a teacup.

Joze rose to take the tray from her and set it on the nightstand. Then he took the heating pads and set them around Glorie and plugged them in.

"Maria, get some more blankets, please." Joze sat down on the edge of the bed and held Glorie up, he tried to get some hot tea in her. He only managed a few drops. He set the cup down and rubbed the towel over her hair.

Maria hurried back into the room with more blankets and a blow-dryer.

All night Joze tried to coax hot tea into Glorie while Maria bobbled around wringing her hands until Joze to her to go away she was making him more nervous.

The guys each popped in here and there to see how she was doing. Joze would only grimly shake his head at them.

He climbed in the bed next to Glorie and took her in his arms to give her his body heat. She was now shivering so hard he thought her teeth would shatter with the violent chattering together.

It went on all the next day.

The following day, the shivers and chill left when the fever struck. Joze poured aspirin and water into her but she only grew hotter.

Maria pulled the thermometer out of Glorie's unresponsive mouth and read it.

Joze had her huddled in his arms with her head on his shoulder. "Well?" he asked, his voice low.

"Master Joze," her face wrinkled with worry, her voice hushed and cracking, "it is pushing past102."

"Ah." He stood up lifting Glorie with him.

"What are you doing?" Linc asked sharply coming into the room.

"I'm taking her to the hospital."

"Bro, you can't. They'll arrest you on the spot."

"I have to, I can't let her die, Linc." Joze bundled her up in the blankets and carried her to the door. "Her life is more important than my freedom."

Chapter Thirty-Four

"**A**t least let me and the guys take her, Joze. You stay here."
Linc held his arms out to take Glorie.

Joze snorted. "You think I would drop her with you and run?"
He shook his head. "*Na*. I will not leave her side."

"Joze, please, listen, I'll take her to the hospital, you don't need
to put yourself in that position. "I'll-"

"*Na*. She wouldn't be in this situation if I hadn't fucking
kidnapped her and kept her here." He gazed down at her, his
expression wreathed with regret and sadness. "I'm so sorry, *babi*,
this is all my fault."

"Joze-" Linc tried again.

"Get out of my way." Joze started to muscle past his friend
when he felt Glorie stir.

Pausing, he looked at her. Her lashes threaded thick shadows
on her thin pale face. They flickered then briefly wisped up,
revealing weary, blurry amethyst.

Her hoarse voice hushed and dry, she rasped, "Joze?"

"Oh, *babi*," Joze almost cried. He moved back to the bed and
sat down with her tucked against him. With a gentle finger, he
pushed aside her hair damp with fever.

Linc came to stand next to them. He bent and put his palm on her head. "Bro, I think the fever is breaking." He smiled down at Glorie.

Her lashes wavered, then curled up as she struggled to force her heavy lids up. She looked so tiny and frail in Joze's powerful arms.

Linc quietly asked her, "Hey toots, how you doin'?"

Confusion flickered across Glorie's wan face. A feeble smile was just a faint ghost of a curve to her dry lips. Her blurry eyes flitted to Joze.

Slowly she was becoming aware she was in Joze's arms, wrapped in a blanket on his lap, with Linc staring down at her. They were in Joze's bedroom. On his bed. She suddenly moved to get up.

"It's, okay *babi*," Joze uttered, bundling her tighter against him. "You've been...sick." He glanced at Linc.

Linc said with a relieved grin, "It's good to see you're feeling better, honey." He leaned over and kissed her on her forehead then nodded to Joze and left them alone.

Joze asked her softly, "How are you feeling, *babi?*"

Her brows drew down, puzzled. "I...I don't...how did I get here," she looked at the sweats she was dressed in.

"Ah, you, had a...fall, and got chilled and," Joze didn't want to remind her of her running from him, but he didn't want her to forget their awesome lovemaking either. "How do you feel, Glorie?" he asked again.

"Um," her lips pursed. "I feel like going to the bathroom."

He laughed out loud. "Good. That means you're better. Maria and I gave you sponge baths and rinsed your mouth with minted saltwater, but I bet you can't wait for a hot shower."

She started to move off him but he held her. "Wait, Glorie, you'll be weak, let me help you."

A bit of color brushed her cheeks. "I think I can do this myself," she advised him as she tried to move again.

"*Ie*, but let me get you there, you will be weak." He stood up and carried her to the bathroom then set her on her feet.

Lightheaded, she immediately swayed and reached out to grab the doorframe.

He caught her with his arm around her. "Here wait, just stand still for a minute. Get your bearings." Joze held onto her until she stood steady then he let her go.

Returning to the bedroom, he sat down on the bed and waited for her to come out.

Her face was washed, but she was shaky and pallid.

"Come on, honey, come to bed, let me take care of you." He went to her and helped her walk to the bed and climb back into it.

After stacking pillows behind her so she could sit up, he tucked her in then grabbed a chair and set it next to the bed then sat down. Hunching his back, he rested his elbows on his knees, took her hand and held it.

Peering up at him through wan eyes, Glorie said in a low voice, "I remember, Joze."

His head lowered, shoulders hunched more, he looked up at her from under the ridge of his brow, through his long lashes. "Glorie, listen-"

"Joze, we had a beautiful time, I felt so close with you," her voice was strained, weak, her lids hovered heavy over her tired eyes.

His head hung with guilt. "*Ie.*" He raised his eyes to hers and told her, "It was the best time of my life. Glorie." Scooting his chair as close to the bed as he could get it, he squeezed her hand.

"I didn't mean to insult you. I'm a crass asshole, even my friends told me so. I," he ducked his head in embarrassment. "I was trying to be funny. Trying in a stupid childish way to say I want to be exclusive with you. I don't want you to leave. I want to free you, and have you stay with me of your own free will."

Her pale face was unreadable. Her eyes flickered across his face as she watched him speak. But she kept her mouth closed.

"Glorie," he said, lifting her hand to his lips, he kissed it. "I will free you. As soon as you are fully recovered."

At her skeptical arched brows, his sigh labored and pained, he told her, "I promise. It was wrong what I've done to you. I will let you go even if it means prison for me. I had no right to keep you. It was necessary for me to take you at the time, to get you the hell out of that damned saloon, but I should have taken you to a police station."

The pupils in her crystal eyes flared, she looked from his ashamed eyes to his lips. "Do you really mean that, Joze? You will set me free?"

His head down, he nodded, holding her hand so tightly it was turning white. He raised his head and looked directly at her. His mouth firm, grim, his jaw worked, a vein beat crazily at his temple. "*Ie*, I swear. No matter how you respond to my question, I will still free you."

Weary, yet her brows rose. "What question?"

Joze slid off his chair onto his knees and took both of her hands in his. "*Babi*, Glorie, will you marry me?"

Before she could answer, he took a breath and said, "I love you, Glorie. I want to spend the rest of my life with you. I only wish to take care of you, cherish you, give you everything you could ever need or want. Maybe, if the heavens are aligned, we can build a family together. I never thought I'd ever have, or even want to have children, but with you, it's all I think about. What do you say?"

She was silent so long Joze didn't think she was going to answer him. Then, she asked, "You will let me go, back to my home, even if I say no?"

His heart clenched like a knife stabbed through it. His head dropped, the blond hair flopped over his forehead. Raising his head to regard her, he grit his jaw so hard his face grated like solid steel.

"Yes," he exhaled the word hard. It was tough for him to agree to it. "I love you, Glorie. I will do whatever makes you happy. If that means to not have you…with me, then, whatever you want."

His eyes went from blue to crestfallen grey, the light dimming in them. He waited to hear what she had to say, but he already knew.

Glorie surprised him by asking, "What about your other women?"

Sitting back on his heels, he frowned. "What other women?"

She shrugged. "All other women, you told me you are with a different one every night."

His mouth turned down, scowling. "Glorie, if you were mine, I swear to *Duw, fy cariad,* I love you. I would never even look at another woman. You are all I will ever need, all I want. I want to wake up every single morning forever and open my eyes and see your beautiful head lying on the pillow next to me."

He knew he was gripping her hand too hard, her gaze dropped down to it, but he was afraid when he let go it would be the last time he would get to touch her. Now that she knew he wouldn't hold her here she would be gone before the screen door slammed closed.

"Joze, really, we're going to grow old. I'll put on weight, my hair will turn grey not to mention wrinkles. You won't-"

"*Babi*, sure, your face and body turn me the hell on and I admit looking at you everyday will be no hardship," he chuckled, then his expression sobered.

He went on, "But, my feelings for you started when you were in disguise as a plain Jane wallflower. It was your courage, your utter sweetness, kindness to everyone, your wit, your smile, honey," he grinned, "it was you I fell in love with. Your looks are just frosting on the most delicious cake in the world. I *hope* to grow old with you. You hear me?"

"Would we stay here at the ranch?"

"Huh?" His head flew up. Then his brows lowered. "Yes. No. Whatever you want. If you wanted to live anywhere else, *babi*, that will be our home, wherever you want it to be." He kissed her hands, hope welled in his eyes brightening them to vivid blue.

"I love your ranch, Joze. I've never been so happy, felt so content. I never wanted to be a police officer. I just took the job that was in cyber-crime because it was available. I had no idea they would snatch me out and stick me undercover. It was like living a lie, I hated the subterfuge of it."

He gazed at her, stunned by her gorgeous smile. "You love the ranch, but," he looked pained, and hopeful, "what about me?"

Her eyes stilled, the amethyst glazed with a determined glean. She informed him firmly, "Joze, I will not be bullied by you. I will not be dragged or pushed or forced to eat. I will not be forced to," her gaze lowered then rose with determination. "I am done with being assaulted by anyone. That includes you." She tugged a hand free and jabbed a finger into his chest."

"Ah *babi*," he caught her loose hand then brought them both to his mouth and kissed them tenderly. "I will do my best to treat you as an equal, without pushing you around. It's just," he kissed her fingers again, then his lips pulled in, he petted her hair.

"I care so much for you it makes me worry. Sometimes my own strength gets in my way, and you are so…small, delicate. I will do my best to not haul you around like the beautiful doll that you are."

"Joze," she admonished. "I am not a doll. I am an adult person and I expect to be treated as such."

He looked at her fingers like he wanted to put them in his mouth and suck on them. He nodded. "Yes. I will do my best. So," he licked the ends of each of her fingers, "back to me. What do you feel about me?" He sounded more confident yet a bit of uncertainty lingered, she hadn't yet told him her feelings for him.

Glorie pulled a hand away and trickled her fingertips tenderly down the side of his face.

"When I finally realized you would never hurt me, not deliberately, because at least with me anyway, you're all bluster and no bite. I was able to let my feelings for you fill my heart. I love you, Joze. I want to marry you, stay here," her shoulders bunched shyly, "and raise a family of tow-headed little children, just like their daddy."

Her lips pulled in with hesitation. "I mean, if that's what you want. You mentioned children. Those boys at the rec center just adored you- um," she trailed off at the funny look on his face.

His mouth dropped, he never dare hoped. "Oh *fy Duw*, Glorie, you mean it?"

When she nodded with a loving smile, he got up and sat on the bed. He gathered her up, cuddling her to his chest. "You really mean it?" He looked down at her, her eyes teemed with happy tears.

She nodded. "Yes, Joze."

He kissed her so hard her head bent back, realizing it, he quickly drew away. "I'm sorry, honey, you've been so ill and I'm a brute. You need to rest."

Her sigh happy she agreed, "Yes, I do."

Grinning so hard his cheeks hurt, Joze said, "But I want little fire-haired children with jeweled eyes like their mama." He put his palm on the side of her face cupping it, and held her hand.

"*Babi*, do you…ah…forgive me for what I said to you? I didn't mean it. I was trying to be…" he swallowed hard, "you know. I was just stupid."

Smiling her forgiveness, she said, "Joze, I was being too sensitive. My life these past few months, this," she looked around then back at him, "is all new to me, bizarre, everything, you, I way overreacted."

One brow cocked dryly. "Are you saying I'm bizarre?"

"Ha!" she laughed gaily. "Yeah, you sure are."

Her smile thinned, she turned somber. "I mean, I was so shortly a police officer, then…assaulted, then put undercover, then kidnapped, this ranch," she smiled again, "is a fairytale dream. But, I almost died in the woods, not to talk about the barn and the shootout and, well," she let out a long breath, smiling weakly.

"Bizarre?" He pulled her face toward his. "You think I'm bizarre? I'll give you bizarre."

Releasing her chin, he grabbed her legs, pulled her down the bed, moved over her then latched his lips on hers and kissed her so fiercely they were both breathless with the slamming rush of kaleidoscopic, body shuddering feelings burning up their bodies.

His erection, a long hard staff pressed throbbing against her core made no secret of what he wanted. But, he pulled back, rolled off her and sat up.

He lifted her, propping her back against the headboard.

"Sorry, *babi*, you are a nectar I can't resist tasting, smelling, touching. But you have been so ill. We need to wait until you are recovered."

Sighing, Glorie snuggled cheerfully yet wearily into the pillows. With a wicked little smile she said, "Joze, I can't wait to do what we did the other night again. You said you had more to teach me?"

He choked, sputtered, his eyes sprung wide. "Are you talking about, I mean, do you mean, sex?" His eyes narrowed eagerly, he asked, "You want to do...more things?" He crawled over to sit beside her. The mattress jostled with his weight.

She grinned. "Duh, yeah." Snuggling against him, Glorie said, "It was, wonderful Joze. The feelings, so crazy good, and you," she smiled up at him, moving towards his mouth. "I loved being so close, so intimate, you inside me was," her face burst into a full blush.

He pulled her in close to him, his face spilt with a happy grin. "*Ie*, with you, *babi*, it felt like nothing I've ever experienced before. I've never felt so close to anyone as I did with you. And I want more. Much more. Forever." He hugged her tight. "So, you haven't said if you forgive me for being such an ass?"

She laughed. "Yes. I forgive you. I should have been more patient, Joze. You are trying to be a better man and I didn't give you enough credit for how hard you're trying."

Her head ducked, she said, "I, uh, what we had done was so unbelievably special to me, then I thought that it meant nothing more to you than a- a roll in the hay, no more than one of your other...women." Her eyes welled.

"I felt, used. You got what you wanted then tossed me aside like you have with all your women. I was too ashamed and mortified to stay and confront you."

"*Duw*, *babi*, never, you are the most important thing in the world to me. I'm not used to having feelings...ah, for women. Instead of telling you how much our loving making meant to me, I just, well I was just a crude male. I love you, Glorie. Can we make the term 'my other women' obsolete, toss it out of our vocabulary, please?" Joze cupped her chin, tilting her head up so he could cover her mouth with his.

Other than to shower, he made her stay in bed for two more days before he let her get up.

Another day passed before he would allow her to go outside. She had been excited beyond words to visit with the horses, play with the alpacas, feed the chickens, even chat with the braying donkey.

It was while they ate a picnic lunch out in a secluded area that Joze got on one knee on the blanket and took her hand. He pulled out a ring and slid it on her finger. "I know you agreed to marry me, *fy babi*, Glorie, but I wanted to make it official. Will you do me the biggest honor and marry me? Become my beloved wife?"

Glorie threw her arms around him, the tears started immediately. "Oh Joze, you know I will! Yes!"

Embracing each other, they rolled onto the blanket, made hasty ravenous, all-consuming love, then did it again more leisurely to seal their deal.

Joze and Glorie were just coming in from the pasture when a clamoring of sirens and swirls of red and blue lights came blaring up the drive and circled the house.

Parking haphazardly, police leaped out and ran into the house, guns waving, voices bellowing that they were the police and everyone was to freeze.

Within moments they were ushering people out.

Once outside, they corralled everyone into small groups, then did the same to all of the outbuildings, the barracks the barns, stables. Gathering soldiers, ranch hands as well as the groupie women that were present into clusters, officers stood armed guard over them.

Joze shoved Glorie behind him to protect her as the police approached them with guns drawn.

"Glorie!" one of the plain-clothed men called out.

Joze felt her freeze behind him. He tried to hold her back, but she crept to peek around him.

"Glorie!" the man in the suit called, "come here, honey." He gestured to her to go to him.

But Glorie stayed by Joze's side.

The armed officers slowly circled the pair.

The man held his hand out to her and ordered brusquely, "Glorie, move away from him."

She clung to Joze's arm.

Joze pulled her free and held her away. He recognized the detective. "Honey, go to…him. I don't want you hurt." He raised his hands and set them on his head.

The suit strode over quickly and grabbed Glorie's arm yanking her away from Joze. He pushed her to another officer who clamped a tight hold on her.

"No, Luc! Don't hurt him! Wait-" Glorie cried, fighting to free herself from the officer holding her.

"Jozadak Dekar Kane," Detective Luc Bolton identified him. He stood smirking in front of Joze, his gun aimed at his heart.

Joze said nothing, his eyes were on Glorie as she frantically fought the officer holding her.

"Keep your hands on your head, get down on your knees, Kane," Bolton ordered, "now."

Joze sunk to his knees with his hands on his head.

"No! Luc- wait-" Glorie yelled, "leave him-"

"Get her back," Luc barked at the officer holding Glorie. With great satisfaction, tromping over, he holstered his gun then grabbed first one of Joze's hands, yanked it behind his back, then the other and cuffed them.

He declared, "Jozadak Kane, you are under arrest, listen to your rights." Bolton blathered his rights at him as he jerked Joze to his feet.

Her eyes wide and panicked, Glorie glanced all around. The rest of Joze's men were also held at gunpoint with their hands up, but only Joze was being arrested.

Sloan sneered at her, "It was you, you bitch, you turned him in, you called the fucking cops."

"No! No, I wouldn't!" she cried, looking from Sloan to Linc to Bruno to Calvin to Diego. They all glared at her, accusing.

But then Linc said, "No, she wouldn't turn him in."

"Bullshit-" Sloan barked as Bolton walked Joze to several other waiting officers and shoved him into their custody. "Who else could it be?"

Then Bolton marched over to Glorie and gripped her arm. Turning her to face him, he said, "Honey, are you all right? Did that bastard hurt you?"

She protested, "No, Luc, please." Glorie shook her head adamantly exclaiming, "Please, he did nothing, please, he saved me from-"

Luc pulled her into his arms and put her head against his chest, saying, "Shh, you're safe now, everything will be all right."

Glorie tried to twist out of his grasp but he held her taut. She looked over his arm at Joze. Joze's intense eyes blazed across the yard at her. Some of his men stood off to the side, vilely cursing her.

She cried desperately, "Joze, I didn't-"

The officers took Joze and shoved him into the back of a police car.

Glorie stood watching helplessly as he was taken away. Before she could utter another word, she was whisked to another car, practically shoved inside, and driven away before she could talk to Joze's friends.

They stood on the lawn watching her as she looked back through the window at them, seeing the unforgiving hatred on their faces.

Chapter Thirty-Five

Six Months Later

Glorie didn't see Joze again until the trial. Detective Luc Bolton, her handler, would not allow her visitation. Plus, she was retained in protective custody in case Joze put out a hit on her.

The only people allowed contact with her were her sister, Detective Bolton, and the security people at the safehouse where they were keeping her. Glorie cringed every time she saw Bolton. She was so tired and annoyed at seeing his hard, thin face at the door.

He was tall and angular, had short fine, light brown hair, and zero personality and even less of a sense of humor. He wanted to nail Joze so badly, thus he dissected Glorie endlessly. However, he only showed when Shana wasn't around. Glorie's sister was beyond infuriated at the danger Bolton had put Glorie in.

In fact, Bolton had to crazy spin his wheels to keep his superiors from hanging him for the stunt he'd pulled. Putting a green officer in the line of fire. Having her go after the biggest gangster kingpin in the States.

Well, that was what Bolton had thought about Joze. Glorie still hadn't heard that they'd come up with any concrete evidence against Joze. The only thing that saved Bolton's ass was the fact that they now had Jozadak Kane on trial.

Bolton unceasingly asked her questions over and over about her time with Joze. He was insistent that she must have seen or overheard *something* that could be of value to the trial.

In the courtroom, the prosecutor introduced vague references of Joze's racketeering and other felonious charges. Unfortunately, for the prosecutor, the poor lack of concrete evidence was clearly not sufficient to sway a jury.

Glorie was their trump card. At least they could slap a conviction of kidnapping a law enforcement officer on Joze. Their biggest hope was that with the seriousness of the courtroom scene and the prosecutor slamming her with hard interrogation Glorie would eventually recall something and spit it out and they'd hang Joze.

Luc Bolton sat next to the prosecutor, the two men practically licked their chops and rubbed their hands with greedy glee when Glorie was brought in to testify.

The entire courtroom watched her walk up the aisle.

A deputy held the swinging door for her to pass through. Her hips swayed, feminine yet demure, self-conscious to the max, her stomach was in knots.

Dressed in a flouncy skirt and white frilly blouse, she looked sweet and subtly sexy. Her flaming hair was in a neat French braid that curved over one shoulder and coiled around her breast.

With her hair pulled back, it only made her amethyst eyes appear bigger and glowing with vitality and apprehension.

Exhaling gracefully, she forced her face to remain smooth and calm, and politely thanked the deputy. She walked through the courtroom, her head high, spine straight, regally like a queen and took her seat at the witness stand.

Her head still, her eyes searched the courtroom. She saw Joze's friends glaring at her. Even Bruno's girlfriend, Melissa gazed at her with some doubt on her pretty face.

Daniel caught her eye, and winked. Her shoulders relaxed. She smiled gratefully at him, Daniel believed it wasn't her that had turned Joze in. His recovery from the gunshot had been long and arduous, but Glorie was pleased to see his cheeks were filled with healthy color and his tan was once again solid, a declaration that he was back at work at the ranch.

Then, her eyes found him. Joze was staring at her. Dark brows and long lashes framed his piercing blue gaze, like a laser slicing straight to her across the several dozen feet that separated them. He was wearing an expensive black suit and red tie, his blond hair combed back thick and wavy, the darker sides shaved close.

As she looked at him, his eyes changed, they smoldered to the deep black discs that everyone else found so terrifying, but they made Glorie melt. His expression was granite in his hard, masculine face. She could not tell what he was thinking, whether he hated her guts, or…

The judge was speaking, she blinked to listen, but she couldn't take her eyes off Joze.

Then the prosecutor was standing in front of her. Tall with narrow shoulders, dressed in an inexpensive brown tweed suit with blue tie, he asked the standard questions, her name, her hire date and position in the police force, what her initial position and job was in cyber-surveillance.

She answered all in a polite quiet voice. Joze's gaze never wavered from her.

"Miss Toby," Michael McNeill, the prosecutor continued. His short, dark brown wavy hair looked moussed and had an odd shine to it.

"Office Toby," Glorie corrected politely.

He frowned. Dark brown eyes looked her up and down, hesitated at her breasts pressing against the blouse with the frilly collar, they moved up quickly to her tiny plump lips. His expression indicated that he found it hard to believe this dainty young woman was a police officer.

His thin lips pursed, he nodded. "Uh, of course. Officer Toby, tell us what happened the day Detective Bolton chose you for undercover work. What your task was." Shifting his head sideways, the prosecutor and Luc Bolton shared a discreet smug smile.

"Oh, of course." Glorie tugged her skirt down. She could feel Joze's eyes burning through her clothes, stroking her like she was naked with his flaming gaze.

"Detective Bolton got me hired at the Seraphim Saloon as a barback-cleaner so I could locate Jozadak Kane. And, once I did that, I was tasked to find something on him that he could be prosecuted for and sent to prison."

"And, did you find him?"

"Yes."

"And, did you find evidence of unlawful acts?"

"No."

Prosecutor McNeill's dark untrimmed brows shot up. "No?"

"No."

McNeill's brown eyes narrowed at her. She sat primly, her hands folded in her lap, her shoulders straight. McNeill's gaze followed the braid stalling on her breasts again.

"Mr. McNeill?" The judge's stern voice broke his revelry.

"Yes, Your Honor." McNeill turned from Glorie to go to his table to review his papers but he almost stumbled when he saw the steaming threat permeating from Joze's obsidian orbs, fierce as black bullets aimed at him.

He hesitated, then glared back at Joze and grabbed up his papers. He shuffled through them trying to keep his hands from shaking. He set the papers down, and without glancing in Joze's direction, he stalked back to Glorie.

"Miss, uh, Officer Toby," he cleared his throat, "how did you end up at Mr. Kane's ranch?"

She cleared her throat with a little feminine cough then said, "Well, while I was undercover, it was late one night at the saloon and I was cleaning up. Apparently the employee who said he locked the front door did not. Suddenly, four armed robbers burst in. They grabbed me and tried to break into the vault. They said they were going to-" her cheeks colored prettily, she swallowed.

The slight murmurings in the crowded courtroom silenced as people held their breath, waiting to hear the salacious details of her abduction.

Once the police interviewed the saloon staff and the thugs and studied video and pictures they put two-and-two together and discovered it was in fact Jozadak Kane who had also been undercover. He had been present when the saloon was being burgled.

The news had blasted for weeks about the gangster who had allegedly beaten almost to death a team of thugs that while robbing the saloon were going to assault the young female officer. Then, the notorious gangster had kidnapped the woman himself and kept her prisoner on his ranch for months.

Glorie's lips pulled in, she pressed them together to suppress the terror that assailed her at the remembrance of that harrowing night. Her voice hushed, she went on, "The robbers said that they were going to- to assault me in the car on the way back to their home and then kill me."

"Miss Toby," McNeill interrupted, "we don't need a diatribe of what allegedly-"

"Objection," Joze's lawyer, Thomas Kincaid, said from his table. "He asked her how she found herself at Mr. Kane's residence, she is explaining."

Kincaid sniffed at McNeill then said with steep derision, "The young woman endured a traumatic event. She could have easily been raped and murdered. You would be well to remind yourself of what she suffered in the line of duty." He straightened his jacket sleeves, "And that's *Officer* Toby as the lady said."

"Sustained." The judge frowned at McNeill, then smiled kindly at Glorie. He said sympathetically and with all sincerity, "I am sorry for your travails, Officer Toby. Please, continue."

"Um, thank you Mr. Judge." Glorie smiled shyly at him.

He smiled back. "It's Your Honor."

"Oh. Okay. I'm sorry." She blushed deeper. "I didn't mean to offend you, sir." Her long curly lashes fluttered at him.

"Ahem." Judge Lawrence Merrigan cleared his throat then said kindly, "You didn't my dear, please continue." He glanced up in time to see McNeill rolling his eyes, which earned the prosecutor another frown.

"Yes, sir. Thank you." Glorie took a deep breath, her voice wavered slightly with the remembered fear, "So, as the thug holding me was about to punch me to knock me out so he could carry me without my screaming-"

"Object, Your Honor, she can't say what the man was thinking."

"Oh," Glorie said quickly. "The one man told the man holding me to knock me out so I wouldn't scream, and the man holding me said, 'Okay' and he raised his hand to punch me." Her body roiled in a visible shiver at the memory.

Murmurings in the courtroom increased. The audience's empathy for her terrifying experience was audible.

McNeill said, "Your Honor, I objected, she can't-"

The judge lowered his glasses and glared over them at the prosecutor. "Overruled." He smiled kindly at Glorie. "It sounds like you had a terrible ordeal, would you like to take a break?"

McNeill sputtered, "Your Honor, come on, she's being dramatic, she doesn't need-"

Swinging his head around, Merrigan snapped his glasses off his face and glowered at McNeill. He turned back to Glorie and said softly, "Officer?"

Glorie shook her head. The fiery braid flipped back and forth across her chest. Both prosecutor and judge watched it. "Oh dear, no sir. I certainly do not want to take up the court's valuable time. There are many more trials to be heard, I'm sure. I am fine, sir."

McNeill opened his mouth but shut it at the judge's frown. "Fine," McNeill groused. "Please," he said sarcastically, "continue."

"Um, thank you so much, Mr. Prosecutor. So, this awful man had picked me up and had pulled back his fist to strike me, when suddenly Mr. Kane came from the back room. He had been listening.

He could have run out the back door and saved his own life, I mean there were four of them, all armed."

She glanced warmly at Joze. His face remained impassive, but his gaze never wavered from hers.

"But, to make a long story a little shorter, without a weapon at all, Mr. Kane beat them all up, rescuing me. He feared there might be other thugs lurking outside so he took me with him to keep me safe."

The courtroom sat in stunned silence. All eyes, including judge and jury, turned to Joze, expressions turning from hostile condemnation to admiration.

"Miss, I mean, Officer Toby, you can't know what Mr. Kane was thinking. He could have had another motive for taking you that you weren't aware of. He could have been in cahoots with the hoods."

She shook her head. "It was obvious, Mr. Prosecutor. It all happened so very quickly, and so terrifying. The thugs threatened to kill Mr. Kane as well. Neither Mr. Kane nor I knew if there were others around, there could have been a get-away car waiting out front with more criminals in it. I mean we didn't know.

"The men were talking amongst themselves, they made it clear they weren't even aware who Mr. Kane was. They thought, as did I, that he was a mentally challenged employee that barbacked at the saloon. They planned on killing me, so there was no need for any of them to pretend in front of me. If you don't believe me, Mr. Kane is sitting right there," she said mildly as if he were a bit slow, "you can ask him."

Half the courtroom snickered.

McNeill coughed loudly to break the humor. "Fine. Let's move on. He took you there, allegedly to protect you. But you stayed. For months. Why?"

The amethyst eyes glimmered brightly. They flitted to Joze, the jewel tones warmed at him, then Glorie looked back at McNeill. "I was invited."

Luc Bolton's gasp broke the quiet of the courtroom. His pale blue eyes narrowed in puzzlement.

McNeill did a double-take. "What?" He looked her up and down, narrowed his gaze at her pure complexion, to her innocent eyes. "You were invited? Who invited you?"

Glorie smiled at Joze. He never took his eyes off her but his face remained inscrutable. "Why, Mr. Kane of course."

McNeill stared hard at her. "Why would he do that?"

Glorie grinned coyly, "Mr. McNeill, why do you think?" The courtroom twittered. Glorie saw the corner of Joze's lip twitch.

McNeill swiveled a look back at Luc Bolton, but Bolton was as stymied as he was. "So, then, I don't understand, he's a criminal, why would you stay with him?"

She hesitated then said, "Mr. Kane is a very good looking man, Mr. McNeill." The ladies in the courtroom erupted all babbling at once cooing and giggling about how true that was.

Many a female eye was swooning at the tall, broad-shouldered, hard looking but handsome man. They boldly feasted on the male with the vampire-ish appearance with his white-blond hair and uncanny blue-black eyes sitting at the defense table.

"Order, please," the judge admonished. He waited until the twittering died down then nodded to McNeill. "Please proceed."

McNeill's brown eyes were dark angry slits. His lips pushed out then thinned into a straight line. "Are you telling me, Miss Toby, that you went to Mr. Kane's residence, in a totally different city from where you live, and stayed for months because he invited you and you were attracted to him?"

Glorie smiled a dismayed frown at him. She explained as if he were a child, "Of course not, for heaven's sake Mr. McNeill. I had a job to do. I was to get close to Mr. Kane to dig up dirt on him. The task of observing him at work was blown with the robbery. It was pure luck that he invited me to his home. Can you think of another way I could get close enough to him to spy on his activities and dig up evidence?"

Her eyes flickered to Joze. His brow quirked at her. She prayed that he realized that she was telling a tale. That in truth, she had not been spying on him. Besides, he was the one who had forced her to stay at the ranch.

But, if she told the court that she had eventually become enamored with Joze she would lose all credibility. She would look foolish, a silly cop girl that fell for a disreputable gangster. She wanted to help Joze, to do so, she had to remain in the police persona. Glorie looked back to the prosecutor.

"Your Honor," McNeill said crossly, "please direct the witness to only answer the questions, she is not to question me."

Merrigan's eyes flicked from McNeill to Glorie to McNeill and then warmly back to her. "My dear, please try to avoid asking the State questions."

"Of course, sir, I am sorry." Her long lashes curled down abashed over her eyes. "This is all new to me, I will try my best to behave accordingly. Please forgive me."

"Now, now, my dear," the judge said cheerfully, "you are doing very well. No need to apologize." He glared at McNeill and said coldly, "Continue."

McNeill brushed an aggravated hand over the top of his shiny dark waves. He glanced at Bolton who just blinked impassively at him, then he cleared his throat again.

He moved to Glorie, placed his palms on the front of the witness box and leaned in aggressively close to her. His voice harsh, he said coarsely, "A single young woman living with a young man, it can only be assumed that you two were, uh, intimate." He shook his head with disgusted disapproval. "Sex in the line of duty, hmm? Now, Miss Toby, tell the jury of your sexual-"

She reacted by leaning back with a slight look of fear at him. Her big eyes shot sideways at the judge, her lashes fluttered like she was in distress. In the background, Joze's growl was audible.

The judge glanced at Glorie, the shy pretty young thing that she was. He frowned at McNeill. "Mr. Prosecutor, you need to back up a bit, give the little lady some breathing space." He turned and smiled back at Glorie.

Her lips turned up gratefully. The courtroom broke into twitters again. They could have been back in the 1950's the way the judge and prosecutor were behaving towards Glorie.

Dark red crept up McNeill's neck, he stepped back, his shoulders rigid. "Fine then. Miss Toby-"

"Excuse me, that's Officer Toby, sir," Glorie said in a very shy, feminine voice. She didn't react to the snickers in the room. She knew she didn't look like a cop but she had to keep the jury in that frame of mind to believe her testimony.

It wasn't fair that they were going after Joze when there was no discernable evidence against him, and Glorie would be damned if she'd let the court railroad her into testifying against him. Sure, he was technically guilty of abducting her, but if he hadn't saved her from those ruffians there wouldn't have been anything left to kidnap.

McNeill grit his teeth, a crease deepened across his forehead. Eyes just brown slits of fury, he almost snarled, "*Officer* Toby, did you?"

She blinked, the long curly lashes flapped. "Did I what?"

He sighed loudly. Placing his palms on the counter of the witness stand, his arms out rigid, he said with cold asperity, "Were you intimate these many months while you were living with Mr. Kane? Did you two have sex?"

Appalled, a hand fluttered at her throat, Glorie said with haughty indignation, "Mr. McNeill, how dare you, are you insinuating that I – I- slept with, I mean, oh dear, you are not a gentleman, sir!"

Blushing demurely pink, she moved her hand up in front of her face in ladylike embarrassment. "I most certainly did not sleep with Mr. Kane all those months!" She was being honest, basically, it had only been in that last week they had become truly intimate.

Joze's attorney stood up. Holding his tie against his stomach, he declared, "Your Honor, I must object to this character assassination of this poor young woman who was only laying her life on the line to do her duty. She isn't here to be slandered, to have her virtue be sullied, turned into sensationalized fodder for the tabloids!"

The judge, and the men and women of the jury frowned at McNeill as if he had insulted the young woman's honor.

Joze's lip twitched. Sitting behind him, Linc chuckled.

"No, wait, uh, let's get back to my first question," McNeill sputtered. Dragging a finger around the inside of his collar, he tugged at it, loosening it and the knot of his tie over his anxiously bobbing Adam's apple. He looked to Bolton who rolled his eyes and shrugged.

Trying to salvage his poise, McNeill smiled weakly, then said calmly, "Miss," he bit his tongue and quickly said, "*Officer* Toby, did you find any unlawful activity regarding Mr. Kane that could be used to prosecute him?" He took a deep breath and loudly let it out.

"No."

His head shot up. "No? You were there for several months, are you saying in that time you found nothing that Mr. Kane was doing that was unlawful?"

"No. I did not."

McNeill's brows dragged down hard over his eyes. "Let me ask you this," he shot a wary glance at the judge, "where did you stay when you were at Mr. Kane's house? What room?"

All eyes turned to Glorie.

She said primly, "His house is quite large, like a lodge. There are a lot of rooms in his house and on the property. Many people stayed in it. There are even barracks for the farmhands. I had my own room which had its own bathroom."

Her eyes narrowed gracefully at the prosecutor. "Please feel free to ask anyone that was there, Mr. Kane, the ranch hands, his uncle, the other men and women that were there off and on. Ask his housekeeper, Mrs. Velera, the maids," her gaze slid to Maria sitting between Linc and Daniel. "They will all confirm that I had my own bedroom, that I did not share Mr. Kane's bed for all those months."

Tears in her eyes, Maria nodded a kind, sad smile at Glorie.

"Really, Miss Toby, you expect us to believe that for all those months, you, an attractive young woman and Mr. Kane did not-" he broke off, turned his head slightly glancing at Joze then back at her.

McNeill thought for a minute. Then he decided on a new track to follow. A heinous one that would surely bring damnation down on Kane. He said, "Miss Toby, Mr. Kane is a notorious gangster of obviously loose morals and ethics, he is a big, well-framed man with presentable looks. Did Mr. Kane, uh, assault you, rape you?"

Everyone gasped, mouths dropped. They all looked at Glorie with compassion and pity, some glared at Joze.

He sat impassively, his eyes on Glorie.

Glorie shook her head. "No. I would have said if he had. I repeat, we did not have sex all those months that I was there."

At McNeill's clear disbelief, she held her dainty hands out and said, "Please, call for a lie detector test right now. I will swear, as I have, under oath, that I had my own room and I slept in it every night."

"Really, Miss-"

"Except for one when I was outside at night and got disoriented. I got lost in the woods, in the dark, during a terrible storm. I fell down a ravine and lay unconscious for almost two days. I became very, very ill. I guess I almost died from being out so long in the storm."

A pin could be heard dropped.

McNeill's mouth opened and closed. "Wha- what happened, how did you get back, I mean, what happened?" He couldn't keep his own curiosity out of his voice.

Without looking at Joze, Glorie kept her eyes leveled unwavering at McNeill. She replied, "Mr. Kane and his friends came out in the storm and searched for *fourteen* straight nonstop hours for me. Mr. Kane found me at death's door. He carried me up a hill, in the dark, in the fierce gale back to his home where he nursed me, himself, with hot tea and aspirin, until I was well."

McNeill stood with his mouth open.

No one said a word for a moment. The jury ping-ponged from Glorie to Joze to her.

She looked like the frail, beautiful princess, and Joze looked like the handsome valiant prince who fought dragons to rescue her. You could hear a collective romantic sigh throughout the courtroom.

McNeill spoke, "Uh, Miss Toby-"

The Judge muttered, "Officer Toby."

McNeill forced himself to not roll his eyes. "Yes, yes, *Officer* Toby, are you saying the entire time you were with Mr. Kane you did not have sex with him?" Ignoring the courtroom's angry gasp, McNeill leaned in aggressively towards her again.

"Ahem," the judge cleared his throat with a gruff cough. "Mr. McNeill, the question has been asked and answered, please move on."

Rubbing his chin, McNeill glared at Glorie. She stared back with those big wide innocent eyes. "All right, Miss Toby-"

Almost the entire courtroom, including the judge and jury said in unison, "*Officer* Toby."

Glorie's eyes flicked to Joze, the corner of his mouth was turned up, his gleaming eyes still never left her.

The courtroom laughed around them, some people even high-fived until the judge glared at them.

McNeill's body turned to stone with embarrassment. He waited until the room quieted down again. "All right, *Officer* Toby, do you know that Mr. Kane has been accused of being involved with racketeering, money laundering and a list of other illegal offenses, including murder?"

Glorie smiled like he was silly and rolled her eyes. "Of course, Mr. McNeill." She leaned forward, said again like he was slow, "Didn't you know that? That's why we're all here. That's why I was sent to spy on him in the first place."

The courtroom roared with laughter, the judge had to hammer his mallet for quiet.

His face beet red, fury radiated at her from his little brown eyes, McNeill ground through his grit teeth, "Officer Toby, you're saying you were aware of prior accusations of Mr. Kane's illicit businesses, that is why you were there. You're saying that you lived at Mr. Kane's house for a lengthy period of time and you never heard or saw one iota of evidence that Mr. Kane was involved in illegal activities? Don't you know about his businesses?"

Glorie took a breath, licked her lips, let out the breath. "Mr. McNeill, if you had done your job properly, done your due diligence, you would have discovered that yes, Mr. Kane inherited some illegal enterprises from his father. He did not ask for them, they were foisted upon him."

"I object!' McNeill yelled, he looked at the judge. "She's not answering, she's commenting, she can't-"

The judge smiled. "Ah, Mr. Prosecutor, you opened the door, you asked her what she knew." He smiled at Glorie like she was his favorite granddaughter and said, "Please continue, Officer Toby."

Glorie maintained her ladylike poise. With zero smugness, she nodded demurely at the judge, then said to the prosecutor, "If you had done your research, Mr. McNeill, you would have discovered that although Mr. Kane was given these businesses, he has spent the time since he left the military, you know, protecting our country. He was in a special ops unit, he survived terrible deadly combat."

She smiled over at Joze. "He doesn't like to talk about himself, he gets embarrassed whenever anyone mentions his medals, what a hero he was when he-"

"Miss Toby, please answer the question!" yelling, McNeill's voice was so strained it was getting screechy. He slapped his hands over his ears as the courtroom once again shouted, "*Officer* Toby!"

Glorie looked sweetly contrite. "I'm sorry, Mr. McNeill," her voice softened with just a slight fearful tremor in it. "I understand you are angry with me, but please don't yell at me, it, uh, scares me."

The entire room glared at McNeill.

His face darkened to maroon. Voice cracking, through a held breath he muttered, "Sorry. Please answer the question."

"Of course, Mr. McNeill." Glorie could see Joze had his hand over his mouth, like he was trying to hide a grin.

Glorie smiled at the prosecutor. "Of course. So anyway, as I was saying, when Mr. Kane inherited the businesses, he left the military when his dad was getting sick to help him," she hurried on as McNeill opened his mouth.

"Since he inherited the businesses he has struggled to turn those businesses into legitimate enterprises, those he couldn't, he dismantled or sold. He's fought lethal competitors to protect his people, his employees, plus those businesses gave a lot of jobs to people that weren't aware of the," she thought for a word, 'inappropriate' aspect of them. But to suddenly close a business would hurt a lot of families with little children to feed, so-"

"Okay, all right already, we've got it, Miss- Officer, just answer the question!" McNeill almost shrieked.

She turned to the judge and said sweetly, "Then there are Mr. Kane's charities,"

"I object!" McNeill screamed. "I didn't ask about any charities. I didn't ask what a benevolent kind-hearted person Mr. Kane is. I asked about his businesses. Tell me-"

"Well, now," Judge Merrigan interjected, "it seems that charities can be considered businesses as there are taxes involved on Mr. Kane's part, claiming them that is."

Glorie nodded emphatically. "Yes, Your Honor. In this case, Mr. Kane hires people, with his own money, to work at a rec center to help the young people to keep them off the street at night.

"And they also help the kids with homework and music lessons as well as other things like exercise and learning to prepare healthy meals. They have their big basketball game that all the families attend, then he takes the children out for wings and burgers after and-"

"Enough!" McNeill bellowed with his arms raised to the ceiling in exasperation. The air sailed out of his lungs, his arms dropped. Shaking his head, sighing, he said weakly, "Enough. I'm done with this witness." McNeill stood with his head hanging, trying to keep the rest of what little composure he had.

"I have a question." Joze's attorney rose.

The judge looked at McNeill.

McNeill looked about to cry. He mumbled, "Whatever, I don't care...I mean," he sighed miserably. "I don't object."

In his neat, pinstriped suit, Kincaid smiled widely, friendly at Glorie. "*Officer* Toby, can you tell me, were you the one who contacted the police to tell them where Mr. Kane resided?"

Glorie looked at Joze, she shook her head. "No, I did not." She smiled at Joze, then the attorney. "I honestly didn't know where I was, and I had no access to a phone. I had been blindfolded on my way there. Besides, I was not done at the ranch yet. Even though Mr.

Kane treated me like a gentleman and risked his life, twice, to save mine, I still had a job to do." She glanced back at Joze, their eyes collided.

He finally smiled, allowing his enlarging pupils to shower his love for her from across the room.

"Thank you, Your Honor. That's all." The attorney bowed briefly and took his seat at the defense table.

McNeill stumbled over and plopped down in his own chair. To save face, he pretended to shuffle papers and make notes.

Glorie was excused. She gracefully rose from the witness stand and stepped down then crossed to the gate that separated the audience from the court participants.

The deputy smiled at her as he held the gate open for her to pass through. Again, she thanked him graciously. She glanced around, unsure where to sit.

Daniel motioned for the people next to him to make a space. They shifted down and he nodded his head to her.

Smiling gratefully, Glorie threaded through the people and sat down beside Daniel.

Guy Whaler was called to the stand. He kept his eyes straight ahead. His nose was crooked from the beating Joze had given him. He admitted he was the one who had advised the police where to find Jozadak Kane.

But, although he was frequently at the ranch as an extra hand, as well as he did work for some of Joze's businesses, he admitted he'd never seen anything unlawful going on. But then he hadn't been part of Joze's direct team.

The prosecution had had subpoenaed others from the ranch and Joze's enterprises like Daniel, Linc and Calvin, but they claimed the same as Glorie and Guy. They saw nothing, heard nothing, did nothing illegal.

They were all quickly dismissed after only a few moments of testimony by an extremely irate McNeill.

The trial didn't last much longer.

Chapter Thirty-Six

The jury returned with their verdict. Joze was found innocent of the 46 felonious counts. He was found guilty of only one charge, a misdemeanor count of running a business without a license.

One of the businesses had slipped past Joze's own accountants who took care of all the licensing's, permits, etc. for the many companies.

Because he lost on all the other serious counts, the prosecution refused to barter on the sentencing. A first arrest of a misdemeanor seldom brings jail time. But Joze was sentenced to the maximum, one year in jail.

Glorie gasped, tears sprung.

Daniel put his arm around her. He whispered, "Don't fret, honey, the military was a thousand times tougher than a county jail. With time served and good behavior he should be out in 8 or 9 months."

On the other side of her, Linc patted her knee. He had always believed in her innocence.

As the judge pronounced his sentence, women in the jury and others in the courtroom whipped out tissues, and weeping reverberated around the wood-paneled room.

Glorie stood up and asked if she could approach the bench.

The judge said she could. When she reached him, he smiled kindly down at her. "Yes, Officer Toby?"

"Your Honor, may I please have a minute with Mr. Kane before he's taken away?"

The normally austere judge nodded. He'd fallen for the princess rescued by the prince impression too. And the young woman, so brave, even though she owed her prince her life, she had still stuck to the ethics of her job. "Yes, go ahead, honey, a few minutes."

"Thank you, sir." Glorie hurried over to where Joze was bookended by two deputies that had handcuffed his hands behind his back.

She stood in front of him, gazed up, unsure. After all, he must have thought she'd betrayed him.

But when his eyes glowed at her and he whispered, "*Babi*," she sighed in relief. Glorie wiped at a tear. She wanted to hug him, touch him, kiss him, but she didn't want the people to think she had lied on the stand about their relationship.

"Joze, I never-"

He smiled at her. "I know, honey. I knew it wasn't you. I love you."

The tears started rolling. "I love you, Joze. I'll come and see you as soon as-"

"*Na*." His eyes darkened. "I don't want you to see me like that. I want you to forget about me."

At her shaking head he said, roughly, "I mean it, Glorie. I will refuse to see you. I don't want you wasting your life on me."

"I'll write you then, Joze," she said firmly, she couldn't resist touching his face tenderly.

"*Na*." He shook his head adamantly. "Don't write me. I will not write you back. I won't read your letters, they'll be returned unopened. You will not wait for me. You will not," his voice broke, the ebony in his eyes swelled to sheening black moons.

"Please, *babi*, I mean, Glorie, I don't want you to throw any more of your life away on me. I've already taken enough of it. I'm no good for you. You're too good to be tainted by my convicted existence. Please-" the deputies started to pull him away.

He twisted his head, said over his shoulder, "Please, Glorie, please stay away, I am dead to you-"

She stood like a statue watching until they took him out of sight. Her tears streamed. Although she had professed to just be spying on Joze, the occupants of the courtroom saw the truth. The young couple was clearly in love.

Around her, people sniffed and cried for the handsome, gallant man being taken to a cage, and the broken-hearted princess left behind.

At the prosecution table, McNeill sat slumped over with his face in his hands.

Luc Bolton shoved to his feet and stalked over to Glorie. "You-you little bitch. Your career as a police officer is over. I'm gonna fucking tear you apart, I'm gonna-"

He was suddenly surrounded by Linc, Calvin, Bruno, Diego, Daniel, Sloan, Van, Maria and Melissa, as well as other men and women lurking behind them.

"You have nothing else to say to her, Bolton. Ever," Linc stated coldly, his voice flat.

Van and Daniel moved Glorie slightly away from the detective and behind them. Calvin and Linc made a wall between Bolton and Glorie.

Bolton tried to bluster, but the men tightened ranks until Bolton could no longer see Glorie through the wall of men. He spat curses at them then stormed out of the room.

Sloan moved to stand in front of Glorie. His face wreathed with apology. He asked, "Glorie, can I talk to you?" After the way he yelled and cursed at her, accusing her of being the one to turn in Joze, he didn't expect her to agree.

Graciously, Glorie smiled at him slightly wary. "Of course, Sloan."

His contrite head lowered, he looked up at her. "I just want to say I'm sorry, Glorie. For accusing you. I was so- so afraid for Joze. He could have gotten more than 20 years for what they tried to get on him. You, being a cop and all, and he was holding you captive, I, well, I was wrong.

349

"He trusted you, he never stopped trusting you and I should have seen if he was that way, then it must be the truth. Please accept my apology."

Glorie laughed without regret. "I'm pretty sure my police days are over. And I'm okay with that. It wasn't something I really wanted to do in the first place. I was sort of thrust into the undercover position."

Her smile forgiving, she set a hand on his arm and said, "I accept your apology, Sloan. I can certainly understand you thinking it was me. But I love him as much as the rest of you do." Tears gleamed in her crystal orbs.

"Yeah," Sloan's eyes were wet too. He held his arms out, Glorie went right into them.

Epilogue

As she promised, Glorie wrote Joze every week. Told him she had moved in with her sister for now. Had a job doing cyber-surveillance but with a private detective agency that she could do at home. She told him she'd gotten a few horses.

Her sister's land was extensive with fields and woods, and Glorie and Shana, and sometimes Shana's husband and their friends went riding. They had barbeques and other parties.

She wrote that she kept in touch with Daniel, Linc, Van, Maria and some of the others. Daniel was taking good care of the ranch until Joze was released. She told Joze she would be there waiting for him on that day to take him home even though his friends said they had it covered.

As Joze had said, he did not write her back, or accept her calls, and refused to see her when she had tried to visit him.

But her letters had not been returned to her unopened. So Glorie knew he read them. That meant he still cared.

Much to her sister's chagrin, she was marking off the days on the calendar for when he'd be released.

Her sister believed Joze was a gangster and Glorie deserved better.

Glorie believed there was no better man than Jozadak Kane.

****

Shana Wright answered the doorbell. When she opened the door she could have kicked herself for not looking through the window first.

The man standing there could be a stranger. Well above average height with powerful shoulders, biceps bulging, brawny forearms visible from his rolled up long sleeves.

But she recognized him from Glorie's description. The white blond hair, wavy on top, shaved on the sides, and there was no mistaking those electric blue eyes that Shana felt piercing her brain so palpable, she shivered.

"I'm sorry," Shana said quickly, "we're not buying anything," and she went to close the door.

But, he put his boot in it blocking it from closing. "Shana, I am Joze Kane, I-"

Shana glared coldly at him. "I know who you are. I was being polite. My sister wants nothing to do with you. Go away."

"If I could just speak with Glorie-"

"No. I said she does not want to see you or talk to you. Ever. Now," Shana's eyes narrowed with her threat, "please leave or I will call the police." She waited, anxiously biting her tongue. Obviously a man as big and strong as Joze Kane would not be held off by a simple door.

"I see. If you would please tell her I was by?" Joze moved his foot from the door and held a card out with his name and number printed on it.

Ignoring his outstretched hand and the card Shana closed it in his face. After counting to ten, she ran and peeked out the window.

The big man walked straight and confident, elegant even for such a powerfully built man, but she could tell by the set of his shoulders he was unhappy, depressed even, for being told Glorie didn't want to see him.

Joze climbed in a big, black, very expensive looking SUV and drove off. Just as he rounded the corner Glorie came up beside her sister.

"Who was that?" She asked trying to look out the window.

Shana turned her face so Glorie couldn't see she was lying. "It was no one. A salesman."

"Oh." They can be annoying. You want me to start the meatloaf?"

Anxious to get Glorie away from the window in case Kane returned, Shana said, "Sure. I'll get the potatoes out."

A few days later, Glorie was rambling around aimlessly.

Shana watched her mope from room to room. She knew it was because she missed that gangster. But dammit, she would protect her sister from that criminal. Eventually they would forget about each other. After all, they were hardly Romeo and Juliet.

She said to Glorie, "Listen sis, I know you called the prison and found out he'd been released early and you had hoped, well, but, honey, he's no good, you need to forget about him." Shana hardened her heart at her sister's woebegone expression.

Shana said softly, "Listen honey, clearly he has no interest in seeing you or he would have, uh, you know, called or come to the house by now. Remember, he told you to not contact him, obviously he wants nothing more to do with you." So far Shana had managed to intercept Joze's phone calls and deleted his messages.

Glorie swung her angry glare to her sister. "Shana, I love him with my whole heart. I will never forget him." Slapping at the tears that escaped, she stated firmly, but flatly, "Never."

"Come on, Glo, let's go horseback riding, you'll feel better."

"I don't feel like it." Glorie stared bleakly out the front window.

"Come on, you can't sit there moping and become nothing but a vegetable. I want to go ride and you know Justin hates it when I ride alone. Especially when it's a cloudy day like it is today."

Glorie sighed long and hard. "Yeah, your husband is such a worry wart when it comes to you. Fine, I'll go with you."

The girls saddled up and headed to the far meadow where the wild flowers were blooming.

Even the pretty flowers that normally cheered her even on her gloomiest days did nothing for Glorie. She just stared dispassionately past them. It was a cool day, the sun covered by a thick haze from the low clouds.

Then, Glorie saw another rider coming towards them. It was difficult to see him through the heavy mist. He became clearer as he got closer, Glorie's heart started hammering.

When Joze reached them, Shana tried to move her horse between the pair, she said angrily, "I told you she did not want to see you. Now, go away before I call the law!"

Glorie looked aghast at her sister. "He was here?" Her eyes wide, mouth gaping, she exclaimed, "He came here and you sent him away?" Her head swung to Joze. "You were here?"

He glanced at Shana then nodded soberly to Glorie.

Recalling the knock at the door and Shana telling her it was just a salesman, her sister's deceit came clear. Back to Shana, she said, "You told him I didn't want to see him?" She turned to him, "I- I never said that, Joze-"

"Glorie," Shana's horse's legs were hopping from her trying to keep between Glorie and Joze. "Don't talk to him. He's a convicted criminal, he's no good for you, send him-"

Joze's eyes morphed from blue to smoldering ebony discs. He looked at Shana. She visibly shrunk from him. He said calmly, "Don't you have something to cook back at your house?"

"No!" Shana exclaimed, "I am not leaving my sister alone with the likes of-"

"Go back to the house, Shana," Glorie ordered her quietly, her gaze steady on Joze.

"But-" Shana looked from one to the other.

Their eyes were frozen to each other.

Shana opened her mouth, then snapped it shut with a heavy sigh. She pointed at Joze, her eyes narrowed with anger and threat, she demanded, "Don't you dare hurt her."

Joze's gaze slipped to hers for a brief second, he smiled, then looked back to Glorie.

"Fine." Shana pulled up her reins. "I will be at the house. I can see you from there. My phone will be in my hand if anything happens to her." She turned her horse and headed back to her house.

The couple didn't spare her a glance. They only had eyes for each other.

"She's feisty," Joze said.

Glorie nodded with a grin, "Yes, she is."

Joze climbed off his horse and went to her to help her down.

She slid down his body to her feet where she stayed enveloped in his arms.

He picked up her hand, his thumb stroked the diamond. A faint smile of pleased surprise, he said, "You still wear my ring?"

She rolled her hands up around the back of his neck. "Every time someone," her lip curled sadly, "my sister, or her husband, or my friends told me I should take it off, something inside me burned."

Her shoulder rose slightly, then she lowered it with a brief shrug. "So I didn't."

Her fingers sifted up the back of his hair, she twirled the silky strands between her fingers. "Why are you here Joze if she told you I didn't want to see you?"

He tucked a loose curl behind her ear with his long fingers, then stroked his hand around the side of her face, splaying his fingers along her jaw.

Their gazes connected, held.

Glorie's smile and ease in his arms, her hands around his neck gave him confidence. "I had to come and get you, *fy babi*. I couldn't face the rest of my life without you. I admit when your sister said you refused to see me, well," he rubbed the back of his head, his expression grim.

"I gotta say it killed me. I thought about giving up, just walking away, leaving you alone, like I said when they took me to prison.

But," he drew her face closer to his, his eyes deep onyx with passion and love, they tenderly stroked her soft jeweled orbs.

He stared hard into her eyes and declared, "I couldn't stop loving you. I had to take the chance. I had to hear it from your lips." His mouth quirked, he said, "Plus, I had to see you if only for the last time."

Her head cocked, she said, "Uh huh. And what if I told you to get lost?" They stood in the grass, hazy dew and vapor from the horses mouths mingled, tails swished at a few flies stirred up.

Joze grinned mischievously. "You know me, *babi*, like a dog with a bone. I am unwilling to give you up. I have considered kidnapping you again until you finally give into me, fall for me again. I mean," he shrugged, "it worked the first time." But he hoped she truly wanted him. His stomach tightened as he waited for her response.

Her smile as big as the colorful wildflowers, Glorie said, "I love you, Joze, I've never stopped loving you. I never will."

His gut unclenched in relief, he said, "How soon can we get married?" He wanted to tie her to him as quickly as possible, before common sense made her come to her senses, before she could remember he was a gangster and she was a sweet, brave wonderful woman who deserved only the best of everything, and send him on his way.

Beaming her beautiful smile up at him, she said, "Is tomorrow too soon?"

His eyes flaring with love, Joze declared, "Tomorrow it is." Drawing her into his embrace, he lowered his head capturing her mouth.

She stood on tiptoe, her hands twined behind his head, holding him tight as they melted into an everlasting kiss.

The End

Louise Furley

Please enjoy an excerpt from my book, Wrath of Wolf.

Wrath of Wolf

Chapter One

"*F*or cripe's sake, Ollie," Annabella groused from the passenger seat, "slow down. We have an hour before we have to be at dinner with your stupid family. I wanna stop for a drink. I need fortification to spend even a minute with your pompous father and his imbecilic friends."

Her bulbous bosom rounding over the seatbelt jostled like mad from the swerves and bumps as the car cruised the uneven road.

The Lincoln SUV easily hugged the ancient winding road as it coiled down and around the mountain like a thin black snake. The last of the dropped autumn leaves whooshed behind the vehicle.

The night pitch black, there was nothing to illuminate the shrouded asphalt except the beaming headlights. Even the bordering trees were just dark craggy phantoms looming along both sides of the narrow two-lane road.

Ollie Duncan let out a loud, beleaguered sigh. Thumping a thumb irritably on the steering wheel, he grumbled, "Will you shut it for just one damned second? Nag, nag, nag, I'm tired of your incessant complaining. And FYI, my brothers aren't coming until Christmas."

Her double chin wobbling, Annabella retorted nastily, "Screw you, Ollie, and your father and Talon DeMar that insists on having their special retreats at the lodge.

"Just because all of your father's frat brothers grew up together doesn't mean we have to spend every blasted minute of our time with them. I'm bored out of my tree with the McShanes, Ansberrys and the Burtons and the others."

Ollie nodded, peering into the dark night ensuring he kept the car on his side of the twisting road. "Yeah, the king himself, Talon DeMar and his clan will already be there, and of course Talon's right-hand knight, Stone Cash will be present as well."

"Oh just great." Annabella tipped her head back with a scowl.

"What's your problem now?" Ollie glanced at his wife, then quickly focused back to the obscured windshield, his brows knitted in concentration.

"That bitch Ketherine will be hanging about then, won't she? When Caralina passed, Talon dragged her daughter from her schooling in Italy to run the company with him per Caralina's will. From archeology to building bridges, I bet Ketherine hates every second of it." The scowl turned into a gloating smile.

Ollie shot her a quick frown. "Keti is not a bitch, she's just...kind of...cold."

"Uh huh," Annabella grunted. "Glacier kitten the men call her, Glitty for short." Her coarse laugh a piggish sound, she said, "Glitty Kitty. Even though so much older than Keti, as soon as her little tits sprouted you boys were on her like barbeque sauce on ribs."

Her pudgy lips twisted in antipathy. "They say she's beautiful like a soft icy statue. Michael McShane says a goddess statue. Huh. I think she's butt ugly and too- too-"

"Dainty?" Ollie smiled.

Her eyes narrowed at him, she spat, "No. I was thinking brittle, too slender for most men's tastes. Stick thin like she's

2

still in her teens for Pete's sake. Those green eyes unattractively too big for her fragile face."

A small chuckle, Ollie remarked, "I think you mean delicate. Or even ethereal."

Annabella snorted. "Come on, that is so over-used, so cliché. She's hardly a wraith. Unfortunately her damned curves have filled out since she suddenly left home at 13. She's nothing but ignorant trailer trash from her mother's side of the family.

"Talon, her stepfather put the kibosh on her archeological studies, and rightly so. Honestly, rooting around in the dirt like a sow. I heard he's planning an arranged marriage for her. Good thing. Keep her away from all you horndogs." A jealous sneer pinched Annabella's melon round face.

She prattled on, "I hear Talon wants her to marry Rein van Baer. That old perv was sniffing after the girl when she was barely out of diapers."

His shoulders hunched, Ollie tugged the wheel tightly to the right to keep on the serpentine roadway, he agreed, "I know. Poor Keti did not want to come home to Talon...her bastard of a father, rather stepfather, and be forced to work with him. Her mother left her half of the business to Keti.

"But they each have 50-50 of the company and all documents have to be signed by both. One time Talon tried to forge Keti's signature and he got caught. He was lucky, he only got a slap on the wrist. But he learned his lesson, I'll say."

Ollie leaned over the wheel squinting into the dark. "And Rein van Baer is not that old. Like my dad, he's in his fifties." He shrugged one shoulder. "But compared to young Keti, yeah, he's old." There was silence in the car for a few minutes.

3

His head swiveling as he tried to follow the dark road, Ollie tried to cajole his wife. "It won't be as crowded this year though. Most of the other siblings won't be there. They have work and other shit to attend to. It'll just be the older generation, the basic fathers, their wives and one or two of their children, the younger generation like me at the lodge."

"Yeah, I hear as usual the guys are bringing a plus one."

Ollie nodded. "Yes, a wife, fiancée and a girlfriend or two."

"God," his wife groaned. "I hate this mountain we have to get around to get to the mansion. It's damp and chilling this far north of Oregon. Listen," her whining voice turned to a fake, but gentle coaxing. "There's a bar just past the exit off this ghastly hill. O'Shareef's, we can get a cocktail there."

Rolling his eyes, her husband sniped, "Oh sure. We want to join the party reeking of booze. Leave it to you to know where every watering hole in the Northwest is. Of course everyone is used to you and your all-consuming love of food and alcohol. You just-"

"Look out!" Annabella screeched. A truck suddenly emerged from the gloaming darkness and was barreling straight at them right in their lane.

"Omigod! Omigod!" Ollie yelled as he wrenched the wheel to the right to avoid the truck. But the truck clipped the front bumper and the Duncans' SUV veered sharply off the road.

Annabella's screams were so loud they almost drowned out Ollie's frightened wails as the SUV went flying out of control and crashed through the wooden fence. Pieces of wood shot out in all directions like brown fireworks. Their screams mingled as the car careened wildly for several yards before it flew off the side of the mountain.

The car rolled and bashed over rocks and grass as it tore down the mountain then it suddenly smashed into a tree and that stopped it dead. Metal clanking against the stalwart tree proved Mother Nature was stronger than mankind as the car wrapped around the redwood's thick trunk like a paperclip.

The mangled Lincoln wheezed and rattled then whistling steam plumed from under the crushed hood.

****

He pulled off to the side of the road and carefully parked the stolen tow-truck far over on the shoulder. Climbing out, he closed the door then trod across the grass. "Boy," he muttered, "what a bitch stopping the truck and getting turned around in that skinny driveway. Now, let's see how I did."

Stepping over the pieces of broken fence, he sauntered to the rim of the grassy area and looked down.

"Yowzer," he let out a whistle. "I didn't mean to smash 'em up so much. I thought the fence would stop the car. Shit, I hope they're still breathing or this won't be any fun at all. Now," he put a finger to his chin and pondered.

Mumbling to himself, he said, "Gonna be rough getting them and the car up. Especially that Porky Pig Annabella. Thank God the car's descent was halted so near from the road. Tree ain't looking too happy though," he grinned.

"I guess I can tie a rope around ol' Ollie and the pig and to my truck and drag 'em up the side of the mountain. Okay then, off to work!" He spun around to grab the rope from his vehicle.

****

Ollie's head was pounding, and Annabella's screams weren't helping any. *What the hell is the matter with her now?* He didn't move for a minute trying to get his bearings. "Ahh," the groan scraped out as pain hit, everywhere. Dizziness flooded his brain making him slightly nauseous.

"What the-" He was lying in a funny position. On his stomach but his hips were pushed up over a pillow, oddly shoving his ass up in the air.

He tried to move an arm, then started when he realized he couldn't budge it. His arms were splayed out to the side, and they were bound to a bed frame. He tugged at his legs only to find they were spread apart and also immobilized.

Blinking rapidly, he took in the closest wall. The room had a cabin feel to it with the rough wood walls, and the cowboy lamp on the nightstand beside the bed, he didn't recognize where he was. On the table Ollie saw a box. Squinting at it, he read the title on the lid, it said 'wood burning kit.'

Annabella's screaming went on and on. Only his wife could shriek that piercingly, sound goes right through a man's head. How can he think with her caterwauling?

"Annabella, for crying out loud, shut the hell up!" He cranked his head so he could see more than the mattress he was lying on. "What kind of game are you playing tying me-" His eyes widened in confusion.

On the floor beside the bed, Annabella was on her back, it appeared that her hands were bound behind her. Naked as a beached whale, she was writhing and squirming, and peeling paint with her screams.

She was covered with scrapes and bruises, her hair matted with dirt and dead leaves, and a man was on top of her, banging her. Hard.

Seeing red, the wooziness clearing, Ollie shouted, "Hey! Annabella you slut, what's the matter with you?" His own yelling made his head hurt worse. "You're so freakin' obnoxious to be screwing him while I'm right here!"

He could now feel his entire body ached. The SUV crashing through the fence flashed in his mind. Remembering the car going over a cliff, the last thing he recalled was the Lincoln rolling over and over and-

Annabella stopped screaming, but now she was making gagging, gurgling sounds.

"What-"

The man screwing his wife turned his head and grinned at Ollie. "Oh, took you long enough to come around, Ol." His hands were wrapped around Annabella's throat, and he was squeezing the very life out of her, even as his hips pounded between her sausage fat kicking legs.

"Hey! Stop that!" Ollie could see Annabella's face turning scarlet, her eyes bulging out of her head. "Shit, man, you're killing her! Stop!" Ollie jerked at his binds, struggling to get free and get the freak off his wife.

It was too late. Annabella made no more sounds, no more movements. Her now bone-white face was frozen with the terrified eyes bulging, her tongue lolled out the side of her mouth.

Ollie's brain fizzled and went blank as confusion and horror took his breath. He stared blankly as the man ejaculated into his wife with a moan. Grunting as he pulled from her, the man carefully peeled a condom off, tied it and then bustled to his feet doing his pants up.

Ollie couldn't form a sentence, he stammered, "Wha, wha, wha..."

The man's head fell back honking out a laugh. He grinned at Ollie with dark mirth. "Aren't you the lucky ones

I came upon first?" Peering at Ollie, the man's grin widened at the bound Ollie's bewilderment.

"Ah, you're curious to know what's gonna happen next?" With gloved hands, he pulled a plastic baggie from his pocket. He dropped the condom in the bag, sealed it and tucked it in his pocket.

Ollie blinked at him, his mouth opening and closing like a gasping fish.

"Well," the man said, rolling down the long sleeves of his white shirt and smoothed the cuffs. He chuckled. "I won't keep you in suspense, Ol. I'm going to do the same thing to you as I did to Annabella," he jerked his head at Ollie's dead wife lying like a trussed hog on the floor.

Frowning at her, he remarked, "I don't care much for the fat ones, but," he shrugged, "a man's gotta do what a man's gotta do for the cause, you know what I mean?"

If possible, Ollie's eyes rounded even wider at the man. His gaze lowered to the man's zipper and he gulped. "Y-you're going to- to rape me?"

The man turned to him and nodded gleefully. "Yep. And kill you." He frowned at the dead woman, his lips pulled in.

He looked back to Ollie and smiled. "Oh, don't worry, I'm not going to rape you with my dick, ew, no," he grimaced and shook his head. "I am not a homosexual. You know very well I like the ladies. No, I'll be using that," he looked pointedly towards a wall.

Painfully, Ollie angled his head to see what the man was talking about, and he blanched. His stomach revolted at the sight of the iron rod leaning against the wall. "Wha-" he choked. His eyes twitched back to the male who had just killed his wife.

He said, "Bro," swallowing trying to wet his dry throat, "we- we're practically family! Why?" His voice an

8

anguished cry, tears poured down his cheeks wetting the sheet beneath him.

The man deliberately stepped over Annabella as if she was just a crumpled piece of trash left on the floor and ambled over to the wall and picked up the iron bar.

Tapping the bar against his palm his eyes gleaming with tormenting delight he moved to where Ollie lay trembling.

That was when Ollie fully comprehended that he was buck-naked, his bound legs spread, with his butt pushed up in the air.

"Since you asked so nicely, Ol, I'm gonna tell you why I'm doing this." The man's eyes darkened as the torturous doom of hell stalked into them. He lifted the iron rod and placed it near Ollie's rear end.

Ollie started screaming.

Shaking his head, the man said blithely, "Now Ol, my bro, how can I tell you my story over all that yowling? You need to hush now. So," he began, pushing the bar, speaking like he was telling a fairytale, "a long, long time ago, there was this little boy," he pushed harder.

Ollie screamed so loud the windows rattled.

"Quiet now, Ol, I can't think with all that noise."

9

Dear Reader, thank you for purchasing Jozadak!

I know you could have picked any number of books to read, but you picked this book and for that I am extremely grateful.

I hope you enjoyed this novel, and if you did, please leave a review, *and look for other exciting titles in my name!*

About the Author

Louise Furley loves writing romance with a huge helping of suspense. She finds it exciting to study new lands and learn everything she can about the area and the natives that call it home.

Her idea of fun is researching ideas, studying enigmatic modes of science, archeology, and different ways to kill someone.

Louise Furley

Her Significant Other finds the last to be particularly notable. He remains wary yet gives Louise his full support with her writing adventures.

Sunny Florida is home where Louise is a graduate of St. Thomas University with a master's degree in Mental Health. This degree is essential for exploring the deviant soul, and understanding the mind of a killer, while finding it exhilarating, frightening and sad all at the same time. With artistic license, Louise can be judge, jury, and sometimes executioner!

Louise is the author of numerous published novels. When not researching or writing, she is dreaming of unique plots, and discovering fresh ventures she hasn't yet experienced in the world.

Ride along with her as she travels new and thrilling journeys!

www.ingramcontent.com/pod-product-compliance
Lightning Source LLC
Chambersburg PA
CBHW021432240626
47153CB00001B/125